HEATHER SMITH

DUSK TO DAWN

FATED DARKNESS | BOOK 2

Cover design by MiblArt

Author Photograph by Heather Alvarez

ALSO BY HEATHER SMITH

Fated Darkness

Shadow of Twilight

To Richard

For showing me what true love really is.
A lifetime together could never be enough
for us, but I'll do my best to make
every second count.

CHAPTER 1

FIRST SHIFT

"Christian! Christian! Come here! Quick!"

Christian ran out of their bungalow, his hands caked in flour and eggs. The mixture clung to his face and dripped from his hair.

Amelia rolled her eyes at the sight. She should have known better by now than to rely on him in the kitchen. Yet, he kept insisting he could learn. Get better. The tomato sauce on the ceiling said otherwise.

"What is it? What's wrong?!" Christian panted, his heart beating erratically in his chest.

He scanned the yard, the tree line. Searching for his favorite little girl, running around on her tiny toddler legs. Amelia stood in the middle of the yard, smiling excitedly as she observed a small pup bouncing around the yard, chewing on stuffed plushies.

Christian frowned. When did they get a puppy, and where was his niece? Emery was never not within Amelia's line of sight. So, where had the precocious toddler run off too?

"Mia, where's Emery?" Christian asked.

Amelia pointed to the pup.

The tiny ball of fluff had silver-white fur with a black stripe running down the length of her spine all the way to the tip of her tail. Her tiny teeth were tearing into a teddy bear, gnawing off its ears at the seams. The small pup finally minded him. Her silver eyes widened, catching sight of Christian. The bear fell from her mouth before she bounded over to him, leaping through the air and into his arms. A narrow pink tongue ravaged his face, licking off the flour mixture.

"Isn't she amazing?!" Amelia couldn't help the squeal that escaped her throat.

Her daughter never ceased to amaze.

Christian pulled the puppy away from him, forcing her to withdraw her tongue. The little pup yipped in his arms, panting heavily, her small tail wagging, shaking her body. He looked from the pup to Amelia and back again.

"Emery?" Christian spoke softly to the wolf pup in his arms.

The small were-pup barked in response, squirming in his grasp. He carefully placed the pup back on the ground. The instant her paws touched the earth, she took off, running for her mother, circling her feet, and jumping up on her hind legs.

"She's only three! How is this even possible?" Christian stammered, his mind racing.

Amelia couldn't help but smile at her daughter.

It wasn't unheard of for a pup to shift between age eight and ten. She and her twin were extremely young when they experienced their first shift at age six, but three years old was unheard of. Unprecedented.

"I don't know. One second she was playing, the next, she was chewing on all her toys." Amelia shrugged. "Isn't she stunning? She says her wolf's name is Hailey."

Christian's eyebrows raised. "She can mind link already?"

"Yes, she's extremely excited to talk to her wolf. She says she finally has a friend." Amelia's eyes darkened as her words faded, no longer sparkled with enthusiasm.

It was their sixth home in four years.

They currently resided in a little town outside of Mexico City. The rogues had managed to track them down to each hideout, constantly hunting them. Relentless mutts. They constantly had to be ready to run at a moment's notice which meant no stability, no friends, no ties. Nothing to hold them back.

Christian couldn't help but toss his arm around her shoulder, providing her with a firm squeeze. Amelia leaned into his large frame, leaning her head against his shoulder.

She remembered once upon a time trying to keep Christian from following her. Insisting it would be too dangerous for him. Not to mention what he'd be giving up. Losing his standing in his pack, quite possibly considered a traitor, and running off with his Alpha's mate—to name a few.

Amelia was grateful he didn't listen to her, for his unfailing support. On more than one occasion, they had barely escaped with their lives, especially when they had a baby to consider, but Christian never wavered, never gave up. He was constantly encouraging her to stay strong, to hold on just a bit longer. Without him, she was convinced she'd be dead or captured by now.

Amelia jerked her head to the side. Rey stirred within her mind as they detected a faint scent blowing towards them in the breeze.

"Rogues," Amelia whispered.

Christian straightened beside her. His body went rigid, glancing around at their surroundings on high alert.

"How far?" he demanded.

"Ten minutes." She bent down, beckoning for her daughter to come. "Come on, baby. It's time to go."

"She can't shift back, Mia. The first shift lasts a few days as she gets the hang of it," he reminded her.

"Fuck," Amelia hissed loudly.

He was right. The first shift lasted a few days as the pup got used to the breach of mind and body. Emery and her wolf would require time to grow accustomed to one another. Time they no longer had. It usually took anywhere from three to five days before a pup shifted back to their human form. Given that Emery had only just shifted, she would stay in her wolf skin for a couple of days at the very least—leaving her no other options.

She watched as Christian ran into the house to grab their go-pack. The one bag they always had at the ready with their forged travel papers and money in various currencies.

The scent on the wind was getting more robust, more distinct, which only meant one thing.

They were getting closer.

Amelia stripped out of her clothes, leaving herself as bare as when she first came into the world. Emery observed her mother taking off her clothes and trotted over to her, her little head tilted to the side. Rey came forward as they shifted into her silver wolf.

Come, Emery. It's time to go. Amelia repeated, linking her daughter.

Are we going for a run? Emery hopped up and down on her four little legs.

Her heart fractured.

How could she explain to a three-year-old, they were in danger? Again.

That this was their life. A never-ending cycle of danger and temporary places to rest their head.

Yes, baby, we're going for a run. It's time to find a new home.

Without warning, Amelia picked Emery up by the scruff, grasping her firmly between her teeth. Emery's little body curled in on itself, her tail tucked between her legs as she dangled from her mother's jaws. Christian came running outside, already shifted into his chocolate brown wolf with a backpack hanging from his mouth.

Not bothering to signal, Amelia took off in the opposite direction of the rogue's scent. Rey struck her paws hard against the soft earth. Christian was on her left flank, keeping up with her long and powerful gait.

Emery curled up tighter on herself, swinging wildly from her mother's jaws.

Amelia leaped over a decayed tree causing her pup to whimper at the sudden jolt. Instinctively, she growled at her daughter, cautioning her to keep quiet.

Her daughter's whimpering turned into a sharp yipe. Amelia halted in her tracks. The toddler cry matured into an agonizing gasp of pain.

Amelia blinked her eyes repeatedly.

She was no longer looking through the eyes of her wolf but through her human ones. Her fingers flexed at her sides, indicating she was in fact human and not running through the woods on all fours. She stood in the clearing behind the London Packhouse.

More of a castle than a house. The carved stone towered over them, intimidating anyone daring to look at its foundation.

Looking around the clearing, she finally found the source of the cry that forced her out of her memories. Emery was lying on the ground near the base of the tree line. Her body was nude. Streaks of dirt coated her skin, and her hair resembled more of a bird's nest, filled with leaves and twigs.

Amelia observed her daughter, lessening the distance between them. As she drew closer, she couldn't note any extensive damage. If it were anyone else, something definitely would have been broken, but Emery had been falling out of trees since she could walk.

Emery was past the stages of toddler wobbles and a lanky frame she had yet to grow into.

The girl that lay in a heap before her was nearing adulthood. Reminding her daily of a childhood that was stolen from her. Left to mature quicker than any other her age.

"You okay?" Amelia asked once she finally got close enough.

Emery glared at the tree she had fallen from. The termite house towered over her, standing tall at over forty feet. She had managed to twist her body just in time to prevent breaking anything serious, but that didn't mean it didn't hurt like hell. Her body had shifted back to its human skin shortly after her body made impact—her wolf allowing for time to rest.

"Yeah, I'm okay. My ass is going to be sore, though," Emery complained, rubbing her backside, trying to stretch out the soreness she was already experiencing.

"What happened?" Amelia asked. Looking up, she searched for the point that Emery had crashed through. Discovering a fractured branch, she found the weak point that sent her daughter hurtling towards the earth.

"I misjudged my jump. Landed too far away from the trunk. It ended up snapping beneath my weight." Emery noted her mother's hand offered in front of her. She took it, pulling herself up off the ground.

"You can't afford to make mistakes. I know this is unpleasant, especially in your wolf form, but we do these drills for a reason," Amelia began her lecture.

"Yeah, I know. Use your surroundings to your advantage. Keep your tail up. It helps support your balance. Stay close to the trunk. The limbs are better equipped to carry your weight. The higher up, the less likely they are to identify and smell you. Shall I go on?"

Amelia glared at her daughter, unsure whether she wanted to praise or scold her.

Why did her child have to inherit all of her stubborn snarkiness?

It seemed Emery was blessed with all her good and bad traits. Not to mention what she inherited from her father.

"I think that's enough for today," she said, glancing up at the setting sun. The horizon was painted in hues of purple and orange. Reminding her of home. "You're going to need some ice for your ass. Can't have you too sore for tomorrow."

Emery groaned as she gathered her robe off the trimmed lawn and enclosed it around her exposed body. "You know most girls my age would be worried about finals or parties, hell even boys, but nope, not me. I get to worry about knife throwing, tracking, and tree climbing."

Amelia snorted, unable to contain her smirk. "You're not like most girls. Besides, who are you kidding? You think I didn't know you snuck out last weekend with the Alpha's son?"

"But-how?" Emery stuttered.

Amelia couldn't prevent her eyes from rolling. "You *are* my daughter. You think I didn't pull the same crap on my dad? Honey, I was the *Queen* of Mischief."

"So, it's okay for me to sneak out and go to parties?" Emery raised her brow at her mother.

"That's not what I'm saying, and you know it," she said pointedly. "All I am saying is that I trust you. You're a clever kid. I want you to use your judgment. Don't take any unnecessary risks. Even though I was way worse than you at your age, I also wasn't on the run my entire life. We've managed to live quietly these last two years. I want to keep it that way."

Emery bobbed her head in agreement, lost in thought until she recalled something. "What were you thinking about earlier when I fell? You looked distracted."

Amelia crossed her arms over her chest, pulling her sweater tighter around her body. "I remembered your first shift."

Emery smiled sadly. "With Uncle Christian?"

"Yeah, he was there."

"I miss him so much."

"Me too, baby. Me too."

CHAPTER 2

NIGHTMARES

C hains rattled.

Her wrists pulled sharply against the silver restraints.

The skin was worn away. Blood dripped down her arms. Her cell was gloomy—an endless darkness. Her remaining senses were in overdrive.

The room stank of filth. Her filth and blood. A foul white substance was running down her legs.

Her back was on fire. Her skin was left hanging, torn apart, and shredded.

Remembering the whip lashing against her flesh had her bent over, dry heaving, her stomach already barren. Every move, every breath, sent fresh waves of pain. Her shattered ribs grated against one another. Yet another reminder her healing was dormant.

Her teeth were clenched until her jaw throbbed with its own heartbeat. She was surprised they weren't filed down to the gums.

She briefly remembered the needle entering the soft spot of her neck.

Wolfsbane. The bastards used wolfsbane, making Rey completely unreachable. They were frightened of what might happen if she had access to her wolf—as they should be.

Amelia jerked her head up.

Metal hinges squeaked loudly in the darkness. Heavy footsteps echoed off the stone walls, leather boots tapping on the cement.

She jerked harder on the chains, her movements exacting a fresh swell of agony, tearing open the scabs on her back from the prior nights flogging.

She could smell his arousal—even through the steel door. Her panic and fear were both as good as drugs to him. Affording him a high not even money could buy.

A small chuckle emitted from the back of his throat, amusing himself with the creative ways he would be carving into her. He was imaginative—an artist and her body his canvas. The neat tray of assorted knives and random household objects were his brushes with her blood as his paint.

The sound of a zipper moving down over the bulge filling his pants left her whimpering. The shred of self-preservation she had left had her pulling at the chains even harder.

He snickered at her feeble attempts.

Amelia's hair was yanked back, her scalp burning, eyes tearing as he forced her head up. It didn't matter if she fastened her eyes or kept them open. She couldn't see the man, couldn't see anything. All she could do was smell him—a thick odor of petrol and cigarettes.

"One day, you will enjoy this," the man purred. His voice thick with need and desire.

"Never! You sick fuck!" She spat over her shoulder. The growl that vibrated through her back and rattled her bones informed her of one thing—she still had good aim.

The man snarled, his wolf piercing the veil that separated man from beast.

Tears slipped down her cheeks.

Her screams were swallowed in her private hell.

Amelia bolted upright out of bed.

Sweat dripped down her face and along her neck. Her hair was plastered to her skin, shirt drenched in sweat. She absently rubbed at her wrists. The scar was soft and smooth, pale in contrast to her natural olive tone. The wounds were long healed. But the memories were more than vivid.

The back of her head stung. She reached around, extending her fingers along her scalp. It was as though he had only just gripped her.

The ghost of him haunted her, taunting her.

"I'm alive. I'm okay. I'm safe," Amelia whispered to herself, over and over, until her heart rate slowed to a steadier rhythm.

Glancing around the room, she recognized everything was as it should be.

The lamp beside her was still on, banishing the darkness. Outside her open window, the sky was still black. Stars filled the vast emptiness.

Amelia thought back to a more innocent time before rogues and vague family history, before mates and fate. But she wasn't convinced such a time ever existed.

Sighing deeply, she spread her fingers through her long, silver-blonde hair. The color was growing lighter. Convincing her that one day it would disappear altogether. She leaned back against her headboard before suddenly sitting up again, ears pointed to the window. Her body stiffened, her breathing slow and quiet.

A wolf howled.

Amelia threw her covers off and hurtled out of bed. The sentries roused the alarm. Multiple wolves joined the call, alerting the pack to intruders.

They were here.

Amelia quickly stripped out of her nightgown, throwing the garment to the floor. Ripping open her dresser drawers, she pulled on a pair of jeans and a shirt, jumping in the air as she tugged on her sneakers.

The wood of the adjoining door nearly splintered beneath the force of her hammering fist.

Amelia flung it open and flicked on the lights, bringing the room to life.

"Emery, get up!" she yelled.

A sleeping teenage girl sat up, wearily rubbing at her eyes. "What's going on?"

"Get dressed. Time to go." Amelia entered the walk-in closet without a glance back, pulling down a backpack off the top shelf.

Emery leaped out of bed, her feet striking the cold wood floor. She followed her mother's lead, rapidly changing into similar attire.

Amelia held out the bookbag to her, strapping it on her back.

The bedroom door opened. A familiar face peered inside.

"Ms. Smoke, the rogues are here. A few have slipped through the perimeter. They're coming straight for the house."

Amelia nodded. "We're leaving. Tell your Alpha I said thank you, and I'm sorry."

The man pushed the door open further. The London pack's Beta bowed in submission. This startled her. "It has been an honor, Ms. Smoke. We will hold them off as best we can. Good luck and Goddess speed."

Amelia placed her hand on his shoulder, forcing his eyes up to her. "Thank you, Thomas. We will never forget your kindness."

Thomas briskly nodded before leaving them.

Organized chaos could be heard through the thick stone walls of the ancient castle. The pack herding young and old to the underground passageways. Warriors racing to take position along certain access points. Like a well-oiled machine, the London pack prepared for battle.

A chorus of wolves, savage and wild, sliced through the night.

They were almost here.

"Let's go," Amelia said over her shoulder, throwing open the door and storming her way out into the hall. She didn't bother to check and ensure Emery was following—she knew she was.

The castle was a maze of turns and spiral staircases, endless halls and countless doors leading into rooms long forgotten. They made their way down two levels and through the left wing, encountering little to no traffic.

By the sound of sharp cries and bone-rattling snarls, the fight was already well underway.

They made their way into the library, closing the heavy, hand-carved doors shut behind them. Amelia twisted the key in the door, locking them inside. Warning snarls that dripped with vicious intent vibrated through the walls. They were already in the castle.

"Emery. Go, now." Amelia stood guard in front of the door, her nails lengthening to razor-sharp claws.

"Mom." The girl pleaded, unsure. Run for her life or stand and fight with her mother?

"This is what we've been preparing for. You know what you need to do."

"But—" A small sob escaped her.

Amelia whipped around to face her daughter. She could hear the commotion downstairs growing louder, quickly approaching. She smoothed her daughter's hair down, cupping her face in her hands. "You are brave and strong. You are the daughter of Alphas. I promise you. I will find you, but right now, I need you to run." Her lips were feather-soft on her head. "If I don't get there in 2 hours, you have to go on without me."

Amelia double-checked that the book bag was indeed on her daughter's back before roughly pushing her away. "Now go."

Emery turned her back on her mother and raced for the massive oak bookcases along the far wall. She pulled on the two books that would release the latch, swinging the concealed door open. She caught one last look at her mother. Claws extended, feet planted, prepared to fight.

Emery swiftly closed the bookcase, producing a satisfying click as the latch caught. A thunderous blast of wood splintering could be heard even through the foot-thick walls. Monstrous screams echoed off the stone walls. She pushed through the panic that threatened to overwhelm her and ran through the hidden tunnels.

The estate was ancient and contained countless underground passages, hidden too most. It was the fastest way out of the Packhouse and with any luck, unknown to their enemy.

Emery held tighter to the straps of her backpack as she made sickening twists and turns.

The walls were crumbling around her. Stone mortared centuries past were long forgotten, left to deteriorate and collapse beneath its own weight. She had to choose her footing carefully. Chunks of brick lay scattered along her path, dust heavy in the air, leaving it stale.

Cobwebs obstructed her path, forcing her to push her way through the tacky webs.

The stone floor slanted down at a sinking rate. The air transitioned from musty and stagnant, to damp with a tang of ozone. She slackened her pace as she noted the dewy fresh air caress her face. Currently, she was appreciative of London's contrast drizzle. It would aid in masking her scent and deny trackers the thrill of the hunt.

Emery threw her hood over her head, halting at the end of the tunnel. She listened intently, waiting for the sounds of the intruders. Her wolf hearing caught the sound of water dripping off the trees, the wind brushing through the leaves. But no sign of lurking wolves.

Pushing through the tall bushes, she stepped out from the dense cover and found herself in a thickly condensed wood.

The towering trees provided shelter from the constant wet that was London.

Emery recognized the grounds.

Amelia made sure she practiced their escape route countless times. Always planning for the worst, preparing for endless scenarios. She knew the earth was boggy and where the vulnerable points in the ground were. Through the forest she ran, the ground perfectly mapped in her head.

A howl could be heard in the distance.

Her heart thundered in her chest.

They caught her scent. How the hell did that happen?

Emery forced her legs harder, the forest around her speeding by in a blur. Her wolf wanted to take over, to shift and take the lead, but she knew that would only make their scent stronger.

Staying human was the only option.

Three wolves were catching up to her.

In wolf form, they would have been faster, but she was more clever, capable of outthinking the mindless beasts.

Emery dodged through the bog, waiting for one of them to slip up.

A wolf cried from behind. Mutt must have fallen into a mud pit.

Idiot.

She refused to slow her pace as she charged through the woods.

Two were left, still blundering through the brush, following her tracks. The rogues were daft and dumb, trampling through the forest like a charging heard of rhinos, making the most noise possible.

Emery stopped abruptly, twisting back around and withdrew two silver daggers from her jacket, releasing them with precision. They cleaved through the trees, whistling, piercing into the night.

The ear-piercing cry of two wolves were proof enough the blades hit their mark, the silver searing through their flesh.

A smile played on her lips in silent triumph before she turned back and continued racing for safety. The road was just ahead, dodging between narrow gaps in the trees until she came upon the road—gravel snaking through the woods.

Her feet struck the pavement, a small break in the forest before giant trees took over once more. The motorbike was idly waiting, exactly where Emery left it. Flipping her leg over the side, she straddled the bike, threw her key in the ignition, and kick-started it to life.

The exhaust was muffled for a crotch rocket. She had it modified to run silently, perfect for a quick getaway or sneaking up on someone. The bike purred with sufficient thrust. She leaned down into the metal as it propelled forward into the moonless night.

The connection to her mother remained silent. Emery hadn't been able to mind link Amelia for a while now, but she knew without a doubt she wasn't dead.

Emery pushed the bike further into the night, weaving through the forest until finally breaking free of the seemingly endless trees. A city loomed ahead where gas lamps lined the streets and the sky was illuminated with artificial lighting, erasing the stars.

Steering the bike, she drove until she came upon an abandoned parking garage, driving up the ramps like a demon chased by holy water.

Emery reached the fourth level and pulled into parking spot twenty-eight. Flicking down the kickstand, she switched the bike off and threw her leg over the side. She stretched out her limbs. Escaping death was an adrenaline rush that left her bones aching and stiff.

The garage was silent. Not a single word of chatter could be overheard. There were zero cars idling, waiting for the comfort of home. Only the breeze stirred the air, carrying the lingering scents of stale piss, gas fumes, and burnt rubber.

A thick, cement column dividing her stall from the next reminded her of her task. The one Emery's mother entrusted her with.

She jumped up, the pads of her fingers gripping onto the smooth load-bearing beam until she was able to pull herself up. Swinging her legs up, she tucked her body in, the beam wide enough to conceal a body. She shimmied her way down the shaft to the opposing cement column.

A lumpy shadow could be spotted in the L bracket of the beams.

Emery grabbed the dark form. A solid black bookbag her mother had stashed there the moment they moved into town. She zipped open the bag, confirming its contents, ensuring no one had disturbed the bag since it had been deposited there two years ago. The sack contained stacks of money in various currencies, passports with assumed aliases, and matching fake IDs.

More made-up lives and counterfeit identities.

This particular set identified Emery as Shannon Dirk, daughter of Patty Dirk.

What kind of a name was Dirk? Might as well be Dick. Stupid surname.

Emery's ears perked.

The sound of tires squealing three levels below made her heart freeze, her stomach turned to acid. She zipped the bag shut, tucking herself against the beam, lying as flat as a plank of wood.

Someone pulled their vehicle up beside her bike.

A car door slammed. Sturdy boots walked across the pavement moving in her direction. Emery tucked further into the darkness, imagining her body fusing with the metal, becoming invisible. She fastened her eyes, reaching out to her wolf, masking both of their scents from anyone with sensitivity to smell.

The garage was silent. The footsteps halted. The only thing Emery could detect was her breathing that she was struggling to calm down.

A face appeared before her—she screamed.

"Mom!" Emery shrieked in both fright and relief. Her mother was holding herself up just as she had done, close enough to make out the cuts on her face and the bruise forming along her jaw.

Amelia dropped back down to the garage floor, her hands out for the bag that her daughter threw down to her. She opened the pack, rechecking the contents before securing it shut and flinging it over her shoulder.

"You took too long to mask your scent, and screaming like that would not have saved you," Amelia said flippantly, disappointment evident in her voice.

Emery landed on her feet in front of her mother, standing up straight. "I know. I'm sorry."

What good would screaming have done? That's not what she had been trained to do. "Why didn't you let me know you were coming?"

"I couldn't risk them sensing me using my powers. Besides, it's getting harder for me," Amelia said, glancing away, her eyes remote and cold.

Emery stared after her mother, wondering for the millionth time what she must have been like, before kids, before rogues and constantly fleeing for their lives. The only mother she had ever known was hard, determined, overprotective, and demanding. Always training, always on the run, constantly preparing. It was exhausting but also had saved their lives on numerous occasions. Her mother had given up everything to keep her safe.

She would ensure it was worth it.

"Where to now?"

"Home. We're going home."

CHAPTER 3

SLOWLY FADING

Boston Airport was crowded with men in business suits on their way to early morning meetings, families were urging their children to slow down after their overnight flights and security guards patrolling the terminals.

The airport stunk of sweat, cleaning products, and processed food priced four times its worth. The plane engines vibrated the glass of the windows as a woman spoke over the intercom, announcing yet another terminal change on unsuspecting passengers.

Amelia and Emery exited their plane, their necks stiff and their butt's sore.

Emery looked to her mother. Amelia wore a black wig in public to disguise her unique, silver hair. The bags under those sea-green eyes and loose skin hanging off sharpened cheekbones made her wonder when the last proper meal was. Was Amelia malnourished? Maybe she was.

Those Goddess-given powers had been taking a toll on her body for as long as Emery could remember, and she had been using them a lot lately.

Hopefully, going back to Amelia's ancestral pack would help. But when was life ever that simple?

Amelia had told her almost everything about growing up with the Wandering Moon. Where Emery came from, who her father was, their heritage, and where their powers originated. As the descendants of Rhea, their lineage made them unique and coveted. What her mother didn't know was that Emery had conducted her own research, trying to figure out the origins of their powers. Desperately trying to understand why they'd been hunted all these years.

Emery could remember the night she found out. She had been snooping in a trunk of her mother's things, the sole piece of furniture her mother carted with them everywhere they went. Amelia kept it locked, but what she didn't know was her daughter had taught herself how to pick locks. Getting into the trunk was easy. The contents were a bit more challenging to face. She discovered pictures. Hundreds of photos of people she'd only ever heard of in stories. Her Uncle and his wife with their three kids, her cousins. A yellowing picture of her late grandfather, countless family photos at BBQs, pack gatherings, and holidays spent together.

Emery couldn't help but feel a pang of jealousy.

Amelia tried her best to provide a seemingly normal childhood but moving around every year or two, sometimes running in the middle of the night, didn't exactly allow for a place that felt like home.

In every photo, her mother was smiling. She was joyful, happy with her family and pack. Every so often, Emery felt guilty for existing, for ripping her mother away from her pack and mate.

Maybe it was stupid. But that didn't stop the guilt.

Amelia didn't like to talk about her father, Gabriel. Not that she never did. She was always as candid as she could be and tried her best to answer her questions, but there was always a deep sadness whenever she spoke of him.

Periodically, muffled cries could be heard through the bedroom wall. As though, if anyone knew the true depth of despair buried deep within, the walls so expertly built would be obliterated, exposing a hollow shell.

There had been a few instances where her mother would gasp in pain, clutching at her chest, which seemed to break her further, but she never complained. Not once.

Her mother was the most courageous, strongest person alive. Discovering that book, the one that recounted the history of the first pack, the first mated pair, provided understanding of the genuine hardship and pain Amelia endured. Emery may not be able to understand the full ramifications, being mateless herself, but it did provide clarity of the consequences caused by mates separating—particularly fated mates.

Amelia was silent as they walked through the terminal to the baggage claim.

Emery took in the airport, breathing in the smell of jet fuel and body odor. America was the one country they never dared to enter. The family that lived there were strangers. Didn't even know of her existence. Uncle Damon was the only relative she'd had the pleasure of meeting. But that was nearly a decade ago. Now, nerves set her gut churning.

They were the last ones to arrive at the baggage claim.

The flight they managed to get on at the last minute in London had barely been half-full. Most of the bags had already been claimed. Amelia caught sight of her worn, wooden trunk circling around the automatic belt. It was the only thing she bothered to save from the London Manor.

Emery assisted her in hauling it off the belt, setting it carefully on the thin carpet floor.

Amelia was busy typing away on her phone, texting Goddess knows who, when she looked up smiling.

"He's here," Amelia said, unable to contain her excitement.

Emery tried to ignore the bats beating in her stomach as she seized an end of the trunk, helping her mother outside to the curbside pick-up. Just as they exited the airport, out into the heated, humid, stinking air, a white minivan pulled up, throwing the car in park, causing the car to stutter in protest.

Emery watched as a man exited the van. The silver-blonde and sea-green eyes were identical to her mother.

Amelia couldn't hold herself back, flinging herself into her twins' arms.

Uncle Damon looked exactly like the pictures contained in the trunk set on the pavement. His voice was a bit deeper in person than she remembered hearing through the phone during their weekly chats. Emery barely remembered their first meeting. The memories were buried deep in her subconscious, hidden behind a wall erected to preserve what little remained of her innocence. She hung back, providing her mother a moment to reunite with her brother.

Amelia clung to her brother, fisting his shirt in both her hands, terrified that it was all just a dream. The smell that wafted off the cotton shirt brought forth memories long forgotten. Only now additional scents lingered—his wife and three boys. They were ingrained in him, surrounding him, constantly providing a sense of direction. Home.

Damon looked the same to her, a few additional lines across his forehead, hair cropped shorter than she remembered, but his body had thickened out over the years, adding on additional layers of muscle.

Amelia pulled back.

For once, she didn't care about the tears flooding her eyes. Happiness, a once distant memory, came back, and nothing was going to stop that.

Damon looked at her in the same way, tears slipping down his cheeks, lips pulled up into a goofy grin. She rumpled his hair out of nervous habit before turning back to her daughter.

"Baby, this is your Uncle Damon. Damon, you know Emery," Amelia introduced the two, wiping away the tears.

"You've grown since I last saw you," Damon stepped forward, gathering her in his arms.

Emery stiffened, not used to being treated so familial, but as his scent filled her, she relaxed. He smelled a lot like her mother, only a bit muskier. Even though her entire life consisted of weekly phone calls, talking about everything under the moon, it was still shocking to meet him in person.

Oddly enough, it felt right, like coming home for the first time.

Damon stepped back from two of his favorite women in the world and smiled. Emery looked so much like her mother. The only piece of Gabriel he could see in the girl was her hair, a bit darker than their silver-blonde with black roots, midway through it transitioned from black to blonde. But then again, those eyes were all Gabriel.

Gabriel wasn't a topic his sister brought up, ever. Had never inquired as to how he was or what he had done with his life since she left. Talking about it was painful enough. Why be reminded of what had been given up? But, nevertheless, he thanked the Goddess every day he never had to tell her.

"Let's get out of here," Amelia said, piercing the silence, her eyes scanning their surroundings.

Damon was inclined to agree.

Collectively, he and Amelia loaded the trunk into the back of the van before they all loaded inside. Emery took the middle row while his sister joined him upfront.

"Since when do you drive the van?" Amelia asked, still minding the few people outside of the terminal as they pulled away from the airport.

"Cordie took the boys to their friend's house this morning in the SUV. I didn't have much of a choice."

Amelia barely had time to text Damon their flight's arrival time before boarding the plane. No one knew she was coming, and it had to remain that way.

Being back in Massachusetts, their home state, was sudden and not something considered lightly. But given that her powers were extracting an increasing amount of energy and the resurgence of the rogues, options were limited, if not singular. They needed help and for the first time in seventeen years, hope bloomed.

"Who knows we're here?" Amelia asked.

Emery continued looking out the window. The landscape quickly turned from barren runways to lush greenery as they entered the highway.

"No one. I didn't tell a soul," Damon assured her.

"He'll know soon. There's a reason I've kept an ocean between us."

Emery's ear perked with interest. Were they talking about her father? Was she going to get to meet him? Did she want to?

Damon reached out, grasping her hand, the skin was icy and small, able to feel every bone beneath her thin skin. It was worse than she let on.

Amelia jerked her hand back into her lap, tucking it inside her jacket.

"You lied to me," Damon growled, trying not to startle his niece. "You told me you were okay."

"I'm fine," Amelia growled back.

Damon flinched. Even her growl was diminished. How was this possible? But then again, he couldn't recall the last time they had mind linked. A few years ago, maybe. Amelia had told him they shouldn't try it anymore. Saying it was too hard given the distance. Though it never seemed to bother them in the past. Was her wolf even alive?

"Where's Rey?" Damon asked, trying to mind link his sister. His wolf, Zeke, was beginning to panic, unable to sense their twin.

Amelia sighed, her breath filled with grief and despair. "I don't know."

His knuckles turned white as his death grip on the steering wheel increased. "What do you mean you don't know?"

"I mean, I don't know, Damon. I haven't felt her in over a year."

Emery tried not to indicate her reaction, but her mother's words rocked her to the core. No wonder they hadn't mind linked in so long, no wonder she looked sickly. If her wolf was indeed gone, the human side would die out. It was a slow and painful way to go. Most committed suicide if the wolf half faded.

"I don't want to talk about it," Amelia informed him with finality.

But Damon would have none of that. "I'm taking you to the Packhouse. Our doctor needs to examine you. We have to find a way-"

"No!" Amelia's voice shook the car, a bit of her old self coming to the surface. "No. No one can know we're here."

Damon huffed in annoyance. He didn't care what his sister said. Saving her was all that mattered. "Where am I taking you?"

Amelia offered a slip of paper containing a handwritten address. Damon flicked it open, glancing at it over the wheel. "You're staying in the city? The pack grounds would be safer. We can protect you."

"We're safer hiding amongst the humans. I won't bring my war to your pack, not again. I can handle this, Damon," Amelia told him, trying her best to sound stern and confident, when deep inside, terror reigned. If death came sooner rather than later, leaving Emery unprotected.

Damon swerved the car sharply off the highway, down a ramp, and into the heart of the city. It was only an hour outside of the Wandering Moon's borders, but that still didn't help ease the worry, the doubt. He didn't want to leave his sister, not if her wolf was indeed gone, making her vulnerable.

Damon pulled up to a three-story brownstone in the Boston city heights. The house was easily a hundred years old. The weathered brick and Victorian style were evidence enough. He looked at his sister quizzically.

Amelia noted his look and shrugged her shoulders. "I bought it shortly after I left, just in case I needed a place to come back too."

"You could always come back to your pack. We love you," Damon tried to assure her.

"This has nothing to do with love, Damon. The reason I left is the same reason I can't go back. I won't put them at risk." With that being said, Amelia opened the door and got out of the car.

Damon glanced back at Emery, who gave him a slight shrug, almost as if to say, what's there to do? Amelia was strong-willed, and they both knew it. Damon was going to have to take matters into his own hands, whether his sister liked it or not, but first, he needed to have a private chat with his niece.

Emery got out of the car and followed her mother up the sidewalk to the steps that lead up to the vast brick house. She slipped her hand in her mother's, offering a light squeeze.

"Why don't you go inside, Mom. I'm sure the windows need to be opened to air out the house. I'll help Uncle Damon with the trunk," Emery suggested.

Amelia inclined her head, leaving her daughter on the sidewalk as she walked up the steps, pulled a key from a pocket, and stepped inside the home, leaving the front door open.

Emery turned back to the trunk of the van, her uncle patiently waiting. The look in those eyes were unmistakable— a serious discussion awaited.

"What's going on with your mother?" Damon asked, not to waste any time.

"She's been like this for a while now" The pavement looked exceptionally interesting, rocking back and forth on her heels.

"We talk every week, and you never bothered to tell me?" Damon hissed harshly.

"I couldn't. Mom was always hovering, and I was hoping she'd get better."

"But she hasn't."

Emery shook her head no.

"Do we know what's causing it? Is it poison?"

Emery gnawed her lip. "It's the mate bond."

Damon startled, taken aback, frowning. "The mate bond? How? Why?"

Emery glanced back at the house, tucking silver hair behind an ear, listening for Amelia's familiar footsteps and labored breathing. Muttered curses could be heard from the rear of the house, along with the struggling of a stuck window.

Good, busy meant no eavesdropping.

Emery pulled out a hairpin from a jean pocket, prying it open until it was one long pick. The pin slipped inside the lock on the trunk, twisting and feeling around until she felt the familiar tumblers give way, releasing the lock with a satisfying pop. She flicked off the lock, prying the wooden trunk open and rummaged around inside. Pushing aside stacks of documents, pictures, and other memorabilia, she reached the familiar leather-bound book. Emery plucked it out, handing it to her uncle.

"What is this?" Damon asked, flipping the book over in his hand.

"It's a journal. Rhea's journal," Emery informed him.

Damon's eyes widened. "Rhea, as in *the* Rhea, the first werewolf? The first mated pair?"

Emery nodded her head in confirmation. "Yes. Mom somehow managed to track it down. Rhea used to communicate with the moon goddess through dreams and visions. She recorded everything in that journal. Take it with you, read it. You'll understand."

"Emery?"

Emery startled, hearing her mother calling for her. Quickly easing the lid of the trunk closed, she stuck the lock back on and fastened it shut. Damon tucked the book into a private compartment in the back of the van, hiding it for safekeeping. Collectively, they grabbed each side of the trunk and carried it out of the car and up the front of the house.

"What are you two up to?" Amelia asked, hands on her hips.

"Just catching up with my niece." Damon dismissed the meddling tone as they walked the massive trunk inside the house.

Amelia directed them into the primary sitting room, where they settled the trunk down on the floor in the corner of the room.

Damon dusted his hands off on his jeans, looking around the interior of the house. It was quaint and well put together for a place that hadn't been lived in. He noted the time on his watch, muttering a string of curses.

"Crap, I have to head back. Cordie should be home soon, and if I'm not back before her . . . well, we don't want her asking where I've been, now do we?" Damon asked rhetorically that had Amelia shaking her head adamantly. "I gotta go. You call me if you need me."

Amelia smiled, winding her arms around his waist, and leaned into the familial bond that kept them linked. "Promise. I love you."

"I love you more." Damon turned to his niece, hugging her as well. "I'll see you soon, little bug," he teased before bending down to whisper in her ear. "You call me at the first sign of trouble."

Emery nodded into his shoulder, squeezing in return, and walked with him to the front door, Amelia staying behind searching for something to consume in the kitchen. She watched as he got in his van and pulled away from their house, driving down the street until the minivan was out of view.

She sent a silent prayer to the Goddess, pleading with the mother of their race to spare her mother. No one was dying, especially not for her sake.

CHAPTER 4

FADING INTO SILENCE

I t was late at night. From her window, the moon was a sliver in the sky—the city lights masking the twinkling stars.

Being back in this city, so close to home, both homes, was terrifying and euphoric. Like she could finally take in a deep breath, no longer feeling exhausted and drained, something that had been all too frequent in recent months. A bit of color was indeed returning to her skin. Whether it was due to the proximity of a certain male or near their ancestral lands remained a mystery.

If she concentrated hard enough, the mate bond lay just beneath the surface, faint and fragile. Goddess. The idea of reaching across the bond, caressing the string that tethered her heart to his was all consuming. Would he even recognize it or was he too far gone?

Most nights were spent curled in a ball, heart and soul shredding into unrecognizable pieces. He moved on. The bond that was near its breaking point reminded her of it every time he was with another woman, lost to the throws of passion. The pain in her chest was consuming and bitter. But as the years went on, the pain became less and less as her wolf got weaker and weaker.

The bond more than likely no longer required the words of rejection. Time had done enough damage. And once the bond did finally snap, she wouldn't be far behind, her wolf and body too frail to survive the breaking.

This was why she needed to come back—to deliver Emery back to her family.

After all these years, the last thing Amelia wanted was to put her old pack in danger, again, but Damon would do everything in his power to keep her safe. Emery's father would do the same. She was his daughter, after all, but he didn't even know of her existence, and she wasn't about to involve his pack as well.

One pack in the line of fire was enough.

Besides, Emery was a Wandering Moon wolf, direct descendent of Rhea, and chosen daughter of the Moon Goddess. The Wandering Moon was honor-bound to defend her with their lives. The last surviving female of their line. She was precious, and Amelia would give her last breath to protect her child.

Amelia laid back against the downy, plush pillow, remembering a previous conversation with Rey, her other half, her wolf.

It was almost a year ago, one late night in the London Manor.

Amelia had spent all day training Emery, demonstrating on how to scale trees, jumping, and swinging from branch to branch. They had exhausted themselves physically, but most of the day was watching each other falling to the ground, landing in various painful positions. She was fairly certain she had broken her tail bone, but they persisted anyway. Learning to climb and jump through trees disciplined them to be nimble and adapt to any environment. Exploit any resource, even trees.

Amelia and Emery had eaten dinner together with the rest of the pack before retiring separately to their rooms. The bruises and pain that throbbed to the bone must be what it feels like to be run over by a bulldozer.

As she settled down to bed, the pain started up again. It began much the same. Swelling and building into a crescendo that left her lying in bed, clutching at her chest and gasping for breath. Her heart was shattering, slowly tearing itself to pieces.

Amelia. I can't take much more of this. Rey pleaded with her.

Rey had been begging to go back, back to their mate and pack. They were weakening, their powers becoming increasingly difficult to maintain. They hadn't received dreams from the Moon Goddess in a long while.

Amelia knew something was going on, something had changed, and could feel it in her bones. But she didn't realize how serious it was until a friend of hers, an elder who had access to some of their oldest texts, sent her a journal.

Rhea's personal journal.

Rhea had recorded her initial days as a werewolf. The first female werewolf had received countless visions and dreams, interacting with the Moon Goddess in person. Since Rhea and Ezekial were the first mated pair, the Moon Goddess took it upon herself to explain the workings of the mate bond, explaining their connection, their powers, and the consequences if they spat on that gift.

Together, a fated pair was more potent than any others. The male would receive increased strength and speed, keener senses. But the female would receive a unique sort of ability. She would be capable of healing those she touched, command any wolf, whether they be a member of the pack or not, and she could foresee the future. In the time of Rhea, the Moon Goddess deemed her the true Alpha, and once the mating bond was completed, she would come into her rightful power, complete with a dominating aura.

Amelia read through the journal, noting the distinct similarities to her situation, but what she read next stopped her heart, the blood freezing in their veins. The Moon Goddess forewarned them that if fated mates were to separate without severing the bond completely, the female would grow weak and ultimately die. The mate bond was what fueled her power and that power thrived off their bond. Her wolf was alive because of their power.

One could not survive without the other.

Amelia believed she had survived as long as she had due to dumb luck and the stubborn will to live. But ever since they had discovered the truth, Rey had been pleading with her to go back.

You know we can't! Emery's not ready! she said through gritted teeth, the pain reaching its peak.

Amelia, we're dying! It's not going to matter. We'll be gone. Her father could protect her, Rey begged, trying to appeal to some kind of common sense.

He practically died trying to protect us! Don't you remember that? I miss him too. We can't risk his life again. I won't be able to survive it if something were to happen. She ultimately let out her breath she'd been holding onto, the pain finally ebbing and subsiding.

We won't survive either. Amelia, you are more capable than you know. Your strength comes from your love. Let yourself receive love. That is the true sacrifice. True selflessness comes from being loved and receiving that love with everything you have. Don't forget—

Amelia began to panic. Rey's voice faded into silence.

Rey? She called out. *Rey, can you hear me?*

Rey? "Rey?!" she screamed but was met with absolute and utter quiet.

Amelia could remember the terror like it was yesterday. It had been a year. Some days she could sense a glimmer of Rey. A minor piece of consciousness still holding on in the deepest recesses of their mind.

Ever since that day, she refused to shift, declined to even try, afraid she wouldn't be able to, or worse, it would be the ultimate strain on her wolf. The claws and elongate canines were about all she dared to access, the farthest she was willing to push for.

But being on the same continent, merely a state away from their mate, a faint glimpse of Rey grew a tad brighter, but it was only delaying the inevitable. She could feel it in her heart, her soul. The bond had no more than two weeks left, if it continued to fray as it had been for years and that's if they weren't ambushed, if she didn't have to call on her reserves. The attack on the London Pack Manor took a lot of energy, which was why she brought Emery home.

Emery had tried convincing Amelia to come back sooner. Probably to meet her father. But with no mate of her own, how could she understand? That being with Gabriel again, reforging the bond, would preserve her life and if she did know, that would open a whole other can of worms.

How could Amelia explain to her daughter that the man she was so deeply in love with, her mate, had moved on? Who was having sex almost every night, slowly chipping away at her heart, her soul, and her life.

Yes, reuniting with Gabriel would preserve Amelia's life, but she wasn't about to show up on his doorstep, dying and with their child in tow just to save her own life.

He deserved happiness, even if it meant them never being together.

CHAPTER 5

CONVENIENT
INCONVENIENCE

"Emery! Time to get up!" Amelia yelled up the stairs.

"I'm already up," Emery groaned, stomping down the wood steps in the same clothes from yesterday. "God, you sound like a baboon wailing like that."

Amelia smirked. Emery was customarily a grump in the morning—like father, like daughter.

"Breakfast," she said, pushing a plate filled with eggs, bacon, and sausage in front of her kid.

Emery instantly perked at the sight of food, digging into the plate immediately.

"Hurry up and eat. We have some shopping to do."

"Shopping?" Emery mumbled over a mouth full of food.

"Well, we did leave everything behind in London. We can't live off one set of clothes." Amelia sniffed at her shirt. "We're starting to smell a bit ripe."

Emery chuckled. "I think that smell is all you."

Amelia rejected that. "Anyways. Like I said, shopping. We'll go out and get everything we need."

"But we don't have a car."

"Yes, we do."

"How? When?"

"Don't worry about that. All you need to worry about is getting your tush upstairs, brushing your teeth, and meeting me outside," Amelia said, finishing her mug of coffee in one gulp.

Emery was about to get up to do as directed but stopped, allowing a more extensive look at her mother. The dark bags under those green-blue eyes were no longer as noticeable. The one sullen skin had some color to it and overall appeared better.

"Are you feeling okay? You no longer resemble the Walking Dead," Emery said, gesturing to her face.

"First of all, rude. Second, I managed to get some sleep last night, thank you very much. Third, you're cut off from the tv. We've got enough real-life horror. I don't need you watching it too. Now go, hurry up. I want to be out of here in ten and miss the morning traffic."

Emery disappeared up the stairs, feet pounding into the floor above.

Amelia shook her head laughing before grabbing the backpack off the counter. Inside was a stack of cash, along with their counterfeit passports and IDs, and transferred it to a purse she discovered on the floor of her bedroom closet last night.

The black wig was in there as well, mocking her. She hated wearing it, hated having to conceal a part of her, but it was an additional layer of protection for them. Those silver locks were too noticeable, too easily seen.

Amelia quickly bound her hair. Cutting it was never an option. He liked it long, and honestly, so did she. Flipping her head over and clipping it into place before sitting upright, she ensured her silver hair was completely hidden. She slipped her phone into her back pocket when footsteps pounded down the stairs.

"Slow down. You sound like a herd of elephants," Amelia said in warning. The last thing they needed was for an accident down the stairs.

"Sorry, Momma." Emery smiled, not sorry at all.

Amelia rolled her eyes at the rambunctious teen before giving her a light shove towards the front door. She snatched the purse off the counter, along with a new set of car keys.

Outside, she secured the door, giving a firm tug to ensure it was indeed locked. Parked on the street was a sleek gray Audi sports car. Emery stared at it, mouth gaping open.

"Since when did you find time to buy a car? Since when did we have the money to buy *this* kind of car?" Emery asked in a state of sticker shock.

Amelia frowned, herding Emery towards the vehicle as they both got in. "I told you. When your grandfather died, he left us quite a bit of money. We've never really needed to use any of it since we've been moving from pack to pack over the years. Besides, this'll be yours one day."

Emery was almost afraid to touch it, settling into the expensive car.

The Audi was glossy and pristine with that brand-new car smell of tanned leather and lemons.

Amelia's words should have left her jumping for joy. Any teenager with the prospect of owning this kind of car would be through the roof, but something was off. Amelia was dying, and soon, and she wanted to make sure Emery was taken care of.

The contents settling in her stomach from the morning's breakfast turned sour.

Amelia pushed the start button, the engine purring to life. Without a moment's hesitation, she shifted the car into gear and took off down the road, away from the house, and into the vast city. She kept glancing over at her unusually silent daughter, staring out the window.

"Emmie, what's wrong?"

Emery looked up to discover Amelia smiling with those sad eyes. Even after everything, her mother was constantly smiling, no matter what.

The last thing her mother needed was to be burdened by her anxieties. The worry that just going for a walk would be too taxing. Fear of her dropping dead cooking dinner. So instead, Emery swallowed it all down and chose to focus on a separate issue.

"Aren't you worried we might be noticed? Going out in public, especially this close to Uncle Damon, is a risk," Emery wondered aloud.

"I'm a little worried. I'd be lying if I said I wasn't. No matter what we do, it's a risk, but we can't hide away forever. We've tried that, and it doesn't work," Amelia told her, focusing on the road, weaving in and out of traffic, making their way to the shopping district.

Emery couldn't help but bob her head. They tried hiding in the past, completely isolating themselves. A village in Kenya, a hobble in Columbia, the forests of Bulgaria, even a hut in the northern reaches of Russia. No matter where they hid, somehow, they were inevitably found. It was as though whoever had been pursuing them around the globe could sense them, track them somehow.

"Besides. You and I, we're a team. Right?" She saw her daughter nod in her head fervently out of the corner of her eye. "Right. We've prepared hundreds of scenarios. If something goes awry, we know what to do, and we'll always find each other."

"Always," Emery said meekly, knowing soon enough that wouldn't be possible.

Amelia pulled up to the shopping district, managing to snag a parking spot on the main street, parallel parking the car with ease.

They spent the next few hours in and out of a dozen stores, buying countless outfits, shoes, and accessories.

Emery missed the slow pace of Europe. The difference in culture where life wasn't a rush, where store associates weren't following their every move incessantly offering their help. The leisurely strolls, taking the time to admire and appreciate life's simple moments were a commodity in the states.

They had to make two trips back to the car to drop off bags. They had bought enough to fill each closet in the entire house, enough clothes for any occasion, but none of that mattered. For the first time in a long time, they were relaxing, having fun, and just being a normal mother and daughter out on the town.

After the first drop off at the car, they stopped for ice cream and finally succumbed to their growling stomachs, stopping at a cafe, and enjoying lunch together. Amelia couldn't help the smirk over life's simplicities, Emery catching the eye of an adolescent boy, teasing her over their sandwiches.

Emery produced the deepest shade of red known to man.

Leaving lunch behind, the girls headed back out to the shops, deciding to take one last loop around before calling it a day. Amelia started to feel tired, her bones aching, but she wasn't about to cut their day short, didn't want to end the precious time spent making memories with her kid.

They passed by a series of offices before coming up on the next row of stores. Amelia stopped in front of the first one, a home fragrance store. Their current home could use some candles, and they were running low on lotion. The fall scents wafting from their doors and out onto the streets thawed the ice in her heart just a fraction—cloves, cinnamon, and apples, her favorite.

The scent was familiar and sent her heart racing. The hair along Amelia's neck and arms raised in alarm. Those sea-green eyes widened, brow furrowing as a certain string hummed. For the first time in a year, Rey was stirring in the back of her mind.

Amelia gripped Emery's arm tightly, hauling them away from the store farther down the street.

"Mom! What's wrong?" Emery asked, the panic contagious, trying to jerk her arm free from her mother's death grip.

"Hush!" Amelia hissed in warning, a growl pushing through teeth, instantly quieting her resisting daughter.

They continued walking down the street, their feet moving quickly over the pavement, trying to put as much distance between them and the one Amelia has been desperate to avoid as possible.

Amelia spun on her heels, forcing Emery to meet her gaze. "You are going to cross the street quickly. You are going to double back to cover your scent. I will meet you at the car. Lock yourself inside, and do *not* open the door unless it's me. If I'm not back in half an hour, you call your uncle and drive like hell to his pack. Do you understand me?"

Emery frowned. "What's going on? What's wrong?"

Amelia thrust the set of keys into her hand before finally letting go. "No time. Walk, don't run. You'll look suspicious if you run. Now, go."

Even though defiance and speculation were plain on her daughter's face, thankfully Emery knew better than to question orders. She didn't bother to watch her swiftly cross the road, not needing to. Emery had been trained well and could find her way through a maze if need be.

No, Amelia's task now was to steer him as far away from Emery as possible. His smell was getting closer by the second.

Amelia dodged into an abandoned alley wedged between two towering buildings.

Amelia kept going, pushing further into the more desolate part of the city when a hand reached out, seizing her from behind and pinned her to a rough cement wall. He reached up, ripping the wig off, hurling it down into a muddy puddle, forcing silver-blonde hair to cascade, unrolling past her waist.

For the first time in over a year, Rey was finally stirring, struggling to gain consciousness as the ripples racing along her flesh sent a psychic shock to their heart.

Amelia fastened her eyes, struggling against the bond that was hammering in her chest. The butterflies that were beating in her stomach. The shivers that were racking down each vertebra, slow enough to make her teeth rattle.

Rey's abrupt reappearance was painful. Her mind had grown used to being the sole occupant and was now shoved aside to make room for her wolf once again.

A sharp, rough shake jolted her, skin scraping down the jagged wall. She was terrified to look at him, to see the look on his face, what she might find there may be worse than anything she dared to imagine.

"Look at me!" he growled, shouting.

His Alpha aura expanded around them, flexing angrily, consuming the light filtered between the buildings and bringing forth a darkness that may have once left her shaking. But Amelia knew darkness, understood it. The dark had been her lonely companion these last years, she lived in it and not even his menacing aura could rival her own nightmares.

Even though his Alpha command didn't work, she couldn't help but obey. Gradually, she came face to face with her mate.

His lustrous eyes were sinister, almost black, his wolf near the surface.

Her mate looked much the same as she remembered, except for the additional worry lines across his forehead, the tiny wrinkles at the corner of those stunning silver eyes, and the light, thin scars that marked a warrior's skin. The lovely black hair she spent hours running her fingers through was much the same, except for now it was longer, hanging past the ears, combed back from that furious face.

Gabriel was dressed for business in a dark suit and jade tie. He had filled out over the years, much like her brother, adding on additional layers of rigid muscle.

The key difference was the gold band on the left ring finger.

That hurt worse than dying.

No. Amelia couldn't afford to think like that. Her claim to him was long over.

Good for him.

Amelia needed to be strong, needed to stand her ground. No matter what. She couldn't allow him to affect her or her duty to Emery, their daughter. The one he didn't even know existed.

Holding his gaze firmly with whatever power she had left, Amelia grew her aura and expanded it past his. Licking at the air between them, she forced it back until rays of sunshine flooded back into the alley, until finally he looked away.

Gabriel took a step back, dropping his hands in utter defeat.

Losing his touch was like losing the sun's heat, its warm, comforting presence, leaving her frozen and shaking. Amelia pulled on her jacket, enveloping it tighter around her thin body.

"What do you want, Gabriel?" she spit, trying to sound menacing as though she never cared at all.

Her heart was broken further.

Gabriel flinched at her words. A brief flash of sadness crossed his face before it was rapidly replaced with anger. "That's all you have to say to me?! After seventeen years, that's all I get?"

"What do you want me to say? I'm sorry? Well, I'm not." It wasn't a total lie.

Gabriel growled angrily, his claws extending.

Mate, Rey cried out, her voice frail and faint.

Shh, Rey. It's okay. Save your strength, she begged her wolf.

"Will killing me make you feel better?" Amelia asked, taunting. "Go ahead." She tilted her head, exposing her neck for a final blow, a killing strike. "Kill me."

Gabriel froze. He hadn't expected her to surrender, especially not so easily. It was like she had a death wish. "Why did you abandon me, Amelia? After everything we'd been through, losing a child, we could have faced it together."

Amelia winced. The memory of that night, the blood, the pain haunted her dreams nearly every night. Those jade blue eyes turned cold, noticing the wedding band on his finger. "What do you care? You moved on. You have a new Luna," she said, the words were acid in her mouth. "Why don't you just move on with your life, and I'll do the same with mine."

With one final push, she expanded her Alpha aura even farther, dominating him into submission, until it was no more than a faint band around his body.

Gabriel looked furious over the fact that she was capable of overpowering him, but he was unable to disable her, unable to do a damn thing against it. He backed away from her slowly as though she was a rabid beast.

"This isn't over," he growled, moving farther away towards the entrance of the alley.

"It was over seventeen years ago," Amelia informed him, her voice losing its venom, fatigue building, settling deep in her bones.

Amelia watched as he backed out until he was no longer shrouded in shadows and back on the bustling street. Watched as stared at her, searching for the woman he once knew, once loved, until he was gone from sight.

Darkness clouded her vision. Fog swallowed her mind as her knees shook. She thought to call for help, but who would come? No one.

Blackness swallowed her before she could even think to grab onto anything that might slow her fall.

CHAPTER 6

BACK HOME

E mery was waiting in the car.

Her legs were jigging up and down, fumbling with the keys, contemplating her next move. Those silver eyes surveyed the streets on either side, seeking any sign of her mother. Waiting for that fake wig to come into view, for her mothering-tone to scold her for not doing as she was told—given that her thirty-minute time limit had expired ten minutes ago.

A familiar presence brushed faintly on the edges of her mind, like a feather drifting on the wind, weightless and fleeting. Someone she hadn't felt in a long while.

Mom? Rey? Emery called out. She'd bet their lives it was her mother's wolf.

But as soon as it appeared, it vanished, leaving her even more hollow and alone.

A knot formed in the pit of her stomach. Something was wrong.

Unlocking the car door, she stepped out onto the street, slamming the door shut and securing it. She walked back the way she came, retracing her steps to where she'd last seen her mother. Anxiety increased with every step, fear gnawing at the rational side that reminded her if Amelia was dead, she would know.

As she continued down the lanes of shops, her feet gaining speed with every step, something buzzed in her jean pocket.

Emery answered the call without bothering to check the caller ID.

"Hello?"

"Emery! Thank the Goddess. What's going on?!" Uncle Damon's voice came through the phone.

Emery pushed through the thickening crowds, her pace faster than anyone around, continuing to survey the bustling crowd. No screams, no calls for help—that had to be a good sign.

Right?

"What do you mean?" Emery asked absently, unable to focus, all of her being centered on tracking her mother.

"I thought I sensed Rey for a second, but then the connection just ended. Where is your mother? Put her on the phone."

Emery's stomach twisted in knots. Her throat increasingly dry. "I-I can't find her."

"What do you mean you can't find her?"

"She told me to run. We were in the city shopping. Everything was fine, and then she just grabbed me and told me to go back to the car. She told me to go to you if she didn't make it back in thirty minutes. It's been over forty . . . I can't abandon her, Uncle Damon. I won't."

Emery stopped on the street. A soft gust of wind kissed the rising flush on her skin, releasing a familiar scent—roses and honey.

"I can smell her," Emery said faintly, glancing both ways for oncoming cars before dashing across the street.

"Emery, stay where you are! It could be a trap!"

A car engine roared to life in the background, but none of that mattered. She lifted her nose to the air. Her mother's scent came from a row of stores to the left.

Uncle Damon could barely be heard muttering curses under his breath, cars honking in the distance, muffled through the phone.

Emery's feet were running, pounding into the pavement. Her breathing became labored as fear began to win out.

Uncle Damon was yelling something through the phone but could barely piece the words together. The only sound she could make out was the beating of her heart hammering in her ears.

Emery took a left and then a right, her mother's scent carrying her farther away from pedestrian traffic. She took the last right when she froze.

The sight of a body slumped over in the rough alley halted her dead in her tracks.

She ran to the body, instantly recognizing her mother's long platinum hair.

The plastic slipped through her hands and crashed onto the gravel.

All she could do was scream, scream at her mother to wake up.

With two fingers, she pressed them against Amelia's neck. A pulse was there but barely, so faint not even the rise and fall indicating breath was visible.

Emery pulled her mother's light, frail body onto her lap, cradling her head against her chest.

When had she gotten so thin, lost so much weight? How had she not noticed?

Emery searched for any visible signs of injury but discovered none. She cupped her mother's face with one hand, shaking her head lightly.

"Mom! Mom! Wake up!" Emery yelled.

Amelia's head rolled back, unresponsive and lifeless.

Emery looked around wildly, tears streaming down her face. She couldn't risk yelling for help in case the wrong kind came calling.

Suddenly, she remembered her phone. Frantically looking around, she searched for it.

Where did she drop the damn thing?

Something pushed uncomfortably against her thigh. Reaching around her mother's limp form, she found the phone.

"Uncle Damon! She's barely breathing," Emery cried.

Tires squealed in protest on the other end. "Is she hurt?"

"Not that I can see," Emery informed him. "But she won't wake up. I don't know what's wrong with her."

"I'm almost there." Another pair of skid marks existed in the world.

"I don't know where I am."

"Your mother put a tracker in your phone. I'll be there in two minutes."

If these were any other circumstances, she'd have a few choice words for the both of them, but instead, she sat there, helpless. Tears were soaking into her hair, but none of that mattered.

"Emery!"

Emery glanced up, eyes unable to focus, moisture obscuring her vision. She blinked hard a few times, trying to clear away the annoying, useless moisture.

Damon was running towards her from the other end of the street. He stopped at the sight of his sister limp in his niece's lap. He took in a deep breath before kneeling and gathered Amelia in his arms.

"Get up, Em. It's time to go."

Emery scrambled, snatching her phone off the ground, and running after him.

They came upon a black mustang, the muscle car left running idle.

Emery stepped in front of her uncle, flinging open the back door and slid across the seat arms open. Damon carefully leaned in the car, laying Amelia across the back row, her head resting carefully in Emery's lap.

Damon slammed the door shut, running around the car, and jumped into the driver's seat. He propelled the vehicle forward and peeled off down the street. Emery struggled to buckle herself in, her body shifting and leaning with the car's sharp turns.

"Where are we going?" Emery asked. The bustling city was quickly put behind them.

"I'm taking you back to where you belong. With our pack," Damon said. Those eerily familiar sea-green irises eyed her through the rear-view mirror.

"No. No, we can't! Mom will freak!" she panicked.

A new wave of anxiety began to set in.

"Yea, well, your mother can scold me *after* we save her life." Damon didn't give a rat's ass what his sister thought.

Even though they were an hour outside of the Wandering Moon territory, Emery knew Damon would make it there in half the time, violating every law of the road.

Emery kept her eyes on her mother, counting each breath her body struggled to take in. Goddess only knew what was going on internally. It was as though Amelia's body was shutting down. Her once comforting smell of home was unusual too, laced with spices and apples. Her mother's favorite scent.

All her life her mother always had a candle burning with that same smell.

The light around them dimmed, turning a shade of dark green. Driving down an isolated road, tree canopies reached across the stretch of road, completely concealing them in filtered emerald light.

Emery caught sight of wolves racing alongside the road, running through the woods. Two, five, twelve, soon more wolves than she could count joined the procession— their long-lost pack-mate finally returning.

Emery gazed down at her mother, smiling in sadness. She had always wanted to meet Amelia and Damon's pack, the legendary Wandering Moon Pack, the one they grew up in. She had always imagined her mother bringing her, introducing her to generations of Smoke's.

This was nothing like how she imagined.

Damon pulled the car up in front of the Packhouse.

The building consisted of five stories made of red brick, vines snaked their way up the foundation.

The car doors opened on both sides. Her Uncle reached inside to lift his sister out while Emery exited from the opposite side.

Dozens of wolves gathered around them, staring at her, unsure of who she was. Was she an intruder? Or a friend?

Emery walked around the car, ignoring the hundred pairs of eyes staring into her back as she followed her uncle up the stairs and into the house. Her mother's hand was dangling limply at her side. Uncle Damon took extra care to support her head against his shoulder.

They raced down a hall, away from the main living quarters, away from the familiar scents of a home teaming with life, and into a more sterilized area.

Damon entered a spacious room. A young woman wearing a doctor's coat stood by the bed waiting.

Emery barely paid the doctor any attention before stepping to the other side of the bed, assisting Uncle Damon in laying her mother down on the thin, stiff mattress. Damon stepped back, allowing the doctor to take over as she began checking Amelia's heart rate and blood pressure. Emery held onto her mother's hand, squeezing gently, silently ordering her to stay alive.

"Damon! What happened?"

Emery looked up to discover a woman around the same age as her uncle with shoulder-length strawberry blonde hair bouncing over her shoulders. From the hazel cat eyes and flame tinted blonde hair to the broad shoulders and narrow frame, Emery would recognize her anywhere thanks to the countless pictures her mother possessed.

It was her Aunt Cordelia.

Damon barred her from going any further, but that didn't stop Cordelia from identifying the woman on the bed, her best friend unconscious and hooked up to various monitors and IV fluids.

Tears filled those hazel eyes, Cordelia's hand covering her mouth in shock.

"Amelia!" Cordelia shrieked. "What happened? How is she here? What happened to her?"

"I'll explain everything in a bit," Damon said, trying to reassure her. "But first, I need you to sit with Emery. I'll have guards placed in the hallway and increase the patrols on the border."

"What—why?" Cordelia asked, eyes firmly planted on her seemingly lifeless friend. "Damon, what's going on? Who is Emery?"

Damon directed his wife's head towards the young woman clinging to her mother. "Emery, this is your Aunt Cordie. She's going to stay with you for a bit."

Cordelia's eyes widened, mouth gaping open.

Emery ignored her aunt's stares and stood up from the bed. "Where are you going?" she asked.

Damon looked her straight in the eye. The ones so eerily identical to an Alpha he was dreading to contact.

"I have to make a call."

CHAPTER 7

HAILEY

Emery chased after Damon, pushing past her still stunned Aunt and running after him down the hallway. He was fast, but she was faster.

Emery jumped in front of him, obstructing his path, and swatted the phone out of his hand mid-dial.

The phone shattered across the floor.

"What the hell, Emery?!" Damon shouted.

"I know what you're doing, and you can't!" Emery yelled back. "You do this, and she will *never* forgive you! It's bad enough you brought us here when she strictly told you no, but I will not let you do this to my mother. You call him and everything she's done to protect us goes out the window."

Damon's eyes softened, his anger dissipating. "Emery, she's dying. Not in a few months or a few weeks, but now. Whatever she did in that alley used too much of her power. Whatever she had left of her wolf is nearly gone." Damon was guessing, but from the look on his niece's face, he could tell he was telling her exactly what she knew to be true. "I don't want to do this either, but if he can save my sister's life, then I have to try."

"I can't betray her," Emery's voice broke, shaking her head. "You don't know what it's been like for her. He's moved on."

Damon sucked in a breath, stunned. "How do you know that?"

"Mom is good at hiding a lot of things, but she can't always control when it happens. The pain she feels when he—well, you know," she said, her face blushing red hot.

And just like that, his anger was back ten-fold. "She can feel that? All these years she's known, and she experiences it every time?" By the downward cast of his niece's eyes, he had his answer. "That son of a bitch."

Emery put her hand against his chest, the effect oddly soothing him, dissolving the violence that begged to be unleashed. "Stop. Whatever you're thinking—don't. They've both done this to each other, my mother more than anything, but this was her choice. She did what she thought she had to. She understood the risks, the consequences that might result from her decision. She wasn't blind or dumb, but that doesn't mean it hurts any less."

"I read the book, Emery. I know everything. If your mother doesn't reunite with your father, and soon, she *will* die. Everything she has worked so hard to protect will come undone. You'll be vulnerable and exposed without her. If she had to choose between saving her life to save you or dying and abandoning you to your enemies, which do you think she'd choose?"

Emery was speechless, the words escaping her. Nothing she could say would make any difference. He was right. Amelia had already given up everything to protect her. She wouldn't stop now. Even if it meant doing the one thing she dreaded most in this life.

Confronting her father.

Damon could see that his words had imparted some kind of common sense. He gathered Emery in against his chest, hugging her tight. "I'll find you when I'm done. Okay?"

All Emery could do was nod. She suddenly felt exhausted, her eyes were red and dry as though she'd spent countless hours crying even when her tears had dried.

Emery watched as he retrieved the broken phone off the floor and continued down the hall.

Emery turned back around, back to her mother.

Inside the room, Aunt Cordelia was sitting in the chair waiting beside the bed, holding Amelia's hand. The doctor had attached her to a heart monitor and an IV drip, steadily releasing fluids into her body.

Cordelia looked up at the sound of incoming footsteps and surveyed her niece.

The girl was definitely a Smoke, with enough genes to recognize exactly who the father was.

Looking back down at her best friend, Cordelia couldn't help but feel betrayed. It had been seventeen years since any of them had last seen Amelia—seventeen years without her person, her confidant, her rock.

Now here her niece was. A niece no one knew existed, no one except for her husband. He knew all along, yet oddly enough, she wasn't cross. Considering the circumstances that caused Amelia to disappear in the first place, losing a child, her mate nearly dying, battle to the death to name a few, things must have been more severe than she realized.

Cordelia had always wished Amelia was out there somewhere in the world, enjoying her life, but by the look of her and her wayward daughter, it was far from it.

Cordelia stood up from the chair, gesturing towards the chair. "Here, baby, why don't you come and sit."

All Emery could do was nod, selecting the seat beside her mother.

Cordelia bent down, relaxing her hand over Emery's, offering a reassuring squeeze. "I'm your Aunt Cordie."

"I know." Emery tried to smile, but exhaustion was making it difficult. "Mom told me all about you."

"She did?" Cordelia asked, surprised.

"Of course. She has a lot of pictures of the two of you together. Uncle Damon even managed to send pictures of my cousins. They seem nice."

Cordelia bit the inside of her cheek, trying desperately to keep from crying. The poor child was raised away from everyone that loved her. "They are. Maybe in a little while, you could meet them."

"I'd love that," Emery sighed, leaning back against the chair.

Cordelia took notice of her niece's state, exhausted after such a trivial day. New country, new city, new house, new family. It must all be overwhelming.

"I'm going to get you a bite to eat. I'll be right back," Cordelia whispered, the girl's eyes already fluttering closed.

Behind closed lids, Emery could hear her aunt leave the room, closing the door firmly. She was beyond tired, but an idea came to mind.

Hailey?

I'm here. The other half of her subconscious answered.

Mom's really sick.

I know, pup.

The sadness in her wolf's voice was enough to crack open her heart.

Is there anything we can do? Anything at all? She's done so much for us. Please, we have to try something. Emery begged.

Hailey sighed profoundly. *There may be something we can try, but it might not work. I don't know how far gone her wolf is.*

I'll try anything.

It would only give her a little more time.

I'll take whatever I can get. She just needed her mother to hold on long enough for her uncle to contact him.

Take her hand, Emery.

Emery reached out, clasping her mother's hand in both of hers.

Close your eyes.

Emery obeyed, sealing her eyes shut.

This is going to be just like jump-starting a dead car battery. It won't be enough to sustain her long-term, but it should get her going.

How do we do that? Emery asked.

We're going to heal her.

But she's not injured.

Not physically, no, but her heart has been shattered for years. We're going to use our power as a type of tape to hold it all together. This only works because of our shared power and her being our mother. Never attempt this on anyone else.

Emery bobbed her head in understanding. *Okay, so now what?*

Now we sing and be prepared, this'll take a lot out of us.

Sing?

Emery heard Hailey begin to hum, vibrating through the chambers of their mind.

The song was beautiful and soothing and all too familiar, stirring a distant memory of a familiar voice carrying the same tune more than a few times over the years.

Emery joined in humming along with her wolf, the sound pulsating through her chest. She pushed out her power, through her hands, and into her mother. Forcing the energy into Amelia's body, feeding her heart.

A purple haze clouded her vision. The power receded back into her body like a rubber band snapping back into place.

Emery allowed darkness to swallow her whole. The last thing she heard was the sound of the heart monitor spiking, carrying with it a steady, strong beat.

Amelia was still alive—for now.

Voices broke through her subconscious.

The darkness receded as Amelia focused on the conversation taking place a few feet away. The voices were easily recognizable—her brother and best friend.

Gradually opening her eyes, brilliant fluorescent lighting filled her vision, the pupils taking a moment to dilate and adjust. Adjusting to her surroundings, she experienced a creeping sense of dread. The room, the familiar smells, Damon and Cordelia together, even the land itself called to her, welcoming her home.

"Oh, thank the Goddess," Cordelia sighed in relief.

Amelia tried to speak. Her voice cracked under pressure. Relief swelled within. Seeing Cordelia again for the first time in over seventeen years brought forth a rush of so many conflicting emotions, it was difficult to sort through.

Cordelia rushed to her side, poured a glass of water, and placed the cup between her hands.

Amelia drank from it slowly, the cool liquid soothing down her raw throat.

"What happened? Why am I here?" Amelia asked, fixed on her twin.

"You collapsed, Mia. Emery called me and we brought you here." Damon tried to explain.

Amelia looked around wildly, until she found precisely what she'd been searching for—Emery sleeping peacefully in the chair beside the bed. She smiled lovingly at her child, her reason for breathing. If not for the creature beside her, Amelia wasn't certain where life would have taken her. Being a mother, especially a mother to such an intelligent, brave, and courageous young woman left her more fulfilled than anything else on the planet.

It was as though a piece of Emery was forever engrained on her heart, cocooning the damaged, scared muscle by sheer will. But it wasn't just a mother-daughter bond or even their pesky Goddess power the two of them shared.

It was Emery. A physical piece of her daughter resided inside.

Amelia placed a hand over her heart, recognizing something foreign that shouldn't be there

"What's wrong?" Damon asked, stepping closer, her expression troubling him.

"Emery," Amelia breathed out, eyes stinging. "She tried healing me."

"But how?" Cordelia asked, not sure she was hearing her right.

"Like mother, like daughter." Damon smirked.

"She transferred a piece of her wolf," Amelia said in amazement.

She could feel her daughter's wolf, threads of their life-force entangled with her own.

"I didn't know that was possible," Damon said, looking between the duo.

A stunned Amelia merely shrugged. "Neither did I."

"Can someone please tell me what's going on?" Cordelia sighed dramatically.

"Why did you bring me here, Damon? I told you it was too risky." Amelia ignored her friend for the moment and focused on the big picture.

"What was I supposed to do, Mia? Leave you to die in an alley in the middle of Boston? You *know* Emery would *never* have left you," Damon informed her as if she didn't already know how stubborn and persistent her daughter was.

"I would have been *fine*," Amelia spat, lying through her teeth. She was positive she would never have woken up. "You would have taken care of Emery. Now all you've achieved is holding up a neon flashing light, alerting them to our location."

"You are so unbelievably stubborn!" Damon yelled, throwing his hands in the air. "I don't care what your reasoning is, whatever martyr crap you think you're pulling. I will not let you die. Do you understand me?"

"What do you mean?" Amelia scrunched her face at him, reading between the lines. "What did you do?" For the briefest of moments, she saw the worry, the fear, and lastly, the guilt passing across his face, causing her heart to plummet into her stomach. "You didn't. Please, for Goddess sake, tell me you *didn't* call him!"

"I had too, Mia," Damon said, his voice small, like when they were children and he broke her favorite toy, full of sorrow and guilt. "I had to."

"Momma?" Emery woke, blinking her eyes heavily.

Amelia ignored the enormous elephant in the room and focused on her kid. "Come here, baby," she said, patting the bed beside her.

Emery slowly stood up, sitting down on the thin mattress. "How are you feeling? Are you okay? Did it work?"

"Yes, baby, it worked. You are brilliant, my sweet girl," Amelia smiled warmly, tucking Emery's loose, dark blonde hair back behind her ear. "How are you feeling?"

"A little tired," Emery said with a shrug. "Kinda hungry."

"I bet. It's been a long day," Amelia chuckled.

For the first time in a while, she felt like her old self. Death had taken the day off, no longer knocking on her tire, tapping the watch on its wrist, reminding her that time was almost up.

Even though Rey was still dormant, it didn't deter the fact that she felt better than she had in months, maybe years and Amelia had a sinking feeling it wasn't all thanks to Emery. The land from which she was born thrummed through her, fueling her body, her heart and mind, but most importantly her power. Rhea's power and ultimately, the Goddess that blessed them centuries past.

Everything comes full circle one way or another.

"Please don't be mad at Uncle Damon," Emery said, ignoring the pointed look her mother was executing. "It was my idea."

Now Amelia was the one confused. "What are you talking about?"

"I discovered the book."

"Book?" Amelia was confused, thinking back to a book that Emery could be referring to, but nothing came to mind . . . except, maybe—but no, she couldn't have found it. "What book Emery?" The anger in her tone spiked, pricked by fear and panic.

"I picked the lock."

Even with her werewolf hearing, Emery could barely make out what her mother was mumbling under her breath. Something along the lines of father-daughter.

"I know why this is happening to you. And how to fix it."

"Emery—" Amelia started.

"No, mom. No. Uncle Damon is right. You have given up everything to save me. The Moon Goddess warned Rhea. Separating yourself from your mate would cost you your wolf and you can't live without your wolf. It's possible an ordinary wolf could, but not you."

"Emery, this is not something you need to worry about," Amelia said, trying to assure her pup.

Emery jerked away, standing up off the bed. "No. This is exactly something I need to worry about," she said, her anger rising. "You have given up *everything* for me. You're dying *because* you left your mate—for me. Well, that stops *now*. You can't keep sacrificing your life for me. I'm sixteen years old. I am *not* a defenseless pup."

Amelia stared at her daughter.

Never before had Emery raised her voice in such a way. Sure, they've fought. Emery *is* her child and prone to rebellious stints, but she had never stuck up for herself in such a way.

Amelia was almost proud if it didn't bring along a drowning wave of terror.

Emery stepped forward again, squeezing Amelia's hand. "I know you're scared. I know what's been happening to you. I know you try to hide it, but it's obvious. The bond has caused more damage to you than any poison ever could, and it needs to end. He can fix it."

Amelia blinked back the tears threatening to spill. She thought she had done a better job of hiding it, hiding the bitter betrayal and the crippling agony his infidelity brought on, but clearly, she'd been wrong.

Emery knew all along.

Cordelia observed Amelia at war with herself. Even after all these years, her tells were still the same, biting her lower lip, eyes shifting uncontrollably as a million thoughts raced across that stubborn mind.

Some things never change.

"Damon, why don't you take Emery to the kitchens and get her something to eat?" Cordelia offered softly, motioning for her husband to allow them a moment.

Damon gripped his niece's arms, giving a gentle pull towards the door. "Let's give your mom a minute, okay?"

Emery released her mother, following Damon out, but not before looking back and producing one last smile.

Amelia waited for the door to click shut behind them before letting the dam break. Her emotions from the last few years finally engulfed her. The panic and fear gripped her in its vice, its razor-sharp edges sliced and tore through the last layers of self-defense she had left.

Cordelia climbed onto the bed and wrapped her arms around Amelia's narrow body, hugging her tightly. Tears pooled against her shirt as she cradled her friend against her chest, rocking back and forth.

"He's on his way. Isn't he?" Amelia asked in between sobs.

"Yes," Cordelia confirmed her worst fear.

"He moved on. I can't ask him to uproot his whole life for me."

"Amelia, he's your mate and not just your mate, but your *fated* mate. You two were made for each other, literally. When are you going to learn to stop fighting that?"

"It's been so long since I left. I've done so many terrible things. I've slaughtered hundreds to keep us safe."

"Were they trying to hurt you or Emery?" Cordelia asked, keeping her voice soft and non-judgmental.

"Yes."

"Then it doesn't matter what you did. You did what needed to, to protect your child. Same as any mother would."

Amelia took in a deep, raspy breath, eyes swollen and raw. She couldn't remember the last time she cried, truly cried for no other reason than to unleash the brimming tide of emotion kept locked away behind multiple layers of mental blocks.

Amelia sat up off her friend, trying to sit up straighter.

Cordelia pulled back, giving her space.

"How much longer till he gets here?" Amelia asked, staring down at the hands clasped in her lap.

Cordelia confirmed the time on her watch. "An hour at most."

Fuck. It wasn't enough time. She didn't think that amount of time existed.

A part of her wanted to run, far and fast. Take Emery and disappear but running was no longer an option. It was finally time to stop and face the music.

"I need to speak with Damon and Emery. Now."

CHAPTER 8

REUNITED?

Damon and Emery came back to the room—Emery carried a plate with a turkey club sandwich.

"Here, Momma, I brought you some food." Emery placed the plate on her lap. "You should eat something. You need your strength."

Amelia smiled, lips pulling into a tight, thin line. "Thank you, baby, but first we need to talk."

"Okay," Emery hesitated, sitting down on the arm of the chair still beside the bed, Damon standing behind her.

Cordelia made sure the door was closed, encasing them in the soundproof room.

"Emery, you know your father is coming here," Amelia stated rather than asked.

"Yes."

"While he's here, I need you to promise me that you'll stay hidden. I *will* tell him about you, I promise, I just-"

"I understand. You two have a lot to work through—just promise me one thing."

"Anything."

"No fighting, please. I can't lose you, and I don't know how long my wolf can keep you stable."

Amelia's heart broke. Her actions and choices were hurting her daughter, and she despised it. "I can't make that promise. If you knew our history you'd understand, but I can promise that I will not jump out of bed and try to beat him to death with his own arm."

Emery started to frown only for it to turn into a smirk. That was her mother—a fighter.

Amelia looked at her twin. "How many know were here? Know about Emery?"

"By now? The whole pack," Damon said bluntly. "Our arrival garnered a lot of attention with you looking dead in my arms and all. As for Emery, I'm sure most of them understand she's yours. Your scent is all over her, there's no masking that."

Amelia began to fidget with the sheets on the bed, her mind racing.

"I've already put out a gag order. No one in this pack, without yours or my permission, is allowed to speak of you or Emery," Damon informed her.

"What do you mean?" Amelia's brow furrowed.

"It's all in the journal—you're an Alpha, Amelia. The strongest Alpha in existence. By blood, you retain every right to rule this pack. You're the oldest, so by law, you are Alpha."

"No, I am *not* Alpha. Damon, *you* are the Alpha of our pack. That will never change," she said, swaying her head adamantly.

"As you wish," Damon lowered his head bearing his neck, something no Alpha does, not even for another Alpha.

Amelia wanted to reach over and cuff him upside the head but restrained herself. "Cordelia put Emery in the room beside mine. I want her close, but she can't be in my old room. He may come looking for me there."

Cordelia bowed her head as well, following her husband's lead.

"You two knock it off! Right now!" Amelia shouted, making them all jump.

Amelia forgot whatever she was about to say when her twin's eyes glazed over.

Someone was mind linking him.

Amelia didn't need it confirmed. "He's here."

Damon nodded.

Amelia gathered a deep breath, her stomach threatening to heave the acid lingering in the back of her throat. She reached out for Emery, seizing a hand, and gathering her close. She cupped her face and kissed her on both cheeks before pulling away and looking into her stunning, silver eyes.

"I love you so much."

"I know, Mom." Emery smiled.

The sadness and empathy that radiated from her kid made her fiercely proud yet mournful. Emery's childhood wasn't full of laughter and fun-filled memories. Instead, Emery had been shaped and molded out of hardship, determination, fear, and the sheer will to live.

"Come on, honey. Let's get you out of here," Cordelia gripped Emery's hand, dragging her out of the room and away from the oncoming shit show.

Amelia looked at Damon, a faint smile pulled at her lips. She never realized how much she truly missed him.

"I'm staying with you," Damon informed her.

"I know."

And now they wait.

Amelia glanced down at the sandwich on the plate. There was a strong possibility that if she consumed any kind of sustenance, it might come back up with a vengeance, but Emery was right. Amelia needed her strength and quickly ate the sandwich. She was hungrier than she realized.

The last bite was halfway to her mouth when she froze. The blood in her body solidified, her body stiffened, and her heart hardened. Amelia was certain she could hear an audible popping of stone being made. She couldn't breathe, couldn't move, or speak. Time stood still and for just a moment she hoped.

"Where is she?!" Gabriel's voice boomed down the hallway, the walls vibrating in protest.

Moment over.

Damon stepped closer to her, setting his hand on her shoulder. He produced a gentle squeeze just as the door was nearly knocked off its hinges.

A powerful Alpha consumed the doorway.

Gabriel stood in the entrance, his body shaking as if he was seconds away from shifting into his formidable and extra-large wolf, Zeke. He stepped into the room, eyes taking her in, roaming over every inch of her body.

Amelia couldn't help the intimate blush that graced her cheeks. Even though she had seen him only a few hours ago, she still couldn't believe her eyes.

No memory, no picture, could do the man justice.

"Damon said you were dying," Gabriel said accusingly, as though it was all some ruse to lure him in, but to what end she didn't know.

"It's a bit more complicated than that," Amelia said, regaining her voice. She was proud with how calm she sounded, as though none of it mattered—that having him just mere feet from her didn't make her body itch with the desire to take his hand, to hold him, kiss him, and beg for forgiveness.

This exact moment would define the rest of her life.

"What game are you playing here, Amelia? I tried talking to you earlier, and you used your Alpha aura on me like I'm some Omega. Then I get a call, halfway back to my pack, from *your* brother informing me that you're dying," Gabriel said, sounding more than flustered.

"You used your *Alpha* aura on him?" Damon hissed. His stare glaring daggers. "No wonder why –"

"That's enough," she growled, her stare alone silencing him.

Gabriel didn't miss the odd exchange, glancing between the two of them.

"Damon, can you give us a minute?"

"I don't feel comfortable leaving you."

"I wasn't asking," she ordered him, delivering a warning look.

Damon gritted his teeth, inclining his head in submission before leaving them alone, but not before providing Gabriel a warning look of his own.

"Touch her, and I'll kill you myself," Damon said, with the loaded weight of his aura behind him.

Gabriel didn't bother with a response, except rejecting the fact that he existed and directed his attention back to the woman he once called mate.

Now that there was no longer a chaperone, he approached the side of the bed.

Amelia regarded him carefully like one might do a fellow predator, studying his posture for any sign of attack. She was surprised when he sat in the chair beside her, slumping down into the rigid leather, wringing a hand roughly down his face.

Gabriel looked fatigued—worn out. His hair looked like he had run his hand through it one too many times. Amelia recalled him doing that when something was bothering him.

Guess some habits never die.

"What do you want, Amelia? Why am I here?" he asked, mentally drained.

"I didn't ask you to come."

"No, your brother did. Why?"

"I was unconscious," she said, unsure how to begin, where to start.

"Why? You seemed perfectly fine last I saw you," he said, growling at the way she had commanded him like he was some pup, some mongrel so easily cast aside.

"Using my Alpha aura like that on you. It-it took a lot out of me," she slightly stuttered.

"What do you mean? Why?" he asked.

"My powers, they've been getting harder and harder to use."

"What are you talking about?" Gabriel asked, sick of the run-around. Sick of her dodging his questions and not just speaking plainly.

"I'm dying, Gabe," she whispered hoarsely, using her nickname for him. She hadn't uttered that name in seventeen years, and it felt so good to say. "Rey, she's almost gone."

Gabriel just stared at her, unable to process the meaning of the words. "I don't understand."

Amelia ran her hand through her hair. "The mate bond is killing me," she said with finality, the words finally released out in the open.

Gabriel scoffed. "What mate bond? We haven't been mates in nearly two decades."

Naturally, he wouldn't understand. "Gabe, we're fated mates. You know as well as I, that it's different for us. Separating from you put a strain on my abilities, but over the years, Rey grew weaker. I never formally rejected you, so the bond was still intact, but the more you pulled away, the weaker it made me."

Gabriel stood up, knocking the chair out from underneath him. Amelia flinched in response, somewhat expecting this type of reaction.

"*You* left *me*! And you accuse *me* of pulling away? You did this to yourself, Amelia!"

He wasn't completely inaccurate. "I understand you're angry-"

"Angry? No, I was devastated when you left. You just disappeared without a word, like we meant nothing to each other!" he shouted, his voice vibrating through the walls.

Amelia gnawed her lower lip, eyes cast down, afraid to look him in the eye. Terrified he might be capable of seeing right through her, unlocking all her secrets. The one's buried so deep she wasn't even sure *she* could uncover them.

"I know it might have seemed that way, but-"

"How else should it have *seemed*? Huh? *You* ran away. *You* left your pack, your family, you left *me*. Like we were nothing."

"That is *not* fair."

"Not fair was leaving me behind in a coma, to wake up and find you gone. Not fair was grieving for our child by myself, having to pick up the pieces of my pack without their Luna. Not fair was never being given an explanation or the courtesy of a goodbye," Gabriel's voice trembled.

Amelia looked up at him to find his silver eyes red and wet. Her throat tightened. A heaviness settled on her chest weighing her down.

"It wrecked me," she said, voice breaking, her body trembling, but somehow, she managed to hold firm. "Watching so many of my pack die. I lost a *baby*, Gabe. I felt it die within me and I couldn't do a thing to stop it. You practically *died* trying to defend me. Do you understand what it feels like to witness your mate on the verge of death? You were knocking on death's door! Damon was injured! I was completely alone! I did what I believed was best to keep everyone safe!" And she regretted none of it. If she hadn't left when she did, Emery wouldn't exist.

"You broke me, Amelia," Gabriel declared. "I was a broken man for a long time."

"And you think it was painless for me? I left *everything* and *everyone* I've ever loved!" she yelled. Her anger overpowering her heartache. "Neither of your packs ever suffered another attack after I left. Leaving kept you all safe."

Gabriel froze. They hadn't been attacked in seventeen years. "How do you know that?"

"Because they've been hunting me," she admitted, pushing past the shocking realization he was having. "It's me they wanted all along. They desire my power and lineage to further their own bloodline. But they don't understand the fated mate bond. They don't understand that I'm not physically capable of being with anyone other than you. But they don't care; they merely desire my power."

"You're not making sense," Gabriel shook his head, his mind reeling. "They want you to breed for them?"

"Yes."

Gabriel could feel his wolf shaking with anger. No one would touch their mate.

"But they don't understand the mate bond. I'm incapable of bearing pups."

Gabriel turned to her, brow furrowed. Had something happened to her that made her sterile? Had someone hurt her in their time apart?

Amelia could see she needed to explain further, spell it out for him. "I can only carry *your* pups."

Realization seemed to finally dawn on him. "You can only get pregnant by me? Why?"

"The mate bond prevents it. Those whom the Moon Goddess has chosen are bound by something much deeper and more sacred than law. Its power. The Moon Goddess's power binds us. I can only carry my fated mate's pups. It's the same reason why Rey has all but vanished. Being apart from you this long, you mating with other women is gradually killing our mate bond. It's practically broken."

Her statement left Gabriel gaping, floundering for something to say. "How do you know I've been with other women?"

Of course, that's what he would focus on—time to deliver a dose of reality. "I can feel it, Gabe. Every time."

"Feel it?"

"What are you not understanding?" she asked, now getting annoyed. They had more urgent things to get to besides his active sex life.

"How is it that you've felt it from me, but I've never felt it from you?"

Amelia flinched, his words striking her across the face. "Is that what you believe I've been doing this entire time? Sleeping my way around the world?!"

"No, that's not what-"

"The last time I was intimate with a man was seventeen years ago, with you. Unlike some people, I remained faithful to my mate," she said, spitting on the word mate.

"You abandoned me!" he roared.

"And that excuses you?! That just leaves you room to trample over our bond?! You have no idea why I did what I did, so don't pretend to try and understand. To make excuses for nearly killing me the last few years!" she yelled, throwing the plate at the wall, pottery shattering across the room.

Amelia hadn't realized she stood up off the bed, but now that she was, she could feel her legs wobbling beneath her.

The floor was coming up quickly. Placing her arms out to try and catch herself, she fastened her eyes, bracing for impact. When it didn't come, she could feel strong arms holding her, elevating her up off the floor.

She unclosed her eyes to find herself cradled against his chest, like the way she used to carry Emery to bed. Expecting him to place her back in bed, she was shocked when he instead sat down on the couch along the wall.

Amelia couldn't help but lean into him, enjoying the comfort of his touch, the security of his arms around her. Breathing him in deeply, she couldn't help the grumbling vibrations emitting from her chest—the wolf version of purring. He smelled exactly the way she remembered.

Amelia, Rey called out weakly.

"Rey?" Amelia gasped.

"Rey?" Gabriel repeated.

"I can hear her," Amelia cried, tears slipping down her cheeks.

Rey, I've missed you so much.

I've always been with you. Been trying to hold on. Waiting for mate. Her words were clipped and short, as though the effort to form them took more energy than she had.

I know, Rey. He's here, he's with us.

Gabriel tucked her in closer, propping his chin atop her head. For the first time in a long while, he felt at peace.

"Gabe."

"Yes?"

"There's something else you need to know," Amelia said, running her hand along the thin fabric of his shirt, stroking her fingers down the planes of his chest directly over his heart. She didn't want to ruin whatever this was, whatever this moment meant for them, but she needed to tell him of their daughter.

"What is it?" Gabriel asked, his eyes closed, taking in full breaths of his mate's scent, calming the beast within.

"I-"

A sixth sense tingled in the back of her mind, rippling down her spine and caused all senses to explode ten-fold.

A warning.

Amelia bolted upright, startling Gabriel. Not even a diminished wolf would allow her to forget that smell. She could scent him from miles away, but he was close. Too close.

Pup's in danger.

Rey's voice was the only confirmation she required.

Amelia could feel her inner Moon Goddess, the mothering side of her emerge with one clear desire—protect. "Emery."

CHAPTER 9

MICHAEL

Amelia ripped herself free of Gabriel's grasp. His questions and protests were background noise as she ran out of the room like a bat out of hell.

"Damon!" she screamed through the house.

This wasn't happening, not again, not this soon. They weren't prepared. Rey was barely there. She wasn't strong enough to fight him off.

Damon ran to meet her in the foyer, Cordelia just behind him.

"He's here," she said, eyes wild and frantic.

"What? My patrols haven't said - "

"He can evade them! He can cover his scent!" she informed them, her eyes flicking to the stairs directing up to her daughter. "Cordie."

Cordelia followed her line of sight, instantly recognizing the she-wolf's reaction to protect her pup. "I got her," she took off up the stairs and out of sight.

"How long?" Damon asked her.

"What's going on? Who's *he*?" Gabriel asked, finally catching up, looking between the two of them.

"He's already here," Amelia left them behind to follow, pushing open the front door and stepping outside onto the gravel drive.

The rocks crunched beneath her feet. Amelia searched the grounds for any sign of a deranged wolf on the loose. She scented the air—a foul stench directed her to the tree line.

Michael stepped out. He didn't look aged or changed in any way. The same menacing smile tore at his scarred face as those vicious lifeless eyes fixed on her.

Amelia despised the way he looked at her, like she was something to own, to devour. The scars on her back began to itch, but she resisted the temptation to reach back and touch them, to feel the knotted scar tissue disfiguring her body. She stepped forward in front of both Damon and Gabriel, taking the brunt of his attention.

It was her he wanted.

Amelia noticed movement out of the corner of her eye, members of the Wandering Moon formed a circle around them. "Damon, send them away."

Damon hesitated. "But they could help."

"Now," she hissed, not bothering to wait to know that he was already mind-linking them. The fifty-some odd wolves retreated. Their lips pulled back as every one of them snarled. No one else needed to get hurt.

"Amelia. My beautiful Amelia," Michael called to her drawing the words out seductively, his voice like nails raking down her bones.

"She's mine," Gabriel growled behind her.

Amelia almost smiled at his response but kept her face void of emotion, forcing her eyes to remain on Michael. Never lose track of a viper in your sights.

"Ahh, Gabriel. The mate," Michael said, saying the word mate like it was a joke. "I haven't seen you around in some time. Why haven't you been by her side if she is indeed yours?"

"You need to leave, Michael," Amelia said, her voice ringing out over the space between them, her Alpha aura spiking, reacting to the rage of emotions welling inside. She jerked it back, reigning it in quickly, already feeling drained, knees shaking.

Amelia took another step towards him, narrowing the distance between them, stepping farther away from Damon and Gabriel. If she spoke low enough, then with a bit of luck, Gabriel may be spared any unforgiving details.

"I'm not leaving without you and that pretty daughter of yours," Michael cooed, his words running over her like oil over water.

Amelia felt disgusted being so close to him, the stench seeping from his pores nearly making her gag. "You will not touch my daughter."

"I'll do much more than touch her," Michael said, encircling her like a vulture circling its prey. He sniffed at her, fingered her hair, making her skin crawl. "First, I'll fuck you. Hard. Until you forget that brute of a mate and if you're lucky enough, you'll bear my seed. Then, when I'm finished with you, I'll have my way with your little bitch. I'll make sure my men take their turn with her, but not before I do. You will both submit to your betters."

Rey grew within her mind, expanding, growling, howling to the Moon Goddess, overtaking her human side. Amelia could feel her clothes shredding.

In the blink of an eye, she was towering over Michael. She had lost weight, her figure slim and muscles deteriorated, but that didn't stop her.

Rey let her aura lose, keeping her pack at bay and challenging Michael in one fell swoop.

Michael smirked, expecting this exact reaction. He rapidly shifted into his mud-brown wolf. He was smaller than her, but if she had learned anything from their previous meeting, it was to never underestimate him.

He fought dirty and unconventional.

The two wolves circled each other, Rey snapping at him.

Michael charged first.

Rey was too slow to anticipate, their weakened state limiting their response.

Michael flipped over, landing on her back. Rey tried to knock him off, she bucked and jumped, but his claws dug into her skin, sharp teeth clamped around her neck. Rey flipped herself around, landing on top of him hard enough for him to gasp.

Releasing his hold, she rolled away from his sharp fangs that left holes in her flesh.

Rey got up and charged, unwilling to be taken by surprise again. He was ready for her. Michael dodged to the side before throwing the weight of his body into her side, knocking her off her feet and into a neighboring tree.

The air was forced from her lungs. Struggling to take in air, the impact sent frozen daggers down her throat and into her chest as she tried to breath. Her chest was burning with the effort.

Rey struggled to stand as he continued to circle.

With her back to the pack, Michael and Rey charged at one another, claws extended, raking each other to shreds, teeth meeting flesh. She could taste the blood in her mouth. A burning pain ignited down her side.

Suddenly she bore his weight on her back once more, the force was too much, causing her legs to buckle.

Rey and Amelia were weakening drastically. The brain was no longer able to direct the body. No matter how much Amelia shouted at Rey, directing their movements, nothing happened. Their limbs were leaden, trembling as Michael tried pinning her to the ground. Her legs gave out. A cloud of dirt billowed around them as Rey's body crashed into the earth—an echo of defeat.

It was foolish of them to think they could take him. Rey hadn't been in fighting shape in a long while.

This was a stupid mistake. One that might cost them everything.

One quick twist and it would all be over.

Gabriel witnessed the fight from the bottom of the porch.

Gabriel couldn't recall a single time he'd ever seen Amelia lose. Michael was smaller than her. He *should* be no match for her, and yet he was winning. Her pale silver coat was soaked red. Long claw marks were split open along her side. She was swaying on all fours, barely able to support her weight.

She was so thin. Gabriel's wolf was just beneath the surface, ready to shift and defend his mate, but her Alpha aura was restraining them, holding them back. If her will faded, he could shift at a moment's notice and intervene.

He would fight for her, fight for his mate.

The man pulled a dirty trick, wounding her and jumping on her back, his claws digging into her sides, his mouth clamped around her neck. Gabriel tried to take a step forward, tried to shift. She needed help, but Amelia's will was still imposed on them.

Damon growled beside him, a sound that went beyond human and straight to feral and animalistic, undergoing the same inner conflict.

Gabriel watched as Amelia fell beneath his weight.

The stranger was gearing to make the final break and take her life, snuff her out as though she was nothing more than the flame of a candlestick, but Amelia was more than that. She was fierce and burned brighter than any star in the sky.

No one would take her away, not when he just got her back. He was on his toes pushing against Amelia's aura that contained them all. He could barely feel it, a thin veil between him and the ability to regain control.

Amelia's aura slipped, just enough that he could command the shift, but he froze.

A silver-white wolf came bursting out of the house, straight between him and Damon, charging directly for Amelia. The young she-wolf head-butted the man, knocking him clean off, releasing his prey. She stood over his mates' body, growling at the man, emitting an aura much like Amelia's.

The young she-wolf wasn't anyone he recognized. Her fur was silver, white except for the black stripe running along her spine. Ren was clawing in the back of his mind at the sight of the wolf, but Gabriel forced him back.

"Now!" Damon shouted to his packmates already shifted.

Gabriel didn't need to be told twice. He ran for Amelia, ran to stand in front of her, between the deranged stranger and his mate.

Damon followed suit, standing opposite, providing additional support. The Wandering Moon Pack surrounded them, growling and snarling, snapping their jaws at the intruder.

"Leave now," Damon growled.

The man she named Michael stood his ground, pushing his front paw forward baring his teeth.

The young she-wolf beside him, still hovering over Amelia's weakened form, stomped her paw into the earth, releasing a growl so terrifying it disturbed the ground beneath their feet.

For the first time, Michael looked fearful, eyes widened, pupils dilating.

Still snarling, he backed away slowly until he disappeared through the forest. Damon released the rest of the pack with a piercing whistle, sending the wolves to chase their prey through the brush.

Gabriel turned to Amelia. Her wolf was barely breathing, blood pooled in the dirt. Her once beautiful silver fur was a thick matted burgundy color. He bent down, leaning over to caress the side of her neck, when the young she-wolf turned on him, snarling a warning.

Gabriel narrowed his eyes, growling back. No pup would challenge him.

"Emery," Damon called out.

Emery ignored her name, eyes fixed solely on Gabriel. Lip pulled back, baring her teeth, her chest vibrated with displeasure over his proximity to Amelia, warning him to back away slowly.

Gabriel growled at her again, his wolf ready to shift if she continued to challenge him. This was his mate.

Who did she think she was?

Emery growled back even louder, her Alpha aura growing, extending to blanket Amelia, marking his mate as hers to protect.

Gabriel pulled back, straightening his back. Her silver eyes glared at him.

Who was she?

Damon walked around the young she-wolf. His hands extended in submission.

Who was this girl for Damon to act this way?

"Emery," Damon repeated. She snapped at him as well, making Damon flinch back. "Hailey, you need to let us help her."

The wolf Hailey finally blinked, her face relaxing at the sound of his voice as he addressed the wolf properly.

"She's bleeding. Please, Hailey, let Emery come back. She wouldn't want this," Damon spoke softly to the wolf, reasoning with the beast.

The she-wolf finally backed down, relaxing her defensive position over Amelia's wolf. She backed away, sniffing Amelia's body, licking her wounds. The young wolf stroked her head against her neck, whining into her fur.

Damon stepped towards her, resting his hand into her silky fur over her shoulder. "It's going to be okay. We'll help her, but you can't help like this," he said softly in her ear.

The she-wolf bobbed her head, this time completely stepping away.

Gabriel, eyes fixed on the young she-wolf, approached Amelia cautiously. When he no longer sensed aggression or hint of an attack, he looked down at his mate. He extended his hand along her neck, fingers caressing her fur—just as soft as he remembered.

"Amelia," Gabriel called to her. He needed her to shift back. "Rey."

Amelia went from wolf to human in the blink of an eye. From a fur-covered beast to a nude, exposed woman.

Gabriel accepted a blanket from an anonymous person behind him, shrouding it carefully around her vulnerable body, and lifted her, cradling her in his arms.

He ran with her inside the house and back towards the room they had been arguing in not fifteen minutes ago.

Inside the room, the pack doctor and nurses waited. Gabriel set her down on the bed, laying her head back on a pillow. Those stunning sea-green eyes were closed. Short, shallow breaths slipped between those perfect, full lips. He pet the top of her head, extending his fingers through her matted hair.

His Amelia.

Gabriel stepped back to allow the professionals the freedom to work before he made more of a scene.

"Alpha, please wait out in the hall," the doctor instructed.

Gabriel nodded in silence, vacating the room, and closing the door behind him. Out in the hall, Damon came running, stopping just in front of him.

"The doctor is with her," Gabriel informed him.

Damon nodded his head, leaning back against the wall.

Gabriel's mind was racing. He had more questions than answers, mind buzzing with the day's confusing and conflicting emotions.

Who was that guy? What had he said to Amelia to cause her to change like that? Who was that she-wolf? There was more to the mate bond than Amelia said, and he needed to know everything. He just prayed he'd have the chance.

"Who was that guy?" Gabriel asked Damon, probably one of the only questions he had that the Alpha could answer.

"Michael," he snarled the name in disgust. "He bears a grudge against our family that dates back hundreds of years to the time of Rhea and Ezekial."

"The first mated pair?"

Damon nodded. "The very same."

"But what does that have to do with Amelia? It was like she recognized him."

"You didn't?" Damon asked.

Gabriel's brow furrowed. "I would remember a wolf like that."

"How much of the attack do you remember?"

Gabriel thought back to that night. The same night he had played over and over in his head, trying to figure out what he could have done differently. "I remember the wake being interrupted. We were ambushed. I remember there more Rogues than I'd ever seen in my life, and they were incredibly well prepared. Amelia was fighting. She should have been in the safe room. She should never have gone out there. She couldn't even shift."

Damon bobbed his head, recalling the very same thing, but he knew his sister better than anyone. Pregnant or not, those she loved were in danger, and she wasn't going to sit on the sidelines and do nothing.

"I remember running to her. I could sense someone coming up behind her, but she was too distracted fighting. I jumped in between them and then—nothing. It's all dark from there. Until I woke up," Gabriel said, sighing.

"And she was gone," Damon said, completing the unspoken words.

"And she was gone," Gabriel repeated faintly.

"The wolf that struck you, that put you in a coma. That was Michael. She ran away to keep him from coming back. Both of our packs lost over a hundred wolves. The Twilight Moon Pack nearly lost its Alpha. After she healed you, she couldn't stand around and endure that again. He's been trailing her ever since. She's been moving around the world, managing to keep one step ahead of him thanks to Rey, but Rey hasn't been available as of late," Damon said, explaining as much as he could without revealing the most significant part.

The door opened beside Gabriel, causing both of them to startle. He stood up off the wall in anticipation.

The doctor stepped out, leaving the door cracked open behind her.

"The damage is extensive. The claws managed to puncture a lung, a kidney and break six ribs. Amelia is also bleeding into her stomach. We could attempt surgery, but she's not stable enough," the doctor informed them, eyes welling with unshed tears. Her face told them everything.

Expect the worst.

"I'll heal her."

CHAPTER 10

HEALING

"I'll heal her," Emery informed them. Catching the tail end of the doctor's analysis. She got the gist of it. Her mother was dying.

Cordelia pulled on her arm, bending close to her ear. "You don't know how much energy this will require. She wouldn't want this."

Emery shook her head at her aunt. "I don't care. I won't let her die."

"I'll help you," Uncle Damon said, producing a warm, tired smile that didn't quite reach his eyes. He was nervous, fearful that her mother was too far gone to be helped.

Emery bobbed her head in respect, grateful for the offer. Aunt Cordelia was right. She didn't know how much it would take, but she would give everything to spare her mother.

Nothing less than what her mother had done for her.

She ignored the lingering looks from Gabriel. The questions in his eyes. Refusing to make eye contact, she walked right past him, past the doctor, and into the room.

Amelia lay still in the bed. Her heartbeat was barely registering on the monitor, and the rise and fall of her chest was quick and brief.

Emery sniffed, wiping away the tears that were falling freely. She felt a hand rest against her shoulder, producing a light squeeze.

"Stand on the other side of her. We'll need to stay connected, the three of us," Emery advised him over her shoulder.

Uncle Damon didn't bother responding. He didn't need to. He understood.

Hailey?

We can do this. Her wolf assured her. *But we'll require him too.*

Emery glanced over her shoulder, back to the man left waiting in the hallway. The man who sired her.

What? Why?

We can restore her body, but only he can heal her soul.

Emery didn't bother to oppose her wolf. She already knew she was right.

"We need Gabriel too," she told her uncle.

Damon stiffened in response. He wanted to keep him away from his niece, but at the same time, they had to save Amelia. He turned back to the open door where Gabriel stood waiting on the other side.

"Gabriel," Damon called.

Gabriel poked his head in. "Yeah?"

"Get in here. We need you."

Emery walked over to the right side of the bed. Damon assumed position on her left. Gabriel stepped into the room, awkward and out of place.

"What do you need me for?" Gabriel asked.

"We can heal her body," Emery notified him, not shifting her eyes off her sleeping mother's face. "But that won't mend her heart, her soul. We need you to keep in contact with her. Any physical contact will work. It'll keep her grounded to this plane."

"This plane?" Gabriel asked, not sure of her meaning.

"So, she won't die," Damon told him, keeping it simple and to the point.

"Let's start this," Emery said, effectively ending any further conversation. She laid her hand against her mother's shoulder. With her other, she reached across, clasping her uncle's hand. Near the foot of the bed, she could sense Gabriel moving closer, his hands reaching down, slipping beneath the covers, holding onto the slender feet.

"You remember how to do this, old man?" Emery asked her uncle, slightly smirking, trying to relieve the tension in the room.

"It's been a while, but it's like riding a bike," Damon smiled.

"Oh, you mean you fall off a lot?" she said, laughing at him.

"One time! I fell off one time!" Damon yelled, then remembering where he was, he instantly lowered his voice. "Goodness, did she tell you everything?"

Emery looked back down at her mother, her mood turning somber once more. "Not everything," she shook off the sadness that was threatening to overcome her. Rounding out her shoulders, she looked back up at her uncle. "Ready?"

"Ready," he said with a brief nod.

Emery seized the chance and turned to her father, holding his gaze for but a moment. "Are you ready?"

Gabriel swallowed with difficulty, his Adam's apple bobbing in his throat. "Yes."

Emery took a deep breath. "Here we go."

Fastening her eyes, she reached for her wolf, the power that lay within. Hailey came forward, directing her through the channels of her abilities. The wolf initiated the hum and allowed it to expand, vibrating every cell in her body.

Emery could detect her uncle's hand growing warm in hers.

That was her cue.

Emery began to hum aloud, the song passing between her and Damon, overlapping and dancing, their chords blending into one. She could feel her power pass through Damon and his through her before finally down into her mother.

She didn't know how long they continued like that. It could have been minutes. It could have been hours. She didn't know. But she wasn't about to stop until it was done.

Refusing to leave even a single scratch on her mother's skin.

Emery could detect their combined power and energy push its way into Amelia's body. She recognized the exact moment the puncture to both her lung and kidney were repaired, restoring proper blood flow. The audible sound of bones cracking was sign enough of her ribs being moved back into place, fusing cartilage. The healing began to work on the external injuries, purifying and sealing every gash, cut, and scrape until the open wounds disappeared from her flesh.

Their song ended. The healing complete.

They let go of each other's hands like they were made of lead, too heavy to hold up. Emery could feel herself swaying, her mind grew dizzy and lightheaded, but she had to make sure.

Emery reached out, her hand fumbling and awkward, cupping her mother's face, feeling the softness of her skin.

Rey? Are you there?

Emery was met with silence, her heart sinking in her chest. A tear dropped onto her mother's hospital gown.

Pup?

Emery gasped.

A slight hysterical laugh bubbled on her lips. Damon looked terrified. She could feel Gabriel's panic.

"It's Rey. I can hear her. We did it," she quickly explained in excitement, their relief audible. Fastening her eyes once again, she reached out for Rey once more. The wolf's presence in her mother's mind was faint and weak, but she was there. *Rey, are you okay? Is mom okay?*

I'm here. Amelia is alive. It'll take a bit for her to come back. Today has been long and hard on the both of us.

Emery smiled. *Right, of course. I love you both.*

We love you. And pup.

Yeah?

You did great today. You were a true daughter of the Moon Goddess.

Emery pulled back, opening her eyes, her cheeks damp. "We did it. She's going to be okay."

Her excitement was short lived as the world around her began to spin, darkness taking over once more.

Gabriel observed the adolescent girl. She couldn't be older than sixteen and yet she commanded them as though she possessed a greater authority.

He couldn't place it, but he felt like he recognized her.

Maybe it was because his mate's scent was all over the girl.

Had Amelia adopted her? Was the loss of their child too much to bear that she had to imprint on another that needed her help?

The girl kept her head down, refusing to look him in the eye. He felt offended by this. He was an Alpha, her superior. Instead, she completely ignored him.

What were they even talking about? How could this girl heal Amelia? Damon clearly knows her and is offering his help.

They both walked into Amelia's room, leaving him alone in the hallway with Luna Cordelia.

"It's best to hang back. Let them work," Cordelia said, leaning against the wall across from him.

"Who is that girl?" Gabriel asked.

Cordelia's mouth froze open, unable to produce a sentence that was anything other than a lie. She was spared from responding when Damon's voice called out.

Gabriel extended his head inside the room to find Damon standing behind the girl, his hand resting on her shoulder.

"Yeah?"

"Get in here. We need you," Damon said, not bothering to turn back.

Gabriel hesitantly entered the room.

Damon and the girl walked to stand on either side of the bed.

The heart monitor beeped faintly in the background, her heartbeat too far apart to be normal. She looked dead, or almost. Her skin was pale, barely containing life, and she looked as if she was struggling for air. If he listened carefully enough, he could hear her ragged breathing as blood penetrated one of her lungs.

Now he grasped why she was so terrified. That night, many moons ago, when it was him lying in bed, knocking on death's door and Amelia was the one left to piece him back together.

Seeing her in bed, lifeless, was something he never wanted to see again. If she even got the sniffles, it would be too much.

"What do you need me for?" Gabriel asked, feeling utterly helpless.

What could he possibly do to help?

"We can heal her body," Emery said. Her gaze was fastened on Amelia. "But that won't fix her heart, her soul. We need you to keep in contact with her. Any bodily contact will work. It'll keep her grounded to this plane."

"This plane?" Gabriel asked, not grasping her meaning.

"She won't die," Damon flat out told him.

This seemed to snap something inside of Gabriel. He didn't care what he had going on in his life. At that exact moment, he came to a final decision.

No matter what, he was never letting her go.

"Let's start this," Emery said.

The girl laid her hand against Amelia's shoulder, gripping Damon's hand in hers across the body. Damon was doing the same on his side.

Gabriel stepped forward towards the foot of the bed. He pushed the covers back and wrapped his hands around her feet. They were emaciated and frail between his giant palms. He couldn't believe how much she had changed from the young woman so full of life, fit to confront anyone, to the frail, mature woman before him.

Gabriel could overhear the two of them talking to each other. Their conversation was familiar and teasing, but he didn't pay them any attention. His focus was locked on Amelia, fixed on the rising and falling of her chest, ensuring she was still alive.

If they could repair her body, then he would make it his mission to save her soul.

"Ready?" The girl asked Damon.

"Ready," he said with a curt nod.

For the first time, the girl turned to him, fastening her eyes, her silver eyes, with his. "Are you ready?"

Gabriel felt Ren stir in the back of his mind, slightly taken aback by the color of her eyes. "Yes," he heard himself say.

The girl took a deep breath. "Here we go."

Both she and Damon closed their eyes. He couldn't help but observe the two of them. The hairs along his arms and down the back of his neck rose, standing on end, goose flesh spreading across his body. He could sense the power in the room building, the smell of it burning his nose.

They began to hum—the sound both beautiful and terrifying. The kind of sound that could lure men to their death. He remembered hearing Amelia sing that exact tune when she healed someone, but she was a descendant of Rhea. It even made sense that Damon could do it, being her twin. But this girl, how did she fit into any of this?

His gaze gravitated back to Amelia. Her breathing became more even, now capable of inhaling a full breath. The screen of the monitor was beginning to pick up speed, turning into a more regular heartbeat. His ears picked up a slight cracking sound, her rib cage snapping back into place as her bones healed. Her skin was regaining its rosy olive tone that he loved and watched as every scratch was visible, sealed, ultimately healing, leaving no trace behind.

Suddenly the song ended as quickly as it started. Damon and the girl broke apart. Damon looked weary like he might throw up, swaying where he stood. The girl, on the other hand, looked as if she might drop at any moment.

She reached up, placing her hand against the side of Amelia's face, rubbing her thumb along her jaw. The girl closed her eyes for a moment before she suddenly gasped, startling both Gabriel and Damon.

Gabriel leaned forward, straining to identify what was happening. Was something wrong with her? Did they lose her?

"It's Rey. I can hear her. We did it," she squealed in excitement.

Damon and Gabriel both exhaled in relief.

Gabriel leaned back on his heels, his shoulders slumping forward when he realized something.

This girl was mind-linking Amelia. Was able to speak to her wolf somehow.

He needed answers, and he wanted them now.

"We did it. She's going to be okay," the girl said, tears running down her face before her eyes rolled to the back of her head, and she dropped.

Gabriel dashed to her side, skidding along the floor, seizing her just before she hit the tile.

Damon leaned over the bed, looking down at them. "Is she okay?"

"Yeah, I think she's fainted," Gabriel said.

He stood up, cradling the girl to his chest, her head propped against his shoulder. "Is there somewhere I can take her? She needs rest."

Damon looked at him funny, his gaze flicking between him and the girl. "Her room is the one right next to Amelia's. I can take her if you want," he said, stepping away from the bed.

"It's fine. I've got her. I remember the way," Gabriel said. "I'll be back in a minute."

Damon merely bobbed his head, still staring at them oddly.

Gabriel walked down the hall toward the central part of the house. The few wolves he passed halted and stared until he was out of sight. He walked up the five flights of stairs and down the dimly lit hallway. He recognized Amelia's room as the last door at the end. The closest door to hers would be the one on the left. He twisted the handle and pushed the door open with his foot, strolling right inside.

The room was an ordinary guest bedroom. A simple Queen-size bed was placed in the middle, set between two windows.

Gabriel walked to the bed, carefully setting the girl atop the covers. He grabbed a throw from the end, opening it and spread it across her body, covering her from shoulders to feet.

He finally looked at her, really taking her in. She looked much younger asleep, peaceful and worry-free. He moved the hair from off her face.

The hair was an interesting color. The roots were deep, almost black, quickly transitioning to a dark silver-gray blonde. The coloring reminded him of Amelia—almost.

Zeke tried to push through, but he shoved the beast back.

Gabriel left the room, closing the door firmly behind him.

CHAPTER 11

COMPLETE BETRAYAL

Amelia's eyes opened. Her body was sluggish and heavy as her eyes adjusted to the afternoon sun pooling in through a window. She glanced down at her body.

Someone had fitted her in clothes and was covered from the neck down with a heavy comforter.

Looking around, she found herself back in her childhood bedroom.

The room was scarce and unfurnished, clearly left untouched since it was last occupied. As she took in the room, she discovered Damon sitting beside the bed, dozing off in the most uncomfortable-looking chair.

Amelia reached out with her hand, grazing against his knee, causing him to jerk awake.

"Mia," he breathed in relief. "You're awake. Thank the Goddess."

Amelia struggled to lift herself into a sitting position. Damon immediately jumped up to support her, settling pillows behind her back against the headboard.

"What happened?" Amelia asked, scratching her head and found her hair surprisingly soft and brushed. "And who's been using me as a Barbie?"

Damon chuckled. "Cordelia was in here earlier. She changed your clothes and brushed your hair. You've been asleep for an entire day."

"A day? What the hell happened?"

"What do you remember?"

Amelia thought about it and the only thing that was clear was Gabriel. "I remember Gabriel. We were talking—"

"Yelling," Damon corrected her.

"Fine, we were yelling. And then ..." Amelia gasped in horror, recalling the smell. Michael, he was here. Michael was here. "Where's Emery? Where's my baby? Is she okay? Please tell me she's okay," Amelia begged, fat tears gathered in her eyes.

Damon reached out, massaging her leg through the blanket. "She's fine, Mia. She's unharmed."

Amelia rested her hand over her heart, taking in deep breaths, trying to calm her panic and heart rate. "Where is she? I need to see her."

"She's downstairs spending some time with her cousins," Damon smiled.

Amelia bobbed her head, her mind racing.

"You'd be so proud of her, Mia. Goddess, she reminds me so much of you. Michael was about to kill you. He had his mouth around your neck. He would have snapped it if it hadn't been for Emery."

"Emmie?"

"You never told me how lovely her wolf is. She looks just like you, except for the black in her fur, of course."

"She shifted? In front of everyone?" Amelia asked, too stunned to do anything but gape, her mouth wide open.

"She knocked Michael right off you. You were already passed out," Damon briefed her.

Amelia concealed her face in her hands. What if something had happened to her? "She shouldn't have done that."

"Amelia, she saved your life. She chased him off. You didn't see her, but we did. You've trained her well, Mia. She's got almost as much power as you, maybe more. She used her Alpha aura, and it shook the earth, sending him running with his tail between his legs."

"She did what?" Amelia asked, unable to comprehend what he was declaring.

"Hailey was in absolute control. She's a formidable wolf," Damon said, stating the obvious.

"He'll be back, with numbers," she warned him.

"I know," Damon nodded. "Don't be upset with Emery. Because of your aura, none of us could intervene, not even I could break through. You would have been killed if she hadn't stepped in. She was brilliant, Mia. She even challenged Gabriel."

Amelia's stomach fell out of her ass. "Excuse me?"

Damon swallowed with difficulty, instantly realizing he indeed placed his foot in his mouth. "It was nothing, Amelia. Hailey growled at him a bit. She just wouldn't let him near you."

Amelia pushed the covers off her body, forcing herself out of bed. She swayed as her body readjusted to the upright position, the world may have been spinning.

Damon reached out to aid her, but she swatted his hands away.

Pup saved us. Don't be mad at her.

Amelia froze. *Rey?*

I'm here.

The wolf sounded strong and conscious. Gone was the quiet and silence of lingering death but having Rey back could only mean one thing.

"How-how can I hear Rey? What the hell happened while I was out, Damon?!" she asked, nearly shouting at him.

Damon looked anywhere but at her, avoiding eye contact at all costs. "We healed your body. You were going to die, and Emery suggested that Gabriel help as well, to prevent you from moving on, to keep Rey with you."

How in the hell did Emery know to do all of this? "Where is Gabriel now?"

Damon thought for a moment, probably mind linking one of the pack members. "He's downstairs."

"With Emery?!" Now she was screaming. She tore out of the room, throwing the door wide open.

Damon chased after her. "No, not exactly."

He had his hands extended just in case she fell which seemed to piss her off even more. For someone who had been confined to a bed for nearly twenty-four hours, she was moving relatively well.

Amelia charged down the stairs, her feet hitting the hardwood of the main floor and instantly caught her daughters' scent—roses and vanilla. She followed her nose to the entertainment room, where Emery was playing video games with her oldest cousin, Adrian.

Emery turned around, catching the sound of her mother's familiar footsteps and smell. The emotions her mother emitted into the air made her drop the controller onto the couch and stand up abruptly in alarm.

Adrian yelled out at the TV, his character dying as a result but shut up when he saw the look on his aunt's face. The boy instantly left the females to their drama.

"Mom!" Emery yelped in surprise, ignoring the growing pit in her stomach. Amelia looked furious. "How are you feeling?"

Amelia approached her kid until they were close enough for their noses to almost brush against each other. "Don't you do that. I want to know why you put yourself at risk, exposing yourself to get hurt."

Emery was taken aback. Was she seriously mad? "Mom, I did it to save your life. He was going to kill you. He almost did!"

"That is no excuse! I ordered you to stay in your room. What if he had other wolves with him? You could have been killed!"

"I can't believe you're seriously yelling at me about this," Emery scoffed. "I am not going to apologize for saving your life. You would have done the same thing for me."

"I am your mother. That is my job," Amelia ground her teeth together, trying desperately to keep her voice low.

"Yeah well, I'm an Alpha too," Emery said, standing a bit straighter, ultimately claiming her birthright, her title. "You're the one who drilled me, taught me that being an Alpha means protecting her people at all costs. You don't give up so how can you expect me to? You can't say that you'll die for me and think I won't do the same."

"Being an Alpha means being smart and using that brilliant head I stupidly taught to talk. Michael is *not* to be underestimated, or have you forgotten all those years we spent on the run?"

"Of course, I haven't forgotten. My entire life we've been running from him. That's all I've ever known." Emery turned away from her mother and ran an angry hand through her hair, hurt and frustrated. Turning back around, she felt tears pricking her eyes. "You are all I have in this world. You've taught me how to fight even when the odds are stacked against us, to be brave in the harshest conditions, but you've also taught me that there are bigger things in this world than just you and me. I am *not* running anymore."

Amelia stared at her daughter, wondering when her baby became so fearless. "I just worry for you, Em. I can't lose you."

"I'm not going anywhere. You'll always have me," Emery said, reaching out and gripping her mother's hands.

Amelia swayed their hands between them smiling, but that swiftly vanished as she recalled something, or rather someone looming over them. "I understand that I've taught you to be all these impressive things, but stupid was never one of them."

Emery's eyes hardened. "Stupid is subject to opinion."

"Really? So, you think it was smart, challenging You Know Who?" Amelia hissed, trying to maintain a low volume. "Or did you think I wouldn't find out?"

Emery at least had the decency to lower her gaze. "It was Hailey, not me."

"Don't you pull that crap on me. I know better than anyone how strong our wolves are, but Hailey is under no circumstances in full control. On some level, you wanted to challenge him."

"Maybe I did," she hissed back.

"What is that supposed to mean?" Amelia flinched. Her daughter's words were shocking.

"Hey, is everything okay here?"

Amelia spun around, automatically moving to block Emery. She was so focused on their bickering she hadn't sensed him.

Gabriel stood in the double archway, curiosity furrowing his brow.

Her heart was racing in her chest, her palms sweating.

"We're fine," Amelia informed him, her tone clipped and short.

Gabriel ignored her rudeness, stepping farther into the room. He tried to look over her shoulder at the girl behind, but Amelia readjusted her position following his line of sight.

Emery peeked her head over her mother's shoulders, capturing his eye.

"Hey there. I'm Gabriel. We weren't properly introduced earlier."

Amelia growled in warning. "Back off, Gabe." Even Rey was bristling, perceiving him as a possible threat to their pup.

Gabriel arched his brows, looking between the two. "Is she your daughter?"

Amelia stifled a gasp. She refused to give her or her daughter away, not until she was prepared, and it was on her terms. So alternatively, she kept her mouth shut.

"She's what, sixteen? So, either you adopted her or lied to me when you told me you'd been faithful. Which means you lied about fated mates not being able to reproduce outside of the bond. My vote is for the latter since she looks so much like you. Maybe Christian—"

A hard slap bounced off the walls, ringing in their ears. A red handprint was already forming against his skin.

Amelia didn't remember moving towards him, but it was clear she did from the stinging in her palm.

"How dare you utter his *fucking* name. How dare you accuse *me* of *anything*. I am *not* the one fucking whore's every night," Amelia growled. "And if you ever speak like that in front of my daughter again, you will regret the day the Moon Goddess put me in your path."

Gabriel stared down at her, his eyes black, his body quivering with anger.

Amelia held his gaze. Rey growling and snapping from behind the curtain. She wanted to deliver a taste of the pain they endured over the years. The nights spent alone curled up with their misery over the fact that their mate was screwing others. Wanted him to have a taste of what betrayal tastes and feels like.

"No! Don't go that way!" Cordelia's voice rang down the hall.

Hers and another set of footsteps moved swiftly towards them.

"What's wrong with you, Cordie? I know I heard Gabriel."

Amelia snapped out of their pissing contest. She knew that voice, that high-pitched female tone. She looked to the hall just as a familiar face walked in.

Gabriel spun around hard on his heels, nearly obstructing her view.

But it was too late.

"There he is," the woman sighed in relief. "Gabriel, you didn't come home. I was worried."

"You have got to be fucking kidding me," Amelia scoffed. She could feel her heart shattering.

The overwhelming emotions rising inside were blocking her vision. Everything looked fuzzy and disoriented. Did time stop or was that just her breathing? Was this some sick, cosmic joke or was this karma?

"Amelia?" Kelsey looked around Gabriel, her face a mixture of shock and ignorance.

Amelia shook her head.

Rey was whining, pawing at the sky and howling to the moon.

Mom?

Emery mind linked, but she couldn't answer. "Please. Please tell me you didn't marry her."

Gabriel didn't move. Didn't bother to grace her with an answer. She already had it.

Gabriel had not only betrayed her and their bond, he also married the one friend she made in the Twilight Moon pack. The one person who welcomed her and made a strange place feel like a home.

"A-Amelia," Kelsey stuttered. "We-we didn't think you'd e-ever come back."

"So, you marry my mate?!" she heard herself scream.

It was like she was witnessing someone else's life. Nothing seemed to connect.

"You're the one who left," Kelsey said, trying to defend herself.

Amelia flicked her wrist, the movement so fast, no one grasped what happened until Kelsey lay on the floor, her nose streaming red.

"Emery. Now!" Amelia commanded, not bothering to glance back at the woman she formerly considered her friend and the mate that dared to marry her.

Emery quickly followed after her. They walked past her brother, Cordelia, and a dozen other pack members watching the show. It all rushed past in a blur.

Damon followed behind them as she threw open the front door, stomping out of the house and down onto the drive.

"Amelia, don't leave! Not like this," Damon pleaded with her.

Amelia spun around on her twin. Her eyes flashing red, tear tracks racing down her face. He stepped back as though a razor knife had pierced his heart. He had never seen his sister so devastated, so destroyed.

"You knew! Didn't you? You knew this whole time, and you still brought me here. Brought him here!" she screamed.

"You were dying. What choice did I have?" he heard himself yelling back.

"I would rather die than live with this," she whispered, her hand clutching at her shattered heart. She sounded broken and void of all hope. "This is worse than death."

She faintly recognized Gabriel coming out of the house, standing on the porch steps, looking down on them.

Amelia turned away. She couldn't look at him, her stomach turning to acid.

A Mustang was parked in the driveway. Luckily, it was open and threw herself in the seat. She pulled down the compartment under the steering wheel, exposing the wires of the car. Looking for the two she needed, she stripped the wires back, rubbing them against each other until the car roared to life. She twisted the two ends together and stood up.

Emery was still standing in the driveway facing the Packhouse. She couldn't identify her face facing her back, but the set of her shoulders she knew too well. Her daughter was saddened and upset. Gabriel was staring right at her.

"Emery Grace! Let's go!"

Emery turned away from all of them and got inside the car beside her mother.

Amelia endured one last look at them. All of them traitors.

Sitting back down in the car, she slammed the door shut and peeled out of the driveway.

Damon watched as his sister drove away in his car.

The look of betrayal on her face cut him deeper than any mortal wound ever could. He turned on Gabriel who still stood on the porch, his eyes fixed on the dirt floating in the air that the tires kicked up.

Damon launched himself at him.

Collectively their bodies rolled down the steps onto the gravel, the stones biting into his skin. He managed to land on top, straddling his body, landing shot after shot to the bastard's face.

In a murderous rage, he took it out with his fists.

Gabriel managed to knock him off, his fist meeting his jaw.

Damon skittered in the rocks, struggling to stand and gain a footing. Zeke was close to the surface, ready to shift.

"That's enough!" Cordelia yelled, moving to stand between the two fuming Alphas.

"Cordie, out of the way," Damon growled at his wife.

"I don't want to hurt you," Gabriel urged her, his wolf at the ready.

"Both of you will knock it off *right now*. Damon, this is not how we help your sister or Emery," she said to her husband before spinning around on the ass. She got dangerously close to his face, pointing her finger, and jabbing him in the chest. "And you. You should be ashamed of yourself. We tried to warn you, we told you getting married was a terrible idea. Of all the people, you select the one person in your pack that was closest to her."

Gabriel huffed. His cheeks puffed out as if he was prepared to say something, but Cordelia wasn't having it.

"If you say, 'she left you' one more time, so help you, I will gouge out your eyes with a teaspoon," Cordelia forewarned him.

"Who is *she* to be upset with *me*?!" Gabriel yelled. "When she has a child with another man!"

"Emery is—" Damon started.

"Damon! That's enough!" Cordelia shouted at her husband, her eyes staring daggers at him with a final warning. It was not their truth to reveal.

Damon huffed, storming back inside the house, and slamming the door behind him.

Gabriel's chest rose and fell, anger and confusion battling within.

"Look, Gabriel. I don't know everything that's going on here, but I know for a fact, you know next to nothing. Blaming her for everything isn't the way. She's more willful than you, and she's lived the past seventeen years on the run, alone. She's been through a lot."

"But she didn't have to do it on her own. I would have followed her anywhere," Gabriel admitted aloud. He didn't care that seventeen years had passed. Being near her again brought everything rushing back as though it was only yesterday. Everything he'd tried burying, tried forgetting, slammed back into his heart as if she had never left. It was overwhelming, and he didn't know what to do with it all.

"She knows that which is likely why she never said anything. She would never allow you to abandon your pack for her," Cordelia said, knowing she was right. "Look, I don't know where she's been or what she's been doing, but what I do know is Amelia. My entire life, I have known her, and I have never seen her so hurt. No matter what, that woman never goes back on her word. Shame on you for not having faith in her."

Cordelia left, leaving Gabriel standing in the driveway, alone, beaten inside and out.

CHAPTER 12

COMFORT FOOD

The drive back to the city was quiet.

Emery was anxious the whole drive, unsure whether her mother should be driving or not. Amelia was trying her hardest not to be conspicuous, but it was clear she was still crying. Her hands on the wheel were shaking, and her breathing was ragged. Emery wanted to go back to her father and let her wolf have her way with him, tear him apart, claw into his flesh until only ribbons adorned the lawn.

Hailey was furious. Neither of them enjoyed seeing their mother upset, but they've never seen her cry. Her mother looked devastated, broken, even hopeless. She always knew her mother was in love with him. It was evident every time she spoke about him. She just never believed he could hurt her like that. Plus, it didn't help that he was insinuating she was sleeping around, and Emery was a bastard.

Yeah, his bastard.

Amelia sniffled, switching hands on the wheel to wipe her nose with a napkin she found in the glove compartment. Emery reached over and grasped her hand, forcing her to focus on something other than her grief.

"I'm sorry, Momma," Emery said, her voice small.

Amelia glanced over at her quickly. Her eyes were red, the tip of her nose pink and shiny. She tried to smile, but it was in vain, her mouth incapable between the tears. "No, baby, it's me who's sorry. I'm so ashamed of everything you heard. I'm sorry for so many things."

"Momma, I'm a big girl. I'm just sorry you're hurting. I wish I could have punched the bitch," Emery growled.

"Emery!" Amelia gasped, stifling a laugh. "You are *not* a violent person."

"Not normally, no, but she hurts you, she hurts me," Emery said proudly. "You got her good, though. Snapped her nose clean."

Amelia groaned, rotating her head to the side. "Ugh, I did. I really did," she chuckled, almost as an afterthought. "It felt good, though."

Emery laughed, the mood in the car lightening.

They pulled up beside the brownstone, the Audi parked in its original spot in front of the house. Emery stepped out of the mustang while her mother undid the wires, effectively turning the vehicle off.

"Mom? How did the car get back here?"

Amelia slammed the car door shut, not bothering with locking it. "Our housekeeper went and picked it up for us."

"We don't have a housekeeper," Emery countered.

Amelia smiled a secret smile as they both walked up the steps to the front door. Emery pulled their car keys from her pocket with the house key on it, but before she could get the key in the lock, the door was suddenly pulled open.

Standing in their doorway was a petite, older woman with curling red hair streaked with gray, pulled up in a bun on her head and wore an apron over a black dress. Her face was pleasant and welcoming. The woman reminded Emery of those grandmas you see in a baking commercial.

"Ms. McKready, meet my daughter, Emery. Emery, this is Ms. McKready," Amelia said, introducing them.

Emery smiled wide, remembering hearing stories of the pack's old cook. "It's nice to meet you, ma'am."

Ms. McKready smiled warmly. "Nice to see someone teaching young folk some manners. Come on in. I've prepared dinner. Chicken Noodle Soup."

Emery walked inside the house, taking her shoes off at the door. The smell of chicken stock and vegetables permeating the air made her stomach rumble. "It smells amazing."

Amelia came in behind her, giving Ms. McKready a big hug.

Ms. McKready pulled back, placing her hands on Amelia's shoulders, turning her this way and that. "You look like hell, darling."

"I feel like it," Amelia snorted.

"You're too thin."

"Well, that's what happens when you're dying. Or were. Maybe, still am. I don't know," Amelia said, motioning her off.

"Well, we'll have to get some meat back on your bones. Why don't you two go and get washed up? Dinner is in an hour, and I made sure to put away all your shopping in your rooms," Ms. McKready instructed, gesturing towards the stairs.

Emery looked to her mother for guidance, and from the look of her, she wasn't going to argue.

"You're a saint," Amelia said, placing her hands together, praying.

Emery couldn't help but smile. Her mother deserved to have someone take care of her for once.

"Come on, Em. You heard Ms. McKready," Amelia said, already heading up the stairs.

Emery followed behind her. "It'll be nice to take a shower and wear something that's mine," she said, gesturing towards the clothes Aunt Cordelia gave her. "I know what you mean."

Emery and Amelia broke off, going their separate ways down the hall at the top of the stairs. They each had separate bathrooms, so they wouldn't be seeing each other until dinner.

Emery entered her room. It had been tidied since she was last there. She walked over to the dresser and pulled open the top drawer closest to her. Inside were most of the clothes they had purchased in the city. Emery picked out a pair of sweatpants, a tank top, and underwear.

They weren't leaving the house anytime soon, so why not get comfy?

She went into her adjoining bathroom and turned on the shower to the hottest setting before stripping out of the too big clothing. She pulled her brush out of the top drawer in the vanity, running it through her hair.

Looking at herself in the mirror, she saw herself differently. After finally meeting her father in person, she could see where her black roots come from, his being jet-black. It was intriguing how her hair achieved that. It wasn't black, it wasn't her mother's silver blond, but a combination of the two.

Running her finger down her nose, she knew that was from her mother, thin and pointy. Her silver eyes, clearly her father, including the cat-eye shape. The plump, pouty lips, and stubborn chin, all her mother, but the bushy eyebrows and thin face was her father.

Stepping into the scalding hot shower, she moved under the flowing water, allowing the heat to relax her muscles. She had thought of a million scenarios for meeting Gabriel for the first time—the day's events were nothing close to what she imagined. She wasn't sure what to think of the man seeing as how she barely knew him, but she wasn't impressed by what she had seen so far. She was confident she didn't like him at all.

Amelia was her world, her fiercest protector, her champion, and confidant, and he all but called her a whore to her face. Her mother, a whore. The woman who had never brought a man around once, let alone go out on a date. She wasn't even sure her mother ever even went out for a night by herself let alone with someone of the opposite sex.

Amelia took her duty seriously. Being a mother was her sole job, and she excelled, sometimes too well.

Her mind continued running wild as she got out of the shower, freshly scrubbed, and smelling like the vanilla body wash left in the shower. Drying off her body as well as she could, she winded her hair up in the towel before changing into her clothes. She sat down on her bed and pulled the phone out of the backpack she had managed to keep with her these last few days.

The phone showed eleven text messages and four missed calls, all from her Uncle Damon, since he was the only one aside from her mother with her number. She quickly flipped through the messages.

They were all pretty much the same. Wondering where they were, if they were okay, how much of an idiot he was.

Honestly, she didn't blame her uncle.

Yeah, he probably should have informed her mother about Gabriel being married, especially since his wife *was* her mother's friend.

Talk about messed up.

The whole situation was screwed up, to be frank.

It's going to be okay. Hailey said gently, like a warm glowing light in her troubled world.

Emery sighed. *Goddess, I hope so. Mom deserves to be happy.*

We all do.

Emery bobbed her head. She was right.

Opening her phone, she sent her uncle a brief message. She didn't want to leave him worrying, so she sent him a brief text letting him know they were home. Leaving it at that, she sent the message.

Tucking the phone into her pocket, she vacated her room, following the savory aroma of chicken broth downstairs and headed directly for the kitchen.

Down in the kitchen, her mother was already sitting at the island, eating from a steaming bowl set in front of her. She was wearing almost the same clothes as she was, with the additional sweatshirt hiding her scars.

It's a wonder where she got her fashion sense from.

"Hey baby," Amelia said, not bothering to look up from her bowl.

Ms. McKready pushed a bowl in front of the seat beside her mother. "Sit. Eat."

Emery obeyed, sitting on the stool, and leaning over her soup. She inhaled sharply, the thyme, rosemary, and chicken flooded her nose. She shivered with delight over the comfort food, picked up her spoon, and dug in.

"Uncle Damon tried calling," Emery said privately over their food.

Amelia didn't move or make a sound, merely continued eating her soup.

"He says he's sorry, and he wants us to go back to the pack."

"We're not going anywhere," Amelia said flatly.

Emery frowned. She knew her tone meant the conversation was over, but she wasn't backing down. "Don't you think we're stronger in numbers? You and I both know Michael will come back. Being on our own has never worked. We need help."

"Emery. I appreciate your input, but I do not want to talk about this right now," Amelia said sharply. Her face relaxed as she gathered a deep breath. "Please, just eat your food. We can talk more about it in the morning."

Emery nibbled her bottom lip, nodding. She wasn't going to give up, but she knew her mother had more than enough on her mind at the moment.

"Do you wanna cuddle on the couch and watch a movie or some TV? We can find something good to rent," Emery offered, the tension already evaporating.

Amelia smiled over her spoon. The heat from the broth rose and swirled around her olive skin. "What kind of movie do you have in mind?"

"We could watch munchkins in Munchkin Land or some sexy vampires?" Emery wiggled her eyebrows.

Amelia nearly gagged. "Vampires are nothing like what the media portrays them as. They don't sparkle and they don't have emotional switches. They are cruel, cunning, and terribly formal."

Emery rolled her eyes. "I think it would be interesting to meet a vampire."

"And it would be the last thing you ever do. There's a reason our species don't mix. They stick to themselves, and we stay with our own. That's the way it's always been."

"Have you ever met one?"

"A long time ago." Amelia barely remembered the time she ran into a vampire and to this day she still wasn't sure why he hadn't ripped her throat out. "I don't know how I walked away but I did."

"What happened?" Emery leaned forward on her hand, curiosity getting the better of her.

"This isn't story time, Emery. All you need to know about vampires is to stay away from them. Far away."

"Why do we hate them so much?"

"Vampires tried exterminating us. They failed, but it took us a while to rebuild."

"But why? What reason did they have?"

"We never knew. Still don't. That's why if you ever come upon a vampire, I want you to run, hard and fast."

"How will I know if someone's a vampire? Don't they look normal?"

"Yes, but there are subtle differences, you just have to pay attention. Most of it is in their personality. They are distant, more reserved, and formal in the way they dress and act. But the biggest red flag there is that they smell cold."

"Cold?" Emery frowned.

"Yeah, I don't know how else to explain it." Amelia shrugged her shoulders.

Emery pondered that bit of information, curious as to what it meant. "Munchkin Land it is."

Amelia chuckled. "Sure, baby."

Emery finished her bowl, placing it in the sink before going into the sitting room, tucking herself in on the couch, and flipping on the television. She messed around with the remote, figuring out the new system in search of her favorite movie.

When she was younger, the Wicked Witch used to terrify her. Flying monkeys and witches on brooms used to plague her nightmares, but as she got older, the horrors she'd seen in real life were worse than anything conjured from the Land of Oz.

Now, it reminded her of simpler times when a green-faced woman with a black hat was her most dreaded nightmare. Monsters didn't dress up in silly costumes and melt into puddles. They wore a face as ordinary as anyone, making them harder to detect.

She found the movie on the TVs On-Demand, purchased it, and hit play.

The theatrical music started immediately, along with the opening credits.

Amelia made her way into the room, two hot mugs in hand. She handed her one, the glass scalding to the touch. Emery took it and placed it on the coffee table in front of her, allowing it a chance to cool before attempting to drink.

Her mother sat down beside her, cradling the mug with both hands as if the heat from the small pottery was forcing heat into her body. Emery curled up against her side, breathing her in deeply. Roses and honey.

Amelia wrapped her arm around her, tucking her in against her body. She may be a teenager, but she was a Momma's girl through and through. She didn't require a father. Her mother was all she needed.

The Munchkins of MunchkinLand emerged from their homes, thanking Dorothy for dropping her house on the Wicked Witch when the doorbell rang.

Both Amelia and Emery looked at each other oddly. Emery shrugged her shoulders, having no idea who it could be. Her mother wasn't expecting anyone either.

Amelia stood up, setting her mug down on the table, before walking out of the room. Emery was too engrossed in the movie to notice the gleaming knife her mother pulled out of her slipper boots, lining it up along her forearm, hiding it in the shadow of her body.

CHAPTER 13

TELL YOU A STORY

A melia unlocked the door and pulled it open.

The night was surprisingly cool.

Standing on her porch was Cordelia. Her friend was dressed casually, wrapped in a cream sweater to keep off the chilly night air. She glanced behind Cordelia, down to the street.

The mustang was gone, replaced with a white minivan.

"Damon dropped me off. He was afraid you'd drive his mustang off the bay bridge."

Cordelia was trying to be funny, lighten the mood, but it wasn't working.

"Driving it off the bridge would require work. I was just going to leave it unlocked in the hopes that someone would steal it," Amelia stated.

Cordelia chuckled. "There's the Amelia I know and love."

Amelia crossed her arms over her chest, not feeling the humor. "What do you want, Cordie?"

Cordelia sighed with more than just physical exhaustion. "I think it's time you and I talked," she started. "I haven't seen my best friend in seventeen years. I miss you."

"Mom?"

Amelia turned around to find Emery standing in the hall just behind her, trying to look over her shoulder to see who was at the door.

"It's okay, baby. Go back to your movie. I'm going to step outside for a few."

"Hey, Aunt Cordie," Emery called out.

"Hey honey," Cordelia smiled genuinely.

"Emery," Amelia said, refocusing her kids' attention.

"Yeah, I hear you. I'm going."

Amelia watched as her daughter disappeared, the scarecrow's voice telling Dorothy how much he wanted a brain.

She stepped outside into the brisk air, securing the front door behind her. Gesturing to the porch steps, both women took a seat side-by-side.

Amelia hugged her arms, the cold biting into her skin. Even through the thin sweatshirt, it was cold. She could feel Cordelia's eyes watching her, taking in every detail. She could only imagine what she looked like to her friend. Probably half the woman she once knew. She was no longer the spunky teenager—fearless and impulsive.

"You look tired," Cordelia said, breaking the silence.

Amelia ran her hand through her still damp hair, now cold to the touch. "It's been a long few years."

Cordelia merely nodded her head, acknowledging the time that passed between them.

"If there's something you want to say, Cordie, just say it," Amelia was nervous, having an idea of where this was leading, the stray glances to the sweater concealing her scars were enough of a clue. "You saw my back."

Cordelia met her gaze, eyes brimming with unshed tears.

Amelia looked away. She couldn't stand seeing the pity, the look that told her she was a victim.

"Please, don't cry, Cordie," Amelia begged.

Cordelia took in a steadying breath, wiping the wetness from her face.

They sat in silence for some time. Maybe it was minutes, perhaps an hour, but together they sat until Cordelia regained her voice.

"I'm not going to ask you what happened, Mia. If you want to tell me, I'll listen to anything and everything you have to say. I'll cry with you, scream with you, whatever you need, but from what I saw when I changed your clothes, those scars are old. Like maybe eight years old."

Amelia scrunched her face, ultimately looking at her friend again. How did she know it had been eight years? Damon would never have mentioned a word to anyone without her permission.

"I'm going to tell you a story," Cordelia started, settling back against the wooden pillar of the awning over their heads. "Over eight years ago, it was a day like any other. The boys were young. We had just enrolled Adrian for soccer. Damon got caught up with pack stuff, so he had to meet us at the field for his game. But he never showed."

Amelia frowned. That didn't sound like her brother.

"I know what you're thinking. Damon is not one to skip family functions. No matter what's going on. But he did. When we got home after the game, Damon was nowhere to be found. Dominik told us that he got a phone call and just left. No word of where he was going or when he'd be back. He was just gone. I went crazy. He was an Alpha. The boys weren't old enough to help lead. Dominik had been given no notice. How could he just leave us like that? I started to believe that he was cheating on me, but I would know if he was. I'd be able to feel it. Or maybe the pack was getting to be too much. But that didn't make sense either. The pack hadn't had issues in years, no conflicts to speak of."

Amelia gnawed her lower lip, shivering, but not from the cold.

"I didn't hear from my husband for two agonizing weeks: no phone call, text, e-mail, nothing. Then one day, he just showed up. Pulled his car into the driveway and walked into the house as if nothing had happened. As if he hadn't abandoned us for two weeks with no word as to whether he was alive or not," Cordelia informed her. Her voice was remarkably steady. There was no upset, anger, nothing.

"Damon was enraged for a while after that. He refused to talk about where he'd gone or what he'd been doing, but he was angry. He would scream at the kids for no reason. The pack became terrified of him. He even wrecked his brand-new car in a blinding fit of rage. I was furious with him for a while. I couldn't comprehend why he wouldn't tell me. I was his wife, his mate, his Luna, and still, he said nothing," she said matter of factly.

"That's when it hit me," Cordelia met her gaze, her eyes soft and so full of love it hurt to look at. "I may be his Luna, but there was only one other person in this entire world Damon felt more connected to. He left us for you, and something had to have happened to you to make me terrified of my husband."

Amelia turned away, hugging her arms tightly.

"I didn't know about Emery at the time, but I'm glad you had your brother with you. I can't imagine what you've been through these last seventeen years, but I do know that you're the strongest, most courageous woman I've ever known."

"The kind of strength I have is not something I'd ever wish on anyone," Amelia said, her tone harsh and empty.

Cordelia bit the inside of her cheek. "I know. But you're here now. You don't have to do this alone anymore."

"It's not that simple, Cordie. I can't put the packs at risk again. We were nearly wiped out the last time we were attacked. Damon and Gabriel were nearly killed. I lost a baby for fuck's sake," Amelia hissed bitterly. She didn't speak of the baby she lost. The last time she talked about it was ten years ago when Emery asked about her birth.

Cordelia's eyes widened.

Shit.

"You really did lose a baby?" Cordelia asked in disbelief.

"I was expecting twins," Amelia informed her. "And if I hadn't left when I did, I would never have been a mother."

Cordelia bobbed her head. "I get that Mia, I do. Being a mother is one of the most rewarding, frustrating, energy-consuming jobs in this life. But it's been seventeen years since all of that went down. The packs never stopped training. The Warriors have continued learning new rogue tactics and they're more efficient with weapons. We're prepared."

"It's not that simple," Amelia sighed. Scared to admit just how truly terrified she was.

"Gabriel still doesn't know. Don't you think it's time?"

Amelia continued staring at the concrete beneath her feet, the cracked patterns splitting the cement. How could she reveal to the love of her life that she ran away with his child? That she raised their daughter on her own without him.

"I don't know how. He'll kill me," she heard herself whisper, fear wrapping around her heart, clutching her in its grasp.

Cordelia chuckled, tucking hair behind Amelia's ear, and leaned against her friend.

Amelia was surprised by the gesture, surprised that she wasn't freaking out at being touched. Instead, it felt comforting, warm, and pleasant. The same way she felt when she was around her twin.

"He won't kill you. He could never hurt you. You know that. Pissed, yes. But he'll understand. Eventually."

Amelia groaned, placing her face in her hands. If Gabriel knew Emery was his, she'd never escape him.

"Listen, I don't understand all of your reasonings. Or even what's going on inside that mind of yours. But I do have one last thing to say," Cordelia said, braving the risk to reach out and clasp her hand. "Do you really think the Moon Goddess would have gone so far as to weaken you to the point of death if she didn't want the fated pair to end up together again?"

CHAPTER 14

NO MORE RUNNING

Twilight was waning. The night took over, engulfing the forest in total darkness. Wolves howled in the distance.

The smell of rot and decay filled the air.

The woods felt familiar. Beneath the stench of Rogue, the scent of pine and sap could be detected.

Twilight Moon Territory.

They're coming.

The ground shook with the impact of hundreds of wolves racing towards one another. Her wolf itched to join them, to join in the fight that surrounded them when an eerily familiar voice whispered in the wind, raising the hair along her arms.

"Amelia."

She looked around, surrounded by nothing but shadows and darkness.

But she *knew* that voice.

"Mom?"

She was sure of it. She hadn't heard her mother's voice in over twenty-nine years, and yet it was unmistakable.

It was her.

"When dusk fades into twilight, the sun will rise, and darkness will descend. Be brave, my sweet girl."

Her feet shifted into paws and ran through the forest, the sound of her mother's voice fading all around her.

"Mom!"

Amelia jolted awake, sitting up out of bed. Her heart was racing in her chest. A cold sweat broke out across her forehead. She couldn't remember the last time she had a vision, but there was no mistaking it.

Rey was restless, agitated, like a muzzled wolf. She longed to be free.

Rey.

I saw it too.

What if we're not ready?

I don't think it matters. They'll attack anyway.

Rey was right. That much, the dream conveyed.

The Twilight Moon Pack would be attacked by an entire army of Rogues, worse than the last time and it wouldn't matter if she was there or not. She could run, and her pack would still be slaughtered.

No more running. Rey said firmly.

No more running. Amelia confirmed.

No matter what her personal issues were, the pack was more important. It was finally time to confront Michael and her past.

We can do this, Amelia. Rey tried comforting her human, sensing the anxiety. *It's high time we ended this. We've let that man control too much of our life already. He cost us our mate. Don't allow him to cost us our pack. Pup is old enough now. We can do this.*

Amelia took in a deep breath, fastening her eyes, willing herself into a sound mind.

One thing was certain, Michael had taken enough from them. She lost Gabriel, but she still had her daughter, and even though she hadn't been a part of the pack for some years, they were still her family, still her responsibility.

Amelia got out of bed, the sun already rising above the horizon, peeking through the trees.

It was time to confront her fears and do the next right thing. Preserving her family.

She pulled out a suitcase from the closet and began to dump all her clothes in with haste.

Emery stumbled down the stairs, sleep still at the forefront of her mind. In these moments, she looked so much like her father.

Amelia pushed aside the thought. If she was going back to his pack, she needed to stay focused. Winning this war, that is what was important. Nothing else could distract her from that simple truth.

It was already noon. Given that she had awoken with the sun, she had plenty of time to pack everything they'd require and arranged for the house to be closed since they likely wouldn't be returning any time soon.

She sipped on her coffee, watching over her mug as Emery made her way to the island, sitting on one of the bar stools. Emery immediately reached for the cocoa puffs she had set out for her, pouring herself a hefty bowl of chocolatey goodness.

Emery ate in silence as Amelia continued draining the caffeine from her cup.

The dream still plagued her. She could practically hear her mother's voice echoing in the chambers of her mind. Of all the people to reach out to her, she never expected it to be her. The last time she received a vision, it was the Goddess's voice she heard. So why now? Why her mom?

Emery glanced up from the bowl of sugar she called breakfast and took notice of her mother observing her. She examined the adjoining family room and spotted her mother's belongings, packed and ready to leave.

Her daughter frowned. Her brows drawn together in confusion. "We're leaving?"

"Yes," Amelia replied calmly.

"Where are we running to next?" Emery asked, the disappointment evident in her voice.

"We're not running anywhere. We're driving."

Emery's confusion continued to grow. "I don't get it. What do you mean driving?"

"It's time to go home. To the Twilight Moon. Your father's pack."

"What? Why?"

"I had a vision last night," Amelia started by admitting the truth. It was the least she deserved. Her powers, their powers, were no secret to her daughter. If she were to find her fated mate, then she would gain the same powers she had. "The rogues are going to attack the Twilight Moon Pack soon."

Emery sat up straighter in her seat, sleep erased from her mind. "What? But can we run? We can lead them away."

Amelia shook her head. "It won't matter. There's no more running for us. Even if we're not there, Michael will still attack. He has an army of rogues. His numbers are far greater than the first time he attacked." She walked around the large island, leaning back on the white quartz counters beside her daughter. "We can't run anymore. I've stolen your entire childhood from you because of my decision for us to run."

"You kept me alive, kept me safe," Emery tried defending her.

"Even still. I'm tired of running, and I refuse to let the Twilight Moon suffer because of the choices I've made. We'll stand and face Michael together," Amelia pushed off the counter, setting her now empty cup in the sink. "We have to warn the pack and prepare them for what's to come."

"We can help them train. We've been fighting off rogues my whole life," Emery said, a smirk playing on her lips.

Amelia smiled proudly. Her daughter possessed the similar fierce look of a warrior that she once possessed. She taught her everything she knew, and then some—experience being the best sort of practice.

"Yes. I don't think we have long before Michael's army shows up. Every second counts."

Emery stood up off her stool. A fierce look of determination settled over her features. "I'll go pack."

"We're leaving as soon as you're done."

Amelia didn't even get to finish her sentence before Emery was already racing up the stairs. If an attack was imminent on the Twilight Moon, they couldn't do it alone.

Two packs were better than one.

Damon. She reached out with her mind, looking for the bond that tethered her to her twin.

Amelia? Damon's voice sounded unsure. *Are you okay? I'm so sorry for yesterday. For all of it. I should have told you. I should never have—*

Damon. It's okay. Cordie told me everything. But that's not why I'm contacting you.

Okay. He said, dragging out the word.

Amelia filled him in on her dream, the warning, even the fact that it was their mother who contacted her.

Mom? Are you sure? Damon asked, skeptical.

Damon, it was her. I'm positive. It's not just that I could hear her. I felt her.

Man, you get all the cool powers.

Yes, because I thoroughly enjoy having nightmares of death and destruction.

Point taken. Damon quickly shut up. *So, an attack, you say?*

She waited for him to think it through. What she was asking for wasn't an easy choice for an Alpha to make.

I can be there tomorrow with a hundred wolves. Is that enough?

She stood corrected.

A hundred wolves, are you sure? What about your pack?

Mia, if you say there's going to be a massacre on Twilight Moon lands, then that's a risk I have to take. I'll be leaving a hundred-fifty warriors to defend our lands, but if Michael is coming for you, I will be there.

Amelia couldn't resist the smile that filled her face, her brother's unwavering support shouldn't come as a surprise, and yet it did.

Are you sure about this? he asked.

He wasn't referencing the attack. *It doesn't matter how I feel or what I believe. This is about the survival of my daughter's pack. I may no longer be their Luna, but their blood still runs in her veins. They treated me like family, no matter how brief and I won't let them down.*

CHAPTER 15

WELCOME HOME

Emery required a grand total of twenty-two minutes to shove all her belongings into a suitcase. Unfortunately, the poor girl packed like her mother and was sure to expect an explosion of clothes and accessories when she finally opened the bag back up.

She was eager to get on the road and meet her pack. The pack she would have been born into if not for Michael.

Michael stole her dreams of having a happy family, a peaceful, ignorant childhood, hell, even siblings. Instead, they spent her entire life trying to stay one step ahead of the deranged man.

The drive would last around four hours, but who knew what was possible with her mother behind the wheel.

They were only about an hour out, and Amelia hadn't stopped fidgeting the entire way.

Emery noted her constant movement from the corner of her eyes. Altering her position in the seat, fiddling with her hair, readjusting her shirt. She finally had enough when she began to mess with the radio.

"Mom! Relax!" Emery shouted and instantly regretted it.

Naturally, her mother was nervous. Neither of them had any clue as to what they were walking into. Her mother hadn't even bothered to inform Gabriel they were on the way.

In all honesty, Emery was thrilled to see the Twilight Packs lands. Her mother recounted numerous stories from when she lived there, and she couldn't believe she was finally getting the chance to see the place for herself. Whether her father claimed her as his or not, they were still her pack by blood.

But that didn't change the way Emery felt about him. She was furious for the way he behaved back at the Wandering Moon. The way he spoke to her mother struck a nerve. Once that bell was rung, it was hard to stop the vibrations. She couldn't forgive him anytime soon.

Uncle Damon had been informed of their plans. He was planning to send over a hundred warriors tomorrow, including the Alpha himself. Uncle Damon would do anything for her mother, that much she was certain.

The next few days, weeks even would prove to be interesting for everyone involved. Between her mother's sudden reappearance, the lost heir to the Twilight Moon, and half the force of a neighboring pack arriving at their border, there was one thing she was sure of—nothing would ever be the same again.

Emery glanced over at her mother, now silent and finally still. Her eyes were remote looking off in the distance. Her grip on the wheel left her knuckles white. She reached out, rubbing the tension from her mother's hands. The last thing they needed was to wreck the car.

"Momma, are you okay?"

Amelia glanced at her quickly before devoting her attention back to the road. "I'm fine."

"No, you're not. You're terrified."

That seemed to sadden her mother as she let out a deep sigh. "Listen carefully, Em. These next few days will be tense. I don't know how we'll be received but just know, I won't let anyone hurt you."

"I won't let anyone hurt you either," Emery promised. "I don't care who they are. You always have me by your side."

Amelia smirked. Her eyes still focused on the road in front of them. "You're the best, kid. You know that don't you? I don't know how I ever got so lucky."

"The feeling is mutual. I got the best mom in the world."

Amelia nudged her shoulder, the tension in the car improving significantly.

Emery gazed out the car window. The American Beech trees, with their speckled branches of burning orange and fire reds were on full display, perfectly showcasing upstate Fall. The streaks of color zoomed past in a blur as the car broke the speeding limits through the winding roads. The white trunks stood out amongst the fallen leaves littering the floor.

The beautiful view and full forest looming over the road reminded her of a time they had fled to Germany, hiding in a small village out in the country, in the middle of nowhere, surrounded by forest much similar to this. The winding road, the endless miles of trees and wildlife brought back a rush of memories.

The village was small and secluded, tucked away in a distant mountain ridge. The moon used to rise over the mountain peak and illuminate the entire village. It was stunning and mystifying. It certainly explained how some of the more prominent fairytales developed out of Europe involving the woods, a full moon, and things that go bump in the night. The ancient land was a strange place after dark.

Emery was lost in her memories. The thought of schnitzel flooded her mouth when a sudden movement in the car snapped her out of the memory of delectable German foods.

She took note of her mother sitting up straighter, more alert. Those sea-green eyes scanned the tree line, searching for something.

Pine and sap. The smell invaded the car.

Amelia froze, her heart rate increased drastically.

Emery wanted to ask what was wrong when she detected wolves following alongside the vehicle. First four, then fifteen, thirty.

"Mom?"

"It's fine, baby. It's okay. Just keep calm and keep your wolf at bay. We're not looking for a fight."

Her mother's warning was explicit. Show no reason for them to attack.

As they continued down the road, a substantial house came into view. Upon approach, the house only grew in size.

It was enormous. Five stories tall, farmhouse style.

"It's exactly the same," Amelia breathed, leaning into the wheel, peering through the windshield to get a proper look.

Her mother pulled the car around the circle driveway, parking directly in front of the porch steps leading up to the front door. She began to fidget with her hair that hung loosely over her shoulders, twisting it until it only draped on one side. Amelia's top seemed to lay wrong as she began to play with the fit of it. Her mother opted for a fitted shirt that hugged her curves perfectly but still managed to cover the scars on her back.

Emery couldn't help but smirk at her mother's efforts. She was nervous but also clearly looking to impress. But trying was futile. It didn't matter if Amelia wore baggy sweats, or a glorious ball gown made with her exact measurements—her mother was beautiful no matter what.

"Here we go," Amelia huffed.

"You got this, Mom," Emery encouraged her, executing her bravest smile.

Amelia nodded once before exiting the car.

Emery followed suit.

Outside, the smell of pine and sap was overwhelming—the Twilight Moons scent. The thirty-odd wolves who had followed them through the territory had grown more prominent in size, now reaching a number closer to seventy, all surrounding their car, blocking any chance of escape. Most were wolves, but some in human form had joined the gathering, curious of the invaders.

Hailey was bristling inside, feeling cornered and threatened.

Emery looked to her mother for guidance, trying to observe her reaction to all of it. Amelia had barely gotten out of the vehicle when gasps erupted all around them. Whispers of recognition floated on a soft breeze that whistled through the trees, shocked to discover her mother back on pack lands.

A stocky woman came running out of the house, bouncing down the steps. Her hair was grayer than brown, and tears streamed down her face. The woman ran to Amelia, winding her arms around her tightly.

Emery made her way around the car, taking up her mother's flank. The strangers surrounding them made her skin itch with the desire to shift.

"Moon Goddess, bless you! I thought I'd never see you again!" The woman cried into her mother's shoulder.

Amelia wrapped her arms around her in a familiar hug. Some of the stress from her shoulders faded away.

"Lena," Amelia breathed, relief evident in her voice. "It's so good to see you."

Lena pulled away and took notice of Emery at her side. "And who is this beauty?"

Amelia wrapped her arm around her daughter, tucking her in closely. "Lena, this is Emery. My daughter."

Emery could hear more whispers amongst the wolves and pack members surrounding them, but that's not what held her attention.

Lena's mouth dropped open, looking between herself and Amelia. The resemblance was unmistakable between mother and daughter, but what she focused on most was the silver eyes, the same shade as her father's.

"You-your, daughter?" Lena asked, stunned.

Amelia smiled, bobbing her head. "Em, this is Lena, the one I told you about."

Emery bore her hand politely to the woman, "It's nice to finally meet you, Ms. Lena. My mother has told me a lot about you. I hope I'll get to try your lasagna while we're here. It's all she talks about."

"I do not," Amelia grumbled, bumping her with her hip.

"Yes, of course! I'd be honored to make whatever your heart desires. I'm so glad to meet you my dear and to have your mother back!" Lena couldn't contain her glee, nearly bouncing up and down, shaking her hand vigorously.

Amelia finally looked around at all the wolves gathered.

The moment she lifted her head to make eye contact with the crowd, every wolf present bowed in submission. Emery and Amelia both turned around in a slow circle, and sure enough, every wolf and human alike followed suit, the word Luna ringing in the air.

Amelia was stunned.

Emery was bewildered and confused. What in the hell was going on?

"Lena," Amelia whispered to the woman beside her. "What is this?"

"The pack has never forgotten you. Whether Gabriel is married or not, you are his fated mate. The pack would never accept another Luna, not so long as you're alive. Gabriel never performed the Luna ceremony with her," Lena informed them, whispering softly.

Amelia was speechless, mouth gaping open.

Emery was pleasantly surprised. She had thought the worst of this pack, expecting a fight, a confrontation, something. But instead, they were greeted with nothing but respect.

Emery was kind of falling in love with the Twilight Moon Pack.

Or not.

Gabriel finally made an appearance, stepping out of the Packhouse, onto the porch, and down the steps. His walk was deliberate and controlled.

A complete farce is more like it.

His intense eyes revealed he was shocked to see them, along with the anger that boiled just beneath the surface, the tang of it permeated the air between them.

Emery kept an eye on her mother and couldn't help but smile.

On the outside, she looked like a woman in complete control, in charge of her emotions. Her shoulders were pulled back, head held high, hands clasped in front of her ever so casually. She looked to be at ease.

If only they perceived what brewed beneath the surface. What she kept locked away, buried so deep even Emery could barely detect the turmoil that battled inside her mother.

"What are you doing here, Amelia?" Gabriel called to her, halting a few feet before them. His arms were crossed over his chest, feet shoulder's width apart, prepared for a fight.

Amelia regarded him, taking in his stance.

Did he seriously expect her to attack? She honestly wasn't expecting such a hostile reaction, but if this was how he wanted it to be, then so be it.

You got this, mom. Emery linked her mother, offering her all the support she needed.

"We need to talk, Gabe. Somethings coming and we need-"

Gabriel laughed, his voice booming, jarring her to the core. It was a laugh that crept down her spine, unsettling every part of her.

"There is no *we*, Amelia. This is *my* pack, and you have no authority here. I want you off my land," Gabriel held firmly. His posture stiff and eyes unyielding.

The gathering crowd around them began murmuring amongst themselves. Tensions were running high, and even though they showed her respect upon arrival, now that their Alpha was present, they would, of course, side with him. She needed to keep things civil.

Amelia held her ground and took a risk stepping towards him. She wasn't sure if she could take him in a fight. Her body hadn't been in top fighting condition for a while, but if it came down to it, she would do what it takes to win, even if she had to make him submit.

"I'm going to keep this short since neither one of us can stand each other at the moment," Amelia stated the obvious. "The Moon Goddess sent me a vision. Michael and his pack of Rogues will be here within the week, and they *will* attack in full force. Over a hundred Rogues."

"And why should I believe you? I'm surprised you haven't scampered away like you did the last time," Gabriel wafted his hand at her in a dismissive gesture. "Take your daughter and leave. It's what you're good at."

Amelia was seeing red. Her old temperament was coming back in full force in front of the man she once called mate. If anyone could break her cool, it would be this obstinate, ignorant man.

"You arrogant bastard," she shook her head in disappointment. "I'm here to help you!"

"Help me?! When have you helped me?! A lot has changed in the last seventeen years, sweetheart. Now I won't tell you again, take your mutt and leave my land," Gabriel growled.

Amelia flexed her hands at her side.

Rey was growling in her mind. Her wolf's aura grew around her.

How dare he dismiss them! How dare he speak about their pup like that!

Gabriel didn't back down from her intimidating aura. Even though it was flexing around her, sparking with anger, licking the air in warning to everyone around them.

Emery was the only one unphased, her posture poised at the ready to defend herself and her mother.

"How dare you speak about her like that!" Amelia shoved him hard, causing him to stumble back.

The wolves around them gasped, twitching with uncertainty. Unsure whether to help or stand back.

Gabriel recovered his composure and merely stood there. The mere fact that she had laid hands on him could be perceived as a challenge for his position. But he was completely impassive.

"I'll say whatever I like. Tell me, is Christian her father?"

Amelia flinched at his words. A verbal slap to the face, a piercing pain lanced her heart. He was still as clueless as ever.

"Christian was the father she deserved," she said, selecting her words wisely. Knowing full well it would be his tipping point.

Gabriel shook with anger. His eyes were no longer their familiar pools of silver, instead they were swirls of onyx—his wolf entirely in control.

The Alpha before her shifted, clothes shredding in the process and stood towering over her on all fours. His obsidian fur bristled with fury, raising along the length of his spine. His canines snapped, biting the air in front of him in warning.

Ren, his wolf, had grown more monstrous than she remembered. His body was lined with rigid muscle, thick and bulging beneath silky fur. Ren was a stunning wolf but given the fact that his lips were pulled back, revealing sharp teeth left her bracing for an attack.

Rey whimpered softly at the sight of her mate. It had been so long since she'd seen Ren, but she couldn't forget the threat to her pup. She would not forgive them so easily.

"I'm sorry, Em," Amelia called over her shoulder. Knowing this next part was not going to be easy or a pretty sight to watch.

"It's okay, Mom. I believe in you."

Her daughter's confidence was enough.

Directing her attention back to the massive wolf in front of her, she snickered.

"You are the most stubborn, idiotic man I have ever met!"

Gabriel jerked his head, his fur shaking in the wind.

Amelia knew it was best to stay in her human form. She couldn't risk anyone seeing the scars on her back and to be honest, she wasn't even sure if she could force the shift even if she wanted. Besides, she needed to be able to continue speaking.

It was now or never to reveal her longest kept secret.

The link is still there, Rey informed her.

Seriously? Amelia was shocked. How could she still mind-link him?

It's there. I can talk to Ren.

Amelia reached out through their bond, and sure enough, it was there. Faint but present.

"Gabriel, listen to me. The Rogues are coming. They'll be here in a few days. I'm not running. I'm staying here. I want to help," she said, trying to convince him, forcing her words through the mind link as well for extra emphasis.

Why should I believe you?! You were my mate once. You've done nothing but lie to me, and you dare come here and bring another man's child to my land!

Amelia barely had time to respond before the enormous wolf charged for her. She stood prepared, but he veered left, back behind her.

He was going for Emery.

Rey pushed forward, pure instinct taking over. Amelia twisted where she stood, lunging for the man she formerly called mate.

No one threatens their pup. Not even him.

Amelia grabbed onto the Alpha's tail, using every bit of strength she had, wrenching him back and swinging him to their left, away from her daughter. Gabriel landed hard on his side but jumped back on all fours, ready to charge again. She stood her ground in front of her pup, digging her heels into the earth.

The other pack members were circling them, producing a ring, boxing her in.

This was bad.

How dare you try to attack our pup! Rey screamed through the mind link, causing Gabriel to wince at her words.

It had been nearly two decades since the bond was used, and it hurt the both of them to use it.

Gabriel lunged forward again.

This time Amelia was done playing games. He meant business and so did she.

Amelia charged forward to confront him, forcing her body into his side, knocking him off balance.

"That's enough! Do you have any sense?!" Amelia yelled, winded.

Gabriel snapped at the air between them, too close.

On instinct, Amelia snapped her fist out. One, two, three hits to his jaw. Her knuckles screamed in protest, but it felt good to release the years of anger and pain on the man who had caused so much of it.

Their link was bleeding together on both sides. Amelia was not just linking with Gabriel but Emery as well, and the same for Gabriel. His mind connection blended with that of his pack.

Everyone present witnessed the inner turmoil between the two Alphas.

Gabriel swayed his head, trying to remove the fog that was threatening to overcome him. Amelia took advantage of the moment of hesitation and launched herself forward. She latched onto his back, digging the claws that sprouted from the tips of her fingers into his sides, holding on as he bucked, trying to force her off.

"You're a thick-headed fool! You wouldn't recognize the truth if it pricked you in the ass! You didn't know I was pregnant for weeks! You're blind to everything around you!" Amelia screamed, causing him to buck even harder, flinging her off.

Amelia landed hard on her side. The impact knocked the breath from her lungs.

Gabriel seized the opening, pinning her to the ground with a large paw to her chest. Snarling, his jaw snapped a hair's breadth from her face, spit hitting her face as his hot breath fanned her flushed skin.

"Stop it!" Emery screamed from the sidelines. "Don't hurt her!"

Amelia relaxed beneath him. Her daughter's panicked voice was distant. The smell of the man dominating her overwhelmed all sense of propriety, swimming through her body until it flooded her system.

It was now or never.

"She's our daughter, Gabe. She's yours."

Amelia was convinced she could hear his heart stop. His blood ran cold.

Whispers around them grew more urgent. Every pack member understood the declaration.

The pressure on her chest lessened. She pushed him off, causing him to stumble and could practically hear the thoughts churning inside his stubborn mind—the inner battle between man and wolf.

Ren already knew, Rey spoke up.

And yet he still tried to attack her, Amelia didn't care. They still tried to hurt their pup.

Ren wasn't in control. Gabriel was.

Amelia didn't care who did what. She was furious.

Approaching him with caution, she planted her feet in the earth, unwavering, unyielding, positioning herself between her mate and her daughter.

"Emery is your daughter, Gabe. I never betrayed you, and I never cheated. Those are your flaws, not mine. And the fact that you can't see the resemblance makes me wonder if you have eyes at all."

"He sees what he wants to see," Emery said aloud, her voice ringing through the yard.

Gabriel's head snapped up at the sound. It was as though he was seeing her for the first time. The identical silver eyes, black roots, square jaw, all of it. It was all him.

How could you do this? How could you keep our child from me?! Gabriel yelled, turning the brunt of his anger on the woman in front of him.

"If I didn't leave when I did, we would never have had children. I would have lost her too and been left barren. Michael requires us both. I did what was best for her survival," Amelia informed him, her words void of emotion. "We don't have time for this. Michael will be here soon. Damon is arriving tomorrow with more warriors."

Damon's coming? Gabriel asked, his voice remote.

"Keep up, Gabe. It's time to get off your ass and do some work."

Gabriel snarled, growling in warning at the disrespect.

"You don't like that, do you? Beats being called a whore," Amelia snarled as well, Rey emphasizing with her own growl of displeasure.

Gabriel disregarded her, glancing back where their daughter still stood.

"Eyes over here!" Amelia snapped, refocusing his attention. "You don't get to look at her. You have been a real son of a bitch since I came back. Most of it, I deserve. But not her. So, let me remind you of something. She is *my* daughter, and if you say another thing that in any way hurts her feelings, I will show you exactly what I've learned over the last few years, and trust me, you won't enjoy it."

Amelia turned her back on the ass and approached her daughter.

Lena had her arms wrapped around the teenager. Probably both to restrain her and provide comfort. She owed her kid a serious apology. No child should have to witness what she just saw. She sure wasn't winning any mom of the year awards, that was for sure.

"Come on, Em," Amelia said softly, winding her arm around her daughter's shoulders, gathering her into the crook of her body.

Emery followed her mother up the porch steps and into the house. Leaving her dumb-struck father on the lawn surrounded by his pack and went in search of their rooms.

CHAPTER 16

YOU'RE SAFE HERE

T he Packhouse hadn't changed much since she left for her father's funeral, forever altering her life.

The notable change she detected were additional pictures hanging on the wall. Kelsey dressed in white, smiling on her memorable day. Gabriel beside her in a black suit and tie, his mouth turned up into her favorite grin.

The picture was a fresh knife between the ribs, twisting deeper and severing major vessels, ensuring she knew of its presence with every breath she took.

Amelia felt a small hand run down her arm, the touch instantly quieting her heart and mind. She fastened her eyes, enjoying the fragrant scent of roses and vanilla.

No matter what, Amelia had her daughter. She didn't need anyone else.

Amelia turned around. Emery stood just behind her. Her gaze fastened on the same picture. Amelia winded her arm around Emery's shoulders, issuing a soft squeeze. It pained her to see the hurt on her kid's face. This was supposed to be her home, her pack.

Now they truly were outsiders—lone wolves.

Amelia directed them down the hall to where she recalled the guest rooms to be and walked past his office. The door that was long ago replaced after she kicked it in, splintering wood throughout the room. It took them weeks to remove all the fragments from the couch.

A few doors down, she stopped at one of the more spacious suites reserved for visiting Alphas and pushed open the door. It was a lofty room with a King size bed and adjoining bathroom.

This'll do.

Amelia deposited her bag on the bed, taking in the space.

Curiosity tickled the back of her mind, recalling what the bedroom on the top floor looked like. Had he trashed her bookcase? Had all her books been donated or worse burned? The room was probably furnished for the happily wedded couple, complete with Kelsey's quirky, brightly colored tastes.

Tears pricked her eyes at the thought.

"Mom?"

Emery's voice swiftly pulled her out of her misery. She breathed in deeply before turning to face her daughter, a smile plastered on her face. She needed to be strong for her, for the both of them.

"Do you want to stay here with me? Or you can have the room next door. I believe it's the same size," Amelia said, trying to think back on the layout of the rooms.

"I'll take the room next door. Don't want to bring any boys back to a room I share with my mom," Emery teased, her eyes twinkling in the fluorescent lighting, a smirk tugging on her pale rosy lips.

Leave it to Emery to make light of a situation after nearly watching her parents tear each other's throats out. Amelia wasn't sure if she should be awed or terrified by her adaptability.

"Ha ha. You are very funny," Amelia laughed sarcastically, twining her arm around her daughter's shoulders, squeezing tightly against her own body. "You do know I'll snap any boy in half that tries to touch you. I'm too young to be a grandma."

"Eww! Mom! I was kidding!" Emery shivered in disgust.

Fortunately for Amelia, Emery hadn't expressed much interest in boys yet. Even though she was sixteen and most girls her age were already exploring their sexuality, Emery had always stayed close, keeping to herself. Probably due to constantly running from Michael, but Amelia figured it had to do with their lineage. Most likely, somewhere in this world, she had a fated mate waiting for her, just like she had at one time—perks of being one of Rhea's descendants. Emery's wolf, Hailey, would prevent her from mating with anyone until she finally meets her true mate.

Good thing for her. It wasn't something either of them needed to worry about just yet. At least, she hoped.

"Knock, knock."

Amelia looked towards her door to discover a burly man taking up the doorway. His hair was peppered with more gray than she remembered. A deep scar ran down the left side of his face, one she didn't recall him having. But all in all, he was the same man whose forearm she snapped her first day at the Twilight Moon.

"Rick!" Amelia squealed.

Abandoning her daughter, she ran and jumped into the towering man's arms.

A rush of memories overcame her. The countless hours they invested in training. How relieved she felt when she finally earned his and the other warriors respect. He had been her fiercest advocate after that training session. One woman versus fifty men certainly was a day to remember.

His brawny arms wrapped around her, engulfing her in a tight bear hug. Ordinarily, she refused to be touched by anyone aside from Emery, but at that moment, she didn't care. She was overcome with the welcome she was receiving, and she honestly missed everyone there.

The man was all muscle, thick and hard beneath her. She was confident she'd have bruises afterward.

Rick let her go, allowing her to slide back down onto her feet. The older man was well over a foot taller than her, his sturdy frame towering over hers. She nudged his shoulder, smiling so hard her cheeks hurt.

"Love the salt and pepper look, old man," Amelia mocked him, rocking back on her heels.

"Yeah, well, a lot happens in seventeen years."

His words shocked her, but his face was all smiles and warmth—no intention of causing offense.

"And I can see why," Rick said, nodding over her shoulder. "So, the rumors are true. You have a daughter."

Amelia turned back to Emery who stood waiting, taking in the exchange between her and the big man. Her face was a mixture of awe and confusion. Amelia didn't blame her. She couldn't remember the last time she hugged someone that wasn't family.

"Emery, this is Rick. Rick is one of the warriors here. He always had my back. Rick, this is my daughter, Emery Grace Smoke," Amelia said proudly. She had to admit; she loved introducing her daughter, finally, after all these years.

Emery smiled in greeting, offering a slight wave.

"Grace, that's a lovely name. Gabriel's mother?" Rick asked curiously.

All she could do was nod.

The topic of Gabriel was still fresh. Especially back in this house—his house.

Rick's face softened, a warm, encouraging smile spread across his face, making his laugh lines more apparent around his kind brown eyes. The movement tugged at the faded scar down the side of his face.

"What happened there?" Amelia asked, pointing to the scar.

"The Rogue attack. One tried flaying me alive, but don't worry. I killed the bastard in kind," Rick chuckled, shaking his entire frame.

"I'm so sorry, Rick. I should have been there to heal you," Amelia said, shaking her head.

Rick reached out, setting a broad hand that engulfed her shoulder. "Don't worry about it, princess. You had more than enough going on that day. I was the least of your worries. Besides, scars from battle are an honor to bear."

Amelia tried to smile, tugging on the bottom of her shirt. The scars on her back were a constant reminder of her own battles. One's she could never be proud of, let alone flaunt to anyone.

Rick noted her fidgeting, his eyes fixed on her hands, or more accurately, her wrists. He carefully grasped her hands in his, his thumbs brushing along the faded ridges circling the thin, bony flesh.

Amelia gnawed her lower lip, afraid to meet his gaze. She wanted to wrench her hands away but was more fearful of appearing weak and revealing her darkest secret—what happened to her during those days she was locked away in that dark cell buried beneath the earth.

"You're safe here, princess."

The tone in his voice seized her heart.

Not thinking twice, she looked. Rick's face was utterly composed and encouraging. His tone, even and soft, but she could identify a rage within him lying just beneath the warm exterior. Somehow, he knew. Maybe not everything, but he had an inkling of just how she received those scars.

A throat cleared behind Rick.

Amelia jerked her hands away, concealing them behind her back. She could sense Emery moving closer behind her as the smell of apples and cinnamon wafted up her nose.

Rick stepped to the side, unblocking the doorway.

Gabriel stood out in the hall, his gaze flicking between Rick, Amelia, and Emery. It looked as though he found the time to change, wearing a fresh set of clothes.

"I'll see you later, Ella," Rick smiled down at Amelia before vacating the room, bowing to Gabriel in passing.

"Don't go far!" Amelia called out, halting Rick where he was before completely disappearing from view. "Gather the head warriors. There'll be a meeting in ten minutes."

Rick nodded in acknowledgment and left down the hall.

"I'm going to get our stuff from the car," Emery said behind her, providing her arm with a light squeeze.

"Get someone to help you, the trunk-"

"I know, it's delicate. This isn't my first rodeo, Mom," Emery smirked, rolling her eyes.

Amelia flicked her wrist, smacking her daughter's butt as she passed. "You know you're not too old for a beating."

Emery glanced back at her mother, her silver eyes full of mischief, provoking her with a smile. "You wish you could take me."

Amelia stomped after her, causing Emery to laugh, running out of her room and past Gabriel. For the first time in a long while, she felt giddy. Watching her daughter laugh and joke was music to her ears, filling her with joy.

Amelia could feel his eyes on her, observing her curiously. Straightening herself, she walked back towards the bed and began to fidget with her bag.

Gabriel's boots tapped against the wood floor, moving closer towards her.

"I missed that smile."

Amelia directed her eyes to the bag in her hands, playing with the zipper. Was he seriously trying to flirt after what just occurred out on the front lawn? But it didn't seem to matter what she thought as her heart hammered in her chest. The blood in her veins boiled at the sound of his voice. Even after all these years, he still had the same effect on her body. But lucky enough for her, she gained control of those urges' years ago.

The trigger of her time in that cell did the trick.

"What do you want, Gabe?" Amelia asked, gripping her left wrist in her hand, digging her nails into the scars. The pain, the reminder of her torture, was the perfect distraction she needed, forcing her body to forget the mate bond and focus on what was happening around them— war.

"You should be on the top floor. These rooms are for outsiders," Gabriel said.

Amelia finally looked up at him. Her blue-green eyes confronted his silver ones. The pressure of nails pushing into the scars restrained her, keeping her grounded and centered.

"I have no rank. No position, no title. I'm a lone wolf and have been since I broke with the Wandering Moon. I will sleep here in the guest quarters until this is all done," she surprised herself with how cold she sounded.

Mate. Rey chimed in, her presence weak, but could feel her wolf's spirit growing stronger now that they were back in this house. Being closer to Gabriel would be beneficial for Rey. The strain of distance no longer burdening their bond.

I know, Rey. It's okay. Amelia said, trying to calm her wolf.

Amelia made to move past Gabriel when his arm stretched out, gripping her, pulling her in close. Contact with others, especially men, inevitably caused her a brief moment of panic. The urge to fight or flight. But being that it was Gabriel, her mate, her soul's other half, his touch soothed her every nerve. Her mind turned pleasantly numb as his scent overwhelmed her.

She dug her nails further into her skin.

We can't lose focus! She practically screamed at herself.

But it's Gabriel, Rey started.

No, Rey! We have a job to do. The Moon Goddess sent us a vision, and that is what we are here for. Or did you forget the countless nights we spent dying in agony?!

She could almost see her wolf hanging her head low in submission. The mention of the Moon Goddess was precisely the push her wolf needed.

You're right. He weakened us for over a decade. The mission comes first. Rey said, her tone determined and full of steel.

That's my girl.

Amelia finally locked eyes with him.

He stood patiently waiting. Realizing she must be conversing with her wolf since she was taking so long.

Amelia glared at him harshly, causing him to flinch.

"Get your hands off me," Amelia growled, including the bite of her aura.

Gabriel jerked his hand away and took a few steps back, arms raised in surrender. "I just want to talk. There's so much I need to know. About you, about our daughter."

His pleading voice struck a chord in her heart. The piece of her that somehow, someway still bonded them. The pesky mate bond that tortured her for years and now he was playing its last string that tethered them together.

"I know I can't avoid you forever, but the safety of our packs is at stake, and that has to take priority. We can talk about Emery and us later." Without providing him the chance to respond, Amelia walked past him.

The conference room was only a few doors down. It was a reasonably sized room. A giant table took up most of the space with enough chairs to fit over twenty wolves. A large flat screen tv occupied the far wall. Other than that, the room was bare except for the thirty-odd wolves waiting.

Gabriel followed closely, closing the door behind them.

The room went silent, conversation ceasing at the sound of the door clicking shut. All eyes turned. The head members of the pack and a few council members that resided inside the territory were already seated.

Amelia advanced to the head of the table to address everyone present. Gabriel stayed off to the side which surprised her. He was willingly surrendering control of the room to her. In the brief time she was with him, not once had he ever given up that easily.

But it didn't matter now. What mattered was the imminent threat looming over them.

"I know you all must be wondering why you're all here. Why I'm here," Amelia started, making sure to maintain eye contact with as many of them as she could. "As you know, seventeen years ago. A large group of rogues attacked the Wandering Moon. We lost a few of our own. Many were injured."

The men and women around the room bobbed their heads in remembrance. Most of them had been there, in the thick of the fight. She glimpsed Rick amongst the group, inclining his head, encouraging her to continue.

"In less than a week, another group, a more considerable group, will be attacking. Here."

The room instantly filled with noise. The wolves were speaking over one another, firing questions, accusations, declarations of strength. She elevated her hands to quiet them and the room went silent once again.

At least she still had some of her power.

"I know this because I am the descendant of Rhea and Ezekial, and as the mate in a fated pair, I receive visions from the Moon Goddess," she ignored the whispers amongst the wolves in front of her and continued. There could be no more secrets. Not with everyone's life on the line. "I know this is hard for most of you to understand. Rhea and Ezekial are stories we tell our children. But it's all true. All the stories are true."

"How can we trust you? You ran away from your pack and your mate. Stealing our Alpha's child away from its home, it's father," an elderly gentleman spoke out.

Amelia barely recognized him but knew by the insignia on his collar; he was a council member. She noticed Gabriel visibly flinch at the elder man's words. Could taste his desire to lash out at the man, but instead, he stayed silent, leaning back against the wall.

That was fine. She didn't need anyone to defend her.

"I have done nothing but be honest with all of you from the beginning. Some of you might remember me. I was only here for a short time, but in that time, this pack became my family, and I loved you all," Amelia confessed, filled with conviction. "You're right. I did run after the attack at my brother's pack, but not because I was afraid and not because I didn't want to be here. I left because the Moon Goddess warned me that I would lose my child and never have another if I didn't. If I stayed, our fates were decided, and our pack would have been wiped off the map. I chose to run to protect us all."

"Where have you been this whole time?" A female warrior spoke out, a fair-haired young woman she didn't recognize.

"Everywhere. Nowhere. From the moment I left, they've hunted me. The man who is after us is named Michael. He has over a hundred Rogues under his command. I have no idea how he manages them, but he does. He's been chasing my daughter and I around the world for the past seventeen years," she informed them, not wanting to go into too much detail.

"Look, I know you all have a lot of questions. But right now, we need to focus on Michael and the Rogues. Michael already came after me at my brother's pack a few days ago. But now, it won't matter if I'm here or in China. He is coming here, and he will attack. I'm here to make sure we stand a chance. I won't allow anyone else to be hurt."

"Why is he coming here? What does he want?" Someone said from within the group, but the face of the voice eluded her.

"He thinks my heart is here. He wants to hurt me in the worst way possible. But Michael doesn't understand the fated mate bond. Not many do. He doesn't realize it's already broken," Amelia swallowed with difficulty, preventing her eyes from gazing in his direction. She couldn't allow him to see her lie. "I've managed to keep him away this long, but now he's done waiting. He's coming here in hopes of capturing me and my daughter."

"What do we do?" Rick asked, speaking up.

Amelia glanced towards Gabriel. His face was an impassive one, cold and unyielding, conveying nothing. "My brother will be here tomorrow with over a hundred warriors of his own. Training will begin immediately. Every warrior, twice a day. We need to be ready. We need a meeting with the entire pack.," she said, directly towards the Alpha. Gabriel nodded in agreement. "Those with families that want to leave should do so. For the rest, it's time to hunker down. If Michael wants a fight, we'll give him one."

CHAPTER 17

PACK MEETING

Shortly after speaking with the higher-ranking members of the pack, Gabriel stepped to the front of the room, allotting everyone one hour before the pack was expected to meet outside in the backyard.

At the minimum, one person from every household was required to attend.

Gabriel dismissed them all, allowing them time to spread the word. Lucky for them, this was one of the key reasons the pack link was essential. Information could spread at the speed of light.

Amelia hung back, allowing the others to leave first. Most inclined their heads in submission, addressing her as Luna in passing. A few glared at her from under hooded eyes, afraid to meet her gaze head-on. The few elders in attendance shook her hand, welcoming her back.

Amelia realized Gabriel hadn't moved from his position against the wall. His broad arms crossed over his chest. His lustrous eyes never wavered, focused intently on her position. She could detect them roaming her body, noting all the things that changed over the years and what little remained the same. Shivers licked down her spine in response. She squeezed her knees, keeping them from shaking or showing any sign of weakness.

"I think those with pups, elders and families, should be able to evacuate. Neighboring packs can take them in until this mess is over with," Amelia studied the map laid out on the table, marking the boundaries of neighboring packs. There were five in New York alone, not to mention the ones in the surrounding states.

"Good. Reduces casualties. And you're certain they're coming here? Not attacking elsewhere?"

"Positive," she confirmed. The Moon Goddess was plain in her warning. "They surprised us last time. We won't make that mistake again."

"We'll be okay, Amelia. We've been warned this time," Gabriel pushed himself off the wall, leaning against a chair, his arms bulging with the effort.

Amelia held her breath, keeping herself from breathing him in. It was worse than she remembered. Her body screamed at her to go to him and Rey wasn't helping either, whimpering in the back of her mind.

"You don't know them like I do. They've been hounding me for nearly two decades. I've had too many close calls to count," she rubbed at her wrists absently. His eyes flicked to her hands before she could gather them behind her back, not wanting to spark unwanted attention. "They could be here tomorrow. No more than a week for sure. It'll never be enough time to prepare. He's had years to get ready. We have days."

She could tell Gabriel wanted to say something to reassure her, taking a step in her direction, forcing her to move back.

"We should get outside. Most should be out there already," Amelia said, keeping her head down as she sidestepped him, putting as much distance between them as possible.

Outside in the hallway, she could finally breathe. Her lungs took in gulps of air, but she could never escape him fully. His scent was everywhere in the house.

"Mom?"

Amelia looked over to find Emery standing near the front door. She offered her daughter an encouraging smile, narrowing the distance between them. Securing her arm through Emery's, she hauled her towards the rear of the house.

"What's going on?" Emery asked.

"We're having a pack meeting. Letting everyone know what's going on."

"That's good," Emery said, her voice distracted, her eyes wandering over those heading outside.

Amelia noticed many of the pack were looking back at them—curious eyes staring boldly.

"What's wrong, hun?" Amelia asked, noting the tension in Emery's neck and shoulders.

"People keep looking at me. It's making me nervous," Emery confessed.

Amelia pulled her in closer to her side. She felt terrible for her pup. She should feel confident and secure in her father's pack, but she hadn't grown up here, none of them knew her.

"I know, baby. But you're their Alpha's daughter. My daughter. Your eyes-"

"I know. They're just like his," Emery said, cutting her off. "I know you used to tell me that, that I look like him and my eyes were the same. But it's different seeing it up close. I don't know how you could look at me. Being reminded of him every second of the day."

Amelia froze, stopping before they made it out the back door and towed her away from the others. She gripped her by the shoulders, forcing her daughter to look at her. Emery was right. She had the exact shade of silver and eye shape. She bore his high cheekbones and square jaw.

Emery was the perfect blend of the two of them.

"I don't ever want to hear you speak like that again. I was blessed the moment I knew you were coming. I lost your twin, but the Moon Goddess spared you for a reason. I don't care if you're the exact replica of your father. You are perfect the way you are. I don't look at you and get sad. I'm honored he's your father. I wished he could have raised you, but fate had other plans for us, and I don't regret a moment of it." Amelia felt out of breath. Tears pricked the corner of her eyes. "Did I ever make you feel like I was upset with having you?" Amelia asked, almost afraid of the answer.

"No, never," Emery answered without hesitation.

"Then believe in that. It was a joy to watch you grow up," she cupped her daughter's face, rubbing her thumb along her jaw. "And you possess the most exquisite eyes I've ever seen."

"You're mother's right."

Amelia and Emery both snapped up to find Gabriel a few feet away, observing them. Amelia straightened herself. From the corner of her eye, she noted Emery smiling shyly.

The way he was glancing at them made her chest feel heavy and warm. Something stirred within herself that she hadn't experienced in a long time, and it made her nervous. He was married. She couldn't forget that. No matter what the mate bond wanted from them, she refused to be the other woman.

Amelia cleared her throat, breaking the odd look on his face as his eyes finally focused on hers.

"The meeting?" she asked, nodding towards the back door.

Gabriel straightened. He still had a strange glint in his eyes that she couldn't pinpoint, and his hair was grown out. It was no longer combed back and kept short as she remembered, but now hung loosely over his eyes, past the tips of his ears.

Amelia clenched her fists at her sides, digging her nails into her palms as her and Emery followed him outside, his large frame blocking their view, projecting a large shadow over them. Amelia didn't recall him being quite so large when they were together, yet somehow, he was more intimidating, more grown-up, and handsome, and she hated that she noticed such things.

Gabriel veered left, where a small platform was raised off the ground, offering the speaker a more elevated view of the grounds and people gathered. The moment his boots touched the wood structure, the pack went quiet. Amelia was inspired by how quickly the entire pack had gathered, given that most of them had barely an hour's notice. There were easily five hundred members present—a balanced count of both sexes, along with a few pups clinging to their parents.

Amelia couldn't help but feel nostalgia over the sight of young pups. Emery's childhood was gone in the blink of an eye, stolen by their circumstances. She'd been training her daughter how to hide, run, and fight since she could walk. It was how they learned to keep one step ahead of their enemies, but what she wouldn't have given to have been able to enjoy those simple years with her pup.

Gabriel's voice removed her from the past and transferred her attention back to the present.

"Thank you all for coming on such short notice. I'm sure some of you have heard by now, but for those of you who haven't, listen up. Most of you remember the rogues that attacked the Wandering Moon seventeen years ago. We lost a lot of good wolves that day," Gabriel's gaze flicked towards Amelia before turning back to his pack. "The rogues have made us their next target. In less than a week, a large pack of rogues will be striking us, here, on our territory."

The pack began to murmur amongst themselves, whispering harshly to their neighbors, family, and friends. Amelia could see the panic begin to set in. Could see the terror in the families and children. Unable to stop herself, she stepped forward beside Gabriel, Emery sticking closely beside her.

Gabriel elevated his eyebrow but didn't move to stop her.

"Listen up!" Amelia shouted over the boisterous chattering of the pack, forcing them into silence. "I know this is scary. Most of you weren't there when the Wandering Moon was attacked, but I was. We can handle this that I promise you. Alpha Damon is coming tomorrow with over a hundred warriors to support the Twilight Moon. You are not alone."

Gabriel directed his attention back to the pack, addressing them himself. "Those of you with families will be allowed to leave. We will be coordinating with neighboring packs to secure you all a sheltered place to stay if you wish to wait this out elsewhere. If you wish to leave, you have until the day after tomorrow to gather your things and head to your assigned safe harbor. As for my warriors, I will need every one of you, but if you choose to leave with your loved ones, I understand."

Amelia looked out over the crowd and noted the fierce determination in the warrior's eyes. Many of them lit up at the prospect of battle. The muscles in their neck and arms were straining to fight. She could remember that feeling. Remember the itch to fight with teeth and claws, to battle her way to victory. But running and practically dying had stolen some of that fierceness. Currently, she was battle-weary but more determined than ever to see this through.

"I am sorry for leaving you all the way I did last time," Amelia said, finally speaking. "Circumstances forced my hand, and I did what I believed was best, but I can assure you, I am not abandoning you to fight this alone."

Emery slipped her hand in her mother's, issuing a firm squeeze. A gentle smile pulled at her daughter's lips, encouraging her to be strong.

Amelia turned back to the pack. The crowd focused on her. Hundreds of pairs of eyes were considering her, assessing the woman she had become. "The warriors who will be staying behind to defend the Twilight Moon territory will begin training twice a day, every day until the rogue's attack. They will be here within the week. Time is not on our side so let's make every second count."

Gabriel bobbed his head in agreement. "You all are dismissed. Get with Kaleb if you wish to leave. Warriors, stay where you are. Training begins now."

Amelia watched as the gathering broke up. The families began to disperse, bidding the warriors good luck and goodbye as they separated. As the numbers dwindled, the warriors were left standing in the backyard, over two-hundred-fifty strong. She was shocked by their numbers. The last time she was on their land, the pack had a little over one-hundred-fifty, but now their numbers had doubled, with over half being women.

She was thoroughly surprised and oddly moved. In all that time she was gone, the Twilight Moon had thrived, grown, encouraging its women to advance through the ranks. It was all she ever wanted. To see the women, flourish and grow, taking their place among the pack with blood and sweat, no matter where that may be.

Gabriel cleared his throat beside her.

Amelia glanced his way. The way he was examining her left gooseflesh spreading across her skin. He was surveying her carefully, monitoring how she observed the pack, the warriors, the apparent changes that had taken place after her departure.

Amelia rolled her shoulders back, straightening her spine to stand tall and erect. She stepped forward on the platform, garnishing the attention of the warriors before her. Emery followed suit, standing strong, chin propped high. Whether they liked it or not, this was her pack as well.

"Thank you all for staying and being willing to help fight the rogues. We have a lot to cover and not a lot of time. I won't waste your time so let's get started. I want you all to break off into groups of five, two against five. Let's see what y'all got. Emery and I will be observing you. This allows us to assess you and see what areas we need to work on," Amelia explained to them.

"What makes you so qualified to instruct us?"

Amelia examined the crowd for the voice but didn't recognize it. It was masculine, but that didn't assist her in narrowing it down. Nonetheless, it was a valid question.

"Emery has been fighting rogues since she could walk. She's learned how to run, how to hide her scent, and how to fight them. I've been evading rogues for the last seventeen years and combating them when I need to. You won't find two better-qualified teachers," Amelia absently rubbed the scars along her wrist before hiding them behind her back.

Emery looked out over the crowd and narrowed her eyes at the blatant disrespect to her mother.

Amelia recognized that look.

"I'm fairly sure my mother gave you her answer," Emery spoke up, raising her voice. Hailey came forward in her tone, emphasizing her command. "Now move it!"

CHAPTER 18

FEAR

Gabriel stood off to the side, watching, observing his mate and daughter. The way they roved around one another, talked, and responded, anticipating the other's needs. He was witnessing an intimate dance between mother and daughter. One they had performed numerous times before. Finishing each other's sentences, even the looks they offered one another in silent communication. The mind link wasn't needed. It was obvious to anyone who paid attention that they were close and accustomed to training together. He couldn't imagine what they had experienced over the last seventeen years—the obstacles they had to overcome.

His anger rose to the surface at the mere thought of what they may have encountered. How close had the rogues gotten? What if one of them had been injured? He would never have known, never had known about his daughter, why his mate abandoned him and his pack—none of it.

A part of him wanted to be mad at Amelia, wanted to blame her and condemn her for hiding their child. Allowed him to continue believing that she had miscarried all those years ago when in reality, had run off with their child to be raised without him.

But the other half, the more reasonable half, could acknowledge why she did it. He could understand why she kept their daughter a secret. Hiding Emery not just from him, but from Michael and the rogues as well—the real threat.

Though he wanted to learn everything he could about his daughter, her mannerisms and personality, fighting style, did she prefer cake or ice cream, the way she held herself with such confidence just like her mother, he couldn't prevent his mind or gaze from wandering towards his mate.

Gabriel couldn't help but notice how much she'd changed. The girl he once knew was free-spirited, independent, and carefree, but the woman before him had grown—changed in ways he could barely wrap his mind around.

Where she once wore as little clothing as possible, she was covered from head to toe, wearing black yoga pants and a matching jacket that hugged every inch of her body, concealing her skin but not her figure. Time had done nothing to quench the thirst for his mate. Her hips had grown wider thanks to childbirth, her breasts fuller and more prominent than he remembered, but the rest of her was lean and thin, agile, and limber.

From her posture alone, he could tell she was more reserved. She wasn't as innocent and welcoming. Standing apart from the group, she observed silently from the side, pointing out mistakes as they were being made. Her back was rigid, clutching her hands behind her back as she addressed his warriors, reminding him of a cobra, patiently waiting to strike.

The silver of her hair had lightened over the years. It was more silver than blonde, making her look ethereal in every way. He could have sworn he caught sight of strange scars circling her wrists that she had been rubbing at mindlessly, causing him to be more curious as to what she had been up to these last seventeen years.

Emery was currently demonstrating the best way to scale up the side of a tree, only to twist through the air and land on the back of a wolf. Amelia was standing back as their daughter took the lead, explaining to the warriors what the point of the demonstration was and how it could aid them against the rogues.

Even he had to admit; it could prove to be highly effective. He had never considered climbing a tree to attack from above. It was genius.

They were using one of his warriors as part of the demonstration. Emery personally showed them the best way to twist their bodies away from the trunk of the tree to get the best grip on the back of a wolf. She even went as far as to demonstrate in both human and wolf form, proving that it could be executed no matter what shape they took.

Gabriel couldn't help the pride swelling within him, puffing out his chest. His daughter was magnificent. She was intelligent, resilient, independent, beautiful, and a fighter, just like her mother.

Amelia was off to the side, helping one of his more junior members, when he noticed her freeze. Her back stiffened, eyes widened and nostrils flaring. Her eye color was shifting like she was battling with her wolf, struggling with something.

Their bond was extremely fragile. The little stunt in the front yard drained their already weakened bond. Even though she looked healthier than the first time he saw her in the alley, their link was barely detectable. But she was still his mate.

Gabriel could sense her panic, smell her fear—metallic and biting cold. Ren could sense the battle raging within between human and wolf. Rey was trying to force her way to the surface, fight or flight mode taking over their instincts.

Just as he was about to step off the deck and approach, he noticed Emery break off from the group of warriors she was working with and beeline straight for her mother. Standing side-by-side, they looked practically identical, all except for the black roots of her hair and silver eyes. Emery was almost an exact copy of his mate.

Emery wound her arm around her mother's waist, rubbing her back softly, whispering into her ear. No matter how good his hearing was, he couldn't manage a word that she said. Amelia's lips barely moved, but it must have been enough. Emery's silver iris flicked towards the woods before running from the clearing and disappearing into the trees.

Amelia stood frozen where she stood, her nails digging into the tender flesh of the underside of her wrist. He couldn't remember that being one of her nervous habits. He was used to her tucking the hair behind her ear, that raging temper, and how comfortable she was with herself.

The woman in front of him was unrecognizable and wild.

Just as quickly as she left, Emery came jogging into the clearing and back to her group of warriors like nothing happened. Amelia was back to managing the young wolf, utterly unphased by whatever had just occurred.

On the outside, she may look calm and collected, but even from where he stood, he could taste the waves of anxiety rolling off her, coating his tongue with its thick, heavy scent.

Movement out of the corner of his eye seized his attention.

One of his warriors, Jonathan, an older man nearing retirement, walked out of the woods where Emery had disappeared. The man looked bewildered and ashamed. His brown eyes glanced towards his daughter and back to the ground in front of him.

Before he could rejoin the training, Gabriel called out to him.

"Jonathon."

Jonathan tilted his head at the sound of his Alpha's voice and approached the dais. Gabriel stepped off the deck, standing at eye level with the man.

"Yes, Alpha?"

"What happened in the woods?" Gabriel asked him point-blank.

"I was in the woods, taking a smoke break," Jonathan started, "when the Luna, excuse me, Ms. Smoke's daughter ran up to me and asked me to stop. I didn't know Ms. Smoke was allergic."

"Emery is allergic to cigarette smoke?" Gabriel asked, confused.

"Not Emery, Sir. Amelia. She said Amelia was allergic."

Gabriel nodded at him in thanks before dismissing him back to training.

Now he was more than confused. He recalled their first date. Taking her to the bar near his old duty station. The air was chalked full of smoke, and not once did she bat an eye at it. Besides, that look in her eye wasn't from an allergic reaction.

It was fear.

CHAPTER 19

CONFESSIONS

Amelia nearly stumbled into the house through the back door and straightened herself before her physical pain became too obvious to those around her. She couldn't remember the last time she had exercised with such fierce determination. It had been a long time since she felt capable enough to force her body past its limits, and now she was paying for it, dearly.

The entire time she worked with the pack, she could feel his eyes following her every movement. Amelia should have been devoting her attention to the warriors and their training, but instead she was zeroed in on him. She tried not to pay him any mind, but she couldn't prevent the way her body reacted to the way those silver eyes followed her. Her skin still tingled. His gaze left a trail blazing along her flesh. It made her want to squirm and run into his arms all at once.

Mentally, she continued to scold herself and Rey—the wolf was not helping in the slightest. Constantly ordering her to go to him, talk to him, something. Talking was the last thing she wanted to do. She remembered how often their talking sessions resulted in bodily contact and that was no longer an option.

Then, she had to go and have a panic attack in the middle of training. Like that was something she needed broadcasted. She could scarcely remember the last time she had a panic attack. But the moment the smell of cigarette smoke entered her nostrils, stroking the back of her throat, she nearly hurled right then and there, curling into the fetal position.

The fact that Emery had to help her through it left her feeling ashamed and weak. Rey attempted to push through, to prevent her mind from turning on itself, but Amelia refused to let her fears consume her. They had controlled enough, and she would not let it rule her life any further.

Dinner was a quick affair. She managed to eat hastily, packing away enough carbs to get her through tomorrow's training. The buzz of chatter around the dining hall left her feeling agitated. The pains of a headache began forming. She hadn't been surrounded by so many wolves in a long while. Even when she stayed with other packs Amelia kept herself removed.

It was all a bit overwhelming.

Gabriel stayed off to the side, which she appreciated. Amelia was relieved he wasn't trying to pressure her, asking questions she wasn't sure she was ready to answer.

Emery stayed by her side throughout the meal making small talk. Her daughter seemed to grow more comfortable with each passing minute, learning each of the pack's names and ranks. This was her pack, and not even twenty-four hours on its land, she was flourishing, blooming into the Alpha wolf she was destined to be.

"I'm going to step outside for some air," Amelia whispered to Emery before pushing her chair back from the table and standing up.

Amelia made sure to move as quietly as she could manage, slipping out of the dining hall and making her way out the front door and onto the porch. She settled herself down on the porch swing, tucked away in the corner, and leaned back, gazing up at the silver stars twinkling against the onyx night.

The outdoors was peaceful as she listened to the crickets singing, owls hooting from their nests, and bats flapping overhead hunting for their next meal. The Twilight Moons territory was far enough away from the city that the Milky Way illuminated the night sky.

Amelia became entranced, tracing the constellation of Ophiuchus when she heard footsteps walking softly on the wood deck. She'd recognize that gait anywhere. The power behind the muscle as he took each step.

He stopped and leaned back on the railing of the porch.

Amelia looked towards him only to find those silver eyes glowing in the darkness directed solely at her. She wasn't sure what to expect from him and that left her uneasy. Would he yell? Ask her questions she couldn't satisfy? What did he want from her?

"You did a magnificent job raising her."

Amelia's eyes widened, eyebrows arched in speculation. That was not what she expected from him.

She shrugged her shoulders, brushing it off as a fluke.

"I got lucky. She's a great kid," Amelia said casually.

"I think you had a little more to do with it than that. From what I've seen, she's a lot like you. At least the you that I used to know," Gabriel crossed his arms across his chest, leaning back against a thick timber column.

Amelia shrugged her shoulders once again. He wasn't mistaken. She was no longer the girl he once knew. That girl was more relaxed, quick to fight with not a care in the world. The woman she was now was damaged, broken, and unsure of herself.

"Emery is a lot like the both of us. Even though she didn't grow up with you, she would do something that instantly reminded me of you every day. Whether it was a facial expression, her mannerisms, and of course her eyes, your eyes," Amelia's voice trailed off, catching herself before she said too much.

"I don't know how I didn't notice sooner," Gabriel ran his hand down his face, combing his hair back from his eyes. "I was just so focused on having you back I couldn't see straight. Now I just feel like an idiot."

Amelia chuckled. "Wouldn't be the first time. You never realized I was pregnant in the first place until my brother blurted it out."

Gabriel groaned in response, twisting his head back for dramatic effect. "Don't remind me. I don't even have a good enough excuse for that. I guess I have a history of being clueless when it comes to you."

She couldn't help the smile that spread across her face as she remembered their countless arguments, make-up sessions, and then back to fighting like cats and dogs. It was endless, but she secretly loved it.

"That's an understatement. You were just too caught up in your head to notice," Amelia pointed out.

"That's no excuse for not realizing my mate was carrying my pup," Gabriel stated, his smile faltering at the memory of their last day together. "What happened, Amelia?"

She pulled her knees up to her chest, hugging them tight against her body, a slight shiver rippled over her skin. "What do you mean?"

"The day of the battle. After it was all over. What happened? Why did you leave? Why did you lie about losing our child?"

Amelia took in a deep breath as she held his gaze. His face was full of hurt and confusion as he desperately tried to understand what drove her actions that day so many years ago. Of all the things he could have asked about, this was one of the easier ones to discuss.

"Where do you want me to start?" Amelia finally asked him.

"The beginning. Why did you join the fight? You promised me you'd stay back in the bunker. Do you know how terrified I was when I learned you were out there fighting?"

Amelia ran her fingers through her long, silver-blonde hair as the memories of that day resurfaced—the feel of the silver blades in her hands, snapping the neck of any wolf that tried to kill her and protecting her pack mates.

It was all worth it.

"The Moon Goddess had been sending me dreams about the rogues for months. The night before the attack, after my father's service, she came to me in person. She told me if I didn't act, then my pack, my mate, and my child, would all die. I didn't know what she wanted from me. That damn woman is too cryptic, offering zero explanation or direction as to what to do. How was I supposed to change fate?"

"You never told me about that," Gabriel sighed.

"There was so much going on that day it slipped my mind. I felt agitated all day. I couldn't settle down. I couldn't calm my nerves."

"I remember. You injured your hand."

"Shortly after that, I had this sickening feeling in my gut. I told Dominik to increase the patrols. I couldn't explain it; I just knew something was going to happen. That's when I had a vision. I could see the shadows of wolves all around me. Snapping and snarling in warning. That was when I scented them."

"Damon got your mind link. I was right next to him when we got your warning," Gabriel said, bobbing his head in remembrance.

"I didn't have any intention to fight. I was carrying our pup, and I didn't want to put it in jeopardy, not after the attack we had at home. I couldn't do that again. But after I got the last few pack members into the bunker, I knew I had to do more. Something inside of me was telling me, no, demanding me to help," Amelia said, trying to explain herself. "What if that was what the Moon Goddess meant. What if I was the difference between our pack being eliminated and winning? I had to take that chance."

"You could have died," Gabriel growled, his anger rising at the memory of feeling his mate getting injured and being unable to reach her in time. How terrified he felt, how helpless.

"I know. But so could you, so could my brother and the hundreds of warriors defending our packs. What makes my life more important than anyone else's?"

"Because you're my mate. Our Luna. Not to mention the fact that you were carrying our pup!"

Amelia flinched at the rising tone of his voice, casting her eyes down to the wood floorboards. "I did what I believed was necessary."

"And you leaving, was that something else you thought was necessary?"

Amelia raised her sea-green eyes to confront his silver ones. She held his gaze hard and long, challenging him.

The air became thick between the two of them as their auras battled for dominance. She could feel his aura, red and pulsating with unrequited anger, trying to dominate her calm and sturdy violet one, but no matter how hard he tried, she was unyielding.

"You may disagree with my choices but leaving was my only option. The Moon Goddess told me that by joining the fight, I changed our fate, but if I stayed, then I only prolonged the inevitable. If I stayed, the attacks would continue, you would die protecting me, and I would lose the child we had left. I would never be able to bear children again."

Gabriel swayed his head, trying to comprehend everything she was revealing. "What do you mean the child you had left?"

"I never lied, Gabe," Amelia stood up off the swing, her hand resting on her empty womb. "I did lose a baby that day. Our baby."

"But Emery…"

"Not Emery," she shook her head. "Her twin. I lost her twin."

"But—"

"I didn't know until it was too late. The doctor managed to save one of our babies, and I couldn't risk losing the one we had left. Even if I couldn't be with you, I knew I needed to keep that part of you alive. She's important."

Amelia hadn't realized she'd been eliminating the distance between them until she found herself standing a hair's breadth from him, between his parted knees. Her hand automatically reached out, cupping his face in the palm of her hand. The familiar sparks raced up her arm, delivering a jolt to her heart.

Gabriel fastened his eyes on contact, savoring the scent that clung to her skin. Goddess, how he missed her.

"I'm sorry you had to go through that alone. I never knew," Gabriel whispered, a single tear slipped from his eyes and down his cheek. Before it could fall, Amelia wiped it away with the pad of her thumb, her own eyes sparkling.

"I've always loved you, Gabe. From the moment we met I knew you were my life. I've loved you through everything I've endured since we parted. Every sleepless night, every tantrum, even the days I was convinced I would die from the pain of feeling you mate with someone else, I loved you. You've always had my heart and always will, but you're married now, and I'm happy for you. I didn't come here to disrupt your life. Once this is all done, Emery can stay if that's what she chooses. She deserves the chance to know you, to know her pack. But if we win, I'll leave, and you'll never have to see me again."

Amelia slowly leaned in and brushed her lips against his cheek, the stubble scratching against her skin. Even if he was no longer hers, even though they could never be together again, she felt liberated, finally getting that off her chest.

She released her hand from his face and left him on the porch, heading back inside.

A part of her wanted him to chase after her. Wanted him to tell her he loved her too. But she was almost relieved he didn't.

That would only make leaving harder.

He would always be her mate, but he had moved on. Their time had passed.

Gabriel stayed out on the porch longer than he realized. His hand rested against the side of his face, marking the exact spot she touched. Her scent still lingered in the air in front of him, and all he wanted was to bask in it, bask in the woman it belonged to.

"Gabriel?"

Gabriel inclined his head, his eyes finally focused on a figure standing in the entranceway.

"Kelsey?"

Kelsey stepped out of the door frame towards him, wrapping herself tighter in her jacket. "Are you coming to bed? It's getting late."

"Yeah, I'll be right up," he said on autopilot.

Kelsey bobbed her head silently before going back inside, leaving the door open behind her.

Gabriel pushed himself off the railing and inside the house, securing the door behind him. He looked at the stairs that would lead him up to his room—to Kelsey.

Unable to help himself, he walked down the hall to the guest quarters until he was standing in front of her door. The mate bond pulled at him, propelling him towards his mate that laid within.

He cracked the door open, surprised to find it unlocked. Within, the light was on, but Amelia was soundly sleeping, wrapped tightly in blankets. He couldn't help but smirk at the sight. Even after all these years, she was still the most exquisite woman he'd ever seen. Not even sleep could hold onto her worries. Her face looked much younger and relaxed than he'd seen these last few days.

Smiling, Gabriel flicked off the light and shut the door quietly behind him.

CHAPTER 20

WHO TURNED OFF THE LIGHT?

Emery sat back on the sofa, sipping on her soda. A few of the other juvenile wolves approached her with idle chit chat, but she couldn't keep up with their chatter, unable to follow the people or places. Besides, her mind was more focused on the front door than the gossip happening around her, wondering how it was going outside.

She had seen her mother walk out to clear her head. Amelia didn't do well in crowds, and she could tell throughout dinner that it was becoming overwhelming. But not long after her mother left, so did her father, following the same general direction.

After some time, Emery noticed her mother come back inside, shutting the door behind her. She looked weary, bone-tired, and almost sad. Her mother didn't look up, but instead headed down the hall towards their rooms.

Not long after Amelia had entered, Gabriel had reappeared. He looked upset as well, but a slight smirk played on his lips, surprising her. Emery noted the inner conflict as his eyes flicked back and forth between the stairs and the hall that would lead him to her mother.

Emery ducked down in her seat, hoping to escape his notice.

On the one hand, she felt bad for her father. Felt bad that he never knew he had a child, and now there they were, suddenly in his life. But the other half was angry with him. Angry over the spiteful things he insinuated about her and her mother that caused a raging fire to burn in her veins.

Once she heard his footsteps retreating upstairs, did she finally sit up. She didn't know what time it was, but she did know she was exhausted. They had even more training the next day, and she needed her sleep.

Heading down the hall, she passed her mother's room.

Emery paused at the door and placed a hand against the wood. Staying silent and completely still, she listened through to the other side. Her mother's soft snores were confirmation enough.

Amelia's screams startled her out of a dreamless sleep.

Emery knew that sound, recognized its panic and fear, it's pain and anguish. She bolted out of bed, tripping over the sheets that tangled around her legs. She kicked herself loose and tore out of her room like a mad devil. She barely comprehended Gabriel in the hall, running for her mother's room.

Emery pushed past him inside.

The room was pitch black.

"Who turned off the light?!" Emery shrieked.

"I—I did. I checked on her, and it was on," Gabriel stuttered, fumbling with the light switch until the light flicked on, eliminating the shadows in the room.

Emery ran to the bed. Her mother was tangled in the sheets, skin dripping wet, and face contorted in agony.

Amelia screamed again, her voice guttural and manic, forcing her heart to hammer in her chest. She hated when her mother suffered these nightmares.

"Mom!" Emery seized Amelia by the shoulders, elevating her off the bed and shook her hard. "Mom, you have to wake up!" She gathered her against her chest, her mother fighting against her, beating on her back, but Emery sat there, taking it. She noted Gabriel trying to approach. "Get back! Don't touch her!"

Gabriel froze where he was, his eyes wide and terrified.

Stroking the ends of her hair and rubbing circles in her back, she hummed their healing song.

That was the one sure thing to lure her out.

"It's okay, Mom. You're safe. You're here. You're okay," Emery recited the familiar words, the exact words she'd heard a hundred times. The same words Amelia repeated to herself whenever she had an episode. "You're safe. You're here. You're okay."

Amelia began to settle down, calming steadily in her arms.

Emery placed her back on the pillows. Her mother's face no longer frowning or in pain but peaceful and soft. She tucked a stray piece of hair behind an ear and pulled the covers back over her body before kissing her softly on the head.

Emery stood up quietly from the bed, knowing full well her mother wouldn't remember a thing and would likely sleep half the day away. She gestured for Gabriel to leave ahead of her—their presence was no longer needed.

Ensuring the light was still on, banishing the shadows from the room, Emery closed the door softly behind her.

Emery exhaled a deep sigh. Half the time, she wasn't sure how these episodes would go or what it would take to pull her mother from her nightmares. Periodically they lasted much longer and required more patience, but Emery was always willing to wait them out.

She leaned back against the door and noticed Gabriel still standing in the hallway. He was frowning, brows scrunched in confusion, clearly having no idea what just happened or why.

"You look like you need a drink," Emery said.

She headed down the hallway and downstairs to the communal room, not bothering to wait and see if he followed. Somehow, she knew he would.

Emery went straight for the cupboard in the corner of the room, remembering distinctly coming upon an aged bottle of bourbon. She pulled the bottle out from behind a stack of books. It was concealed well, but not well enough. Flipping the bottle in her hand and catching it, she headed for the kitchen.

Reaching up on her toes, she pulled out two small cups and set them down, the glasses clinking against the marble counters. Pouring two stiff drinks, she slid one across the island just as Gabriel walked in.

"Your mother lets you drink?" Gabriel asked, his eyebrow arched, eyeing the drink in her hand and the one already waiting for him.

Emery shrugged her shoulders, taking a small sip from her glass. The alcohol burned down her throat, soothing her nerves and the shaking she was struggling to hide. "No, not really. But what she doesn't know won't hurt her."

Gabriel chuckled, taking the drink, and devoured it in one shot.

Emery slid the bottle across the counter to him.

He grasped it, pouring himself another. "You're just like your mother. She was pretty rebellious as well."

Emery smiled. "Mom says I'm a lot like you."

"Really?" Gabriel asked, taken aback.

Emery nodded, sipping the brown liquor. "Sometimes. Mostly when I'm getting into things, I shouldn't. I have a knack with locks."

Gabriel beamed, remembering the first time he slipped into Amelia's rooms. How furious she was that he picked the lock to her room. "I hope you don't drink too much. You *are* underage."

Emery couldn't help but give him a challenging look, unsure how she felt about him sounding like a father. "I pretty much grew up in Europe where the legal drinking age is like fourteen."

"I highly doubt it's that young," Gabriel scoffed.

"It's pretty out there," she said into her glass before finishing the amber liquid, setting the glass down in the sink. "Besides, I rarely drink anyway. Only when I can't sleep or on nights like tonight."

Gabriel frowned. "Does this happen often?"

Emery shrugged absently. "Not so much anymore. She—she just doesn't do well in the dark," she could feel him looking at her. He wanted answers, probably had thousands of questions to ask. "Please don't ask me."

Gabriel shook his head. "I won't. I would never ask you to betray your mother," he assured her. "I just have one question."

Emery hesitated, dreading whatever it was he was about to ask.

"What happened to Christian?"

Emery's eyes instantly watered.

The memory of her uncle was blurred, fading from memory the older she got. She hated that she could barely remember his goofy laugh, the way he smelled when he would tuck her in at night.

But one thing she would never forget was his sacrifice.

"He died when I was eight. He fought for her." She smiled at him softly. "Good night."

CHAPTER 21

IF YOU WERE GONE

Amelia awoke feeling exhausted, her throat parched and scratchy. Dark scenes flashed through her mind; silver chains glinting of torch light, a needle full of wolfsbane entering the bloodstream, foul, and clammy hands tracing over the planes of her body.

A nightmare.

That would be the reason for the sore throat. She only wished she wasn't a screaming loon, waking up the entire house.

Amelia got out of bed, stretching her stiff, sore muscles as she stood. Working out with the warriors yesterday had her using muscles that hadn't been exercised in a long while.

A steaming hot shower was all she needed.

Stripping off her clothes, she flipped on the shower and immediately stepped in, the heat already steaming the room. The hot water ran in rivets down her back, relaxing her muscles and melting the tension from her shoulders. She leaned back into the water further, allowing it to stream down her face, savoring the heat her body greedily absorbed.

Quickly showering and drying off, Amelia wiped the moisture from the mirror and stared at the stranger looking back at her.

Although she looked better than she had in London, she still barely recognized the woman that was her reflection. The years hadn't been kind to her, and it showed in the numerous scars painted along her skin, knotted marks around her wrist from pulling against restraints for days on end, he knife marks sliced up and down along her forearms and thighs when they tried to bleed her dry. Not to mention the whiplashes that wrapped around her upper arms, shoulders, and ribs thanks to the leather whip he enjoyed using on her so much.

Amelia's body was a roadmap of her torture, his pleasure, and she despised it, hated how disgusting and damaged she looked. Hated how even after eight years she could still feel his touch on her exposed flesh, as though he had permanently branded her with his scent and touch. In every way imaginable, her torturer had manipulated her body in ways she dared not remember, ways her mind revolted against and wisely chose to block from memory.

There was a reason she repressed the memories as best as she could. Reliving them in her nightmares was bad enough. That was out of her control. But during waking hours it was best to deny the event ever took place.

There had been no time for therapy, doctors, or Goddess forbid, a rape kit. She had to heal on the run and barely kept out of their reach for the following two years. After losing Christian, there were days Amelia wasn't sure she could do it alone. He had been her rock, her best friend, her brother for all those years, and then he was just gone.

It was all too much.

Laughter from out in the hallway startled her.

Glancing up, she found tears leaving tracks down her cheeks. Hastily wiping them away, she inclined her head to the bedroom door. The Packhouse was already awake and buzzing with activity.

Damon would be arriving soon, and given the way they parted, she was anxious to see him again.

Amelia left her towel on the bathroom floor and changed into her workout clothes for the day. Putting on a fitted sports bra, a long sleeve shirt, and leggings, she plaited her hair back into a long braid.

Ensuring every inch of skin was covered, she left her bedroom and headed directly for the kitchen.

The grand living room was occupied with families gathering to say their goodbyes before departing for neighboring packs. Amelia still couldn't contain her surprise and awe over Gabriel's willingness to allow members of his pack to flee Twilight territory and move to the safety of other packs.

To some, this would be deemed as weak. As though Gabriel, an Alpha, was unable to defend his pack. But to her, it was selfless and putting his pack first ahead of his pride.

There will be casualties in this battle. Not everyone will survive, and not all can fight. So why not allow those with families and elders to evacuate before the worst of it begins?

Inside the kitchen, Amelia went straight for the pot of coffee and poured herself a large cup, actively avoiding the dining hall and those inside. She was still unsure who may have overheard her outburst last night and she was not prepared to find out just yet. Although curious as to what Emery was up to, she knew her pup would sniff her out if need be.

Mia.

Amelia nearly dropped the hot mug from her hand at the sound of her brother's voice in her head.

Christ, Damon, you scared the shit out of me.

Sorry. I just wanted to let you know we'll be arriving in thirty minutes.

Amelia couldn't help the sigh of relief that passed through her lips. Even though her brother always came through, it was still a comfort to know her twin was close by with his warriors.

Having them as added defense would tip the scale in their favor.

Thanks, Damon. I'll see you outside.

Closing the link, Amelia pushed off the counter and made her way to the front door. Before she could reach for the handle, she recognized Kaleb, Gabriel's Beta.

"Kaleb," Amelia called.

Kaleb froze mid-stride at the sound of her voice. Turning back to her, he instantly stood at attention, hands behind his back, neck bent in submission.

"Kaleb, stop," Amelia motioned her hands at him, hoping to get him to quit the formalities. They were beginning to make her feel uncomfortable. Especially given that Gabriel had a wife walking around somewhere. "I just wanted to inform you that my brother and his team of warriors will be arriving in half an hour. I haven't seen Gabriel, so can you please let him know?'

"Of course, Luna," Kaleb inclined his head before turning away.

"I'm not you're Luna!" Amelia grumbled loudly after him, but his back was already turned. She had the sudden urge to stamp her feet in annoyance and almost smiled. The idea made her giddy and reminiscent of the times when that was her typical reaction.

In all honesty, she wasn't confident she was up for a one on one with Gabriel just yet. After their discussion last night, she wasn't sure where either of them stood. She still couldn't believe she told him she was in love with him and always had been. Maybe not the smartest thing to admit, but she felt better now that it was out there.

Though he didn't know everything about their time apart, at least he understood the important bits. But he was married now, and that mattered. Even if Kelsey was keeping out of sight. Not that she could blame her since she had broken her nose last meeting.

A discussion between them was bound to happen at some point. They couldn't avoid each other forever. Amelia wasn't even sure what she'd say to her.

Initially, she was devastated. Kelsey was her closest friend apart from Christian last she lived here. Just the idea of Kelsey and Gabriel together was enough to turn her stomach sour and her blood boiling.

Of all the people for them to choose, why did they have to choose each other?

Outside, the air was crisp and clear.

Sitting down on the porch steps, she cradled the coffee mug between her hands, absorbing its warmth. She sipped on the bitter liquid, desperate for the rush of caffeine to fuel her veins. It was going to be a long day and she'd take all the help she could get.

Emmie.

Mom? You're awake already? Emery linked her without hesitation.

Uncle Damon is almost here.

Crap! I haven't even showered yet!

Emery forcefully closed the link in a state of panic.

Amelia chuckled.

She was so preoccupied with her daughter's antics that she didn't catch the wood creaking beneath solid weight or the smell of cloves filling the air. It wasn't until his arm brushed against hers, causing the familiar sparks to race across her forearm that she nearly dumped the contents of the mug in her lap.

"Sorry," Gabriel stifled a laugh. "Didn't mean to startle you."

Amelia forced herself to take in a deep breath through the mouth, refusing to scent him. Her heart was pounding inside her chest, racing as though she'd run ten miles.

Being so close to him again was excruciating. The mate bond that still tethered them to one another had no care for marriage vows or past trauma. It demanded their union no matter the consequences. It was torture to resist but resist she did, no matter how badly she wanted to fold into his tender embrace and take comfort in his broad frame the way she once did.

"It's alright. I was just linking Emery," she briefed him.

"Ah, yes. Kaleb notified me. Your brother is almost here."

Amelia bobbed her head, afraid to speak in his presence. She already said too much last night and knew better than to trust herself around him. It was almost as though her heart and mind had disregarded everything they had endured over the last seventeen years. He had betrayed her, betrayed their bond, even betrayed the Moon Goddess. They were a fated pair and more than just mates. They were literally made for one another, and he didn't care.

She sipped her coffee, keeping her gaze fixed straight ahead into the woods, listening intently for the sound of gravel crunching under tires. But instead, she heard Gabriel scenting the air loudly beside her and couldn't help but glance at him sideways.

Rey was stirring in her mind, becoming more and more active with their proximity. She was getting stronger, which meant maybe they had a fighting chance when Michael did finally arrive.

"Since when do you drink coffee? You used to hate it," Gabriel asked, crinkling his nose.

Amelia nearly snorted at him before catching herself. "When you raise a rambunctious, precocious pup on your own, you learn to accept all the help you can get. Some days coffee was the only thing that kept either of us alive," she chuckled at the memories of chasing a small pup around the yard. Emery was always a wild one, so full of energy. It was a wonder some days how they lasted so long.

She noticed his face fall at her words. The last thing she wanted to do was rub salt in a wound, and that was precisely what she did. Before she could apologize, Gabriel surprised her yet again.

"Can you tell me more about her? When she was younger?" Gabriel asked.

Amelia nodded. "Of course. Goddess, where to start?" she wondered, thinking back through the years.

"The beginning is always a good place," he said, settling back against the wood steps.

"I highly doubt you want to hear about my pregnancy or her birth," Amelia said flippantly.

"I want to know everything, Snow. I missed a lot these last few years, and I want to know it all."

Amelia's heart stuttered in her chest at. Snow, the name only he used for her. She hadn't heard that nickname since before she left.

Without thought, she reached out and grasped his hand.

"I never wanted you to miss any of it. I wish you could have been there through every hiccup, contraction, and runny nose, but if I had stayed, you would have died. I truly believe that. I could live in a world where we aren't together. I do live in it. But I could never survive and continue to breathe if you were gone."

Gabriel's eyes widened at her words. Amelia withdrew her hand out of his, suddenly feeling incredibly self-conscious and aware, like a bucket of frozen water had been dumped on her head.

This was why she couldn't be trusted around him.

He needs to know how we feel. Rey spoke up.

I don't even know how I feel!

Yes, you do. You just don't want to admit it.

He's married. He cheated on us! Or did you forget?

Of course not. But we don't know what he went through either.

Amelia blocked her wolf from saying any more. She hated it when she made sense, and right now, she didn't want to hear it or acknowledge it. She could see Gabriel's lips twitching like he was searching for the words, desperate to respond.

The sound of gravel crunching shifted their attention.

Multiple SUVs pulled up the drive, followed by two buses. The first black SUV parked in front of the house, parallel to the porch steps they were sitting on.

Amelia placed her mug down on the porch and stood up, rubbing her hands on her leggings. She was feeling oddly nervous at seeing her brother again. They hadn't exactly parted on good terms last she saw him.

The front passenger door opened.

Damon stepped out, shutting the door closed firmly behind him.

Amelia exhaled loudly at the sight of her twin. "Damon."

CHAPTER 22

DÉJÀ VU

Amelia ran into her brother's arms, clutching him tightly.

Damon's grip around her waist held her just as close.

Concealing her face in his neck, she breathed her twin in deeply. Instantly comforted by the familiar scent.

A part of her felt like she should be upset with him. He had kept things from her for years, but on the other hand, what good would it have done to know that Gabriel had moved on and got married. It only would have distracted her.

Damon would never willingly inflict such emotional distress on her if he could prevent it.

"I'm sorry, Mia. I should have told you. I should have—"

"Hush," Amelia said, silencing him. She pulled back, lowering her arms to her side. "You have nothing to apologize for. I understand why you never said anything. It's not your fault. I'm sorry for behaving the way I did and taking it out on you."

"Well, my car. You took it out on my car. I shouldn't be surprised that you know how to hotwire a car, but I was," Damon corrected her with a chuckle.

"I was going to let it get stolen, but then you had to ruin my master plan by picking it up," Amelia rolled her eyes dramatically.

"So sorry I spoiled your plans," Damon smiled.

He glanced over her shoulder to find Gabriel standing on the porch, witnessing the siblings exchange. Instantly, she noticed Damon's body was rigid.

If he had been in wolf form, she was certain his hackles would be raised, and ears pulled back in warning.

"Alpha Gabriel," Damon nodded, acknowledging the man's existence.

"Alpha Damon. Thank you for coming," Gabriel said coldly, crossing his arms across his chest.

Amelia diverted her attention away from that of her mate. The way his muscles flexed as he crossed his arms aroused something inside of her, she was *not* comfortable with. Turning back towards the vehicles that were still unloading the dozens of warriors and their baggage, she finally noticed one key member.

"Cordie?! What are you doing here? Who's watching the boys?" Amelia asked, her voice rising an octave higher than normal.

She was shocked to discover her best friend on Twilight territory. Cordelia wasn't a fighter, and the fact that she had come during a time of war made her uneasy. She couldn't bear the idea of something happening to her.

"Dominik stayed behind. He's watching over the boys. Come on, let's go inside and get something to eat. I'm starving!" Cordelia looped their arms, dragging her past Gabriel and inside the house without an explanation.

Amelia felt unsure, leaving Damon and Gabriel behind. The testosterone floating in the air between them achieved hazardous levels, but Cordelia maintained her grip on her arm, tight and unyielding.

Thankfully she heard the soft padding of shoes sticking close behind her as Damon followed them to the dining hall. The hall was filled with warriors devouring their first meal of the day, anticipating a tedious, arduous day.

If only they knew.

Amelia stopped at the open entranceway, halting Cordelia beside her. "Heads up, warriors! Wandering Moon has arrived. Training will start in thirty minutes."

The pack quickly quieted down, only to scurry when announced their time limit. Most began to eat more rapidly. Others skittered off to their room to get changed.

The smell of food entered her nostrils, causing her stomach to growl. She didn't realize how hungry she truly was until that moment. Amelia snatched a plate, stacking it high with pancakes, bacon, and sausage, and occupied a seat at an empty table near the windows.

The food was fresh and steaming.

Unable to stop herself, she quickly began to eat, knowing she would require every ounce of energy. She tried to ignore the lingering stares from both packs present, but those weren't the set of eyes that set her nerves on edge. It was as though every cell in her body was attuned to him, focused, and moving with him as he entered the room and sat at a table farthest from her, but those eyes never relented.

Damon sat down beside her, Cordelia sitting across the table. They both dug into their meal.

Damon leaned over, trying to swipe a piece of bacon from her plate when Amelia lightly pierced his hand with her fork.

"Hands off," she growled at her twin. "Do *not* touch my food."

"Gosh, so territorial," Damon teased, "you would think it's gold."

"Bacon is a very important food group I'll have you know. Besides, you should know better than to try and swipe food from my plate. How many times as kids did I beat you to a pulp for trying the very same thing?" Amelia asked, thrusting a thick piece of bacon in her mouth.

Cordelia snorted a laugh. "She's right. You two were always getting into fights over food. Not like there wasn't plenty to go around, but I think you secretly enjoyed getting pummeled," she said, calling out her husband.

Damon pouted, shoving pancakes in his mouth. "I did not get pummeled," he grumbled with his mouth full.

Amelia and Cordelia both smirked at one another before saying in unison, "Yeah, you did."

All three of them ended up laughing, garnering even more attention, but at that moment, Amelia didn't care. For once, she felt light and at ease. Sitting down at breakfast with her brother and sister-in-law reminded her of old times. Back before the war, kids, and mates. Back when life was uncomplicated, and their biggest worry was not being late to training, finishing homework for history class, and avoiding their father on weekends when their hangovers were obvious.

An acute pain flared near her heart.

Amelia suddenly had a strong sense of deja vu. Sitting at the table with two of the people closest to her in the world reminded her of the early days in the Twilight Moon Pack. The days where she grew close to Christian and Kelsey.

Kelsey had reminded her most of Cordelia, but Christian was her brother in every way but blood.

The last time she was in the dining hall was with Christian before they ran. Before, he abandoned everything for her so that she wouldn't be alone. Before he deserted his pack and Alpha only to keep her safe and protected. Before he placed his life on the line to remove her from the clutches of their enemies.

"Mia?"

Amelia's eyes focused on Cordelia, her voice removing her from an overwhelming pit of memories. Damon set his hand against her back, rubbing soothing circles against her skin through the thin jacket. Feeling more grounded and present, she felt a cold wetness on her face. Reaching up, she swiped at her cheek to find tears. She looked at the wetness on her fingers in surprise.

Sniffling sharply, she wiped away the remaining traces of tears and smiled as best she could. "I'm okay. Just got lost for a minute."

"It's okay. We get it," Cordelia smiled gently.

Amelia tried to brush the memories to the back of her mind, but like a parasite they lingered, taunting her, tainting her mood. She was still outraged at the world for losing him. Christian was one of the best men in her life, and his death still haunted her. If it hadn't been for her, he would still be alive.

Standing up abruptly, the room quieted. Amelia could feel his eyes on her, noting her appearance. She knew all too well he wouldn't miss the red tinge to her nose—the dead giveaway of her emotions.

Ignoring all the stares, she forced her way outside.

She was pissed and needed to punch something.

CHAPTER 23

EXPOSED

Outside, Amelia spotted Emery, already stretching, and waiting for training to begin.

"Hey, mom," Emery smiled at her approach.

"Hey, baby," Amelia tried to smile but failed, her blood singing, urging her to water the earth red.

"What's going on? What's wrong?" Emery stood up straighter, her eyes flitting around at their surroundings as though expecting an attack.

"It's nothing, baby. I'm okay."

"Bullshit," Emery said, ignoring his mother's raised brow. "Your nose is red. You've been crying."

Amelia wiped at her nose absently, annoyed with her own body for betraying her. "It's nothing, hun. I swear. Just this place brings up a lot of memories. I had a moment."

"How did you sleep?"

Dread lined her stomach in lead. Nothing could ever just be simple.

"I knew I woke you up. How loud was I? Did I wake the whole house?"

"No, no, nothing like that. I managed to calm you down fairly quickly, and you went right back to sleep."

"I'm sorry, Em. I hate that you have to deal with this. You shouldn't have to see me like that," Amelia rubbed at the back of her neck in shame. She hated having her daughter see her so weak, so vulnerable. It was bad enough Emery witnessed the results of her torture at a tender age, but to continuously have to deal with the trauma all these years was taxing on the both of them.

"It's fine, Mom. I'm just glad I was able to get to you so quickly," Emery shrugged her shoulders as though to say it was no big deal.

"Did anyone else see?" Amelia asked again, afraid of the answer.

"Only Gabriel. He heard your screams and came down."

Amelia frowned. "That's odd. He didn't mention it when I saw him this morning."

"Morning, Emmie."

"Uncle Damon," Emery beamed.

Amelia looked back over her shoulder to discover Damon coming up behind her. She noticed Cordelia was hanging back on the back porch, her head bent low, whispering with none other than Kelsey.

Rey surged forward at the sight of their mate's wife, hackles raised and fur bristling. Amelia couldn't help the snarl that slipped past her lips. The sound surprised not just those around her but herself as well. She fastened her mouth into a tight line.

Rey, knock it off. Now is not the time. Amelia scolded her other half.

Just give me two minutes with the bitch. I'll put her mangy wolf in her proper place, and I can promise you it is not at our mate's side. Rey growled.

Amelia placed her fingers on the side of her head, a slight headache forming as Rey's anger and fury overcame her.

"Mia, everything okay?" Damon asked in a hushed tone.

Looking up, she found more and more warriors gathering around them.

The last thing they needed was for Amelia to cause a scene with Gabriel's wife.

They needed to display unity, not division.

"I'm fine, just Rey, she's giving me a headache," Amelia groaned out, her eyes still locked on Kelsey.

Damon followed her line of sight and made a grunting noise that seemed to mean he understood. "Does that mean you're not up for a fight? I'd like to get back at you for saying you used to pummel me, cause if I remember correctly, we both took our fair share of hits."

"Fair share?! I kicked your ass on a regular basis, and you know it!"

Damon chuckled. "Feeling better?"

Amelia straightened her back, the headache disappeared. Damon distracted her long enough for her to force Rey back. "Yes, thank you," she smiled, "and I'm totally going to make you eat your words. I'd hate to embarrass you in front of your wife and warriors, but that won't stop me from thoroughly enjoying mopping the floor with your punk ass."

"Oh, you wish," Damon snickered.

Emery giggled beside them, her face lighting up as though it was Christmas, and in a way for her, it was. This was her first real interaction with her uncle, her family, and in person, nonetheless. The time after her stint of torture didn't count and she hated how much Emery had missed out on growing up away from her pack, her family.

"All the warriors are gathered," Kaleb approached, standing at attention in front of her.

"Thank you, Kaleb," Amelia smiled at him before addressing the substantial number of warriors that seemed to take over the training grounds. "Ten miles, let's go!"

The run was brisk and fast-paced, pushing the warriors to their limits.

Amelia needed to assess how long and how fast they could push themselves. Endurance was critical in battle. They couldn't afford to be slow or winded, which would only mean certain death for any one of them.

Back in the clearing, Amelia provided them a few minutes to catch their breath and grab a drink while she laid out weapons on a table set up near the back porch.

Emery helped, polishing the blades, and applying a disgusting smelling substance to the serrated edge of the metal with a thin cloth. She wore gloves to protect her skin, but nothing could save them from the smell.

The warriors gathered closer towards the deck, the smell luring them in.

It was hard to miss. Even as young pups, werewolves were trained from an early age to avoid wolfsbane, yet there they were, applying it to their blades.

Just another lesson she took away from her torture.

Amelia could feel his eyes on her as he stood behind her just off to the side, watching intently. She checked over Emery's work, ensuring each blade was coated thoroughly. Emery was no fool. She knew not to mess around with the toxic substance and kept the knives in pristine condition.

Looking up from the table, Amelia discovered all eyes on her. Most of the warriors bore questioning expressions. Some were downright disgusted. How dare she have the nerve to possess such a hazardous substance so close to so many Were's.

Picking up a coated blade, she twirled it in her hand, actively avoiding the infected metal.

"How many here are trained in handling knives?" Amelia asked, her voice ringing out over the clearing.

Every warrior in attendance extended their hand.

Amelia was surprised and seriously impressed. A flare of pride filled her.

"Great," flipping the knife in the air, she expertly snatched it by the hilt, but not before a few gasps could be heard. "Now, working with blades is great. Gives us an advantage over the savageness of rogues, especially if it's silver. I know silver puts us on edge, but handle it correctly, and it won't bite. Just make sure to put the pointy end in your enemy, not yourself."

This received a few chuckles.

"I'm sure you're all wondering why I'm using wolfsbane. Not even a newborn could escape its potent smell. It makes our eyes water just being in proximity. If it gets in our bloodstream, it blocks our wolves from being able to contact us, slows our healing down to that of a human, and is extremely painful. Imagine sand being injected into your veins."

She noticed the majority of the warrior's wince at her comparison. She didn't blame them. It *was* excruciating. As though her veins were dry, rubbing together with every beat of her heart as it desperately tried to rid itself of the poison.

"Now, I know some of you may be wary of working with wolfsbane, and you should be. I won't ask anyone if they're not comfortable but working with wolfsbane coated blades has a serious advantage. Even the worst of shots could put a rogue on its back. If a coated blade grazes a wolf, the effects are immediate. It doesn't have to be a kill shot. One slice with wolfsbane would incapacitate them long enough to eliminate them."

"Have you used it on rogues?" a male in the crowd shouted.

Amelia gave Emery a side glance, a slight smirk playing on both sets of lips. "Both of us have used wolfsbane in recent years. As I said, it's extremely effective. Most of the time, we were on the run and didn't have time to stay back and fight. One throw of a wolfsbane knife saved our lives many times."

"For those of you okay with handling wolfsbane, come on up. I'll show you how to apply the substance properly and how to store it, so it doesn't get on anything you touch," Emery said, breaking off from her mother and moving towards another table, this one larger and covered in an assortment of knives, blades, and throwing stars.

Amelia could practically hear Gabriel's mind churning. His curiosity was piqued.

"As for the rest of you, time to pair off. Three on one. Make sure to mix it up, men and women," Amelia said, emphasizing the need to keep the odds mixed.

Stepping down off the porch, she headed directly for her brother, who was already standing by the other two wolves she was in search of.

"Just the men I was looking for," Amelia smirked, her voice full of intent.

Damon caught her eye and immediately shook his head, catching a glimpse into her mind and understanding her intentions. "Oh no. No, no, no. No, Mia."

"Oh, come on, Damon! It's been so long," she whined.

Amelia needed to spar, needed to work out and hard. What better way to start than against three of the strongest warriors she knew? Damon was basically an extension of herself, Kaleb was stealthy and fast on his feet, and then there was Rick, one-hundred percent brute strength.

"That's exactly why I'm saying no. You haven't been at your best in a while. I will not be responsible for hurting you," Damon said.

Amelia looked from Damon to Kaleb to Rick. The three of them stood before her, all denying her the chance to work out, to release her frustrations, and she was not having it. One way or another, she'd get them to cooperate.

"Look, I need practice. So, the three of you can participate willingly or not. Don't make me pull rank. I may not have any standing with a pack, but I'm pretty sure my wolf still outranks two out of three of you. Unless that is, you're afraid to have your asses handed to you," Amelia raised a brow, challenging the men before her.

They may be humans, but their animalistic side never backed down from a challenge, no matter the circumstance or rank. Rick was already ridding himself of his jacket, rolling his shoulders back.

"Just remember, you asked for this, Princess," Rick grumbled, cracking his neck.

Kaleb still looked apprehensive. "I don't know about this, Luna."

Amelia held herself back from glancing at Kelsey. "First off, not your Luna. Stop calling me that. Second, I promise I'll try not to beat you to a pulp."

Kaleb smirked at the challenge, shedding his jacket as well, dropping it on the grass.

Turning back to her brother, she detected his hesitance. "I need practice, Damon. I promise you I can handle it."

"If you get hurt, I'm telling," Damon pointed at her.

Amelia rolled her eyes. "Yeah, yeah. Let's go."

Emery stepped away from the warriors practicing with the weapons. She overheard her mother convincing Uncle Damon, Kaleb, and Rick to spar. Nerves began to settle in the pit of her stomach.

Ordinarily, Amelia could handle herself perfectly well, but she hadn't been in top fighting shape in nearly two years. Her body was still recovering from its near-death experience that happened only a few days ago.

Gabriel moved to stand beside her. Emery could feel the worry rolling off him in waves, probably from similar concerns. Aunt Cordelia and Kelsey, her father's wife, stood off to the side, taking an interest in the proceedings as well. She hoped her mother would put on a proper show for the wicked stepmother.

Amelia stood in the center of the three men. Each of them circled her slowly, stalking, taking in her stance, her posture, assessing where and how to strike first. She surveyed each of them and noticed that Rick favored his left side, the slight slant of his shoulders was a dead giveaway.

Kaleb lunged first, followed by Rick. Amelia dodged Kaleb's punch and side-stepped Rick's massive frame. Damon caught her off guard as she was busy trading blows with them, striking her from behind.

Falling to her knees, Amelia sat up and glanced back at him—a growl slipped past her lips.

Damon's smirk instantly fell, turning into a look that screamed whoops.

Amelia pushed off the ground, leaping through the air, her right fist aimed for his jaw. Damon knocked it aside, missing the left hook already hitting his ribs. Spinning back with her leg, she struck Kaleb in the gut just as he ran for her blind side.

Amelia punched, kicked, jabbed, flipped, and dodged hit after hit. Perspiration collected between her shoulder blades, working up a serious sweat as she tried to fend off the three of them. Rick's nose was bleeding from a hit he took to the face, Kaleb was overcompensating for the cracked ribs she heard when she landed a blow, and Damon was limping after a kick to the side of his knee.

The three of them surrounded her once more, each of them taking a breath before the next attack.

Amelia was tiring quickly. Her stamina was not what it once was, but that was the point. She needed to get back into fighting shape and fast, and the quickest way she could was to push her body past its limits.

Damon and Kaleb ran at her from the front, forcing her to dodge fists, parry elbows, and deflect kicks, her body growing heavier by the second leaving her flank open to Rick's assault from behind.

The back of her shirt tore beneath razor-sharp claws, but luckily avoided skin.

The fact that one of them had come close to drawing blood brought forth a new level of rage. The blood in her veins steamed. A rolling boil of outrage surged deep inside, battering her control, and carefully shielded trauma.

The others seemed to be able to sense it as they instantly stopped their attack.

Amelia smiled, her elongated canines catching the light as Rey came forward without entirely shifting.

Damon took one look at his sister and felt his stomach bottom out. "Shit."

Amelia snapped forward like a viper, going for the biggest prey first. Claws extended, she gripped onto Rick's shoulders, piercing flesh, blood streaming from the puncture wounds. Binding her legs around his waist, she gained enough leverage to punch him hard. One, two, three shots to the temple and the biggest warrior she knew crumpled to the ground.

Leaping off before he made impact with the ground, she ran directly for Kaleb. Flipping through the air, she seized hold of his neck with her thighs before rotating her body down, taking him with her. The fall knocked the wind from his lungs, leaving him gasping for breath. She kicked out with the heel of her foot, making contact with the ribs that were already splintered. He yelled in pain before she got up, leaving him to whimper in the dust.

"Stay down," Amelia advised before turning back to the final target.

Damon sprinted towards her just as she did.

They each blocked, dodging feet, and avoiding leg swipes. He was tiring but not faster than she was. She had to end this soon, or else she'd be the one on her back conceding and that she would *not* let happen.

Rey growled strongly in warning, startling Damon, providing her the opening she needed. Amelia ducked, throwing her shoulder and upper body into his torso, knocking the air from his body with such force she could hear him gasping, struggling to breathe as they landed hard on the compact earth. She straddled her brother, aiming a kill shot for his throat before she stopped herself, hovering just above his trachea.

"You're dead," Amelia declared in victory before jumping off and standing as the victor.

Glancing around, she discovered quite a crowd of onlookers.

Amelia could feel her pride expanding, swelling until it left her warm and standing on cloud nine. Some were clapping, others smiling, hollering her name. She turned in a circle, taking it all in until she noted her brother's face.

Wide-eyed and stunned.

It froze her in place. Her back was to the house when a breeze picked up, kissing the exposed skin of her back, sending a paralyzing fear to cascade down her spine and take root in her stomach until she was sure she had turned to stone.

Amelia twisted around, praying to the Goddess that none of this was real. This wasn't happening. Looking over her shoulder, she could make out the pieces of fabric hanging in shreds down her back, exposing the knotted whip marks to everyone present.

She could hear hissing all around as the warriors took notice of the scars. Some wolves were even growling, angered by what they could see. Amelia felt ashamed and embarrassed with her body on display. It was like being whipped all over again. Tendons and gaping flesh peeled away until only bone was left, laid bare for everyone to witness just what made her tick, and what could break her. Her mind began to spiral and turn on itself, whispering vile and torturous things until one growl in particular bit into her soul, chasing the demons away—even if for just a moment.

Turning back to him, confronting him head-on, she could see him shaking with anger, hurt, and confusion. His Alpha aura grew rapidly around him as Ren came more forward, making those around him cower, their tail tucked firmly between their legs.

Amelia flinched as she felt something soft and large wrap around her shoulders. Looking back, she found Rick placing his jacket around her, covering her back from prying eyes. She couldn't stand to see the hurt, the pity in his eyes—any of their eyes.

Wrapping the jacket more firmly around her, Amelia buried herself further into the material and shoved past a row of warriors, disappearing into the woods.

CHAPTER 24

TO KNOW OR NOT TO KNOW

D amon looked off into the woods where his sister disappeared. He wanted to run after her, wanted to be there for her, but there was someone else he needed to make sure wouldn't do anything foolish.

Looking up onto the back porch, he could see Gabriel was fuming, his eyes shifting between human and wolf, his body unstable with the conflicting emotions coursing through him.

Emery stood beside him, looking up at her father and around at the pack. It was apparent how upset she was with the way they all looked at her mother.

Amelia didn't need anyone's pity.

His niece finally made eye contact, her silver eyes pleading with him on what to do.

Damon nudged his head in Gabriel's direction, encouraging her to talk to him. He looked back towards the woods, his twin's scent already growing faint. He inclined his head in Amelia's direction, letting Emery know he was going after her mother before he himself disappeared among the brush.

Emery looked out among the pack's warriors.

Most were standing around, whispering amongst themselves on what they witnessed, trying to decipher what it might mean. From what she could overhear, most of them hit the hammer on the nail, but she couldn't stand them talking behind her mother's back. None of them understood an ounce of what she went through, and she would not allow them to continue to talk about her as she was anything less than a fighter, a warrior tried and true.

"That's enough! Everyone get back to training!" Emery ordered, making the warriors halt their gossip.

She turned to her dad, whose aura was still flexing around him, expanding, and contracting as he dealt with wave after wave of emotion.

"Sweetie."

Emery looked back behind them to discover Kelsey trying to approach the Alpha slowly.

Gabriel snarled at her, snapping his jaws in her direction, advising her not to come any closer. Kelsey immediately bared her neck in submission and backed away to a reasonable distance.

"Gabriel," Emery spoke softly, trying to gain his attention.

Gabriel looked down at her, his eyes a bottomless pit of darkness, and growled. His human side was nearly forced to the back of his mind as his wolf pushed to take over, but that wouldn't help anyone given the situation.

So, Emery decided to do what was necessary. She called on her wolf Hailey and pushed her aura around them, brushing against his. They released their scent, allowing him to recognize his kin, his flesh and blood.

Gabriel's eyes began to focus, shifting from the darkest shade of onyx to that of his silver color. Staring down at her, he blanched. "Emery—," he started.

"I know. It's okay," she reached out to him, laying her hand on his forearm.

The connection between them was instant. If she didn't recognize it before, she sure did now. Gabriel was her father in every way, whether she liked it or not. Aside from the resemblance, the bond between them was forged. It wasn't like a mate bond that resembled fireworks dancing beneath the skin. This was more of a leaden weight that slid into place within her heart and mind, solidifying his place in her life.

Emery could tell by the look in his eyes; he felt it too. "Let's go inside. Okay?"

Gabriel merely nodded, allowing her to lead him away, into the house and to his office. He felt himself being guided towards the couch and sat down on the leather cushions.

Emery couldn't help but feel her heart crack. He looked so lost, so distraught, as though he was utterly consumed by the past and where it all went wrong.

"What can I do to help?" Emery found herself asking.

Gabriel finally looked up, his eyes focusing on hers. "What happened, Em? I would never ask you to betray your mother, but those scars, her nightmares, the way she's changed... that's not just from being on the run for seventeen years. I know what makes those kinds of scars. What happened to my mate?"

Emery swallowed with difficulty, pushing back the increasing pressure in the back of her eyes. The sound of his voice, the desperation cracked a fissure so deep she was convinced it would ever close. She wrung her hands together in her lap and moistened her lips to remove the sudden dryness.

"All I can tell you is what I know. What I saw—"

"You were there?!" Gabriel asked, his voice rising to a deafening level.

"No, no," she shook her head adamantly. "I was only about eight at the time. They didn't get me, just mom. She was gone for five days, but it felt like weeks."

"Five days?" Gabriel asked, his mind churning. "Eight years ago?"

"Yeah. Uncle Christian went insane looking for her."

"Where was he? Why wasn't he with her?"

"Uncle Christian was in town getting supplies. He was the one less likely to be spotted, so he was always the one to go into town and get groceries. Mom stayed home with me. We were in Canada at the time, high up in the mountains," she explained.

"You were so close," Gabriel said. His voice sounded distant.

"That was the last time we were in North America, until now that is," Emery observed him as he sat there, his arms resting against his legs, bent over himself. "Anyways, mom and I were outside playing when she scented them, but they were closer than they should have been. Somehow, we didn't catch their scent until they were mere feet from our door. Mom sent me into the house to hide, down in a hidey-hole she made in our basement. I waited there for hours," he glanced at her curiously. "I couldn't leave until someone came and let me out," Emery answered the unspoken question.

"Uncle Christian finally found me, but mom was gone, nowhere to be found. There was blood in the backyard, a lot of blood, some of it was hers along with a few rogue bodies, but no mom. Uncle Christian did everything he could to find her. He used all of his contacts, tracked her until he got lucky enough to encounter a rogue. I wasn't allowed in the room with the rogue in the house, but I could hear the screams. He convinced him to shift back and tell him where they were detaining her. Uncle Christian told me he'd be back. He told me he'd save her, and she would come back to me," tears slipped down her face silently. Emery kept her eyes fastened on a drawing of the Packhouse that hung on the wall across from them, afraid to look at her father, afraid to see what he thought. "I waited an entire day, but he never came back. I left the house. I knew I wasn't supposed to, but I didn't know what else to do. They kept the phones hidden from me in case I accidentally called someone I wasn't supposed to. I couldn't call for help."

Emery wiped the moisture from her face, trying desperately to take deep, calming breaths. "That was when I heard a whimper. It was coming from the bushes at the edge of the property."

"You must have been so scared," Gabriel said, his voice breaking her out of her memories.

Emery finally chanced a glance in his direction and discovered him observing her intently. His eyes were gentle, brimming with unshed tears. "I was. I could scent blood and other smells I couldn't explain, but underneath it all, I could smell my mom. I don't remember much after that. I barely remember getting her into the house, but somehow, we managed. I got her to tell me where the phone was, and I called Uncle Damon. He was the only person I was allowed to speak with, and I knew mom trusted him. He reached us in six hours."

"Damon," Gabriel said simply, as though that was the only answer he'd ever need.

"When he came, he got mom cleaned up, and that meant we could assess the extent of her injuries ..." her voice trailed off as the memories assaulted her mind. Emery had tried her best over the years to repress them, but there were some things that no matter how badly she wished, would never disappear.

"I don't want to know," Gabriel stood up off the couch abruptly, pacing in front of her.

Emery watched as he experienced a battle of wills.

A part of him needed to know every gory detail. Needed to know how she was hurt, where every stroke of the blade pierced her skin, every lashing tore open her flesh, but most of all, as a man, he needed to know if another had touched her in ways no woman should ever be touched. While the other part revolted, refusing to envision what happened, how someone could inflict such damage on a beautiful soul.

"There's not much I know beyond that. Mom never talked about it. Uncle Damon stayed with us for two weeks, but he kept me away from her most of that time. He tried his best to use their powers to heal her, but they had pumped so much wolfsbane into her system he couldn't kick start her wolf's healing abilities."

"They injected her with wolfsbane?" Gabriel growled.

If Emery were anyone else, she would have been on her back, belly up in submission. Thankfully she was his daughter, and that made her an Alpha too. She could stand toe to toe with him and not bat an eye. The fury was plain as day on his face. Wolfsbane was lethal to wolves. In small doses it dulls the senses and forces compliance but it's agonizing, most wish for a quick death. Her mother was fortunate she hadn't died.

"Yes. They pushed it into her system so she couldn't fight back. Even they knew how powerful she was with her wolf. They didn't want her to heal…" she said, her voice drifting off.

"What do you mean?" Gabriel asked, unable to grasp her meaning.

Emery swallowed with difficulty. Her gaze fastened on her hands tucked in her lap. "They lashed her. Whipped her until bone was exposed, until her skin was hanging off her back in ribbons. They sliced into her skin so that she would bleed, making her too weak to fight."

Gabriel growled even louder, striking his fist into the office wall.

A decent-sized hole exposed the support beams in the wall. Drywall floated in the air.

Emery stood up off the couch to stand in front of him.

"Look, I'm not telling you all of this just for you to be pissed. I'm telling you so that you might be able to understand what she went through. She doesn't need or want your pity. My mother is the most capable woman alive and to treat her any differently is an insult to her and the torture she had to endure," Emery lectured him, giving him a dose of reality.

Gabriel exhaled loudly, pulling his fist back from the damage he inflicted. "So Christian, he…."

"He died getting my mother out of that hell hole. He held the rogues back, so they couldn't chase after her, giving her enough time to get away. He never came back," Emery crossed her arms across her chest, suppressing the shudder that was working its way through her body.

Gabriel extended his fingers through his hair, pulling at the roots in frustration. "I'm so sorry, Emery. I'm sorry I wasn't there to protect you or your mother."

"It's not your fault," Emery instinctively reached out, grasping his hand. "None of this is your fault. Not mine or my mom's. This is all on Michael and this sick, twisted grudge match."

Gabriel bobbed his head solemnly.

They stood in silence for some time.

Emery waited, minding him as he chewed on his bottom lip. Something was eating him up inside, but she decided it was best to wait and let him find the words in his own time. All the while, she kept a tight hold on his hand. She may not have a mate bond to calm him, but it seemed the paternal bond would do in a pinch.

"I just need to know one more thing," Gabriel started hesitantly. Emery immediately felt uneasy. "Did they … they didn't, you know, violate her, did they?"

Emery stiffened. Her stomach coiled in on itself. "Would it matter to you if they did?"

"No," Gabriel said automatically. "I just need to know how to handle this. Should I be more gentle?"

She took in another deep breath from the umpteenth time that day. "Just be patient with her. The nightmares come and go, but the trauma is always there."

Gabriel nodded his head in understanding, his silver eyes turning a deeper shade of molten metal.

Emery's heart bled for both of her parents.

CHAPTER 25

SURVIVING ISN'T LIVING

Damon followed the scent of his twin. Her familiar smell mixed with the bitter tang of disgust and loathing.

He followed her a few hundred yards past the tree line to discover her sitting on a decayed tree, knocked to the earth, split from its roots. Rick's jacket was still wrapped around her petite frame.

He approached her cautiously, afraid to startle her. Moving around the fallen tree, he stepped in her line of sight and sat down beside her on the crumbling bark.

Amelia merely sat there silently, her hands clasped in her lap, staring down at the forest floor.

"Mia," he called to her softly.

Amelia didn't move or acknowledge him. No shifting of the eyes or change in breathing, no indication at all that she heard him.

"Amelia," he placed his hand softly against the small of her back, reinforcing his presence. "I'm here. What's going on?"

"Everyone saw."

Her monotone voice left him uneasy. "Yes."

"I feel so ashamed. None of them will ever be able to look at me the same."

"Yes, they will. You have nothing to be ashamed of."

"Don't I?"

"No," Damon said firmly. "Yes, something horrible happened to you, but you came out the other side. You survived," he said, squeezing her shoulders.

Amelia finally turned towards him, her eyes hollow and blank. "Did I? Did I survive what they did to me?"

"What do you mean?" he asked, confused.

"Yes, I'm breathing. I'm physically alive, but is surviving, living? I've been a shell of who I once was. Those five days haunt me every day. Some days I wish they had just killed me."

"Don't say that," Damon growled, shocked that she would ever think such a thing, let alone say it aloud. "How could you even say such a thing? What about Emery? Or Gabriel? What about me? Do you know what losing you would do to us?"

"How am I of any use to you like this? Rey is still weak. My body is a roadmap of everything they did to me. I can't even smell smoke without having a panic attack. The nightmares still wake me up screaming. I can still feel his touch on my body, Damon! Everything he did to me, every grunt and thrust, it's like I can still feel him inside of me! So, tell me, tell me how I'm not damaged!"

Damon was at a crossroads between his heart shattering for his sister and wanting to murder the bastard that dared lay a hand on her. Amelia was the most precious werewolf alive, and they violated her in the harshest ways imaginable.

He stared into his sister's eyes, the same shade as his own, and found himself mirroring her. Tears streamed down their faces as they allowed the grief and sorrow to wash over them. He placed his hands on both sides of her face and wiped away the tears with the pads of his thumb.

"Now you listen to me carefully, Amelia Rhea. You are the most radiant, courageous, resilient woman I have ever known. I don't care how many scars you carry on your body. None of them touch your spirit or your soul," Amelia sniffled loudly, the tears still streaming, but he continued.

"Did you forget I was there with you after you came back? I saw what they did. I cleaned every inch of that man's filth off you. If Christian hadn't slain them, I would have flayed them alive. But that didn't stop you from being an incredible mother. You didn't allow the fact that they broke nearly every bone in your body, to stop you from raising that stunning daughter of yours. Because of you, she's alive, thriving, and fighting just as hard as we did when we were her age."

Amelia chuckled at that, giving him hope and encouraging him to go on. He stroked her disheveled hair back from her face, tucking it behind her ear and cupping the back of her neck, directing her attention to him.

"You are not damaged, Amelia. Yes, you have some scars, and not all of them healed correctly, but here, in this pack, you have a chance to correct that. The sister I knew and grew up with is still in there," he said, placing his hand over her heart. "She's a little dusty and rough around the edges, but she never left."

Amelia tilted her head, resting against his. She couldn't hold back the tears from flowing. The last few days had released a flood gate after all these years, and nothing could bottle them back up.

"What would I do without you?" Amelia wondered aloud.

"Oh, you'd definitely be lost."

Amelia chuckled, pulling back. She wiped the moisture from her face with the sleeve of Rick's jacket. It would need to be laundered.

She sighed loudly, looking up into the cloudless sky above the tree canopy.

"I knew I couldn't hide it forever. I just thought I had more time," she confessed.

"I know. But once the genies out of the bottle—"

"You can't put it back in. I know," Amelia bobbed her head, understanding his meaning. "I can't hide from my past anymore."

Damon merely sat there, giving her the time she needed to come to grips with the new reality placed before her.

"Being back here, in this pack, that house, with him. Goddess, it's like I never left," she wound her arms around herself, rubbing warmth into her body. "Being away from him for so long, I almost forgot the intensity of the bond, but now … I don't recall it being this intense."

"Have you considered trying again with him?" Damon asked innocently.

"He's married, Damon. Me being back doesn't change that fact. I will not be the other woman, the home wrecker, even if he is my mate. He made his choice."

"He didn't know, Amelia. He didn't know everything he does now. What if he wants this? What if he wants you?"

"Those are some pretty big ifs," Amelia said in disbelief. "Besides, he knew we were mates when he married her. He knew we were fated, and he made his choice. Showing up on his doorstep with his long-lost daughter and a traumatic past shouldn't matter."

They really were perfectly matched.

"You may not think it matters, but I can promise you, to him, it does. For all he knew, you were never coming back, you had moved on and found some tanned muscled man in Barbados, living your life. If you were to give it another chance, reforging the mate bond could heal you completely. You'd be stronger. He's the only one that can help you."

Amelia merely swayed her head in denial, infuriating him beyond belief. "That chapter of my life has passed. Maybe all I was ever meant to be was a mother. To continue Rhea's line and allow it to flourish under my daughter," she said, looking off into the woods, her expression blank. "I'm okay with that."

Damon nearly rolled his eyes so hard they could have stuck in the back of his head. It was moments like these that he wanted a piano to drop from the sky and land on her head. "That's the biggest crock of shit I've ever heard."

Amelia shrugged her shoulders. "Either way, it's true. He's moved on, and now it's time for me to do the same."

CHAPTER 26

I WILL ALWAYS FIND YOU

Amelia made her way back to the house in a bit of a fog. Her head was swarming with all that she and Damon had discussed.

She hadn't openly talked about her time being held captive to anyone. Never broached the topic or dared to even whisper about that nightmare, afraid to shed light on it, beckoning it from the darkness and consume her. These days, her mind was her own worst enemy, and now that her back was quite literally exposed to the world, it was doing a bang-up job.

As Amelia approached the house, she could feel the eyes on her, following her movements. Hushed whispers could be heard, floating through the air, mocking, and taunting her, but she ignored them all, keeping her head down and focused on the ground she wished would open and swallow her whole.

Maybe hell had a vacancy.

Once inside the four walls of her room, she shut the door firmly, experiencing a sense of relief and safety as the lock clicked into place. Placing her back against the cool wood, she leaned on the door, her head producing a muffled thump.

At that moment, all she wanted to do was curl in a ball on her bed, allow the comforter to encase her body like a tomb, and forget about the world as she drifted off into oblivion. But not even sleep could offer her peace.

Amelia briefly wondered where Emery was but opted against linking her. It was like one bitch slap to the face after another, affecting her daughter just as much as it did her. No matter how much she wanted to shelter Emery from the harsh realities of their world, she'd done a shit job of it.

Emery had been on the front lines since the moment she was born. Over her short sixteen years of life, her daughter had had to run away at a moment's notice, hide under the foundation of houses, train and train, and train so that one day she could defend herself. Her kid had even killed to save their lives.

What kind of mother did that make her?

Pushing off the door, she made her way towards the bathroom.

Wallowing in self-pity and the past would do nothing but make her spiral. With Michael so close to attacking, she couldn't afford to lose her head to her own conflicting emotions.

Inside the bathroom, Amelia pulled off Rick's oversize jacket that nearly devoured her narrow frame. Pitching it down on the floor, she turned her back to the mirror, taking in the full extent of her clothes. Her top was indeed shredded beyond repair, exposing nearly every millimeter of damaged flesh.

Pulling off what was left of her clothes and discarding them in a pile, she flipped the shower on, stepping inside before even allowing the water to warm. She stood there under the rainfall showerhead as the water gradually heated to a scalding temperature and her muscles began to relax. Washing the day's filth and anxiety from her body, she scrubbed vigorously at her skin, eliminating every trace of the pack's curious stares and looks of pity and sympathy.

Amelia turned the shower off and stepped out, wrapping a towel around her body. The soft, plush material was soothing against her skin, her arms brushing against it as she walked back to the sink.

Her hair hung around her, now looking completely white. Whatever color she once had was now almost gone, leaving her hair an old lady silver. Some days she appreciated it but mostly, she just felt old. This merely added to the fire of feeling damaged and worn.

Completely ignoring the scars along her arms, sides, and back, she refused to look in the mirror any longer as she headed inside her room for a fresh set of clothes but what she found there stopped her dead.

Amelia froze where she stood, her foot halfway through a step, practically making her stumble. Her heart hammered against her sternum as her mind raced. The blood in her veins was singing, urging her to move, luring her in his direction, but instead, she regripped her towel.

A distraught and disheveled-looking Gabriel sat on the foot of her bed, his head in his hands, leaning against his knees. She could tell by the rugged styling of his hair he had been spreading his fingers through it continuously, nearly making it spike straight up. Her hands twitched at her side, desperate to extend her fingers through the silky locks. To remember the touch of its softness as she gripped it near the base of his neck.

Although their bond was still incredibly fragile, straining from the distance and pain they put one another through, she could taste just a twinge of grief and regret in the back of her throat. He was hurting, which in turn made her ache. She wanted to reach out to him, pull his head against her breast and embrace him tightly over her heart. She wanted to draw circles into his back, play with his hair as his arms encircled her waist, causing her to feel like she'd finally come home.

But none of that was possible.

"Gabriel, what are you doing here?" Amelia asked, recovering her voice.

Gabriel lifted his head from his hands as though he never heard her exiting the bathroom. His silver eyes rose to meet hers, and she was shocked to discover them brimming with wetness. It was like a cold, electrical shock to her nervous system.

"Amelia—" he stood up from the bed, arms outstretched begging for an embrace, executing a single step in her direction before she backed away, raising a hand that urged him to stop.

"What are you doing in my room?" Amelia asked again, fairly certain she had secured it.

"I need to talk to you."

"The door was locked. You can't just barge in my room whenever you feel like."

"Would you have let me in otherwise?" Gabriel asked, eyebrows elevated.

Words escaped her.

Of course, she wouldn't have let him in. It was bad enough having to be in the same house as him and seeing him every day, train with him, eat meals, pack meetings, even noting his eyes on her on their morning runs—it was all too much.

But being alone with him in her room was beyond her comprehension.

A part of her was terrified. Terrified of having a man in her room, alone with a man and no witnesses. But he wasn't just any man. He was Gabriel. He was her fate, her mate, and whether she liked it or not, the man that still completely possessed her soul.

"That's what I thought," Gabriel said, filling in the silence that lingered between them.

Amelia sighed profoundly, rubbing the pads of her fingers against her temples. "Look, Gabe. It's been a long day. Can we not do this right now?"

She headed for the door. The doorknob was just within her grasp when she felt the familiar tingles as he gripped her arm, pulling her back towards him.

"No. It's been seventeen years. Seventeen years I had to go on without you. Seventeen years I had to wonder where you were. Have you moved on? Were you happy? A part of me wished that for you. Wished for you to be able to find happiness and peace. No one in the world deserved it more. But the other half. The selfish, angry, bitter, dominant half loathed the idea of you being happy without me. I hated you for leaving me behind. I was so angry with you that I nearly burnt my house down, twice. There were so many nights Kaleb had to pick me up off the floor and dump me in my bed, since I was too drunk to move. I almost lost my pack over losing you, Amelia. I nearly let it all go, going mad with where you were."

Amelia just stood there, shell-shocked. Her breathing was shallow and short as she experienced the waves of pain, anguish, misery, and self-loathing that rippled off the man before her. She was about to respond with something, anything, when he placed his fingers against her lips, effectively silencing her. The breath in her throat caught at such an intimate touch.

"Then, come to find out. You weren't happy at all. You hadn't moved on or experienced the world or even found an ounce of happiness. Instead, I learned you gave birth to our daughter without me, in the middle of a war I knew nothing about. You spent all that time we were apart, on the run, defending and protecting our child, but at what cost?"

Gabriel released her arm, only to caress the back of his knuckles against the exposed skin of her upper back, along the knotted scars.

Automatically, Amelia rolled her head back, eyes closing instantly as her stomach fluttered and blood rose to her face. She felt flushed and feverish, a tight sensation budding in the pit of her abdomen as she pinched her knees together.

Her eyes flew open wide. The familiar yet alarming need that burned through her sex had her nearly stumble back, away from his touch. Turning her back to him, she bound her arms around herself, rubbing at them, trying to rid the feeling from her skin.

"I can't, Gabe. I can't talk about this," Amelia's voice came out softer, weaker than she wanted, but the creeping feeling of being aroused terrified her.

"Why not? You can't hide from me anymore, Snow. I let you walk away once before. I was too stubborn and pig-headed to chase after you, but I will not make the same mistake twice. I will always find you. I will follow you to hell if I have to, but I will not live another moment of my life without you."

The tone of his voice had her spinning back around.

Gabriel sounded resolute. Firm yet impassioned. His convictions paralyzed her with fear, wanting, and anxiety. She shook her head from all the confusing thoughts skipping through her mind.

"Gabe, you can't. You're married," Amelia said with finality.

"Do you honestly think I care? She's not you. She's not my mate. You are my heart, Snow. It's always been yours."

Gabriel reached out his hand, wanting to cup her cheek, but once again, she jerked back out of reach.

Finally, a spark of something warm and familiar fueled her veins. She was enraged.

"It's a little late to be saying that now! You say I'm your heart, but you go and marry my best friend. The woman I was closest to when we were together!" Amelia yelled, jerking her hand wildly in the air while trying to keep her towel secured around her. "How could you do such a thing?! How could you marry her?!"

Clamping down on her lip hard, she hated herself as the tears slipped down her cheeks. She hated looking weak, especially in front of him, but how dare he declare those things to her when he made such irreversible choices.

Rey growled in the back of her mind. Her wolf was furious with their mate.

"I did what I believed was best for my pack at the time," he growled, growing more and more frustrated. "I needed help getting my pack back under control, back into fighting shape. I let everything fall apart around me for years after you left. Meanwhile, Kaleb and Kelsey took the reins and were there for my pack when I couldn't. I owed her."

"So, you marry her? Fuck her?! Did you fuck Kaleb too?" Amelia screamed, her anger growing expansive.

"I'm not proud of that, but I did what I thought was best for my pack. They needed someone at my side, someone to help with the leadership, and Kelsey could do that. She was good with the Luna duties, but never once did I consider officiating her. There's only one Luna in this pack, and it's not her."

"But you still married her. You made vows. Tying yourself to her forever," she cried out, her voice catching in her throat as mucus thickened in the back of her mouth. She regretted how upset she was getting. How her body was betraying her at every turn, but there was no going back, they were past the point of no return.

"I know," Gabriel growled, twisting his hand through his hair viciously, pulling at the roots. "Do you want me to say I was lonely? Cause I was. Do you want me to tell you I enjoyed fucking someone that wasn't you? Well, I didn't. Did you know Ren hasn't spoken to me in twelve years, not until the moment I smelled your perfect scent on the streets of Boston, crying mate? He hated me for what I've done, but not as much as I despised myself."

"And that's supposed to make it all better? Because your wolf knew better than you, was more loyal than you ever were, that just nullifies everything you did?"

"That's not what I'm saying," he said, tossing his head. "I know I fucked up, but in some ways, you did too. You took our child away from her father. Raised her without me. Left me completely in the dark and expected what? For me to wait around for you? It's been seventeen years, Amelia. I didn't think you were ever coming back!"

Amelia scoffed, twisting her face away from him as she angrily wiped the tears from her face with the backs of her hands.

"I'm sorry I wasn't there for you when you needed me most. I'm sorry I wasn't there to protect you and Emery. I'm sorry I couldn't avenge you and had the first thing you saw when the light touched your skin as you escaped that horrible place, be my face. I wish I could tear that bastard limb from limb until he begged for your forgiveness, but I'll always be indebted to Christian."

Amelia flung her head up. His words caressed her soul like a warm autumn breeze—tender and soothing.

Gabriel knew more than she'd have liked. Probably thanks to Emery, but Amelia didn't care.

Gabriel had been narrowing the distance between them again, his words distracting her enough not to notice. Not until his hands were already resting against her shoulders, cupping the back of her neck, threading through the hairs at the nape of her neck.

"I am so sorry you had to go through what you did. I wish I could have tended your wounds and breathed life back into your body," his lips lowered, feathering against her cheek as he moved down her neck. "I wish I could have kissed every mark he made upon your gorgeous body and reassured you just how perfect you are."

His lips brushed against her fading mark. The mark he produced upon her the night they were first intimate with one another. The night she gave him her innocence and allowed him to seal their fate. The touch of his breath against her skin, the brush of his bold lips against her mark sent a trail of fire burning straight to her core. She tilted her head back in response, unable to contain the way her body melted at his touch.

"Because you are perfect, Amelia. No matter what scars your body carries or what stories they have to tell, you are the most stunning creature on the planet. Your scars tell the world how strong you are, how fiercely you love, and how your courage knows no bounds."

Gabriel pressed his lips firmly against the mark he left upon her skin over seventeen years ago before opening his mouth and marking circles with his tongue against her delicious skin.

Amelia couldn't help the moan that slipped past her lips. Her hands gripped onto his biceps.

The world was tipping around her as the universe shifted on its axis.

"Gabe," she whispered, her throat already husky and thick.

"Shh."

Gabriel breathed against her skin as he moved his lips back up her through, along her jaw, and hovered just above her lips.

Amelia lazily exposed her eyes to discover pools of silver staring down at her hungrily.

"It was never the mate bond that drew me to you, Snow. From the moment my eyes first saw you, I knew you were mine without ever having to touch you. I want you, my beautiful Goddess. I want all of you."

"But—"

"No. No buts. We've waited long enough. Seventeen years was too long to be apart," he said firmly, holding her gaze. "You are mine, Amelia. Always. You are my heart and soul. My forever. My past and future, and if there is something beyond this world, we'll be together there too, because we're fated, my love."

Without warning, Gabriel descended on her. His hands gripped her waist, his fingers digging into her skin through the thin, cotton towel. Gathering her into his body, her chest pressed against his, Amelia could feel the warm pressure of his lips crashing down on hers.

At first, Amelia tried to push away, pulling out of his grip, his touch that should be revolted by the state of her body. She had been violated in the most shocking ways imaginable, and yet, he was kissing her, caressing her. The pressure on her waist only increased, holding her firmly against him.

His lips were firm against hers, unyielding and selfish. Somehow, she didn't care.

It had been so long since she had kissed anyone.

The last time being the moment she said goodbye to an unconscious Gabriel, lying in a hospital bed, beckoning death. But this, this was much different.

Gabriel's touch sparked something familiar, a feeling she had unknowingly desired for nearly two decades. Lust, desire, want, and love crawled their way throughout her icy, scared, and damaged heart. White noise saturated her mind as everything around them seemed to cease to exist.

All that mattered was the two of them.

Amelia's arms roamed over his broad, rigid arms, over his shoulders that were knotted with muscled, and around his neck, brushing against the soft hair. Her body molded against his, melting into his frame as something clicked in place within her heart.

Home. She was home.

Her lips parted without her permission as something desperate and primal took control. Not needing any further invite, Gabriel slipped his tongue past her teeth, supplying her with the taste of him, igniting a trail of hunger straight to her core. They wildly grabbed at one another. His hands roamed over her ass, squeezing the supple firmness. Her hands desperately gripped his face, neck, and shoulders, retaining the taste and feel of what it was like to be loved and wanted, rediscovering which touch could plunge them over the edge the fastest.

Gabriel was the first to pull away, his breath fanned across her face as he struggled to draw in oxygen. Amelia felt just as winded, her cheeks flushed and warm.

The kiss was unexpected, intense, and breathtaking, but all too short—she craved more.

Untangling from one another, Amelia regripped the towel that had started to slip as she hugged herself. Trying to erase the stinging feeling against her skin from his lack of touch.

Gabriel looked down at her, his eyes hooded with desire and need. She knew how much he still wanted her, how the bond was pulling on the both of them to fix their fragile link, reforging their connection. She was surprised that he was the one to pull away first, unable to help the bitter sting of rejection that shadowed her mind and plagued her nerves, that is until his lips parted.

"I love you, Amelia."

Amelia's eyes widened. Her mouth left gaping in surprise as he left her room, leaving her alone to a hurricane of thoughts.

CHAPTER 27

MAKE EVEN SATAN BLUSH

A melia stared at her closed bedroom door. The very one Gabriel had just exited through.

Her swollen lips stung from the pressure of his mouth on hers. Her body was humming with electricity. He left his handprints all over her body, permanently marking her as his that left her on fire. She pinched her knees shut, unable to help the excitable warmth spreading in her most sensitive places.

Rey was purring like a mewling kitten in the back of her mind.

Amelia was left feeling confused and uncertain. For years, she had been telling herself that Gabriel had moved on. Almost every night curled in the fetal position in bed was proof enough, but did that mean he was happy?

She could be angry all she wanted, but she still had no idea why he did the things he did.

Didn't it matter that he loved her?

Everything he had just confessed meant the world and yet left her even more confused. It didn't change that he was still married and that most definitely bothered her. Of all the people, why Kelsey? Because he felt he owed her? What does that have to do with marrying someone?!

Amelia was growing more annoyed by the second. She was aggravated that Gabriel had taken advantage of the situation and kissed her. But the other part of her was thrilled he did. She had always wondered what it would be like to kiss him again, just one more time, and wondered if it would be the same as before. Would she feel the same, familiar spark race across her skin as her body demanded more from him? Satiate the bond that was damaged. The one that cried out to be fixed and reunited in every way imaginable?

Amelia rubbed her hands along her arms, brushing her thumb against the places where his skin made contact. She could have sworn their bond was broken enough for the mark not to have any effect, but boy was she wrong. All he had to do was breathe against the faded scar, and she was putty in his hands, ready for him to mold and do with her as he will.

Glancing up at the clock on the wall, Amelia noted the time. Dinner would be starting promptly, and she was still only dressed in a thin towel.

She dropped the towel where she stood and crossed over to her duffel bag she had yet to unpack and pulled out a clean outfit. As she was pulling down her black t-shirt over her head, adjusting the tail of the shirt to conceal her, she heard the doorknob of her bedroom being turned.

Amelia glanced over her shoulder to find her daughter entering the room, closing the door once she was inside.

Right away, she could tell Emery was nervous, anxious about something. It likely had something to do with her back being put on display earlier in the day.

"Hey, Momma," Emery spoke, playing with the end of her shirt, fisting it in her hands—a tell-tale sign of nerves.

Amelia diminished the distance between them, taking her hands in her own, soothing her. "It's okay, baby, I'm okay."

Emery seemed to release a deep breath of air. Her shoulders instantly relaxing. "Okay, that's good."

Guilt quickly attacked her.

Emery shouldn't have to bear such responsibilities.

Amelia reached up and tucked a strand of her beautifully unique black and silver hair back from her face and behind her ear. "I'm sorry you had to see that back there. I shouldn't have run off like that and left you—"

"No," Emery said, cutting her off, "don't blame yourself, please. I know you wanted to keep what happened to you a secret, but maybe it's for the best that it's out in the open. Maybe you can finally move forward with your life instead of constantly looking back."

"Emery—"

"No, Mom. You didn't see Gabriel. You didn't hear him cry or watch him put his fist through a wall. He loves you, Momma. Nothing could ever change that for him, and I know it's the same for you," Emery stated, looking deep into her mother's sea-green eyes.

Amelia lowered her head, pushing back the stinging sensation at the back of her eyes. The fact that Gabriel had cried and lashed out troubled her more than she could express. Instead, she resorted to her usual defense mechanism, sarcasm.

"When did my kid become so wise?" she chuckled.

"Around the time my mother taught me to talk," Emery smirked.

Amelia laughed out loud. Emery was sometimes too clever for her own good. "Come on, punk, let's go grab some dinner before all the ravenous wolves take it all."

Emery giggled.

Amelia draped her arm around her shoulders, escorting her out of the bedroom and towards the dining hall.

The Packhouse was in full swing for dinner. Some were already heading back to their room for the night, while most were moseying about inside.

As they made their way within the packed hall, the silence became deafening as all conversations came to a screeching halt. Dozens of eyes followed her around the room, whispers filled the air, and the stench of pity and shame reeked like a decaying skunk.

Amelia was about to turn tail and flee back to her room, unable to stomach the judgment and sympathy oozing from her old pack when she heard a deep, low growl that vibrated throughout the room.

Glancing behind her, she found Gabriel.

The minute his Alpha tone was used, the pack instantly resumed conversation and stopped staring. She inclined her head in thanks but noticed Emery was beaming at her father. Amelia couldn't remember the last time she had seen such a smile grace her daughter's face. It was one made of pride, adoration, and surprisingly affection.

A pang of jealousy crept down her spine. She was thrilled for her daughter. Happy that she could connect with her father so quickly and that they were getting along, but that didn't mean she didn't harbor the nagging feeling of being left out. Amelia was all Emery had, was all she knew. A part of her couldn't help but wonder if she might connect better with her father than they ever had.

Emery glanced at her mother, a puzzled expression on her face. "Mom?"

Amelia tried to smile but failed. "It's nothing, baby."

"It's not nothing, Mom. You forget we're linked. I can hear what you're thinking," Emery said, her eyebrow elevated.

"You know you're not supposed to do that whenever you feel like it. People's thoughts are private, and you need to respect that. One of these days, it's going to bite you in the ass," Amelia growled in warning, a bit annoyed.

"I didn't do it on purpose, but when I could sense you feeling jealous and sad, I couldn't help it, and I'm glad I did," Emery squeezed her mother's hand tightly. "I like Gabriel, but I barely know him. I hope that changes. I think he'd be a great dad, but you will never lose me. You're my best friend, Mom. I'd burn the world for you."

Amelia snorted at her daughter's dramatics but couldn't help the sigh of relief. "Gabriel is a great guy and would be an amazing dad to you. And I'd burn the world for you too, kid."

They gathered their plates and stocked them with lasagna and breadsticks before finding Damon and Cordelia tucked away at the table they'd sat at earlier that day. Amelia sat down beside her brother while Emery accepted the seat beside her Aunt.

Conversation was kept light. The incident from earlier in the day was strictly avoided at all costs. Damon managed to swap a few jokes, and all those at the table laughed and enjoyed the fantastic meal Lena made.

The entire time Amelia sat there with her family. She couldn't help the tingling sensation that crawled its way over her skin. She knew he was observing her closely, but she was appreciative of him for keeping his distance. Everything was happening so fast. She felt like she had been ejected from a plane cruising thousands of feet over the earth and forgot her parachute, free-falling to the ground below.

The question was, was Gabriel her savior or her downfall?

Cordelia was telling a story about the time her boys had covered Damon's mustang in sticky notes as a prank when the entire dining hall went silent. Amelia looked up to identify what had caused the disturbance and froze.

Kelsey stood at the entrance of the hall. Her back erect, neatly manicured hands folded in front of her, looking confident and sure of herself.

Rey bucked at the sight of her, fighting against the bonds that held her back from taking over completely, like a wild beast yanking and fighting against a chain meant to hold them back. Rey battled for control, wanting to phase right then and there and put the bitch in her place.

Amelia gripped onto the arms of her chair in a death grip, her knuckles turning white as she tried to reign in her wolf.

Her mate's wife began approaching their table with steady, deliberate strides. Amelia couldn't help the low snarl that slipped past her elongating canines. She was trying her darndest not to phase and tear her to shreds, but the fact that she was getting closer with each step was making that increasingly difficult.

Kelsey stopped at the head of the table.

Every pair of eyes were focused on them, waiting to see what might unfold—the Alpha's wife vs the Alpha's mate. Amelia could just make out Gabriel in the far corner standing up out of his chair but hesitating, waiting as well.

Amelia stood up.

The chair squeaked in protest as it was pushed back along the hardwood floor. The sound like a knife pic being jammed in her eye.

Amelia was losing the battle with her wolf and could detect Damon and Emery shifting uneasily beside her, ready to support her if it turned violent, and the way Rey was swearing enough to make even Satan blush only confirmed the worst—she was losing.

Fur began to sprout from her skin. Her Alpha aura was beyond her control as rage took over. In the blink of an eye, she would be her true self, her wolf, and there was nothing this pathetic she-wolf could do to prevent her from ripping out her jugular, but she stopped mid-shift, never expecting those words to leave Kelsey's mouth.

"Ella, can we talk?"

CHAPTER 28

WHY?

Amelia stood frozen, shocked. Her anger instantly melted away.

Rey settled into the back of her mind, watching curiously.

All Amelia could do was bob her head yes and follow Kelsey out of the hall. Curious on-lookers watched as they left the room. She could sense Emery's apprehension over letting her go alone, but with a wave of her hand, Amelia let her know she'd be okay.

Amelia followed Kelsey out of the dining hall and up the flights of stairs. She wasn't sure what the woman's point was or what she could want to talk about but worry gnawed at her.

The nerves that wreaked havoc on her stomach only increased as they neared the Alphas floor. What was Kelsey getting at? Was she trying to plunge the knife just a little deeper by showing her what was once her room, decorated for the happily married couple? Her fury began to boil again as Kelsey pulled out a key from her jean pocket and slid it into the door.

Amelia stopped where she stood, curious as to why the room was secured. Her key looked shiny and new, barely a scratch on it as though it was rarely used.

Without a word, Kelsey pushed open the door to the Alpha's room and stepped inside, holding the door open for Amelia to follow.

Amelia hesitated out in the hall. She didn't want to go inside, didn't want to see the place that she had invested countless hours with her mate buried deep inside, lost in the throes of passion. The place she had offered all of herself to a man she thought she'd spend the rest of her life with. She didn't want to see Kelsey's things where hers had been, but curiosity won out.

It always did.

Taking in a deep breath, Amelia pushed through her anxieties and entered Gabriel's room and what she found inside nearly knocked her down to her knees. Tears unwillingly filled her eyes as she choked on the flood of emotions devouring her.

Everything in the room was exactly the way she had left it.

The bookcase, her bookcase Gabriel had custom made for the room, was still intact with all her books in order, just as she had arranged them. She approached the pieces of her childhood slowly. Her fingers ran over the familiar books. Not even a hint of dust appeared on them.

To her surprise, there were a few recent additions to her collection. Rare volumes of classic books, bound in cracked leather, the pages fragile to the touch. But what shocked her the most was the added collection of various aged Narnia books. The covers were so detailed and mesmerizing she couldn't help but hold one in her hands.

They must have cost a fortune.

Placing the book back on the shelf carefully, something on Gabriel's nightstand captured her eye. In a simple frame was a picture of her, laughing. Amelia couldn't recall Gabriel ever taking a photo of her. She couldn't even remember the day it may have been taken, but she looked so carefree, happy. Her hand clasped her shirt over her chest as her heart ached fiercely. She wasn't sure whether she wanted to scream and cry, curl in a ball, or run down those stairs and leap into his arms, but instead, she stayed firm as tears rolled down her cheeks.

Kelsey stayed near the door, standing silently as Amelia took in everything around her.

"You sleep in here?" Amelia asked, her voice coming out broken and pathetic sounding.

Kelsey automatically shook her head no. "No. No one is allowed in here. I sleep across the hall."

Amelia frowned at that bit of information. Why would they sleep separately? Why would he hold onto her things but get married? She knew well enough that he was sexually active. Was that just to satisfy a carnal need, or was there something else?

Once again, curiosity won out as Amelia went for the closet. She opened the door, flicked the light switch on, and her stomach plummeted to the floor.

It was exactly as she had left it.

Gabriel's clothes had evolved over the years, naturally, but her side had been left untouched. All her clothes, shoes, everything was the same. She thought he would have thrown it all away, desperate to be rid of any memory associated with her, but no, instead it was left untouched, waiting.

Somehow, that made everything so much worse.

Amelia vacated the closet, her anger rising.

Anger was the easiest of emotions to deal with, and right now, it was all dialed to rage. She stopped just in front of Kelsey, wiping the backs of her hands across her face to remove the tear stains, but it was useless as more continued to flow.

"Why? Why show me all of this? It's bad enough I thought you were my friend. Then you went ahead and married my mate. *My* fated mate! And now this? Why?"

Kelsey didn't seem fazed by her anger as she stood passive and sorrow filled. "I may be bound by law to Gabriel, but you, Amelia, have always had his heart. He's yours and always has been."

"Then why marry him?! Why, Kelsey? Tell me that much? Why would you marry my mate?" Amelia sobbed, unable to help the break in her voice.

"I'm so sorry, Amelia. I never meant to hurt you," Kelsey sighed heavily. "But there's something you should know."

"I don't want to hear it. I don't want to hear your excuses."

"Almost a decade ago, Gabriel nearly died."

Amelia frowned. Her tears stopped as her eyebrow rose, the anger instantly turned down a hundred notches. She couldn't remember detecting anything of the sort from their bond during the time they were apart.

The only thing she ever sensed from him was the cheating.

"What are you talking about? I never felt anything of the sort," Amelia exacerbated.

"It was random. There was no warning, no signs, nothing. Yet, one day during a pack meeting, Gabriel just dropped straight to the floor like a bag of bricks. Just like that, he was out, slipped into a coma," Kelsey informed her.

Amelia continued to frown, refusing to believe her. If something like that had happened to Gabriel, she would have been the first to know. She would have felt it. But Kelsey continued anyway.

"The doctors didn't know what to make of it. They ran every test known to wolf and man. There was no disease or poison. His body, organs, brain, were all healthy and normal, and yet, he wouldn't wake up. He was unconscious for five days."

Amelia's eyes widened.

A queasy feeling enveloped her, leaving her feeling unclean and dirty. She wanted desperately to wash her skin, flush her body of the unwanted touches, the assault, all of it. Winding her arms around herself, she hugged her elbows tightly.

"It wasn't until he started crying out in his sleep, calling your name, that I realized the mate bond was responsible. He would call out for you, wince like he was in constant pain. We were terrified. Kaleb and I took turns watching over him. Those were the longest five days of my life. We didn't know if he'd live or not, if *you* would live or not. There were times he would scream for hours straight, and there was nothing we could do to help. Not even sedation would keep him down."

Amelia watched as Kelsey quickly wiped away a stray tear before continuing.

"On the fifth day, Gabriel just woke up. He had no memory of what happened. He didn't remember the hundreds of times he called for you or the endless screaming. One minute he was unconscious, and the next, he was up and walking like nothing. The doctor tried to explain that the only thing that made sense was the mate bond, but he had never seen such an aggressive reaction. You can't imagine the terror Gabriel felt. It was so potent it trickled through the pack link until every wolf linked was running around the territory like chickens with their heads cut off. If he had been in a coma for five days, screaming so loud and long enough that he lost his voice for weeks, he couldn't imagine you'd been through. But the doctor assured him you were still alive. If you had died, he would have felt your bond being severed."

"Why are you telling me all of this?" Amelia asked, her voice barely above a whisper, not trusting herself to speak any louder.

"After his coma, Gabriel became nervous for the pack. He was still single, without a Luna and heir, but as you know, I wasn't capable of getting pregnant," Kelsey shrugged her shoulders sadly.

Amelia couldn't help but feel bad for the woman in front of her. Kelsey would have made a great mother. It wasn't her fault none of them knew about the ties of Amelia's and Gabriel's bond, but in a petty, selfish way, she was glad only she could give the gift of life to him.

"That still doesn't answer my question, Kelsey. Why marry him? Of all people?"

"Gabriel and I grew up together. I always had a bit of a crush on him, but he was always such a hothead. When you came into the picture, I didn't think anything of it. You were his mate, and that was that. I liked you. We were friends, and I trusted you," Kelsey said.

"I trusted you," Amelia jabbed a finger in her direction. "I left the pack to save you all, and this is how you repay my friendship? My trust?"

"We didn't know. I had already been assisting with the Luna duties shortly after you left. After Gabriel's coma, he panicked. He asked me to marry him. He wouldn't make me Luna. His conscience wouldn't allow him, but at least in some way, I was legally his equal."

"So, it was what? Jealousy?"

"I didn't do anything out of spite. You were, *are*, my friend, Ella. Even if I'm not yours, you will always be mine. I'm sorry all of this went down this way. He didn't think he'd ever see you again, and he tried to move on. Can you really blame him for that?"

Amelia wanted to roll her eyes, wanted to smack the woman in front of her until Kelsey saw stars or flying unicorns. To stamp her feet and scream at the world. But none of that would change a thing.

"No, I can't blame him for that," Amelia admitted.

Kelsey looked around the room they stood in. Taking in all of Amelia's things that still decorated Gabriel's room. "I always knew the bond between you two was still there. It used to bother me, that is until I saw the scars on your back, and then it all made sense. Those scars, Gabriel's coma. Your bond runs so much deeper than that of mates."

Amelia looked at her quizzically, not sure where she was going with any of this. "What are you saying?"

"He loves you, Amelia. Always has. Always will. I already defied fate by marrying your mate. I won't stand in the way any longer. He's always been yours."

CHAPTER 29

HER FAIRYTALE

A melia was left standing alone. Kelsey had declared
that she was stepping aside and then abandoned
her to her thoughts in Gabriel's room.

Their room.

She wandered towards the bed, sitting down on his
side of the mattress. Taking in their room, the place where
she once lived, weighed heavily on her mind and heart.
Unable to contain her inquisitive nature, she pulled open
his nightstand drawer.

Inside, she found what was expected; a notepad and
pen, Chapstick, and an extra phone charger, but directly
on top, yellowed with age and wrinkled, was her letter.
The letter she had left him the day she left.

Like a magnet, unable to deny the pull, she retrieved
the letter.

Gabriel's name was inscribed on the front in her sloppy,
cursive writing. Her hands shook as she grasped the fragile
paper between her fingers. Her stomach was performing
acrobatics, her heart beating almost painfully inside her

chest, and her breaths came out sharp and ragged. Of all the things, she had never expected him to hold onto her goodbye letter, but given how he left their room, she shouldn't be too surprised.

Carefully, Amelia unfolded the paper and read over her writing.

Gabriel,

I am so sorry, my love. I'm sorry I left this way. I'm sorry I didn't wait to say goodbye in person. But you and I both know you would never have allowed me to leave if you knew what I was planning. I hope one-day things may change, and I can come back to you, but that may never happen.

To save you, to keep you all safe, I have to leave.

This was the last thing I ever wanted, but if I can save your lives, then this is what I have to do. I'm sorry you'll have to deal with the loss of our child on your own. It kills me that I lost a part of you, a part of us, and I'm sorry I couldn't do more to save it.

You will always have my heart, Gabe. You're not just my mate. You are my soul, my fate, my destiny, and I will always love you.

Your Snow

Amelia took in a deep, quivering breath as she refolded the letter and tucked it away, back in the nightstand. She wiped away the moisture on her face as her eyes leaked from the words of the past. Leaning against her knees, she placed her face in her hands and sobbed.

Her chest ached from the seventeen years of separation. The nights she spent awake in agony as she experienced every moment he was with another woman, Kelsey. The solitary days she spent on the run, defending their daughter, no matter the cost. Losing Christian the way she did. So suddenly. Never getting to say goodbye, thank you, or tell him how much she loved him. He was her best friend, her brother in combat, and without him, she'd surely be dead.

Amelia considered all that Kelsey had told her. The fact that Gabriel had gone into a coma during her torture, her rape. Had experienced every whip of the lash with her, the severe burns of wolfsbane coated blades as they sliced into her skin, every time that monster forced himself inside her, tearing her insides—Gabriel had endured alongside her.

Amelia was grateful he didn't remember any of it. It was bad enough she lived with the memories every day; there was no reason for him to live with that torture as well. It would have haunted him, tormented him more than what had been physically forced on her body.

Although, in some small way, she didn't feel as alone. He may not remember, but the fact that he had spent those five days with her, psychically at least, took the sting of her torture down a notch.

Did that make her selfish? Maybe.

Even though Kelsey had quite literally given Amelia her blessing for her and Gabriel to reforge their bond, that didn't erase the past or the facts. What if the damage was permanent? What if it is permanent and their bond is too far gone, broken beyond repair?

I don't know what to do. Amelia internally cried. Her mind, a raging mess.

It's going to be okay. Rey tried to console her human.

How? How is any of this okay? We're a fucking mess, Rey. A walking disaster. You nearly died and left me all alone for the past two years! Do you have any idea what that's like?

I never left you, Amelia. I heard everything. Saw everything through your eyes. You're more capable than you give yourself credit, but I have never left you and never will. I had to go quiet to provide us more time.

Amelia perked, able to read between the lines her wolf was drawing. *You knew this was going to happen, didn't you? You knew we'd end up back here, back with Gabriel.*

I had a feeling that our suffering wouldn't last forever. It was only a matter of time. Our destiny has always been Gabriel, Amelia. Trust in that. The Moon Goddess has a plan.

Fuck the Moon Goddess and her plans. I'm sick and tired of being given half-ass statements and left to decipher the bullshit she leaves behind. I am not a God, a saint, or a savior. I'm just me, and I've given up enough in this fucking life for her. Amelia growled. Angry, hot tears streamed down her face as her hands fisted in the comforter.

I know you're angry and hurt, Amelia, but there's no fighting fate. It was our fate to be with Gabriel, just as it was our fate to leave and come back.

Amelia rolled her eyes at her wolf, wiping the tear tracks off her face in haste. She was irritated with her wolf, the Moon Goddess, the whole damn world. None of it was fair or right. It didn't make sense for a man to hold a centuries-old grudge over a slight that occurred generations ago. It wasn't right that one of the best men to have ever walked the earth had to die to save her life. It wasn't fair that her daughter had to grow up without a father, on the run, and taught to kill from the time she could walk.

You're right. None of its fair, but life isn't fair, Amelia. Stop living in the past and look at what's right in front of us. Our daughter is healthy and thriving. Our mate is within our reach, wanting to love us. As for Michael, justice will be served. It's only a matter of time. Rey spoke, appealing to Amelia's more rational side.

Amelia felt her rage turn down to a simmer. Still present but manageable. She let out a deep sigh as her wolf's words rang with truth. *What if we're too damaged to love again?*

We'll never know unless we try.

She despised it when her wolf made more sense than she could muster, but Rey had a point. The past was in the past, and that's where it needed to stay.

Getting up from the bed, she took in a few more steading breaths. Glancing in the mirror hanging on the wall over the dresser she made sure all evidence of her sob-fest was gone. Straightening out her shirt and shaking her shoulders to rid the remaining remnants of grief, she left the bedroom and closed the door on her past.

The house was quiet.

Most had dispersed as the pack members winded down for the night. She was able to silently slip out the back of the house into the fresh air of the night. Lucky for her, there was enough light in the backyard to guide her way towards the training yard and out to the shore of the lake.

Sitting down on the pale sand along the beach, she tucked her knees in against her chest, hugging them tightly to her body. The crescent moon reflected off the lake's glassy surface, illuminating the space, surrounding her in an eerie silver. Her eyes stayed locked on the reflection as a sense of calm crept over her, settling her frazzled nerves.

Amelia startled violently as a soft, plush woven blanket wrapped around her shoulders. Looking up, she found Gabriel standing over her, hands raised in surrender.

"I'm sorry," he apologized, sitting down beside her. "I didn't mean to startle you."

Amelia pulled the blanket tighter around her frame. She hadn't realized just how cold she was and was grateful for the instant warmth the heavily woven fabric provided. "No, it's okay. Thank you."

Gabriel tried to smile at her, tried to offer her additional comfort, but his lips couldn't quite manage it.

The day weighed heavily on the both of them.

"I'm glad to see you and Kelsey are both in one piece."

Amelia glanced at him sideways. Unsure how to decipher his comment.

A part of her was jealous. Jealous that Kelsey got to spend the last seventeen years with her mate, in his bed, and as his wife. The other part of her wanted to march back into the house and beat Kelsey so bloody that not even her wolf could heal her face. But what good would that do?

"You've changed," Gabriel commented solemnly.

Amelia fully turned his way, looking at him curiously. "What do you mean?"

"The Amelia I knew would have snapped her neck the moment you found out about us, but not before mauling her. Then you probably would have castrated me," Gabriel said with a smirk.

"I definitely would have caused you irreversible damage," Amelia smiled, imagining the pain she would have inflicted on them both. "But I'm not eighteen anymore. I've grown up, Gabe. A lot about me has changed and not all for the better."

Gabriel disregarded her last comment as he stared down at his folded hands. "What happened to you, Amelia? I need to know."

Amelia sighed profoundly, running her hands through her hair. "Gabe, I don't think that's a good idea. It's in the past. What good would it do talking about it now?"

"But it's not in the past. Do you think I don't notice how you freeze whenever a man brushes past you? How reserved and closed off you've become. That panic attack you had yesterday because someone was smoking nearby. Your nightmares, being afraid of the dark. You live every day in that nightmare. I see it, Snow. I see all of you."

Amelia took in a quivering breath. The oxygen rattled in her chest as her heart slammed against her breastbone. She wasn't the only one who had changed during their time apart. The old Gabriel had never been so observant or attuned to her emotions. He was always so literal, a brutish caveman. She had to spell everything out for him.

"I don't even know where to start," Amelia whispered into the dark of night. Afraid that the creatures birthed in darkness might overhear.

"You can start wherever you like. The beginning, the end."

"Well, there's a lot I blocked out. I barely recall being taken. I don't even know how they found us so quickly. Their timing was almost too perfect. Christian had gone into town, and I was home alone with Emery," she started, remembering that day eight years ago. "All I remember is that there were too many of them. I tried to fight them off. I don't even remember how Emery got away; I'm just glad she did."

"So am I," Gabriel said. Trying to restrain his anger from seeping into his voice. Just the mere thought of someone laying hands on his daughter was enough to make him want to hunt down every Rogue alive and rip them apart with his bare hands.

"When I was held captive, I couldn't speak to Rey. They kept me drugged. Wolfsbane and human medicine, so I couldn't heal, couldn't mind link. They wanted me weak so that I couldn't fight back, and I couldn't. No matter how hard I tried," Amelia rubbed absently at the knotted scars around her wrists. The scars produced from hours pulling on her cuffs, trying to tear the silver chains from the stone walls.

Gabriel watched her. Observed how her eyes looked distant as she was swept away in those terrifying memories he asked her to relive. The way she would touch the scars on her hands. The ones he guessed were from being suspended from a ceiling, held at their mercy.

"They kept me sensory-deprived the entire time. I was locked away somewhere with no light, no sound. No food or water. I had no sense of time. It felt like I was locked away for years, not days. The only way I knew I was alive was when he would come and visit me."

Bile rose to the back of her throat. The man that had been her torturer, her rapist, haunted her dreams and waking hours. Still fresh in her mind as though he was standing before her. She dug her nails into the scars on her wrists to remind herself she was far away from him. He was dead and could never touch her again.

"You don't have to—," Gabriel started.

Amelia swayed her head. "No, I want to. I've never talked to anyone about this, and it's beyond time I do. If

I can't tell my mate, then who can I tell?" she chuckled half-heartedly.

Gabriel couldn't help but smile. He shouldn't feel hopeful at a time like this, but a part of him was.

"He spent the next five days torturing me, raping me. The other rogues wanted to take turns with me, but he wouldn't let them. He wasn't even supposed to touch me until Michael got there, but he didn't care. He told me he wanted a taste of the Moon Goddess for himself. They wanted my lineage, my heirs, but not Emery. She was of your blood, and if they had found her, they would have eliminated her, but now that she's of age, they'll want her for the same reason."

Amelia ignored Gabriel's growls at her last statement and continued. "I don't remember much about what happened when Christian came. Somehow, he found me, naked and bleeding, filthy and almost dead. I lost a lot of blood. I wasn't healing, and my wounds had begun to fester. I didn't have to tell him what they did. The evidence was all over me and it sent Christian into such a rage even I was terrified of him. I remember Christian delivering me the head of the man who violated me. He wanted to make sure I knew he was dead and could never touch me again."

Gabriel tilted his head to the night sky and breathed in the brisk air deeply. "I should have known better. I should have known Christian was a good man and hadn't taken my mate away from me," he admitted aloud. "I wish I could say thank you to him. I wish there was some way I could make it up to him. Without him, I don't think I would have ever seen you again or known about our daughter."

Amelia reached up and brushed a stray tear off his scratchy cheek. She left her hand there, lingering against his warm flesh, cupping his face.

Gabriel leaned into her touch, fastening his eyes as sparks danced across his skin.

"You couldn't have known. It's only natural for you to assume that there was something else going on between Christian and me. He didn't blame you. You were his Alpha, first and foremost. He just wanted to make you proud."

"What happened to him, Amelia?" he asked her, finally unclosing his eyes to meet her gaze.

Amelia trailed her hand away to envelop them around herself, tucking her body farther into the blanket. "He managed to get me out of the chains, but they were silver. They burned him, but he didn't care. When he finally got me free, the rogues had realized what was going on and began to attack. I couldn't help. I couldn't do anything. I couldn't even hold up my own body weight. Yet, somehow, Christian managed to keep them at bay and get me out of that hole. He shoved a knife in my hands and told me to run. The rogues just kept coming, and there was no way we could have gotten away together. He sacrificed his life to save mine.

"Somehow, I managed to get back to the house where I left Emery. I didn't know if she was still alive or if Christian had moved her, but it was the last place I had seen her. The next few days are a blur. I was out of it for nearly a week. I was still too heavily drugged. The wolfsbane took weeks to leave my system so I couldn't heal properly, hence my scars. Damon came when Emery found me in the bushes and nursed me back to health as much as he could, but he couldn't stay forever. He had his pack, his own family to take care of. When my back finally closed, he went back to the Wandering Moon, and Emery and I fled to Australia."

"Why Australia?" Gabriel asked randomly.

"When I was a teenager, I tried to generate as many contacts as I could. I had planned to travel and thought it would be good to have a few friends around the world in case I ever got into trouble."

"Knowing you, that would have been very likely."

"Exactly," Amelia smirked. "The Alpha in Sydney took us in while I healed and waited for Rey to come back. Took her three months."

"Alpha Quinn?" Gabriel asked, eyebrow arched.

"You know her?" Amelia couldn't conceal the surprise in her voice. Alpha females were virtually unheard of, and most of the werewolf community barely tolerated her.

"I've met her at the annual Conference a few times. She's a tough woman," Gabriel said, a hint of admiration laced in his voice.

"She really is. She doesn't allow anyone's opinions of her to stop her from doing her job."

"Kind of like someone else I know."

Amelia chuckled, unable to help the eye roll that followed.

Oddly enough, she felt relaxed. More relaxed than she could ever remember being. She had always been terrified of talking about her past and believed reliving the trauma would only make things worse. That all the years she'd spent trying to force the memories to the deepest recesses of her mind would suddenly bring them all right back with such force, she'd never be able to put them back, but it was the opposite.

Telling Gabriel practically released her in some way.

With a deep sigh, Amelia leaned into him, setting her head on his broad shoulder. She breathed in his scent, causing her head to swim and her heart to swell. She missed this. Missed him. More than she had ever acknowledged, and it was sheer bliss to be in the moment with him and not worry about anything else.

What she wouldn't give for him to wrap his arms around her and hold her body tight against his. To listen to his steady breathing and feel his heart beating against her cheek as she laid beside him in their bed. To kiss his tender, soft lips without regret or shame. To enjoy his secure, broad hands grip her waist as he made love to her, whispering in her ears as he professed his love.

That was her dream. Her fairytale.

"Goodnight, Gabriel."

Amelia stood up from the ground, placing the blanket in his lap before making her way to the house and turning her back on her past and quite possibly her future. She wanted Gabriel. Of course, she did.

But could she have him?

Slipping inside Emery's room, she checked to make sure her daughter was sound asleep. The faint sounds of her snores told her she was.

Without bothering to change, Amelia slid into the bed beside Emery and tucked the covers around herself. Now and then, Amelia would sleep in the same bed as her daughter. Their bond was the only one she had been truly comfortable with, and sometimes it was the only chance for a peaceful sleep. After the day she had, she needed to smell her pup and curl up beside her.

Amelia's eyes instantly grew drowsy as sleep overcame her.

Amelia awoke to find herself standing at the front of the lake, again. Glancing down at herself, she found a silver, form-fitting satin dress clinging to her curves, billowing in the silent wind. Her skin was flawless, not a scar to be seen. The pigment of her flesh was warm and radiated a pale, intense glow around her.

Movement out of the corner of her eye commanded her attention.

Standing out in the middle of the tranquil lake was a woman. She wore the same dress as Amelia. Her silvered hair reached past her waist, resembling strands of silk as it flowed around her slight, petite frame. She was stunning, alluring, ethereal, and almost an exact copy of herself, like peering in a mirror only a few years younger and very dead.

"Mom?"

CHAPTER 30

LAID BARE

"M om?"

"Amelia, my daughter," the woman called to her. Arms held out in front of her as though expecting an embrace.

Amelia stared at her questioningly.

Did she expect her to walk across the water?

"What is this? What's going on?" Amelia asked.

Looking around, there were no bodies, no carnage, or signs of conflict whatsoever. Just the serene beauty of the forest and her mother standing in the middle of the lake, glowing in the moon's light.

"The Moon Goddess sent me here to speak with you."

"What? Is she too afraid to speak with me herself?" Amelia grumbled.

"Amelia, don't be rude," her mother scolded.

"Emma, it's been a shitty few years. Forgive me if protocol for a deity escapes me," she said with a roll of her eyes.

Emma sighed deeply. Her sea-green eyes brimmed with sadness. She brushed off the fact that Amelia had addressed her by her name.

"Mia, I know these last few years have been rocky—"

"Rocky?! You consider being kidnapped, tortured, and raped a rocky stint in my past? Do you think being separated from my mate and raising our daughter on my own was a breeze? Are you fucking kidding me?!" Amelia shouted, feeling her anger rise.

"Amelia Smoke! I am your mother and—"

"No! My mother died when I was six! This," she waved between the two of them, "I don't know what this is, but I do know it's not real. What are you? A figment of my imagination? A ghost sent here to haunt me, annoy me to death?"

Emma bridged the distance between them faster than she could blink, causing her to startle, taking a step back.

"This is real, Mia. I'm here, and I *am* your mother. The Moon Goddess sent me down here to help you, to guide you. Now, I understand your upset, and you've been through something horrendous and inexcusable, and I am sorry for that. I'm sorry I couldn't be there to protect you," Emma said, brushing a strand of hair from Amelia's forehead.

Amelia couldn't help but lean into her touch. The woman before her even smelled like her mother. Roses, euphoric and straightforward, as it brought back a rush of memories she thought long gone.

"Now tell me, my sweet girl. Why are you holding back with your mate? Why do you deny fate?" Emma asked, folding her hands in front of her.

"I'm not holding back—"

"Yes, you are. Do you think I haven't watched you all these years? You're a lot like me. More than you'll ever know, and I know you, maybe better than you know yourself. I can see you're holding back with Gabriel, but why?"

"If you've been watching me, then you should know damn well why," Amelia said, looking off to the lake behind her, unwilling to look her mother in the eye. "What if he can't get over what happened to me?"

"It sounds to me that it's you who can't move past it," Emma could tell Amelia had something to say, but she stopped her. "I'm not saying you don't have your reasons, but Gabriel has also expressly told you he wants you. Why can't you take his word for it?"

"He's married," Amelia shot back.

"And Gabriel has informed you that won't stand in the way. Even Kelsey relinquished her rights to him. So, try again."

"You really have been paying attention," Amelia grumbled.

"Mm-hmm. That still doesn't answer my question," Emma said, not backing down as she crossed her arms over her chest.

"For a ghost, you are a pain in my ass."

"Amelia."

"Fine," she huffed, extending her hands anxiously through her hair. "I'm scared. Are you happy now?"

"What could you possibly be scared of?"

"Myself. Gabriel. What if it's not the same? What if love isn't enough? Now I have Emery to consider. I don't want her getting hurt."

"Sounds like you're the one afraid of getting hurt," Emma observed. "Yours and Gabriel's relationship will never be the same because you're two different people compared to eighteen years ago. You've both grown up, but that doesn't mean that's a bad thing. Love grows. It evolves and changes as the people in the relationship change. That's life."

Amelia thought about what her mother said. Was she really just making excuses? Could it be that simple?

"Listen carefully, Mia. Only your mate can heal you. You must reforge the bond, or all is lost."

Amelia frowned at her mother as her form began to dissipate, before completely disappearing.

Her eyes opened slowly as she took in her surroundings. She was back in Emery's room, lying beside her sleeping daughter.

Amelia felt restless and agitated thinking back on her dream. How real and lifelike her mother looked, standing before her on the surface of the lake. She was confident that her skin would have been warm and alive if she had reached out to touch her.

Looking beside her, she observed her sleeping child. Emery looked more her age when asleep. When the world's worries were pushed aside, she could finally relax and escape into the dream world. She couldn't be prouder of the young woman beside her. How resilient and strong she was. Some days, she was sure Emery came from someone else. Not able to believe that someone so perfect, so genuine, and kind could have come from her.

Amelia slowly peeled the comforter off her body. Through the curtains, the sun was kissing the horizon.

The house should still be dormant with only the patrols making their rounds along the border and perimeter of the territory.

Feeling the urge to swim, she crept out of the room as quietly as she could, closing the bedroom door behind her. Forgoing a towel, Amelia figured she could shift into her wolf to get back into the house.

The house was eerily peaceful. She could smell the warriors on patrol, but they kept clear of the lake, sticking close to the outer perimeter and the Packhouse. She slipped out the back, padding barefoot across the soft, dewy grass, through the tree line and to the shore of the lake, her toes sinking into the wet sand.

Amelia pulled her top over her head. The cool, crisp fall air bit into her skin, causing the hairs on the back of her neck and arms to rise painfully. The water would be frigid this time of year, but it would be a welcome shock to a troubled mind.

She unhooked her bra and dropped it in a pile on top of her shirt. Stripping off her leggings and underwear in one swoop, she dipped her toes in the water.

"Fuck," she hissed.

The water was glacial and tortuous against her skin.

Taking the plunge, she arched her arms over her head and dove into the water, piercing the calm surface of the lake. The water shocked her system. Every nerve and cell felt like needles were being driven under her flesh. Blood vessels shriveled on themselves as her body tried to maintain as much of its natural heat as possible.

Amelia pushed through the painful cold, pumping her arms and legs, propelling her forward. She moved her way through the lake in a fluid motion. Her arms steered her as her legs drove her forward, back, and forth across the reflecting surface. Lap after lap, her muscles relaxed and loosened, twisting through the water as though she was half fish, not wolf.

She lost count of the number of laps she completed. Eventually, her body became numb to the cold and warmed due to the physical exertion. Twisting and turning through the frigid water naked left her feeling liberated and free. The liquid reaching every crevice and inch of her body left her rejuvenated and awake.

For the first time in a while, she felt truly alive.

On her last lap, Amelia recognized a familiar presence, standing on the shore, watching. She stopped in the middle of the lake, her head bobbing above the surface. Her breathing was deep and labored, but not from the exercise.

Standing on the shore, observing her intently, was Gabriel with a robe in hand.

Amelia felt nervous and exhilarated all at once. He was standing in her path. The only one that led back to the house.

The sun rose behind her over the trees that littered the territory, casting the forest around them in a bright, warm, orange light. Against Gabriel's tan skin, he looked even more handsome, if that was even possible. She wanted to get out of the lake and run her hands down the length of his taut biceps, relive the experience of having his hands grip her waist in that familiar, intimate way she loved. But the warriors would be arriving soon, ready to swap out with fresh bodies, which meant eyes and ears all around.

Amelia slowly swam her way back to shore. Her arms moved with idle strokes, dragging her lower half behind her until her toes could touch the cold, slimy sand. Walking out of the water, she kept her arms frozen at her side, refusing to cover herself in front of her mate—the man who once knew every inch of her flesh thoroughly.

She stood before him in all her glory. Every slice of the blade on her thighs, arms, and stomach was laid bare before him. The dozens upon dozens of knotted scars from the whip that crisscrossed across her back, down the sides of her ribs and back of her arms, were finally out in the open. The cigarette burns placed randomly across her flesh, saw daylight for the first time.

His silver eyes roamed her body, taking in every scar, cut, and burn, but also the more intimate memories marked across her body. The stretch marks that lined her stomach and hips from her pregnancy. The c-section scar that resided just above her pubic bone from her near-fatal delivery. At first, his eyes flashed black as they took in the damage, but slowly they softened to a pool of molten silver.

Amelia turned, exposing her deeply scarred back. She could hear fallen, dead leaves crunching underfoot as his boots carried him closer. Warm, large, calloused hands wrapped around her slight shoulders, causing her to close her eyes on contact, relishing in the feel of his skin on hers.

A soft, plush material wrapped around her frame as he laid the robe across her back and fastened it in front of her. She turned slowly back towards him, thrusting her arms through the sleeves.

Looking up, she met his gaze with her own and discovered him staring down at her. She smiled gently—adoration and love plain as day on her face.

"Thank you."

CHAPTER 31

HIDE AND SEEK

Amelia pulled a fitted tank over her head.

No more jackets. No more hiding. Those closest to her already knew her past, and the rest had guessed. It was no longer a secret, so why bother?

Amelia wandered out to the backyard for training, all the while her head in a fog. Feeling more confused than ever, she couldn't help but feel Gabriel's lingering eyes roaming all over her body. The thought of her morning swim still imprinted in her mind. She hadn't been naked in front of a man in years.

It both thrilled and terrified her.

Training had begun. She was so lost in her thoughts that she hadn't realized she was sparing with another wolf until he swiped her feet out from underneath her, making her land forcefully on her back, knocking the air from her lungs with enough force to leave her gasping. The man straddled her body, poised for a kill shot when a loud, threatening growl erupted around them.

The warning was enough to shock oxygen into her body.

The warrior that had her pinned to the earth quickly scrambled off, backing away quicker than she could comprehend.

Amelia pulled herself up onto her elbows, her back protesting in agony as her lungs felt as though they were on fire with each breath she struggled to take. A hand moved in front of her face, offering help up.

Without thinking, she took it, placing her hand in his.

Pure, unadulterated strength hoisted her off the ground and set her down on her own two feet.

Amelia felt breathless but not from the hit she took. She looked up into pools of silver that looked down at her with such emotion. It was enough to crack open her soul and thaw her heart. Unconsciously, she moistened her lips, desperate to bring moisture back to her mouth but regretted it instantly as Gabriel flicked his gaze down to her mouth. The spicy scent of apples and spice-filled her mouth, making her insides hum with desire.

She tossed her head, trying to clear the fog as she pushed herself back away from him. "I'm fine," she said, brushing her hands against her thighs, secretly trying to remove the lingering hum between her legs and the growing dampness.

She needed a distraction—a big one and not the one that could slip between her thighs and make her scream.

The fuck is wrong with me?! Amelia internally screamed.

We want our mate. Rey stated the obvious.

Now is not the time for that shit!

"Emery!" Amelia shouted over the clearing, startling everyone around her, including Gabriel.

Emery stepped forward from one of the nearby groups and approached her mother. Her eyebrow was arched high, looking suspiciously between both her parents.

At that moment, Amelia cursed the Moon Goddess for their extraordinary sense of smell.

"Yes, Mom?" Emery asked, a knowing smirk pulled at those sweet lips.

"Drill twenty-three." Was all Amelia had to say to get her daughter to roll her eyes. "Careful, I'll make you join them."

Emery stood up straighter, the annoyance instantly vanishing from her face. "I don't think they're ready."

"They're gonna have to be." Amelia shrugged her shoulders.

"We're going to have a lot of people cleaning toilets."

"We'll have the cleanest shitters in the entire northeast."

Gabriel just looked back and forth between his mate and daughter, unable to follow their banter. "What the hell are you two talking about?"

"Just a game we like to play," Amelia said, barely glancing his way.

"Yeah, a game of torture," Emery grumbled.

"Oh, hush yourself. It'll be me and you against all of them."

This seemed to perk Emery up right away. The teenager began to bounce on the balls of her feet, suddenly looking extremely eager.

Gabriel instantly became wary. "I don't know if this sounds like a good idea."

"You don't even know what we're talking about," Amelia frowned.

"It'll be fun!" Emery said excitedly.

"Just ten seconds ago, you didn't seem so enthused," Gabriel pointed out.

"True, but that's because I always lose. It's never fun to always lose. But now, I won't," Emery rubbed her hands together in anticipation, almost giddy with the anxiety that was beginning to permeate the air as the three-hundred-something warriors began to take notice that something new was underfoot.

"Amelia—" Gabriel started.

"Hush and watch." Amelia ignored him before turning on the gathering warriors. "All warriors, shift now!"

Unable to deny the command, every man and woman shifted into their wolves, shredding their clothes in the process.

"Amelia," Gabriel groaned, striking his hand to his forehead.

Amelia grimaced as tatters of clothes floated to the ground, littering the earth. "Yeah, shit. My bad," she said. Unfortunately, she hadn't thought that through. "All well, too late now."

"Mom," Emery rolled her eyes.

"Yes, yes, I know. We'll deal with it later," Amelia mumbled under her breath, directing her attention back to the wolves shifted in front of her. "Sorry, guys! I didn't think that through, but I promise you, it'll be worth it! We're going to engage in a game of tag."

The hundreds of wolves before her tilted their heads to the side with curiosity. Some even whined in protest.

"Now, now, no whining," Amelia chided the warriors. "I haven't even gotten to the best part. Whoever tags Emery or me will get to spend the rest of the day as Alpha."

"Snow," Gabriel growled in warning, clearly not appreciating her offering his position as though it was a bone being dangled in front of the maws of a dog.

Amelia looked back at him over her shoulder and fluttered her eyelashes. "Don't you trust me?"

"Yes, but—"

"Good," she smirked before turning back to the wolves. "Now, if Emery or I tag you, you're out. The first fifty wolves to be tagged will spend the rest of the day cleaning the Packhouse from top to bottom, giving our outstanding omegas the day off. In one hour, if there are any wolves left standing, I owe you a drink."

Most of the warriors began to bounce on the pads of their feet, eager to get started.

Cocky fuckers. Amelia remarked internally.

This is going to be fun. Emery linked her.

"We'll give you a fifteen-minute head start. Go!"

Amelia barely had a chance to release them before over three hundred wolves took off at a sprint in every direction of the territory. She found Damon off to the side, discussing privately with Cordelia.

"Come on, Damon. You too," Amelia jerked her head towards the tree line.

"Seriously?"

"Even Alpha's have a thing or two to learn. Now come on. Chop-chop." Amelia clapped her hands together as Damon began to undress, grumbling the whole way until he shifted into his wolf and took off, disappearing into the trees. "You too, Gabe."

Gabriel smirked, knowing he'd be next. He slowly pulled his shirt over his head, allowing his muscles to flex and ripple beneath his taut, tanned skin as he eliminated the thin cotton from his body.

Amelia couldn't help but watch, nearly licking her lips, biting on the thin, tender skin. Gabriel knew precisely what he was doing, and he was doing it almost too well. He smirked knowingly before backing into the tree line, disappearing amongst the crowded brush.

"You okay there, Mom? Need a cold shower?"

Amelia snapped her head in her daughter's direction, glaring at her, but she at least had the dignity to keep her mouth shut. Her kid wasn't wrong. A cold shower didn't sound so bad, but she was sure not even glacial waters could sooth the pounding warmth between her legs.

"Shut it, kid. Let's go."

Emery rolled her eyes one more time for good measure before riding herself of her clothes alongside her mother and phased into their wolves effortlessly.

Amelia was a bit slower, but the shift was nearly painless as her bones rearranged themselves, elongating and shortening where necessary. She twitched her nose, whiskers tickling her face.

Amelia took in the sight of her daughter. No matter how many times she observed Hailey, her daughter's wolf always blew her away. She was a perfect blend of both her and Gabriel. The black stripe that ran down her back, from the crown of her head to the tip of her tail, the silver eyes, or the snow-white fur. She was stunning.

Mom, you're staring again. Emery's voice rang in her head.

Sorry, hun. Amelia said, shaking out her fur, flexing her claws into the earth, kneading it beneath her paws. *You know what to do. Show 'em what we're made of.*

Emery took off towards the left side of the clearing as Amelia headed straight into the right side of the territory.

Striking her paws into the compact earth, she allowed Rey to come forward, taking over the hunt altogether. Breathing in the air deeply and taking in each scent, she distinguished them on the back of her tongue and discovered a group of warriors clumped together.

Are they even trying? Amelia asked, exasperated.

Guess they really want to clean. Rey commented.

Amelia chuckled as she sprinted in their direction. The wind was with her, blowing their scent straight up her nostrils, and carrying her scent away from them.

They were a hundred yards dead ahead. She sprinted even faster, bouncing on the pads of her paws to reduce noise. Jumping off the sides of trees, one after the other, she sailed over a group of four juveniles and landed in front of them, startling each of them out of their skins. Once they regained their bearings, they looked prepared to attack, poised back on their hunches.

Amelia snickered, swaying her head at them. That was when each of them began to feel the sting as the air hit the deep cuts along their shoulders. First blood had been drawn, and they were dismissed. She stayed long enough to see their heads droop in defeat before taking off back into the thick of it.

She ran through the woods, using claws and teeth to secure her grip and leap from one to the next. Each wolf she scratched with her claws never saw her coming. They could hear her, even smell her in some instances, but not once did they see her until it was too late. She was a ghost. A whisper in the wind. Unattainable and unsuspecting.

In the first fifteen minutes, Amelia and Emery had over half the wolves knocked out.

Are they even trying? Emery asked, laughing through their link.

Poor pups never see it coming. Amelia chuckled.

Looking down, she spotted a chestnut-colored wolf with a grizzly scar down the side of his face. Amelia almost snorted, which would have sounded ridiculous as a wolf, and given away her position. As silent as a hawk, she leaped down to swipe him on the shoulder.

Rick looked up at her, teeth bared, a growl vibrating deep in his chest until he realized it was her.

Amelia gave him a wolfy grin before disappearing back into the greenery.

The next twenty minutes were spent much the same. Hunting down the remaining wolves, but she still hadn't come upon the one wolf she was truly hunting. Somehow, he was evading her.

Got Uncle Damon! Emery cheered, mentally patting herself on the back.

Great! Now you can rub that in his face for the rest of your life. Amelia smiled, laughing internally at what her brother must have looked like when Emery caught him.

You know I will.

That left just one wolf. One pesky, onyx-colored Alpha.

A faint breeze picked up, brushing against the silky fur on her face, directing her to his location. She advanced her way carefully through the brush until she identified his monstrous, raven wolf just beneath her. Retracting her claws, she dropped from the tree.

Gabriel didn't realize until it was too late. His head twisted behind him just as she landed on his back, restraining him on the leaf-littered floor. Collapsing to the ground under the force of her fall, the air in his lungs was forced out.

Amelia laid on top of him for a moment as they both tried to catch their breath. It took a great deal of concentration and balance to leap through the trees, and man, was she out of practice. But she did feel a sort of victory for capturing him. He was the last wolf standing, and she was proud it was her that caught him.

Laying on top of him, being so close physically, awakened every cell in her body. She could feel the muscles in his legs tense beneath her. The rising and falling of his chest cavity shook, and although it was faint, she could barely make out their mind link.

He was laughing.

Without giving it a second thought, Amelia grazed her teeth along his shoulder, drawing first blood.

Gabriel froze. His breath hitched in his throat, and his heart raced erratically. She injured him just beneath the mark she had left on him all those years ago, and it stunned him.

Amelia licked his face roughly before getting off his body and trotting away, swishing her tail behind her. She wasn't sure where her flirtatious side had come from or why she had behaved the way she did, but she was starting to feel like her old self again, and it felt empowering.

Back at the clearing, nearly every warrior looked defeated. Even Damon was sulking off the side while Emery stood beside him, giddy and proud. They had already shifted back into their human form, awaiting further instruction.

Amelia ducked behind an overgrown bush, finding clothes already waiting for her. Silently thanking Emery, she pulled her clothes on before stepping out and addressing the pack.

"Now, I don't know about you, but that was fun," Amelia smirked, hands on her hips as she stood before over three hundred pouting warriors.

"Tag is a game for pups," one of the older warriors grumbled off to the side.

"Don't be a sore loser, David. You're just upset you got bested by a teenager," Rick spoke out from the front of the group, his voice full of mockery.

Amelia glanced over at Emery, who stood tall, hands clasped in front of her, with the broadest shit-eating grin on her face. That's her girl.

"Does anyone know how you were tagged out?" Amelia asked the group.

The warriors began to murmur amongst themselves, some speaking out.

"I didn't see you till you already tagged me."

"It was like you came out of nowhere."

"It was pretty creepy if you ask me."

Amelia couldn't help but smirk at their comments. She may be out of shape, but at least she still had something to offer these seasoned warriors.

"So, no one has any ideas?" she asked them all again.

The warriors all stood stunned, incapable of answering.

"Trees."

Spinning around, she discovered a shirtless Gabriel making his way from the tree line wearing only basketball shorts that hung loosely on his hips. His abs tapered off into a V that disappeared beneath the hem of his shorts. She couldn't prevent her eyes from wandering all over his body, suddenly feeling blisteringly hot.

Turning back to the warriors, trying to ignore the rising flush to her face, she addressed them. "A deals a deal. The first fifty warriors tagged out, have fun in the house! The rest of you, shift back into your wolf and practice your tree climbing. Use your tail for balance, and make sure you know exactly where you're going to land before you jump."

The warriors that had been tagged first headed for the house where the awaiting Omega's stood, eager for their day off. The remaining warriors were already shifting back into their wolves and making their way to the trees.

Amelia could feel Gabriel approaching her. Could sense he wanted to talk, but she moved towards the house, trying to put as much distance between them as possible. She needed to cool off and fast.

CHAPTER 32

GENERATIONS

Amelia beelined for the dining room, where refreshments and snacks were. She scooped up a cold bottle of water and began chugging it down. Her skin felt hot. Her cheeks flushed crimson red, and warmth pooled between her legs. At this point, she wasn't even convinced an ice bath would help.

A familiar pull tugged at her heart, along with the familiar scent of roses and vanilla that flooded her mouth. She turned around to discover Emery approaching her. Her eyebrows arched high with a knowing smirk playing on her lips.

"Mom," Emery smiled.

"Don't start, kid," Amelia advised her, guzzling the remainder of the water.

Emery held her hands up in surrender, chuckling softly. "I'm not saying anything. I just wanted to see how you were doing with everything."

Amelia flung the empty plastic bottle into the recycling bin before tugging on the end of her braid. "Honestly. I'm confused, frustrated and confused."

Emery's smile fell from her face into one of complete sympathy and understanding. "I know, Momma," she said, rubbing her mother's arm.

Amelia couldn't help but lean into her daughter's touch. Their bond hummed to life between them, connecting them in a way that ran deeper than blood. She noted her eyes fluttering closed when a flurry of movement caught her attention.

Footsteps landed heavily on the wood floor, getting closer and closer.

Cordelia practically ran into the room, her shoes scuffing over the floor as she tried to move as fast as her load would allow. A towering stack of leather-bound journals was cradled in her arms against her chest. Kelsey was following closely behind, carrying a similar stack. Both women dumped the books onto one of the tables, creating a mighty pile of leather and paper.

"What's all this?" Amelia asked, picking up one of the journals lying on top of the pile and flipping through it. She'd recognize her mother's handwriting anywhere. "Cordie?"

"Mia! You're here, great!" Cordelia yelled. Her voice was a strange high-pitched, squeaking noise that was sure to alert the wolves outside.

"What's going on? What are you doing with these?" Amelia asked, gesturing towards the massive pile of journals.

Emery picked up one of the books on the table and flipped through it, her eyes widening. "Where did you get these? These are our ancestor's journals."

"Ever since you came back, I've been looking into your ancestry. Trying to find a way to defeat Michael," Cordelia said excitedly. "This problem with him dates back to Rhea and Ezekial. They fought his ancestors."

"Yeah, and lost," Emery commented under her breath.

"What's all the commotion? We could hear you clear out in the training field," Damon called out, jogging into the dining hall followed closely by Gabriel.

Gabriel's brows were furrowed together in confusion, making clear eye contact. Amelia shrugged her shoulders. Showing him, she was just as baffled as they were.

"Hush," Cordelia waved off her spouse, ignoring his entrance. "Anyways. I remember Damon telling me back when your father passed you had found journals left by your mother. So, I wondered, what if prior generations had done the same thing? I dug through the attic and found dozens of journals! This is barely even a fifth of what I found. The rest are upstairs in our room."

"You found more?" Amelia asked, disbelief clear in her voice. She looked at the already impressive pile of journals and couldn't imagine there being any more of the ancient, tattered words of the past.

"Way more! Generations of Rhea's descendants recorded their lives, but more specifically their end, dating back to Rhea's daughter," Cordelia informed them, her excitement contagious.

Amelia couldn't help the way her heart was racing in her chest, skipping every other beat. The fact that there had been dozens of journals stashed away in her family's attic all these years, possibly referencing their powers, the feud with Michael's line, all of it, left her hopeful and a bit bitter.

"What did you find?" Gabriel asked.

"Well, most of the women were brutally murdered in some way. Stabbings, blitz attacks, rogues, kidnapped and tortured, you name it. Some were left unharmed, usually the ones with weaker wolves and not much in the way of power," Cordelia informed them.

"But that's not Amelia. Her wolf is exceptionally powerful," Damon pointed out. "Emery isn't far behind."

"Exactly. Which is why Michael and his pack of mutts have been trying so desperately to get their hands on her, and now that Emery is of age, they'll be coming for her too," Cordelia said.

A deep growl vibrated from his chest, escaping Gabriel's mouth. His top lip curled up into a snarl. Amelia took immediate notice of the dangerous ground they were touching on. She had already been captured once before, and the thought of Emery having to go through even a minute of that was enough to leave her wanting to burn every one of their enemies alive.

"Get to the point, Cordie," Amelia advised her.

"Right. I managed to date the journals and found the oldest one I could," Cordelia rummaged through the pile of journals on the table, only to pull one out that looked like it belonged in a museum and not on their dining room table. The leather was cracked and dried with age. The pages yellowed and tattered.

Amelia took the journal and carefully opened the book. The spine cracked, protesting the movement. The paper felt brittle to the touch but thicker and more coarse like parchment. The writing was loopy and formal, written in a way that only a few could perform in today's age. Reading over the first few lines, she recognized a signature at the bottom of the page.

"Who's Remy?" Amelia asked, not recognizing the name.

"Rhea's daughter," Kelsey said, finally speaking.

Amelia's eyes widened as she looked down at the journal cradled in the palm of her hands. To hold something so sacred, so priceless, left her head swimming. If only she had discovered the journals years ago, what it could have meant for them, for her.

"Remy was only a toddler when Rhea was killed. This journal was Rhea's, but Remy completed it years later when she became old enough," Kelsey told them.

"When Rhea had been killed, her mate Ezekial had already been dead a few years. We know that the mate bond was created to make the pair stronger," Cordelia said.

"The male becomes more aware, stronger, faster," Kelsey said, side-eyeing Gabriel.

"Right, while the female can see the future, has visions, and can heal at great distances. They balance each other," Cordelia arched her brow at the fated pair before her.

"But, since Ezekial was already dead, it was a miracle she survived the bond breaking."

"Then how did she?" Emery asked, unable to curb her curiosity.

"The bond with her child was greater," Cordelia filled in. "She had already had their child, and the bond between mother and daughter was strong enough to sustain her. But, without her fated mate, she was weak, which is why the New Moon Pack's Alpha was able to kill her."

"Remy wrote in the journal that if she had been older when the opposing Alpha came, two female Alpha's and her fated mate could have beaten the New Moon Pack altogether," Kelsey told them.

"Wait, what are you saying?" Amelia asked. Her brain was lagging with all the information before her.

"It takes two generations and a fated pair to defeat Michael."

"Wait, wait. Hold the brakes," Emery said with a wave of her hands. "You're saying that to defeat Michael and the rogues, Gabriel, my mom, and I have to confront him together?"

"According to what we've read, yes. That's the theory," Cordelia said, confirming her suspicions.

"What do you mean, theory?" Gabriel asked, skepticism in his voice.

"It's what previous generations believed would work. But typically, the fated mate or descendant was killed before anything could be tested," Cordelia shrugged her shoulders.

Amelia wasn't sure what to think or what to make of anything they were saying. Her mind was racing. The words of her dead mother from last night replayed over and over. That bastard ghost knew it would come to this, that it had something to do with the pesky mate bond.

"Yeah, but we're all alive," Emery said, frowning. "We have the two generations and the fated mate pair."

"She's right, Mia," Cordelia said. "By running, you managed to keep yourself and Emery alive. Saving both generations."

"And you made sure to heal Gabriel before leaving, ensuring his survival," Kelsey added. "Saving the fated pair."

"Yeah, but the bond is nearly severed. The fated pair are barely mates," Damon said, instantly receiving a warning look from his wife, forcing him to direct his gaze down to the floor. Not even an Alpha could ignore his Luna.

It hurt, but it was true. Amelia looked away, unwilling to make eye contact with him. She could feel Gabriel's eyes scrutinizing her, seeking any sign of hope, but was she ready to give him that?

"That's the thing," Cordelia started, her voice hesitant and reserved. "The mate bond would have to be reforged. You can't win without it. You need to be at your full strength, Amelia, and you can only do that with him by your side as your mate."

"If you reconnect with Gabriel, reinforcing your bond, and with Emery by your side, you'd be the most powerful Alpha. In theory, with enough motivation, you could essentially order the Rogues away along with Michael," Kelsey said with a sort of finality.

Gabriel could see the panic building in Amelia's eyes. Emery was maintaining a watchful eye on her mother, observing her like a hawk. He noticed their daughter inching closer to her mother, seeking to console her. He was startled with how in sync they were and felt nothing short of pride, but Amelia had him worried.

They all required time to think.

"I think that's enough information for tonight," Gabriel said, using a commanding tone. Leaving the conversation closed for the night. The last thing he wanted was for her to feel pressured in any way, trapped. If she chose him, he wanted her to do it because that's what she wanted.

Amelia glanced up, thanking him with a smile before disappearing from the room. Cordelia and Kelsey gathered the books, restacking them and hauling them away. Damon followed his wife, and Kelsey looked back at him with a supporting smile.

Meanwhile, Emery hung back, waiting for the others to leave. He could tell that she wanted to say something but couldn't quite find the words.

"I don't like the idea of you being anywhere near this fight. Even if it is the only way we can win," Gabriel said. He noticed her need to protest, to stake her claim in this battle and prove her worth. "But your mother trained you well. You're a formidable warrior."

Emery's mouth hung halfway open, ready to protest and argue her need to be there on the battlefield beside her parents, but apparently, she didn't have to. Instead, she smiled shyly, unsure of what to say. "Thank you."

Gabriel sighed profoundly, spreading his fingers through his unruly raven hair. "What do you think of all this?"

Emery looked towards the direction her mother had left. Amelia had all but fled from the room, and that left her somewhat disappointed. "I just want mom to be happy. She deserves it. She deserves to be loved."

Gabriel grunted in agreement. That was all he desired as well. He just hoped Amelia's happiness left room for him.

Looking down at his daughter, a wave of regret engulfed him. "I'm sorry for the way we met. I was an ass, and you didn't deserve that."

"It's okay—"

"No, it's not. I should have known right away that you were my daughter. I've been known in the past to be blind," Gabriel groaned, rolling his eyes.

"So, I've heard," Emery chuckled.

"Anyways, my point is. I'm glad we met. I don't like the way it happened, but I'm proud to have you as my daughter."

"Honestly, I understand why you reacted the way you did. You had no clue I even existed. Why would you think I was yours?"

"Even still, I'm sorry."

Emery smiled, nudging him in the side. She didn't expect such a softie to lie beneath the hard exterior of the Alpha of the Twilight Pack. "I appreciate that."

Gabriel returned the smile, massaging the back of his neck as a strange awkwardness grew between them.

"I'm gonna go find Mom," Emery said, bobbing her head in the direction of the front door.

"Yeah, good idea," Gabriel breathed a sigh of relief. Grateful to her for shattering the budding silence.

In all seriousness, Emery relaxed her hand on his arm, giving him a light squeeze. "It'll all work out. You'll see."

CHAPTER 33

FACE YOUR FEARS

E mery made her way out the front door, finding her
mother sitting on the front porch steps, cradling
a mug between her hands. Scenting the air, she
couldn't detect the fruity aroma of herbal tea or the bitter
tang of coffee.

Instead, it was sweet molasses.

Grinning at her mother, she snuck up behind her,
snatching the cup from her hands and taking a quick sip
before handing it back.

Amelia smacked her arm in response as Emery sat
down beside her.

The wood porch creaked beneath their movements as
they both made themselves comfortable.

Taking a long sip from her cup, Amelia allowed the
liquor to burn down the back of her throat before exhaling.
Her breath released a frosty pale smoke against the cool
night air. The alcohol was working its magic through
her system, numbing her to the cold and the conflicting
emotions fighting within.

Emery rubbed her hands against her arms roughly, trying to force blood to the surface of her skin to keep her warm. Looking out over the front yard, she experienced an odd sense of calm wash over her.

"I can see this place being home."

Amelia looked to her daughter, caught off guard by her words. Suddenly, the cold was creeping through her veins. "Really?"

Emery bobbed her head slowly, taking in the pack grounds and the home behind her. Never had she felt so comfortable and safe. "Yeah, I think so."

Amelia took another swig from her mug, consuming its contents, before setting it down on the deck. "What do you want to do after this?"

Emery frowned, confused. "What do you mean?"

"I mean, what do you want to do, Emery? Say we win this battle. What do you want to do next? Do you want to stay here?" Amelia asked. Her heart constricted in her chest.

Emery's eyebrows elevated in speculation, suddenly unsure of herself. "Do I even have that option?"

Amelia rubbed her daughter's back, spreading her fingers down her spine like the way she used to when she was an infant, trying to lull her to sleep in her crib. "Of course, you do, baby. You're old enough now to make these decisions. We've run long enough. If we defeat Michael, there's no need for that anymore."

"Right," Emery said absently, almost as though winning wasn't something she had considered. "I hadn't thought of that."

"It's time to start thinking, my love. You have your whole life ahead of you once we're done with all this

Michael business. This is your pack. Your father's pack and it'll be yours one day." Amelia ran her hand through her daughter's brilliant silver-gray hair. The strands were like silk through her fingers. "So, what do you want?"

Emery took in a deep breath, wringing her hands together, leaning against her knees. "I just want you to be happy, Momma."

"Emery," Amelia groaned.

"No. You talked. Now it's my turn," Emery said, shaking off her mother's hand on her back. She turned side-faced, facing her mother head-on, and held her gaze with her own. "From the moment we stepped foot on this territory, it's like you've been waking up from a deep sleep. A woman I never knew has been buried deep beneath the layers of self-doubt, motherhood, and past trauma and I've come to realize you've been a walking shell of yourself my entire life."

"Emmie," Amelia sighed. A stinging sensation pricked at her eyes as her throat constricted, barely allowing her to take in a single breath.

"You've been missing your other half. The other half of your soul," Emery said, wetness glistening in her lustrous eyes. "Every single person here can see the connection between the two of you. You're electric. Every time he walks into a room, I see you. I see the way your body moves to face him. The way you subconsciously seek him in a crowd. It's the same way for him. So, why deny yourself? What is holding you back?"

"It's complicated, Em—"

"No, it's not. You make it complicated in your head. It could be simple if you just allow it," Emery stood up suddenly from the porch steps and left her mother alone outside, leaving her without looking back.

Amelia was left flabbergasted. Emery wasn't one to just leave like that. The situation was getting to her daughter more than she let on, which left her full of guilt. Emery was right. She needed to own up to her feelings and woman up.

Pushing off the deck, she stood up. Her boots crunched against the gravel drive as she forged her way towards the tree line, leaving the shelter of the lighted house and disappearing into the deep shadows.

Fear crept down her spine. She had avoided darkness at all costs since her kidnapping, felt suffocated by it as panic strangled her. Leaving her breathless and desperate for air.

This time she knocked it back to the recesses of her mind and focused on her breathing. Taking deep, steadying breaths, she pushed past her fear and anxiety and allowed her feet to support her soundlessly through the woods.

The further she moved away from the Packhouse, the darker her surroundings became. The shadows moved around her. Taking on shapes that seemed to follow her through the brush. Amelia tried to reject them, directing her eyes straight in front of her, but she couldn't ignore the feeling she was being followed.

Looking to the side, the shadows seemed to be taking shape, molding into something substantial and life-like. She squinted at the growing forms of gray and charcoal against the blanket of night, unsure of what she was witnessing.

That is until she heard the growls.

The shapes moved through the woods on all sides of her without a sound. Their paws advanced them forward on the forest floor, and yet the ground didn't stir. The leaves never crunch under the pressure of their weight.

It wasn't until a light grey wolf edged towards her that she recognized what they were. It would have brushed against her leg, except for all she felt was a faint whisper of wind against her skin. The light gray wolf looked up, making eye contact with the same shade of sea-green eyes.

Amelia took in a shallow breath. Her heart froze in her chest. She'd never understand how she knew, but she was certain the wolf beside her was her mother. Reaching out with her hand, she extended her finger along the spine of the wolf. If she concentrated intently enough, she could almost feel the soft fur that should be there and the warmth radiating from her body.

Wolves of all sizes and colors closed in around her. There were dozens of them, moving silently through the woods at her side, trailing behind her, and leading in front. Every single one of them were women, and each of them radiated power, blanketing the air around them in a purple haze.

The air was charged, like ozone stirring the atmosphere before a lightning storm.

At that moment, she felt out of body, as though she was floating above the ground. She knew she was walking, but she couldn't feel the connection between her brain and feet. As if her body was moving of its own volition, and she was merely an observer.

Out of the darkness, a woman appeared just ahead of her, shrouded in a pearly light of the full, pregnant moon above.

She stood waiting.

Amelia glanced around as she noticed the wolves disappearing, blending back in with the shadows of the forest. Her mother beside her hesitated but eventually turned away with a nod of her head, encouraging her to continue.

The woman was like a beacon of hope in the darkness. Her hair was as colorless as the moon, and she wore a shimmering silver dress draped against her pale skin. The air surrounding her was radiant and humming with a power that Amelia felt drawn to, connected to.

Stepping up beside the woman, Amelia stopped.

Facing forward, afraid to meet the woman directly, she directed her gaze straight into the surrounding darkness. She restrained her tongue, afraid to say something offensive or improper. After all these years, the millions of horrific, offensive things she had imagined flinging at the Goddess completely escaped her and silence ensued.

"Don't keep quiet on my behalf."

Amelia couldn't help but turn towards the woman, inclining her head to the side. It was as if she had read her mind.

"I can't read your mind, but I know you, Amelia. I imagine you have a few choice words for me after all these years. You've never held back before. Why start now?" the Moon Goddess asked curiously.

"I never thought I'd be face to face with you. You seemed to enjoy tormenting my dreams. Disappearing after offering me some half-assed prediction," Amelia said tautly, trying to keep from sounding bitter or annoyed, which she was failing miserably at.

The Goddess chuckled, amused. "There's some of your fire. I was wondering if it had been extinguished."

Amelia snapped her mouth shut, turning back towards the darkness. She didn't want the mother of them all to see how much that statement hurt her.

"Why do you deny the gifts I've given you?"

Amelia jerked her head back towards the deity beside her, frowning. "What are you talking about? I've embraced my powers just as you told me to. I've done everything you've asked."

"And your mate? What about him?"

"What do you mean?"

"Your mate is the other half of your soul. An extension of yourself. One cannot be whole without the other and will continue to suffer until reunited."

If Amelia were her wolf, she was sure her fur would be bristling. Rey, the most loyal of the two of them, was even snarling in the back of her mind. "May I remind you that it's because of you I left my mate behind," she growled.

"Yes, and where would you have been had you not left? Dead? Your daughter certainly would have been," the Goddess said matter-of-factly.

"Exactly! So, why punish me for it?" Amelia nearly yelled as she tried to reign in her emotions.

"You punish yourself, sister."

Amelia frowned at the Goddesses words. Her eyebrows scrunched together in confusion. But before she could ask what she meant—she was cut off.

"I never said to leave him forever, and now that you're back, you deny yourself. Why?" the Moon Goddess asked. Her charcoal eyes, the exact color of the craters adorning the surface of the moon, inspected her face for answers.

Amelia couldn't help but look away. The woman's stare was too honest to bear.

"What if he finds me disgusting? I'm tainted. Deformed," she heard herself almost whisper. Repeating the words that ran through her head on a constant loop, constantly telling her she was damaged. She couldn't help her insecurities.

The Goddess sighed profoundly. A deep, sad release of breath frosted the air. "You have endured more trials and pain than anyone should have had to, but you did so with strength, and it has only made you stronger. You have been broken for too long."

The Goddesses' words cut deep, hurting Amelia, but even she could appreciate the truth. She had let her trauma govern her life.

"But you don't have to live that way anymore," the Goddess said, cutting through her thoughts. "Did you know that your mate prayed to me every night that you've been away? Begging me for you to return."

Amelia swayed her head silently. Her eyes were wide with surprise. Even after the years apart and the betrayals endured on both ends, he still wanted her.

"Do not deny yourself any further. I do not wish to see another one of my sisters and daughters murdered. Break the cycle and confront your fears. There is a dawn after twilight. The sun always rises, casting the shadows away. Let love heal you."

The Moon Goddess was already fading away before her very eyes. The light was receding with her, shrouding her in darkness once again and leaving her alone to her thoughts.

A steady calm took over her as she replayed the deity's words over and over in her head.

Break the cycle. Let love heal you. She repeated to herself.

A force beyond her ken pulled at her heart, calling to her soul, urging her forward. Amelia looked off into the distance where her body cried, demanding for her to go.

A song played through her veins, dancing in her blood, tuning her heart to match its rhythm.

Go. Rey urged her.

No more hesitation. No more doubts or insecurities or letting fear govern her. She pushed off with her feet, digging into the soft earth as they propelled her forward. She ran as hard as she could.

Towards her fate.

CHAPTER 34

MINE

*A*re we doing the right thing? Amelia questioned, her heart hammering in her chest.

The Packhouse was nearly in sight.

Yes. Don't second guess this. It's what we need, what we want. Rey urged her on with not an ounce of doubt in her voice.

Amelia pounded up the porch steps. Her boots thudded against the wood planks, making them creak in protest as she threw open the front door, flinging it shut behind her. Her eyes searched around the room frantically.

She ignored the wiggling eyebrows of her brother and sister-in-law, who were sitting on the couch, journals in hand. Emery sat across from them, hiding her blushing face behind the faded pages of a book. Kelsey sat beside her and, with sad eyes, smiled and bobbed her head.

Amelia nodded in response. Silently thanking her before turning towards the stairs and following the scent of her mate.

The smell of home.

Sprinting up the steps, the taste of apples watered her mouth, leading her to his bedroom—their bedroom. Before her thoughts could cloud her decision-making, she forced the door open and secured it behind her.

Upon first glance the room was empty. Her heart bottomed out as disappointment crept through her system. Her head drooped as she turned for the door, ready to leave when footsteps gripped her attention.

Gabriel stepped out of the bathroom, steam enveloping him in a pale mist. The only thing concealing him was a thin cotton towel around his waist. Drops of water glistened against his chest and arms. His hair was dripping on his shoulders, like the only thing he'd done to it was run a towel through.

Amelia swallowed with difficulty at the sight of him. The lower part of her belly cramped tightly with desire. Having him so close and half-naked left her nearly speechless.

Gabriel arched a brow. Looking behind her as though there was a fire. Some kind of emergency to warrant her panicked presence. "What's wrong? Are you okay?"

Disregarding him, Amelia took a step closer. Her hands were shaking, so she clasped them behind her back. A part of her was eager to reach out and stroke him. Make sure he was real, that she was really doing this. Whereas the other part of her, the part that had assured her she was damaged and not good enough for him, advised her to flee. But she forced that small, wicked voice to the back of her mind.

She wanted this. Wanted him and always would.

"I'm not going to apologize for leaving because I'm not," Amelia said firmly, taking slow, deliberate steps in his direction. "I lost one baby, and I was not going to lose another. If I had stayed, you would have been killed. Our pack would have been wiped out."

Gabriel inclined his head steadily, taking in each word she said. "I know."

"These last seventeen years weren't easy for me. I killed countless wolves to keep our daughter safe."

"You did what you had to."

"I was hurt," she whispered. "Badly, and I don't know if those scars will ever heal."

Amelia hadn't realized she'd diminished the distance between them until his hands reached out, snaking around her waist, drawing her against him. She could feel the rise and fall of his chest with each breath. Her blood felt like gasoline being lit on fire, growing into a raging inferno that begged to grow brighter.

"We'll face the darkness together," Gabriel said. His voice grew deeper and huskier by the second.

"I never touched another man. My body has always belonged to you."

"And my heart has always been yours."

"And mine yours."

Amelia barely got the words out before his lips came crashing down. Her arms reached up, wrapping around his neck, pressing him firmly against her. Her mouth opened automatically, allowing him to taste her as their tongues snaked around one another. She would never get enough of him. Not for as long as she'd live.

Gabriel's hands gripped her waist, her hips, her ass. Roaming up and down her back, her sides tangling in her hair. His lips traveled away from her mouth, leaving her breathless, gasping for air as he moved down her jawline, sucking on her neck and across her collarbone.

Amelia moaned. Her breathing came out ragged and rough. Her skin felt electric wherever he touched. Her nose was filled with his scent, his musk. He ground his pelvis against her, pressing his erection into her lower stomach, leaving her clenching, and soaked.

Gabriel's fingers played with the hem of her tank before cleaving it straight down the front of her. The thin cotton fell to the floor in tatters, leaving her in only her sports bra and shorts. His lips made his way across her cleavage that spilled out of the top of her bra.

Tilting her head back, she provided him better access. His tongue flicked out, tasting the saltiness of her skin, drawing patterns against her sensitive flesh. She heard fabric rip before the frosty air of the room stung her skin, making her nipples swell. She bit back a hiss when his eager mouth wrapped around the tip of her breast. The contrast between cold and hot was startling and highly erotic.

Gabriel swirled his tongue against her flesh, softly nipping, rolling her nipple between his teeth. Amelia moaned at the friction, grinding herself against him wantonly. His fingers plunged beneath the waistband of her shorts, hauling them down along with her panties in one fell swoop.

He stood up, withdrawing a few steps back. Amelia suddenly felt exposed and grew cold. His silver eyes grew dilated as he stood there, taking in every inch of her. Subconsciously, her hands moved to conceal herself, feeling timid and insecure, but stopped when a deep, threatening growl emitted from his chest.

"Don't do that," Gabriel warned, his voice deep and commanding. "You're perfect, and nothing could ever change that."

Amelia felt herself relax. His words loosened the tension in her body as her arms moved away allowing him to take his fill.

Gabriel reached around the front of him, loosening the towel and allowed it to drop, circling his feet. His erection sprung out, standing at attention. She noted a drip of cum seeping from the tip, begging to be licked, craving attention.

Memory did not do him justice.

Nerves fluttered in her stomach. She wanted to reach out and wrap her mouth around that silky, thick cock. Mount the hunk of man before her and ride him until she split in half, but what if she couldn't?

Gabriel must have sensed her anxiety and reduced the distance between them faster than she could follow. Gripping her in his arms, he set her head against his chest and placed a gentle kiss against her brow.

"Don't be nervous, my love. We'll take this as slow as you need. Or we don't have to do anything at all. It's completely up to you," he said against her hair, rubbing soothing circles against the base of her neck.

Amelia tilted her head up. "No. I want this. I want you."

A faint smile tugged at his lips before he leaned in, placing a tender kiss on her mouth. Amelia kissed him back. This kiss was distinct from the last. It was gentler and less desperate, slow, and deliberate. His touch, his taste soothed her frazzled nerves.

His hands reached behind her thighs, lifting her off the ground. She bound her legs around his waist automatically, instantly feeling the head of him against her core. Fresh excitement ripped through her, erasing any doubt she may have had. They were made for one another, fitting together perfectly. They always had and always will.

Gabriel sat back on the bed, enabling her to straddle his waist. In their current position, she had all the control. Whether she took him in was entirely up to her. The pace and tempo would be at her discretion. He was offering her absolute control.

The tip of his cock was lined up perfectly with her entrance. She was already dripping wet for him, but she stayed poised, hovering above. Gabriel's mouth was slightly perched open, waiting for her next move.

Amelia looked down into his silver orbs. He looked at her with so much love and desire she thought her heart might explode. She extended her fingers through his still-damp hair, savoring the feel and texture. The stubble along his chin and jawline was soft and dark, just like that of his wolf. Age had been gracious to him, making him even more handsome if that was even possible.

"I love you, Amelia," Gabriel said, breaking her out of her head.

His words sent a shock through her body and straight to her heart, jump-starting her for the first time in seventeen years. A genuine smile crept on her face as her eyes burned alive.

"I love you."

Amelia sank down on his length. Her body stretched to accommodate his girth as she took in all of him. Gabriel twisted his head back, his eyes fastened, groaning at the sensation.

She breathed in deeply, pushing back the slight panic that was beginning to bubble inside. Her eyes closed as her mind dragged her back to that wretched hole—her torture chamber.

"Snow."

Her eyes snapped open at the sound of his voice. She could tell he could see the panic etched on her face. She hadn't realized she froze halfway down his shaft—her body tense and rigid.

Gabriel raised his hand slowly, revealing with an open palm he meant no harm. He brushed the tips of his fingers down her neck, rubbing his thumb along her jaw. Amelia could feel her panic subside at the touch, grounding her to the present, to him.

"Look at me, Snow. You're here with me," Gabriel assured her. His voice soothing and patient.

Amelia bobbed her head, leaning into his touch. Keeping her eyes locked on his, she felt her body finally relax, allowing him to sink in until she bottomed out. She had never felt so full, so complete.

"That's my girl," Gabriel moaned, encouraging her.

Amelia lifted her hips, putting more weight on her knees as she pushed up, only to sink back down slowly. His hand tightened around the back of her neck, digging his fingers into her flesh. She moved up and down the length of him a few more times as her body adjusted to the size and feel of him beneath her, all the while he kept his gaze solely on her. Not once did he stray or take pleasure in her. Directing his focus solely on her, holding her to this place and time.

As the panic receded, Amelia began to feel something else. Something she hadn't felt in so long that she was frightened it was only a dream. Desire and pleasure started to burn in her core as the head of his cock stroked her sweet spot. As the last bit of tension escaped her body, she rolled her head back, moaning loudly as she ground her pelvis against his.

Gabriel bit back a groan as he witnessed her take pleasure in their bodies joined together—at last.

Amelia felt as though a fever was taking control. Leaving her hotter and hotter, needing more and more. She raised her hips higher and faster, picking up the pace. This time Gabriel let out a moan, unable to hold back any longer. She smirked, taking pleasure in the fact that he was capable of losing himself in her. This made her move even swifter, bottoming out on him harder.

Unable to help himself, Gabriel thrust his hips in response.

"Fuck," Amelia moaned. Sweat dripped down her back between her shoulder blades as the air around them became heated, electrically charged.

"You feel so amazing, Snow. Fuck, I missed you," Gabriel panted before pulling her down. He needed to taste her, devour her.

Amelia rode him harder with more enthusiasm. Her hands gripped the back of his neck, threading through his hair, tugging sharply at the roots. His tongue pushed into her mouth, tasting her, savoring her.

"I need more, Gabe. I need you," Amelia groaned into his mouth.

"Are you sure?" Gabriel asked, pulling back to get a proper look at her, but her face related everything he needed to know. She was ready.

"Yes," she breathed. "Fuck me, and don't be gentle."

Gabriel hoisted her off his lap and twisted them around. He directed her over the bed, lifting her ass in the air until her knees were perched on the bed. Amelia looked over her shoulder, gazing at him through hooded eyes. He ran his hand down the length of her spine, caressing her knotted scars. Each of them was beautiful and a testament of her strength.

She shivered beneath his touch, fully aware of the scars on her back, but his touch declared everything. He found her beautiful, desirable. She had never felt more loved or cared for in her life. His hands gripped her waist before plunging his cock between her folds, burying himself as deep as possible.

Amelia nearly yelled, moaning as the tip of him throbbed against the entrance of her womb. Without waiting for her to adjust, he pulled out and forced himself back in, harder and faster. Her breasts bounced against the bed as he took his pleasure, expanding her only to pull out and repeat all over again.

He gripped her ass, her hips, her waist. Dominating her like never before. Desperate and filled with a longing the both of them couldn't explain.

She was nearing her release. The pressure increased between her legs as the friction continued to grow. She matched each of his thrusts, slamming her pelvis back against his. Looking for the desired friction she required each time, his balls slapped against her sensitive bundle of nerves.

Gabriel pulled out, leaving her suddenly empty as her orgasm began to fade rapidly. She looked back over her shoulder, ready to scold him when he flipped her over, laying her on her back against the soft mattress.

Amelia lifted herself on her elbows, her eyebrow arched. "What are you—"

"When we cum, we do it together. Not fucking you from behind like an animal. But instead, making love to the woman of my dreams."

Her eyes widened as she examined his face, looking for any hint of sarcasm. But there was none. He gradually moved on top of her as her knees parted, allowing him in. He lined himself up with her entrance before pushing back inside.

Amelia's back arched at the sensation, pressing her chest against his. Gabriel laced his fingers with hers, pinning her hands above her head as he steadily moved inside her. He sat up, gazing down at her, his eyes locking with hers. She fastened her sea-green eyes onto his silver ones, their bodies synced, moving fluidly with one another.

The pressure was already building quickly. She was so close she could taste it, and judging by the bulging vein in his neck, he was close as well.

"Gabe," Amelia called to him, begging him to let her cum.

"Snow," Gabriel called back, thrusting harder.

Amelia slipped her hands from his grasp, winding her arms around his neck, and lured him down until their bodies were flushed. He braced his body, his hands on both sides of her head as she kissed him, desperate to consume all of him.

His cock throbbed against her walls as she tightened around him, demanding her release. His movements became sloppier, more rapid. Stars exploded behind her eyes as her canines elongated.

Breaking from his lips, she shifted his head and plunged her teeth into his faded mark.

Gabriel spasmed above her. She bit more firmly into his skin as he orgasmed, spilling his seed within her. Her pleasure shot straight up her spine, leaving her mind clouded and disoriented, forcing her to bite harder into his flesh.

With each second that passed, her canines buried in the spot between his neck and shoulder, the bond between them flared to life. In the blink of an eye, every emotion, thought, and memory passed from him to her. Betrayal, longing, desire, and love engulfed her. It was overwhelming. She pushed against his chest, trying to retract her teeth when she experienced a searing pain in her neck.

A second orgasm tore through her body. This one was painful and arousing all at once. She arched her spine against his sturdy frame that restrained her to the bed. Her knee rose higher as he pushed himself in, burying himself even farther inside. His canines punctured deeper into the delicate tissue of her marking spot, permanently marking her as his for as long they lived.

Amelia freed herself from his flesh, gasping in air. Glancing down at the mark she'd left behind; she couldn't resist the pride. She gently licked up the blood that seeped from the mark, completing it with a kiss. He shivered above her in response before doing the same to hers.

She concealed her face in the crook of his neck, winding her arms around his back. His hands slid between her shoulders and the bed, gripping her firmly against him.

They laid there like that for some time. Wrapped in one another's arms, breathing each other in, basking in the bond reforged between them.

Amelia couldn't help but smile.

"Mine," Gabriel growled, vibrating against her as he caressed his mark with his lips. Lightly pecking and drawing circles against her skin with his tongue.

"Mine," Amelia confirmed, twisting him over onto his back and starting the dance all over again.

CHAPTER 35

WHERE YOU BELONG

The morning light illuminated the room. She could see the orange glow of sunlight from behind closed lids. Reminding her the day had already begun.

Amelia gradually opened her eyes, blinking away the sleep crusted in the corners. Slowly taking in the space around her, she recognized Gabriel's bedroom. Glancing down at her body, she found a thin satin sheet concealing her nude body.

Never again did she think she'd ever feel so liberated, so free. She felt as though her heart had broken free of chains that had been weighing her down since she'd left the pack. The weight of the world was released from her shoulders, liberated from years of self-doubt and sabotage. Gabriel's touch was enough to send her world spinning off its axis in all the best ways.

Amelia was sore between the legs. The mark on her neck stung. She brushed her fingertips against the fresh scar, tender to the touch. Even the feather-soft pressure against the newly made mark was enough to deliver a jolt straight to her core, drenching her in seconds.

The bed beside her stirred in response.

Amelia glanced to her side to discover Gabriel sleeping deeply beside her. He breathed the air in deeply, shifting the sheets. Even in his sleep, Gabriel responded to her arousal.

Propping herself on her elbow, she rolled over onto her side and gazed down at him. His hair was an unruly mess splayed across the pillow, laying across his face. The sheet covered him from the waist down, offering an unobstructed view of his perfectly sculpted v-line, rippling abs, and defined pectorals.

She wasn't sure what she had expected when she imagined sleeping with him again, but memory had not done him justice. He was a gentleman in every way, granting her everything she asked for and more. He had tried to be gentle with her on multiple occasions. Giving her numerous outs, but her need overrode his, forcing him to dominate her as she needed.

Amelia reached out with a hand, gently adjusting the hair from his eyes and face. She spread her finger through his onyx locks, down his sideburns, and scratched against his stubbled jaw.

Gabriel began to stir beneath her touch. Subconsciously leaning into her hand and breathing her in deeply. She smirked, unable to help the giddy flips her stomach was doing.

She leaned further into him, her elbow dipping deeper into the bed, and caressed her lips against his. Starting at the corner of his mouth, she gently kissed his nose, both of his eyes, along his brow, and across his jaw. Before she could make it back to his lips, arms of steel wrapped around her waist, hoisting her off the bed, only to straddle his naked body.

His morning wood was firmly erect between her thighs. Exerting a firm pressure to her already wet folds.

Gabriel gradually exposed his eyes. A playful smirk pursed his lips. His hands gripped tightly on her hips, preventing her from being able to escape even though that was the furthest thing from her mind.

Amelia rotated her hips, grinding her pelvis against his hardened member. Indicating just how much she wanted him buried deep inside. A deep growl resonated from his chest, causing a flurry of goosebumps to race up her arms and down her neck.

"Good morning," Gabriel groaned, his voice husky and deep.

She twisted her long hair to the side, flicking her fingers down the silhouette of her breasts as she did. Her nipples were perky against the crisp cold air of the bedroom.

"Someone's greedy," Gabriel noted, thrusting his hips up, forcing his cock to push through her sensitive lips, and plunging deep into her sex.

Amelia rotated her head back at the feeling. He expanded her to the point of no return. If she wasn't feverish already, she sure was now. Bouncing up and down, she rode him hard. Her breasts matched her movements, slapping against her ribs. Gabriel reached up, taking both of her mounds in his hands, pinching the tip, causing her to hiss.

"Gabe," Amelia moaned. The pressure was already beginning to build between her legs.

"Cum for me, Snow."

Clasping hands, Amelia and Gabriel entered the dining hall together.

Whispers floated around them, wafting in the air. Their marks were distinct and visible for all to see. Not to mention their scent was all over one another. In a room crammed with werewolves, they might as well hold up a neon sign.

Amelia couldn't resist the smile that spread across her face. She concealed her face in his arm, squeezing his hand tightly. A small chuckle vibrated through his chest, kissing her softly on the top of her head.

The warriors present eating before training, began hooting and hollering at their Alpha and Luna. Congratulating them on their reunion.

Amelia spotted her daughter, brother, and sister-in-law, waiting for them at a table along the back wall. They headed directly for them. As soon as she got close enough, Emery ran straight for her, flinging her arms around her narrow frame.

Letting her hand slip from Gabriel's, Amelia winded her arms tightly around her daughter. Burrowing her face in her neck, she breathed in her scent—roses and vanilla. The familiar scent instantly soothed her nerves that left her feeling frazzled and off balanced.

Emery pulled back. Looking up into her sea-green eyes, she tilted her head to the side. "Are you happy?"

Amelia smiled, and for the first time in a long while, it felt genuine. She stepped back into Gabriel's awaiting arms, tucking herself against his side. "Very."

Emery smirked at both of her parents. She was witnessing something every kid dreamed of—her parents back together at last.

"Good." Without warning, she threw her arms around Gabriel's neck, relishing in the familial bond between them, solidifying their tie to one another. "Welcome to the family, Dad," she whispered against his neck.

Amelia's eyebrow rose as her heart fluttered wildly in her chest. She watched her mate closely as it gradually dawned on him that their daughter had called him dad for the first time. A broad grin grew on his face as he held her tighter.

If her heart wasn't inside her chest, she was sure it would be bleeding all over the wood floorboards. This was all she ever wanted. All she dreamed of. To have her family whole and complete. To feel at peace and loved once again, not just for herself but for her daughter as well.

Gabriel pulled back from Emery, only to gather her in beside him, putting him between his two women. Amelia looked up. Her eyebrow arched in curiosity. He was up to something. She could tell by the nerves wracking her system that weren't hers.

Stupid mate bond.

"If I can have everyone's attention," Gabriel called out. His Alpha voice rang clear throughout the room, vibrating the house, ensuring he had all eyes on him. "Tonight, we will be conducting a very special ceremony. One that's been long overdue."

Amelia's heart nearly beat out of her chest. Her breath caught in her throat as he glanced down at her with nothing short of adoration and love.

"Amelia's Luna ceremony will be tonight at sunset. It's past time she was a part of this pack," he announced to all present before looking down into her eyes. "I'm done waiting. This is where you belong, Snow." Gabriel smiled, tucking a loose strand of hair behind her ear.

Amelia fought back the tears that began to overcome her but unfortunately wasn't quick enough as one escaped her control. Gabriel was quick to snatch it, wiping it away with the pad of his thumb before anyone noticed. He gently kissed her cheek. His lips brushed against her flushed skin, awakening a flurry of butterflies in her stomach. He smiled at her brightly before turning back to the warriors.

"We won't just be adding one wolf to our pack, but two. Emery, our daughter, will take her rightful place in her pack." He turned towards his daughter. "You may not have been born here, but this is your home. Your pack."

Every warrior, man, woman, and child, cheered loudly, beating their fists against the table, their chests.

Amelia looked around his broad frame to determine Emery's reaction and couldn't help the tears gathered at what she saw. Emery was in shock and awe. It meant the world to her daughter to belong to a pack. Having moved around so much her entire life, she never understood a pack connection or being able to link. Now she would finally have that chance.

"Training in thirty minutes. That is all." Gabriel dismissed them.

The pack members that were present instantly began talking loudly amongst themselves—chattering excitedly about the after-party that was sure to follow the Luna ceremony.

"We don't have to do this tonight. We can wait—" Amelia started to protest.

"No. I told you, I'm done waiting. We've waited long enough." Gabriel turned towards her, giving her his full attention. "I'm not going into this battle without being able to mind-link both you and Emery. Besides, you both need to be connected to the rest of the pack as well if we want to walk away from this."

Amelia wanted to oppose him, wanted to tell him that it could wait, but he was right. Being linked to the pack during as large of a battle as they were expecting would give everyone peace of mind. She'd be able to call out movements, commands, and directions to the warriors and pack.

Her stomach growled loudly, reminding her earnestly that she still lacked nutrition. She was prepared to join the growing line, filling their plates with delicious breakfast goodies, when a young teen approached her. The girl's eyes were cast down to the wood floor, hands filled with brimming plates of food.

"Alpha, Luna," she said gently. Voice meek and fearful.

"Let me help you." Amelia seized the plates, keeping the food from spilling, toppling to the ground. She quickly set them down on the table beside her before placing her hand beneath the girl's chin, tilting her face up to meet her. "Look at me when you speak. You have nothing to be afraid of."

"Yes, Luna," the girl said, her baby blue eyes too intimidated to hold her gaze.

"What's your name?" Amelia asked, completely aware that most eyes surrounding them were watching intently. Mainly the big bad Alpha beside her.

"Michaela."

"Thank you, Michaela. The food looks amazing. Please convey our thanks to the kitchen staff." Amelia smiled, keeping her voice soft and pleasant.

Michaela finally met her stare. Eyes wide and baffled, as though a compliment from her was beyond her understanding. Amelia was puzzled by the reaction, making her want to get to know the girl more.

Em, Amelia linked.

Emery stepped forward, winding her arm around the teen's shoulders. They looked to be the same age, and Goddess knows her kid had lacked in the friend department. It was past time they set down some roots.

"I love your hair," Emery commented on the girls' onyx black, curly hair as she directed them towards the great room. "I've been thinking of chopping mine off. Is there a hairstylist in the pack?"

Amelia could hear her daughter as she pulled the teen away from the group. She'd have to have a chat with Emery about her hair at a later time. No way was she letting her whack off her gorgeous locks.

Amelia was pulled from her thoughts by a slight pressure against the small of her back, making her glance up into a pair of warm, silver iris. He gestured for her to take a seat at the table where her brother and sister-in-law were waiting. She could tell by the shit-eating grin on her twin's face he was bursting at the seams to make some dirty comment.

Amelia averted his twinkling sea-green eyes as she accepted her seat. Her stomach churned, cramping her side as she inhaled the delicious aroma wafting from the plate in front of her. Pancakes, sausage, bacon, and biscuits were piled high on her plate—all of her favorites in one go.

She wasn't thrilled at the fact that she had been served. She could easily have prepared her own plate and been perfectly content, but she was starving, and waiting a moment longer seemed too long.

Not bothering to wait for Gabriel to eat first, Amelia tore into her food. The bacon was maple-flavored and perfectly cooked, earning a groan of approval as the fat melted in her mouth.

"Would you like to be alone?"

Amelia opened her eyes. Her brother's annoyingly cool tone pulled her from her food ecstasy. She glared at him harshly, gripping her fork tightly in her hand.

"I'm starving," she answered plainly.

"Oh, I bet. All those late-night activities cost you some calories that you couldn't afford to lose. Looking mighty skinny there, Sis." Damon smirked from the other side of the table.

Gabriel reached behind her, winding his arm around her shoulders, offering her a light squeeze, helping to calm her flash of anger she felt burning through her veins.

"She's got a lot more meat than you'd expect," Gabriel said, his voice deep with underlying meaning. "In all the right places."

His breath tickled her skin as he leaned into her, brushing his lips against the mark on her flesh. Gooseflesh quickly spread across her entire body as tingling shivers raced down her spine. Her stomach began to burn with desire as heat flushed her cheeks and across her chest.

Amelia leaned into him, desperate to bear the full pressure of his lips against her warm skin. She was no longer eager for the food left untouched on the table. A different kind of hunger was taking over, and if they weren't careful, they might end up on full display in the dining hall.

Damon gagged loudly, dramatizing the act of throwing up. "That's just gross. Please, stop. I'm begging you."

Amelia peeled herself away from her mate before she really did make a scene and giggled. "You asked for it."

"I did no such thing," Damon scoffed. Directing his eyes away from the newly mated pair and returned to the food in front of him.

Even though the food before her wouldn't satisfy the type of cravings she was having, she knew she'd need the energy for the day's training and tonight's ceremony. She picked her fork back up and resumed her meal.

The four of them sat in comfortable silence as each of them consumed their food. Cordelia kept peeking out from behind her lashes at the mated pair, smiling all the while. She could feel her friend's happiness, and it was infectious. She had never felt so whole, so complete and she never wanted to go back to being the damaged, lone wolf. She was home.

With a sausage link raised to her mouth, Amelia detected the atmosphere in the room instantly change. She set her fork down, back on her plate as her stomach immediately soured.

Kelsey entered the room, walking directly for their table.

Amelia sat up straighter in her chair. Kelsey was still his wife. She had a legal claim on the man beside her. Rey, the animal side of her, wanted to rip her throat out, showing all, he was hers. Only her claim mattered when it came to their mate, but the human side felt guilty and had doubts.

Relax, Snow. It'll be okay. No matter what, we're in this together.

Gabriel's soothing voice rang through her mind, almost instantly soothing her nerves and quieting her wolf. Rey settled, growling with displeasure but no longer forcing her hostility to the forefront of her emotions.

Kelsey stopped just in front of the table with a sad smile on her lips. She pulled out a manilla folder from behind her back and placed it on the wood surface before Gabriel.

Gabriel frowned at the envelope before unsealing it and pulled out a small, neat stack of papers bound together by a single paperclip. He read over the first few pages. His eyebrow arched higher and higher in confusion as he read on.

Amelia peeked over his shoulder, curious as to what he was examining. The words in large print at the top of the first page left her feeling conflicted. Her heart was elated while her stomach was twisting in knots as she read, *Dissolution of Marriage.*

Gabriel looked up at Kelsey, his brows furrowed. "What is this?"

"It's exactly what it looks like. Divorce papers," Kelsey spoke softly, her hands gathered in front of her.

"Why now?" Gabriel asked, leaning back in his chair, the papers still in hand.

"This has been a long time coming, and we both know it. We were never meant to be Gabriel, and with Amelia back," she trailed off, producing a small smile. "This is what's right."

Amelia observed Gabriel closely as he flipped through the small pile of papers. His shoulders were tense as he read through the legalities of their divorce until he reached the final page. She noted him visibly relax.

"You're not taking anything? You just want things to resort back to the way they were before the marriage?" Gabriel asked, skepticism heavy in his voice.

"Why make this messier than it needs to be? Once you sign, it'll be like it never happened." Kelsey pulled out a pen from her back pocket and handed it to him.

Gabriel gripped the pen and flipped through the pages that required his signature, signing with a quick motion of the pen, approving their divorce. Amelia couldn't believe her eyes. Couldn't believe what she was witnessing. How could it be this easy?

He clicked the pen closed before delivering the papers back to Kelsey, signed and ready to be finalized. "Thank you, Kelsey."

Kelsey took their divorce and pen from him before turning away without a word and left the dining hall.

Amelia couldn't alleviate the nagging feeling that was souring the breakfast in her stomach. This shouldn't be how it ended. Kelsey, whether she made the wrong choice or not, deserved more.

Pushing out of her seat, she got up from the table. Gabriel's hand shot out, grasping her wrist.

"Snow," Gabriel said, troubling his head.

Given his tone of voice and the concerned look etched on his face, he had the wrong idea about her intentions. She relaxed a calming hand on his shoulder, issuing a light squeeze.

"I'll be right back," she assured him, kissing him on his head before rushing out of the dining hall.

Amelia detected the once familiar scent of Kelsey and followed it down the hall to Gabriel's office. Stepping inside the room, she found her filing something away in one of the cabinets only to suddenly fling it shut when she realized she wasn't alone.

"Amelia," Kelsey said in a rush, clearly startled.

"Hey, Kels. Look, I feel like this is all going . . . it's so fast," Amelia started but then stopped, unsure of what she wanted to say.

Should she say sorry? Sorry for taking her mate back and for ruining whatever sliver of happiness they had together? She was lost as to what to do.

"Don't do that, Ella. You don't need to feel guilty or sorry for me. Gabriel and I knew. Deep down, we knew. We were a temporary fix to something broken so long ago that could only be fixed by one person. Now that you're back, it would be foolish of me to pretend otherwise. He is my Alpha, first and foremost. No matter what, that's what matters. Doing what's best for my pack," Kelsey informed her. "You taught me that."

"Kelsey," Amelia sighed.

Her heart was hammering in her chest. The last person to call her Ella was Christian. She hadn't heard that nickname in almost ten years. In a peculiar way, it felt good to hear, but it also made her incredibly sad.

Just another reminder of the best friend she had lost.

"I just have one question." Kelsey disturbed her troubled thoughts.

Amelia took in a deep breath, anticipating where this was going. "You can ask me anything."

They owed that to one another.

"Christian. I'd known him since we were pups. He was like a brother to me," Kelsey said, her hands fidgeting in front of her. "Did he die honorably?"

Amelia's breath caught in the back of her throat. Her chest suddenly felt like the weight of an elephant had sat down on it. The pressure was building behind her eyes as she struggled to recall her last moments with him. How hard he fought, how strong he had been for her.

"He died to save me," Amelia said candidly, swallowing back the choking feeling in her throat.

Kelsey bobbed her head sadly as tears welled in her brown eyes. "Then he died defending you. I can't imagine a nobler death. You were more than his friend, Ella. You were his Alpha."

Amelia instantly jerked her head no. "I'm not an Alpha."

"You and I both know that isn't accurate. You may not possess the title, but title or not, it's who you are and always will be. And if he was here right now, he'd tell you he didn't regret a moment of any of it. He chose you."

Amelia hadn't realized Kelsey had been moving towards her. She was too focused on trying not to cry. This wasn't where she had expected their conversation to go. She hadn't talked about Christian this much since his death. She had buried it, ignored the cracks he had left behind in her life and heart.

"Kels." Amelia's voice cracked.

"It's time to forgive him. He sacrificed himself because he knew how important you are. Emery needed you, and he gave his life to ensure your survival. Don't let his sacrifice be in vain. Let Gabriel in," Kelsey said in almost a whisper. Silent tears caressed the tender flesh of her cheeks.

"I'm trying," Amelia whimpered, her head cast down.

"Darkness doesn't last forever. Dawn always comes," Kelsey said before walking out of the office, leaving her alone.

CHAPTER 36

CATCH ME IF YOU CAN

Amelia was thoroughly confused.

Between her mother and the Moon Goddess saying almost the exact same things, she wondered how Kelsey fit into any of it. Her words too precisely matched theirs.

Amelia barely remembered getting changed for training, her mind in a fog.

Somehow, her legs transported her downstairs and out to the training yard. There, she found all the warriors already assembled and stretching for the day's exercise.

Damon could be identified in the middle of the hundreds of wolves. His skin was stretched taut over hard muscle, bouncing on the balls of his feet, rolling his shoulders back. Suddenly, Amelia forgot all about Kelsey and her weird, prophetic statement. Her mind snapped, like a rubber band, bouncing back to the problem in front of her. Their battle with Michael was days away, and they needed to be ready.

Gabriel stood off on the sidelines, working with a group of mixed wolves. He was instructing them on their fighting techniques. Just a few inches higher and a swift kick could incapacitate an opponent. Proper placement of the fingers determined if the hitter was walking away with a broken thumb. They were teaching the females how better to use their small size against a larger aggressor. Waiting for them to strike and stepping into their frame where they couldn't be hit.

Amelia was impressed with his knowledge and skill and couldn't help the ripples that traveled down her body, sending pleasurable tingles across her skin. His head perked up. His nostrils flared as he caught her sweet scent of roses and honey. She captured his eye, smirking devilishly before she turned for her brother.

He was her intended target.

Damon was trading blows with two Twilight Moon wolves. The sound of flesh meeting flesh sent her blood coursing through her veins. Her nose picked up the metallic, rich scent of blood as the ring of cartilage snapping could be heard. One of her brother's opponents was clutching his face, trying to stem the bleeding.

"Clean hit," Amelia noted.

Damon swung around on her, his eyes wide with surprise. She couldn't resist a smirk, loving the fact that she was still able to catch him off guard. The Twilight Moon wolves he was training with backed away from them as Amelia flicked her head. Her brother arched a brow. His sea-green eyes twinkled in the morning sun. He ran his fingers through his hair, pushing the silver strands from his eyes as he sized her up, recognizing precisely what she was up to.

"I don't think you're ready for this," Damon teased.

Amelia chuckled, stretching her arm across her chest, loosening her muscles. She rolled her shoulders back, twisting her neck back and forth until she was satisfied. The smell of vanilla and roses wafted in the air. She caught sight of Emery moving among the gathering crowd, making her way towards her father.

It seemed as if training had ceased with the prospect of a face-off between the twins. Amelia tried to ignore the dozens of pairs of eyes watching. It had been some time since she'd been regarded as a spectacle, and she did not want to disappoint.

Damon must have picked up on her nerves, his smile growing broader and cockier as he folded his arms across his chest.

"We don't have to do this if you're too scared," Damon taunted.

Amelia flicked her wrist, her fist striking fast like a cobra, connecting with his jaw. She jerked her hand back. The flesh resting on her knuckles began to throb as her skin split from the contact. Warm blood seeped from the minor wounds, but her body was numb to the pain as she derived immense satisfaction watching her brother clutch his jaw.

"Okay. I deserved that." Damon stretched his mouth until it popped back in place.

"Are you going to shut up now, or would you rather gossip with the she-wolves?" Amelia asked.

Her brother glared at her before he bounced on his feet, raising his fists in front of his face. She knew she wasn't going to get in another cheap shot like that again, so she raised her hands in the same fashion, ready for him.

They circled each other for some minutes. Assessing, looking for weakness in their defenses, hoping for an opening that could provide an advantage. Amelia narrowed her eyes, her patience wearing thin. The slow dance they were engaging in was not what she had in mind, but Damon was always the observant one, waiting for her to make a move.

Amelia ran forward. Damon stood still, maintaining his ground, waiting for the next hit. She went for his left side and faked a punch. Spinning around, she backhanded him with a clenched fist, landing a blow to his still sore jaw. Turning back to confront him, she could see her brother wincing. The side of his face was already a faint shade of purple.

"Getting tired already?" Amelia asked. A slight smile tugged at her lips.

"That was a lucky shot," Damon snickered. "You don't have the muscle or the stamina to defeat me. You've let yourself go, Sis."

Amelia grit her teeth. Her sea-green eyes shifted before his eyes, turning darker, more animalistic. She noted his pupils widening just before she lashed out. She swung hard, switching between both her hands. She received a glancing blow to the side of her head but managed to deflect the brunt of the force. Her leg connected with his ribs as he left himself open, parrying her left hook. A sick crunching sound could be heard.

Her brother growled deeply. She watched as his eyes shifted to a forest green as he allowed his wolf to take over. Cotton clothing shredded into thin strips, drifting to the torn earth as fur replaced smooth skin.

Amelia stood face to face with her brother's wolf. His silver-gray fur was raised down the ridge of his back. His lips pulled back, revealing sharp, elongated canines as he growled in warning. She chuckled at his pathetic attempt to intimidate her just as she wrenched the thin veil down that separated woman from beast and allowed Rey to surge forward.

She could feel her bones snapping, reshaping, and growing into a form that was as familiar to her as her own body. Her spine elongated, limbs extended until she was standing on all fours.

Rey was thinner than she used to be, but she was still as tall as her twin. Her fur was as pale as the snow that littered the ice caps of the North Pole. She shook her body out, adjusting to her form before digging her claws into the earth, leaning back on her heels, ready and waiting.

You look incredible.

The voice inside her head startled her. She searched for his silky voice in the crowd until she found those sterling silver irises. It had been so long since his voice echoed off the chambers of her mind. She knew they reforged their bond last night but to hear it in effect was something else altogether.

Her heart pounded in her chest. Her ears were perked, standing at attention. Her tail began to swing behind her as her excitement grew. To have the ability to connect with him in a way that wasn't just about their physical needs. It was what she had craved the most all those years alone and on the run. She could feel his soul bleed into hers. His ghostly silver aura blending, mixing with her purple one, made her heart feel exceedingly full. She was certain she had never felt so much love before in her life.

Damon sprung towards her, pushing off with his back paws, throwing his body into hers. It felt like a bulldozer had blind-sided her, connecting with her side, forcing the air from her lungs with so much force she was sure she'd never be able to breathe again. She felt her body skid through the dirt and scattered leaves of the floor. Her throat burned fiercely as though a liquid fire had been poured down her gullet as she tried to drag oxygen back into her body.

Somehow, through the pounding in her head and the blood rushing through her veins loud enough to rival that of Niagara Falls, she could hear a deep, menacing growl. She managed to elevate her head to discover Gabriel challenging her brother. His lip was pulled back as he continued to snarl. The skin along his hands and arms were bristling. His body stuck somewhere between man and wolf.

Damon was visibly divided. He kept glancing back at her with his ears pulled back. A slight whine escaped his muzzle, afraid he had injured her. While on the other hand, he couldn't back down from a challenge. With another Alpha so close and threatening him, he had to confront the potential threat.

Amelia took in a deep breath with what felt like knives sliding down her throat and forced herself off the floor. Using every ounce of strength she had left, she pushed with her hindlegs, launching herself through the air, and onto her brother's back.

Damon howled in surprise as she dug her claws into his flanks, sinking her teeth into his neck. He kicked, bucked, and twisted his head from side to side, trying desperately to get her off. But Amelia clung onto his massive frame for dear life, using her thinner size to her advantage. He had spent the last seventeen years bulking up, giving her more to cling to.

She clamped down harder into his tender flesh, causing him to spasm beneath her. He whimpered as the realization dawned on him.

There was no way she was letting go.

Amelia growled through the fur in her mouth, advising him to submit. She could feel her brother's will to fight. He didn't want to give in. His Alpha side refused to submit to another wolf, but Damon and his wolf Zeke knew better.

Rey would never back down.

Damon leaned forward on his front legs before completely laying down on the ground. Amelia continued to growl through the scruff between her teeth, showing her brother and everyone present her dominance and place in her pack. She was not only a Luna and mated to the Twilight Moon Alpha, but she was also an Alpha in her own right.

It wasn't until her brother was fully laying down on his side, head bent back, completely exposing his neck, that she finally let go. Damon laid still for a moment, his side rising and falling heavily as he fought to regain control of his breathing.

Couldn't you have just drawn first blood? You had to go and make me submit in front of my pack and mate? Damon asked.

You're the one who had to knock me on my ass the one second I wasn't looking.

If you weren't eye-fucking your mate, I would never have had the opening.

Eye fucking or not, it was an ass move.

Damon huffed loudly through his muzzle before sitting up on his front paws. He shook his fur out, trying to erase the sting her teeth and claws left on his body.

Amelia honestly felt bad. It wasn't her intention to shame her brother or wound his pride, but she also couldn't help the fact that she wasn't known to lose when challenged. She watched her brother sulk off the field.

Cordelia scrambled to follow him.

Some recessive part of Amelia wanted to chase after Damon, to make sure he was all right. Instead, her eyes searched for the one man she wanted more. Her blood was up. Her heart raced frantically in her chest as her body hummed with desire.

Catching sight of his onyx hair, she found him watching her. His eyes were molten silver and hungry. She sampled the air, her jaw hanging open, licking her maw, letting her mouth flood with the taste of honey apples and cinnamon.

Do you think you could take me? Amelia asked. Her tail swishing playfully behind her.

All day, every day. Gabriel smirked; his eyebrow elevated. *Come and get me.*

Gabriel didn't waste a moment. Jumping through the air, he phased halfway through. Landing on the pads of his paws, his jet-black fur caught the light, reflecting shades of blue and purple. Her core twisted in knots, lighting a fire deep inside her, begging to be released.

She tried her best to push past her arousal and focus on the wolf in front of her. Even though she was large for a she-wolf, he still towered over her with his thick, muscular frame. She leaned back on her hind legs, ready to spring.

Gabriel just stood there. His head tilted to the side like the cocky man he was. His mouth hung open. Tongue lolled to the side like a pup gearing to play tag.

Amelia narrowed her eyes at him and pushed off the earth, kicking dirt up in her wake as she ran full speed at her mate. She internally smirked as his jaw clamped shut, forced to take her seriously, digging his claws into the grass waiting for her hit.

Rearing back on her hind legs, she swiped him across the jaw with her paw, claws retracted. His head snapped to the side with the blow, just as she headbutted his chest, forcing him back a step.

Gabriel growled in warning. *Careful, Snow. You're pushing it.*

And you'll do what exactly? She taunted.

Gabriel stepped forward with his front left paw, narrowing his eyes, his lip drawn back in a snarl. His ears were flattened back against his head. Black fur bristled down his spine while his tail stood straight up, poised for attack.

Amelia turned her back on him, flicking him in the face with her tail. She glanced back over her shoulder, giving him a wolfy grin.

Catch me if you can.

CHAPTER 37

LASTING MEMORY

The brisk Fall breeze licked across her face but did nothing for the heat that radiated from her body. The earth beneath the pads of her paws was moist, yet she still felt as though she was racing across hot coals.

Amelia could feel his balmy breath on her heels as he chased after her through the dense brush. She tried to run harder, faster, put more distance between them, but he was rapidly approaching.

Smelling for the border, she could barely make out the patrol markers. Hoping it was enough distance from the house, Amelia took control of her body and shifted back into her human skin.

Just as she felt the soft soles of her feet touch the damp earth, something collided with her body. Large, calloused hands wrapped around her legs, hoisting her off the ground and winding them around a naked waist.

Amelia tried to recover her breath as Gabriel restrained her against the nearest tree. A small giggle escaped her before his lips crashed down. His breath scorched her mouth as he slipped his tongue between her teeth. She opened wider to let him in further. Honey apples and cinnamon flooded not only her nose but overwhelmed her taste buds. She would never get enough of him.

His hands roamed over the planes of her body. Cupping her breasts, gripping her hips. He ran the backs of his knuckles down her ribs, leaving her moaning in his mouth. Her breath began to pant wildly. His lips moved down her jaw to his mark along her neck. Sucking on the tender skin, he flicked his tongue along the faint scar.

Amelia flung her head back, crying out into the open air. Her voice carried through the trees. Birds flapped their wings against the air, fleeing from their nests. She wound her arms around his upper back, digging her fingernails into his broad shoulders drawing blood. Threading through his silky, fine hair, she tugged hard on the roots, jerking his head back sharply.

Gabriel hissed in response, digging his nails into the small of her back.

Leaning in, she flicked her tongue up his collarbone, coating her mouth with salt. Making small, circular motions, she sucked on his mark and smirked as his body quivered beneath her. A throaty moan rumbled in his chest and escaped through his lips.

Smirking against his mark, she pulled back, breaking contact. Keeping her fingers wrapped in his hair, she tugged on his head, forcing his eyes open. The silver of his eyes struggled to focus, but eventually, the thin pupils stared hungrily at her.

"This is all I've ever wanted. To be back with you. Back in your arms," Amelia confessed.

His hands moved up her back until they gripped her shoulders. "This is where you belong. I'll never let you go again. I'll watch the world bleed if it means keeping you with me. No matter who gets in my way."

"Gabriel—"

"No. You're mine, and I'll do anything to keep you safe."

The urgent tone to his voice and the fierce look in his eyes, the one that promised he'd keep every word he said, sent her heart racing in her chest.

"I'm not going anywhere. I'm yours. Always."

Gabriel pulled her down, making her sink on his hard member that was perfectly lined up with her entrance. Amelia threw her head back, moaning in ecstasy as her walls stretched, making room for his length and girth. He thrust his hips, bouncing her against his pelvis.

She bit down on her bottom lip hard, stifling the scream that threatened to burst from her lungs. The feeling of being full, so completely connected with his body and soul, sent her head swimming in an ocean of bliss.

Grinding her hips against him rewarded her with a few choice curse words escaping his lips. Grinning, she reached up, grabbing onto the nearest tree limb. Using it as leverage, she lifted herself until just the tip of him was left inside before loosening her hold and sinking back down.

"Fuck," he hissed, moistening his lips.

Amelia continued to use the tree behind her to her advantage, repeating the motion. She began to move more rapidly. His eyes locked on her breasts as they bounced. He leaned in, seizing one with his mouth. Sucking hard, he pulled on the nipple with his teeth, rotating it back and forth. The sensation was like a jolt of lightning straight to her core, causing her to move faster against him.

Her moans were lost to the wind. Her mind was too focused on her movements, the exploding sensation between her legs, and the man before her that she didn't think she'd ever get enough of. They never heard the cracking of twigs or rustling of leaves underfoot, informing them someone was nearing.

"Mom! Aunt Cordelia wants to start getting ready for—," Emery's eyes widened before she screamed, hastily turning her back on the scene before her. "My eyes! What the fuck?!"

Amelia froze. Her blood turned to ice. Her heart stopped in her chest, stuttering between beats. Gabriel went rigid beneath her, silently cursing the world.

"Emery! Get out!" Amelia yelled, finally recovering her voice.

"It's the fucking woods, Mom! We are out!" Emery shrieked, her back still turned. "Good Goddess. I need to bleach my fucking eyes!"

Amelia watched as their daughter ran from the scene of the crime. Her silver hair flew behind her as she beelined in the direction of the house. It felt like hours had passed as she held her breath, waiting for the sounds of feet running through the woods and brush shoved aside to fade.

It wasn't until she felt a shuddering beneath her that she finally released the breath she'd been holding. Only to discover Gabriel laughing hysterically.

"This is so not funny!" Amelia rolled her eyes, slapping his chest.

"No, it's priceless." Gabriel gasped for air.

"How are you laughing? How are you not mortified right now?"

"Just think. She'll never come after us in the woods again."

Amelia thought about it and couldn't help but chuckle along with him. "Seriously. What was she thinking?"

"At least we were able to give her one lasting childhood memory." Gabriel laughed.

She groaned, leaning her forehead in the crook of his neck. "We've scarred her."

"It was bound to happen. I don't plan on letting you up for air very often," Gabriel mumbled, pressing his lips into the warm skin of her arms.

"Gabe," Amelia moaned, requesting more.

She needed him. Her core had died down but was still throbbing inside of her, desperate for release. Not needing to be asked again, he pushed himself back inside until his tip grazed the entrance to her womb.

"More. I need more," Amelia cried, pressing her hips forward.

Gabriel responded in kind, thrusting harder and faster. Their grunts and moans were reduced to panting. Lights flashed behind her eyes as she squeezed them shut, her brain turning to mush as her blood boiled, burning her alive. She clenched down tighter around him. The pressure in her lower abdomen was near its tipping point, and she could tell by his quickened breathing and consistent use of the word fuck, he was close too.

"Snow," Gabriel panted.

"I know," Amelia said, almost giving him permission.

The tips of his fingers buried deep in her flesh, clinging to her slender hips as he pounded into her harder than before. She concealed her face in the crook of his neck, unable to hold on. Her head felt light as the world spun around her. The friction between them was amounting to something she wasn't convinced she'd survive.

Just when she thought she couldn't take it anymore, fireworks went off. The pressure in her core finally released right as she felt him spasm beneath her. Her orgasm struck her in waves, continuously letting her go and then sucking her back in as he rode out his own, moving slower and slower inside her.

Amelia forced her eyes open, trying her best to focus on a large spruce just behind them. She felt dizzy and lightheaded but, at the same time, pleasurably numb. She was sure if she tried to stand on her own two feet, she'd be as frail as a newborn fawn.

Gabriel slowly pulled back. His own eyes glazed over with sensual pleasure. His raven hair stuck to his skin as beads of sweat trickled down his brow and the side of his face. She couldn't help but reach up, stroking the hair from his eyes, slowly spreading her fingers along his scalp.

He fastened his eyes automatically as she played with his hair, moaning with satisfaction. "You keep doing that and I may just fall asleep right here."

Amelia chuckled, ceasing her movements. "We can't have that. We have a party to attend."

Flicking his eyes back open, he smiled proudly. "This is just to make it official. You've always been my Luna. There's never been anyone else that could take your place."

Amelia bit back a snide remark. Knowing it wouldn't alter the past or help heal their scars. Instead, she smiled gently, picking up where she left off with her fingers twirling the hair at the nape of his neck.

"I haven't belonged to a pack in over eighteen years. I'm not sure I even remember the bond. It'll be strange," she admitted.

"You'll be amazing. You were born for this. Being a part of a pack is not something you'd forget."

"Says the man who's been in one pack his entire life," Amelia mumbled under her breath.

So much for personal growth. Rey chided.

"I know I've never been through what you have." Gabriel arranged the hair back from her face and tucked it behind her ear. "I can't imagine what it must have been like. To be cut off from your pack, your family. To be completely isolated."

"It doesn't matter anymore." Amelia shrugged, trying to rid herself of the loneliness that was threatening to creep in. The cold had kept her company for nearly two decades.

His tender hand cupped her face, forcing her to meet his metallic eyes. "It matters to me. I'm sorry, Snow. I'm sorry I couldn't be there for you when you needed me. I'm sorry fate has used us for its own gain and twisted us into someone we no longer recognized. But I promise you now, fate can go fuck itself. Cause no matter what, I will never lose you again."

Amelia buried her nose in his palm. Breathing in deeply, savoring his scent. She kissed his palm softly, swallowing back the lump in her throat.

He was right. Fate had used and abused their bond, their bodies, and their minds. She had been forced into hiding while fear controlled her every action. Whereas Gabriel was left behind, left to wonder how she could betray him, abandon him—twisting his mind and his heart against her.

But not even fate could keep them separated. Even when life had thrown every possible obstacle in their path, they were still each other's light. The one person in all the world to chase away the darkness.

Gabriel held on tightly to her hand as they walked back in the direction of the house. Her body was exposed to the elements as the wind picked up, raising the hairs on her skin.

Just ahead of them, not a hundred yards from the training field, she spotted a neatly folded pile of clothing waiting for them. Amelia arched her brow, curious as to how they seemed to have magically appeared.

Gabriel shrugged his shoulders. "Kaleb wanted to be sure we were decently clothed before returning."

Amelia chuckled, silently thanking their Beta for having the foresight to think of clothes. She quickly tugged on the loose-fitting sweatpants and t-shirt. They were two sizes too big by the way it hung off her shoulders and the countless times she had to roll the waistband, but she was still grateful not to have to walk stark naked through the Packhouse.

The training field was still in full swing. As they pushed through the final tree limbs and out into the open, it was like something out of a movie. The world around her seemed to move in slow motion as all eyes turned on them.

Amelia wished she was a snake. At that moment, she wanted nothing more than to shed her skin and flee. Hundreds of eyes were locked on her, most with a knowing smirk plastered on their faces. But then, as if it never happened, every single one of them went back to what they were doing.

She frowned, trying to settle the unnerving feeling that was beginning to twist her gut. "What happened?" she whispered.

"It's not the first time a couple has run off into the woods for a quickie." Gabriel laughed.

She followed him into the house, her head still swimming. She had been out of pack life for a while if she had forgotten how flippant wolves were with their sexuality. Hell, she used to not give two shits who saw her body, clothed or not.

Amelia caught sight of her daughter's familiar silver-black hair. The back of her head facing her as she sat on the couch beside Cordelia. Her best friend glanced over her shoulder. Her thin lips instantly pulled into a wicked smile as she took in her attire. Patting Emery's thigh, Cordelia inclined her head behind them, forcing Emery to turn around.

"Em," Amelia started.

"Nope." Emery cut her off. "I don't want to hear it. I am already permanently scarred and will require decades of therapy."

Amelia rolled her eyes. "You are so dramatic. No one told you to come looking for us."

"How was I supposed to know my parents would be shagging out in the middle of the woods? It's not like I've ever had to worry about walking in on something like that before!"

"What did you think was happening when he chased after me like that?"

"Not that! Anything but that!"

"You're a tad overdramatic, dear," Amelia huffed in annoyance.

"Girls," Gabriel said, directing the brunt of their attention to him. "Tonight, is a night for celebration. Not fighting. Emery, I'm sorry you had to see that, but things are different now that your mother and I are together. I suggest you link or knock before entering to avoid future uncomfortable situations from occurring again."

"Fine," Emery snapped. "But I want a car."

Amelia barked laughing, her breath catching in her throat forcing her into a coughing fit.

"We'll talk about that later," Gabriel said.

"You can't be serious," Amelia said, her voice hoarse as she struggled for air.

"Mia, it's time to get ready if we want to be on time for the ceremony tonight," Cordelia interjected, sensing a new fight on the horizon.

Amelia turned her attention to her friend sharply. "You're right." She nodded. "But this conversation is not over." She jabbed her finger between her mate and daughter. "Car my ass."

"A bike?" Emery tried, following her mother and Aunt.

"Sure," Amelia said, "a peddle bike."

CHAPTER 38

HAZARDS

"It's perfect."

Amelia stared at the glass mirror, unsure if she was looking at what was supposed to be her reflection or a stranger. She no longer recognized the woman gazing back at her. Her skin was a healthy, rosy color, no longer sunken in along her cheekbones or hollow around her eyes. Her ocean green irises were alive and sparkling. She no longer bore a haunted expression but one of hope.

Gone were the days of having to look over her shoulder, constantly fearing the next attack. Would they capture her again, or would they take her daughter?

Living with that fear does something to a person. It shatters your faith in others, your trust in humanity as panic chokes everything, never daring to hope for a better future. But now, there she was, getting ready for her Luna ceremony. Something she never believed she'd be doing. Not in a million years.

Amelia never allowed herself to dare to dream. On the off nights where she wasn't plagued with nightmares that left her sweating and her throat sore from screaming were the nights she got to see Gabriel. The man she had met all those years ago in front of the Wandering Moon Packhouse.

Of course, he had changed over the years. Whereas once before, he was tall and thin. His youth still evident in the soft frame of his body now stood the bulk of a man. If she ever thought he was muscular before, that was nothing compared to the lean, rippling cords he possessed now. His arms were a bulging mass of strength and power. His chest was clearly defined with clear-cut pectorals. His stomach was as flat as the African Sahara and those abs had to have been carved into his body with a miniature chisel, small enough to bring out each dip and ridge with absolute clarity.

Gabriel's hair had grown out, longer than she could have imagined. She barely remembered telling him years ago that she loved his hair long. She wondered if he did it for her or if he just let it go. Even though it was longer, the strands just barely reaching his shoulders, he always kept it groomed back. It wasn't till the end of the day when he had run his hands through his hair too many times, did it start to fall in his eyes. She would automatically twitch at the sight. Desperate to brush them back and feel the silky strands between the tips of her fingers.

But it wasn't just his body that had changed. He was no longer the young Alpha, fresh from the life of an Army grunt. Hot-headed and quick to lash out. He was an experienced man. Calmer and patient than she could have imagined. From studying her across the room, taking note of the way she rubbed her wrists, the clothes she wore, to the type of mother she had become, he took in everything.

The way his silver, gray eyes tracked her across the room, never missing a flinch or the way her heart began to race when she felt his gaze on her, how his eyes would become molten pools, heated, and setting her skin ablaze. That was one thing that hadn't changed but instead grew stronger, more intense.

Now, there she was, sitting in her bedroom they had once shared, back in the house that had witnessed some of her worst and best moments. The pack had taken in a headstrong, strong-willed stranger. The woman that had evolved from a naive warrior to a scarred, resilient mother was finally being accepted into her pack, her fate. She almost couldn't breathe.

The pad of a thumb brushed softly against the corner of her eye, removing the moisture before it could do any permanent damage to her makeup. Amelia nearly startled, her heart leaping from her chest before she caught sight of Emery standing just beside her, observing her through her reflection in the mirror.

"You look beautiful." Emery smiled. Tears brimming in her eyes.

Amelia went back to her reflection. Once again, analyzing the woman staring back at her. Not only did she look radiant, but she felt it, and that was a gift more treasured than a million compliments.

"Thank you, Cordie." Amelia tried to smile at her friend, who was still adding the last few pearl pins to her hair. She swallowed down the lump that had formed in her throat, trying to ignore the stinging in the back of her eyes. She refused to ruin her best friend's hard work. At least, not until Gabriel saw her.

"Are you ready?"

Amelia looked to her daughter, who stood beside her. Who had always been by her side since the moment she could stand on her own two feet. The young woman who had rescued her from countless nightmares and saved her from losing herself to the darkness that threatened to overcome her constantly.

"I'm so proud of you, Emery."

Emery sniffled before reaching out and gripping her hand. Amelia gave her a soft squeeze, kissing the scarred, calloused skin over her knuckles.

"You two need to stop, or we're going to have to start all over," Cordelia said, her voice a bit nasally as she dabbed at her eyes with a tissue.

"She's right." Amelia took in a deep breath and slowly stood from the vanity, ensuring she had a stable footing in her four-inch heels. She turned towards her best friend and daughter, offering each a smile. "Tonight is not the night for tears. It's a night to celebrate." She took her daughter's hand in her own and gave her a tight squeeze, marveling at her iridescent silver eyes.

"We're home."

The fabric of her dress whispered against her skin as she moved as quickly as she dared down the stairs. It had been over a decade since she last sported heels, and with every step, she was increasingly regretting it. Barefoot would have been her first choice. No fear of face planting down the stairs if there were no shoes threatening to snap her ankles every time she put her foot down.

Amelia kept a hand on the railing, helping her inch her way down the steps. Why the hell Packhouses had so many damn levels remained a mystery to her. While the other hand gathered the silky, shimmering fabric, holding it up away from the ground so as not to be a tripping hazard.

Her mind was too focused on the next step ahead of her, on not embarrassing herself on such a momentous day, that she hadn't registered that she'd reached the main floor. Gooseflesh pimpled her skin. The hairs on the back of her neck stood up, traveling down her spine and across her arms. Looking up, she found the most mesmerizing set of silver eyes taking her in.

Gabriel stood a few feet from the stairs, his hands tucked in his pockets. The perfect picture of elegance and grace in a black suit. The crease perfectly pressed down the center of the legs. His white, button-up shirt was pristine. The perfect shade of purity with the top two buttons left undone to reveal a patch of dark tanned skin and chest hair peeking out beneath the folds of his lapel. The coal jacket was tight across his shoulders and down his arms. She wasn't sure how it didn't rip with every breath he took, but she wasn't complaining. The material showcased the sheer strength and power that resided in his exquisite form. His hair was neatly combed back from the frame of his face but left to curl around the nape of his neck and ears. She could tell he had already run his fingers through it one too many times by the small flyaway that already hung down his brow.

Amelia hadn't realized she'd narrowed the distance between them until her hand automatically rose in front of her, brushing the strand from his eyes and pushing it back into place. She allowed her fingers to run down the length of his hair, twisting the ends as she settled her palm against the back of his neck.

Her mouth filled with warm apples and cinnamon spice. She breathed in deeply, fastening her eyes as she savored him. Never. Regardless of how many years she lived, would she ever get used to the smell of him, the taste of his aura. She would recognize him forever. Until the day she could no longer recall her name and even after that. Somehow, someway, she had a fundamental understanding that she would always know he was hers, and she was his.

Always.

"Even when the world is plunged into perpetual night and the Earth is nothing more than a frozen wasteland, my heart is yours. Even when the Goddess collects my soul and I'm left to walk the night sky, I will find you. In a sea of endless darkness, you are my light. Our souls are bound in this life and beyond. Always," he whispered.

His gaze held her own with such intensity she hadn't realized she'd been crying until the calloused pad of his thumb brushed the stray tears from her face.

"Were you just in my head?" she asked him. Finding her voice to be a bit hoarser than she'd have liked.

The corner of his mouth pulled up into one of his smirks she had dreamed about endlessly. "Maybe a little. I'm finding it easier this time around to slip into your thoughts."

"It's as though our connection is stronger." She finished for him.

"Exactly." He stroked her hair back from her shoulders, exposing the permanent mark freshly visible on her neck.

"You look breathtakingly, enchanting my Snow. I'm not sure what I ever did to deserve such a deadly gift."

"I'm deadly now, am I?" She chuckled, unable to help herself.

"Oh yes," he mumbled against the tender flesh of her shoulder. "I'm afraid I may have to execute anyone who looks at you with wanton desire. You are all too tempting in this dress."

Amelia felt as though her skin was doused in lighter fluid as his breath was a feather-soft touch against her skin. Kindling a fire deep in her stomach. She tilted her head to the side to allow more room as his mouth tasted her flesh, sucking and kissing her mark.

"Don't start something we can't finish," she breathed heavily. "People are waiting."

"Let them wait."

His hands skimmed down her sides, gripping at her hips beneath the thin material of her gown. She knew the dress would leave little to the imagination with the plunging neckline and fabric that clung to her slender frame, but she still hadn't expected such a reaction. She had chosen a dress that kept her back covered. Still not comfortable with laying her scars bare, but maybe one day, she would grow more confident.

"Your scars are a tribute to your bravery and your courage." He pulled back, staring down into her soul. "They're a badge of honor you should never have had to bear, but they are a reminder that you can overcome anything." He dragged the tips of his fingers down the length of her spine, along the knotted scars and chords of tissue the whip had left. "Every one of these is a part of you. Even though the experience was horrifying and terrible and ignites such a rage in me, I'm not sure I'll ever be able to release it. They are beautiful. You are magnificent, and I will tear the throat out of anyone who thinks differently."

Amelia snorted through the thickness building in her throat. Wetness once again gathered in her eyes, threatening to spill. She didn't recall him ever being so expressive, but she didn't care. He was declaring not just what she wanted to hear but what she desperately needed to understand. Her scars didn't define her. They were just as much a part of her as the stretch marks she carried on her stomach and hips.

"You really need to stay out of my head," she commented almost as an afterthought.

"Why? When I'm right?" He spoke against the corner of her mouth, taunting her with the taste of his lips.

If she budged just a fraction of an inch to her right, his lips would be on hers, and she wasn't sure they'd be able to stay on the ever-thinning line they were dangerously playing with. If he kissed her, she was sure she'd beg him to take her back to their room. Unwilling to let them leave until his mouth tasted every inch of her body.

"I'm okay with that." He slipped his hand around her waist and pressed into the small of her back, closing whatever sliver of distance was left between them.

"Good Goddess! This is going to become a recurring problem, isn't it?! The pheromones choking the air in this room are enough to set a pack of hounds in heat. Jesus fucking Christ!" Emery announced.

"Emery Grace! Language!" Amelia turned around to discover her daughter fanning the air in front of her with her hand as though to remove a foul stench from the space before her.

"Can you two at least wait until after the ceremony? Then you can hole up in your soundproof bedroom for eternity," Emery complained, coming to stand beside her mother.

"Sounds perfect," Gabriel purred into her ear.

Emery gagged, forcing Amelia to roll her eyes.

"You are so overdramatic." Amelia shook her head.

"I learned from the best." Emery flashed her a brilliant white smile. "Are we ready?"

Before Amelia could say yes, Gabriel halted her.

"Almost." He got down on his knees, resting on the hardwood floor before her.

She was ready to shout at him to get up when she felt his warm hands wrapping around her thin ankles. The slight pressure of his hand forced her to elevate her foot. Her brow scrunched in confusion as she was about to inquire what on Earth he was doing until she felt the thin straps of her shoes being slipped over her foot. He released her right leg, causing her to stand at an odd angle until he did the same with the left.

The wood was cool beneath her feet. A minor respite against the flush that still clung to her skin. She wiggled her toes. The arches of her feet were no longer straining against the unnatural stretch of the shoes. Even though her dress would now surely drag along the floor, she felt a severe sense of relief at no longer having to worry if she'd be eating dirt in front of her pack.

Gabriel stood back up, the heels in hand. "That's better. Enough of those hazards. Now we can go," he said, pitching them onto a nearby sofa.

Emery arched a brow at her mother, unsure of what to make of the gesture. She was about to ask what that was all about until she noted the unbridled love brimming in her mother's eyes. Eyes that had known such anguish and grief. She knew better than to say a word.

Gabriel tucked his arm through Amelia's as he led her through the house and towards the back doors. Emery went to follow when she felt a gentle pressure on her arm. Aunt Cordelia had managed to slip up behind her unheard and unseen. She wanted to say something but noticed her Aunt's gaze still trailed after her parents.

Emery looked back over her shoulder to watch them. Her mother's shoulders were relaxed. No longer tense with doubt and self-loathing or bone-weary exhaustion. Now she stood tall and proud like the Queen she always knew her to be.

"They are a stunning couple," Cordelia remarked.

Emery continued to watch them as her father opened the door, allowing her mother to pass through first. "No. They are so much more than that."

CHAPTER 39

STAND OR FALL

abriel opened the French doors to reveal the backyard. The sun was setting in the west over the tree line. The sky was painted in radiant violets, burnt oranges, and yellows that reminded her of fields of sunflowers. With the sunlight rapidly retreating, the entire perimeter of the yard was lined with tiki torches stationed every few feet illuminating the hundreds of faces before her.

The entire pack, the ones who hadn't evacuated, were present, to include the supporting Wandering Moon warriors. All of those in attendance were in their finest clothes. The men sported elegant suits, and the women wore stunning gowns. The attire was more formal than she ever remembered with her brother's Alpha ceremony, which left her feeling insecure and unsure.

The moment her slender foot struck the weathered wood of the back porch, hundreds of eyes burned against her skin. Gasps could be heard across the clearing. Whispers drifted on the soft breeze, only to be blown away before they could reach her ears. She squared her shoulders, straightening the length of her spin as she held her head high. Even though the attention screamed for her to run, her fight or flight instincts overwhelming her, she held her ground.

This was her home, and she would fight for it.

Why is everyone dressed so formally? Amelia linked Gabriel.

They wish to honor you. Everyone knows you are more than an ordinary wolf, blessed by the Goddess. Besides, you may be their Luna, but you are my Queen.

The possessiveness in his tone sent delicious shivers down her spine, straight between her legs. She had to pinch her knees together and focus on the soft Earth beneath her feet as she strolled towards the dais.

Amelia walked the path before her, split down the middle of the gathered crowd. Each individual present bowed their head in submission as she passed. Trying to keep her jaw from becoming one with the ground, she kept her eyes forward.

This isn't normal, Gabe.

Relax, Snow. Just breathe.

Amelia bit back the instinct to bite his head off. Instead, for once, she listened and took in a steadying breath as she continued her brief walk to the stage. She wanted to look back and check on Emery. See how she was taking it all in but resisted the urge when she heard her familiar voice in her head.

I'm right behind you, Mom. You got this.

Was her panic that noticeable? Her skin felt like a million fire ants were dancing along her body, tasting her flesh. She wanted so badly to shed her skin, shift into her wolf, and flee into the woods. Once upon a time, such attention wouldn't have phased her. Hell, she would have reveled in it. But now, it was like her own personal hell. Could they see her scars? She was sure her dress had covered them up. However, the ones on her arms and wrists were still visible.

Will you stop twitching? Rey surged forward, causing her step to falter. *They're right. Relax and stop worrying. You're not being dragged out here to be flogged. This is supposed to be a happy ceremony, now snap out of it, or I'll attend the ceremony in your place!*

Rey's words were like being thrown in a tub filled with ice water. Shocking and infusing her with adrenaline, leaving her fully alert. Rey was right. Annoying and a bit harsh, but right. She sucked in a deep breath and took the last few steps towards the dais. A warm hand pressed against her lower back, causing heat to race across her skin, staining her cheeks red. She glanced beside her and was confronted with molten iris and lips pulled into a genuine smile.

Amelia bobbed her head at him once before she gathered her dress in her hands and took the first step up the set of stairs. It was four quick steps before she reached the platform and took her place center stage.

Gabriel came to stand beside her. His hand molded to hers, gripping her tightly. Amelia squeezed him hard, using him as a lifeline. A tether to her present and future.

Emery took her place on Gabriel's right, sandwiching him between both of his girls. Amelia looked down at the first row of spectators and found her brother and Cordelia front and center. Her sister-in-law had her arm threaded through her twins, tears already flowing freely.

Damon merely smiled, allowing his emotions to feed through their familial bond. He was proud. So damn proud.

Amelia's ears heated instantly. She imagined not even the color wheel could determine the shade of red her face might be. If it wasn't for Gabriel initiating the ceremony, she was sure she'd have made some obscene gesture at her brother.

"Welcome, everyone. I know this is last minute, and with a battle on the horizon, it may not be the best timing, but I have come to realize something. Something that I wish I had realized much earlier in life." Gabriel turned towards Emery, his hand squeezing hers to the point that she was sure her fingers might pop, but it didn't hurt. "Life is short, and time with our loved ones is precious. That is why tonight, I present you with my daughter and heir to the Twilight Moon Pack, Emery Grace Smoke Thorne."

Emery gasped. Her eyes widened in shock. "You can't be serious."

"You are my daughter, Emery. Whether I've known you your whole life or a few days, it doesn't change that my blood flows through your veins. I may not have raised you, but that doesn't make you any less a part of this pack. Your mother raised an intelligent, caring, and capable young woman. This is your birthright," Gabriel told her.

Amelia looked over her mate's shoulders to find her daughter shell-shocked. As though his words weren't quite registering. But Gabriel wasted no time and moved forward with the ceremony.

"I, Alpha Gabriel of the Twilight Moon Pack, name you, Emery Grace Smoke Thorne, as my heir and a member of this pack." Gabriel took the blade he held in his hand and pushed the sharp edge into the pad of his thumb. He smudged the blood that already flowed freely from the cut along her lips and across her forehead, marking her as a member of his pack. "You are Twilight Moon Pack, now and forever."

Emery sucked in a breath of air as a current of energy expelled from her the moment she licked the blood from her lips. Her eyes glowed a silver amber as the mind link snapped into place, connecting her with the entirety of the pack.

Howls tore through the air as the pack warriors lifted their faces to the sky and sang a song of welcome. Goosebumps pricked her skin as the sky seemed to come alive with the pack wolves' embrace. Amelia was positive she had never seen her daughter so happy, so utterly complete as she looked in that moment.

Emery wrapped her arms around Gabriel's neck, taking him by surprise. She squeezed him tightly and smiled when she felt his arms encircle her waist.

"Thank you, Dad."

Amelia's heart skipped in her chest. How any of this wasn't a dream, she'd never understand.

"You're welcome, baby." Gabriel pulled away to turn back to their pack, who had grown silent again. "Now that our daughter has joined our pack, that only leaves one thing left to do." He slipped his hand back in hers, entwining their fingers. "This pack has long been without its other half, and I will not waste another moment without my mate, and this pack will not spend another minute without their rightful leaders. We are stronger together. One pack, two Alphas."

Amelia visibly flinched at his words. Her head twisted in his direction as her vision blurred around the edges. She wasn't even sure she was breathing. The night was frosty, and yet her body felt as though it was cooking from the inside out. Her heart hammered in her chest so loudly she couldn't focus on anything else. Her eyes widened as her brows furrowed. He couldn't possibly mean making her an Alpha. That simply wasn't done. No pack, in the history of their entire race, had ever had two Alphas. She wasn't even sure if it was altogether possible.

It's possible.

Amelia focused on Rey's words as confusion tore through her. *But how?*

We were born for this. You just never wanted to admit it.

Amelia took in a deep breath, forcing her heart to slow to a steady rhythm. She found Gabriel and the entire pack waiting, waiting for her to come to terms with what he announced. She glanced down at her now empty hands and found her mate gripping the ceremonial knife in his own. The torchlight glinted off the gold handle. The silver steel seemed to absorb the last remaining rays of dusk as the moon began to rise above them, full and pregnant with raw energy.

"Tonight, the Twilight Moon Pack witnesses a new beginning. Normally this would be a simple Luna ceremony as we take you into the pack as one of our own. But you, Amelia, my mate, my best friend, and partner are anything but simple. You are no ordinary wolf, and I would never ask you to be. You are a daughter of the Goddess, blessed with her power and strength. Your birthright has always been more, and tonight we begin to rectify that." He held his hand out to her, palm up, asking for her own. For her permission.

"Do I have a choice?" Amelia asked, her voice cracking. She wasn't sure if she should laugh or cry. Was this some sort of joke? Could she even be this person? An Alpha.

"You always have a choice," Gabriel promised her.

Amelia took him in. The stubborn set of his jaw and those perfect lips firmly pressed together as he waited. His pupils were wide, tracking every breath she took and taking in her demeanor. His nostrils widened as he took in her scent, as though he was expecting something in particular. Was it fear? Was he trying to see if he could sense her wanting to run? As though she hadn't wanted this.

Since the moment she drove her bike off Wandering Moon territory, she had wanted to belong. She didn't know it then, but now she can acknowledge and understand that she was always meant to be at his side. The years they spent apart, no matter what happened to them while they lived their separate lives, she wanted him. Twilight Pack was her home. Since the instant, she took in his scent at her brother's Alpha ceremony; he was her future, and this pack was hers to protect. There would be no more running. Where would she run to when she was already home?

Amelia placed her hand in the palm of his. The tender flesh was exposed to the brisk air, dark skies, and full moon. She looked up at the night. A blanket of stars winked against the onyx canvas when she spotted a falling star shooting across the sky. The wind kicked up, billowing around her as it lifted the bottom of her dress. Her unbound hair tickled her skin as she followed the curls at the nape of his neck moving with the air. She felt a surge of warmth enveloping her, wrapping around her like a blanket of safety and protection, soothing her frazzled nerves and overworked emotions. It reminded her of what it might have felt like to be held by ...

Be free, my daughter.

Amelia looked around her wildly as the warmth left her as swiftly as it had arrived. Her mother's voice was something she had clung to as a child when the lingering smell on her clothes quickly faded. As she clutched her sweater and the scent swiftly became replaced by her own, she held onto her mother's honeyed voice. Seeing her the other night in the woods had left her bitter and ashamed. Not many get to visit with a deceased parent, and she had squandered her opportunity.

Glancing down to where her brother stood, he looked none the wiser. Merely waiting for her to make her choice just as the hundreds of wolves before her were waiting. She turned back to her mate, tears lining her lashes as she admired his lovely face, now filled with confusion and worry.

"I choose you. I choose our pack," she spoke clearly, allowing her voice to carry over all those present.

Gabriel's smile could light even the darkest of nights. His pearly teeth shone in the dark as his lips pulled back. Small dimples showed along the corner of his mouth, catching her off guard. It wasn't until that moment that she wasn't sure she had ever truly seen him smile. Not fully, at least. She reached up, her hand cupping his cheek as she rubbed the pad of her thumb along the small indent in his skin.

"You're so beautiful," she whispered. She felt wetness on her face but ignored it. He was the most stunning man alive, and she wanted to make sure he knew it.

Gabriel chuckled but leaned into her touch much in the way a flower gravitates towards the sun's rays. "Nothing is more stunning than you."

A small gag could be heard from behind Gabriel.

"Get a room," Emery groaned.

Giggles rose from the crowd causing Amelia to lower her hand. She had practically forgotten where they were and the number of people witnessing their moment. But she wasn't embarrassed. She was grateful.

Gabriel cleared his throat, trying to hide the interrupted arousal that was dancing in his eyes. His hand tightened on hers as he placed the point of the blade in the center of her palm.

'Do you, Amelia Smoke, accept the role of Alpha of the Twilight Moon Pack? To lead its warriors into battle. Nurture its young pups, encouraging and supporting them to one day be respected members of this pack. To lead by example and honor the pack members from the weakest to its strongest. Do you promise to uphold pack tradition, abide by the laws decreed to all werewolves by the Council of Elders, and perform your duties to the best of your ability?"

"I do," Amelia declared as the sting of the blade bloomed in her palm. The silver pierced her flesh, causing blood to pool in the center of her hand.

"I, Gabriel Thorne, Alpha of the Twilight Moon Pack, take you as my Alpha, my partner, and my mate." Gabriel lifted her palm to his mouth. Maintaining eye contact, she could feel his velvety lips wrap around her wound as he took in her blood.

Amelia felt only what could be described as an electrical current that raced down her arm, through her hand, and into him. Gabriel's eyes flew wide as the blood passed his lips. His pupils shrunk until they were barely visible. His silver iris changed before her eyes. The inner layer was pale silver, shimmery, and as iridescent as her gown. Where his eyes had once been entirely silver were now rimmed in a golden band, glowing brilliantly.

Her arms moved beyond her will. Without thought, she seized the knife from his hand and flipped his palm over, facing the sky above. She nicked his flesh with the blade as she studied his changed eyes.

"I, Amelia Smoke, Alpha of the Twilight Moon Pack, promise to stay by your side, stand or fall. You will always have my counsel, honesty, and loyalty." She brought his hand to her mouth, fastening her eyes. She ran her tongue over the superficial cut. The taste and smell of iron overcame her senses. She nearly gagged on the blood when she felt a surge of power stampede through her body, flooding her entire being. Her vision became spotted with brilliant, white lights. Every cell in her body became electrically charged as unstable energy coursed through her.

Her eyes flew open as she gasped, struggling to breathe through the devastating sensation. She felt as though her entire body was awake. Like a giant being awoken from a centuries-long slumber.

"Your eyes," Gabriel gasped, his own wide and full of surprise.

Amelia smiled. Feeling lighter than she had in her entire existence. "I'm sure they look much like yours."

And they did. Her eyes glowed green. A green as deep as the forest and as bright as a freshly bloomed Hellebore rimmed with radiant gold.

We are who we were always meant to be. Rey spoke. Her voice was as deep as the Mariana Trench yet as light as Dandelion seeds on the wind. Her voice resonated power as it vibrated through her mind, down her spine, and into the Earth beneath her feet.

The Earth rumbled and groaned. The trees shook, branches scraped against branches. Leaves brushed against one another so loudly it pressed on her ears. Birds fled from their nests in a panic, squawking and screeching into the night. But that wasn't what drew her attention.

Deep growls sent gooseflesh racing across her skin, sending the hairs on her arms and neck standing straight. Her eyes narrowed, searching for the cause of the noise.

The warriors on the ground were preoccupied with the Earth shaking and oblivious to the shadows that began to move along the edge of the forest. Hundreds of them rose, gathering into a tight formation that was familiar to her. Their maws snapped, teeth cracking against each other as they moved closer towards her. Their growls caused a sense of dread to fill her, but that was quickly replaced with a realization.

Hundreds of shadow wolves gathered along the forest's edge, warning her.

"Amelia, do you see that?"

Amelia snapped her head towards her mate. "You can see them?"

Gabriel merely nodded his head. His eyes were as wide as saucers as he took in the shadow wolves—her ancestors.

"They're here to warn us," Emery said confidently.

Amelia simply nodded her head. "They're coming. Michael is coming. Now."

CHAPTER 40

ONLY THE BEGINNING

The air around her was buzzing with anticipation and purpose.

Once the ground had finally settled, and the pack was no longer trying to maintain their footing, Gabriel was able to link them all, gaining their attention. Based on the scent in the wind Amelia was able to detect, they had an hour before the rogues arrived. Giving them all just enough time to change into fighting gear and assume their positions around the territory.

After Gabriel announced the incoming threat, each of the warriors set off to prepare themselves.

Amelia could taste the eagerness. The thrill of battle permeated the air, but she could also smell their fear, and that was just as needed. Fear meant they had something to lose as well as something to fight for. Rogues didn't have that. They had no self-preservation, no fear of death, which made them deadly but also easier to kill. They weren't desperate to protect themselves in a way that a pack wolf would fight for their life and for those around them.

Emery had already disappeared into the house. She could overhear her mumbling something about trying a new set of knives. Her excitement was palpable.

Damon had left alongside Cordelia with a curt nod of his head. Cordelia, along with Kelsey, was in charge of assembling those who had stayed behind, unable to fight, and getting them to safety in the bunkers beneath the house.

Gabriel wound his arm around her waist, steering her within the house. Inside was a flurry of organized chaos. Warriors were shouting at one another as they assembled the armory, handing out weapons as some left to set up position outside. Others were heading for their rooms to change. While some were giving final goodbyes, just in case.

No one was guaranteed tomorrow.

Amelia watched them all with pride, but also despair. The battle hadn't even begun, and she knew they weren't all going to make it. For some, tonight would be their last night. Each of them would fight for their pack, for her and Emery, with their dying breath, but she could already feel death's presence lingering above. Waiting to claim the first soul that would depart that night. She wanted to flip him the bird.

Gabriel's grip on her waist tightened as they climbed the stairs, heading for their room.

"Don't think like that."

"How can I not? I'm supposed to be their Alpha, and not even two minutes into the job, I'm already leading them to their deaths. I thought we had more time. We've barely trained!" Amelia yelled, flinging open their bedroom door.

"This is war. One that's been a long time coming. Everyone here knows that not everyone will make it, and they're willing to accept that risk. To defend us. To defend you and our daughter. Michael is well past his expiration date, and I look forward to watching you shred him limb from limb." Gabriel shrugged off his jacket and flung it on the bed before working on the buttons of his shirt.

"Oh really? And you're going to do what? Just sit back and watch me do all the work?" Amelia snorted as she stepped into their closet, pulling the zipper down the side of her dress.

"No, I'm going to watch my mate take her revenge on a man that's done more than deserve it. He's your kill, Snow. I'd never take that from you. As much as I would enjoy it, he's all yours."

Amelia poked her head out of the closet, a smirk playing on her lips. "I knew there was a reason I loved you."

Gabriel chuckled. He pulled a loose tee over his head and slipped on some comfortable shorts, allowing for easy movement when fighting and the ability to transform rapidly when he needed to. He was tying his shoes when he caught movement out of the corner of his eye.

Amelia stepped out of the closet in form-fitting yoga pants that stretched from the top of her waist down to her ankles, a tight sports bra, and a tank top. She was already plaiting her hair and wrapping it into a bun on top of her head when she caught him observing her and froze, unsure what could be holding his gaze.

"What's wrong?"

"I'm just disappointed I didn't get to take that dress off you myself. This is not how I figured our night would end. I wanted to be plunging myself deep inside you. See how many times I could make you cum. My bet was six."

"Only six?" Amelia arched a brow, challenging him.

"I'm not sure you could handle more than six. Wouldn't want you to pass out."

Gabriel stalked towards her like a predator would his prey.

Amelia squeezed her knees together, trying to relieve the instant ache that left her wet and wanting. She desperately desired to feel him, to cum with him, to revel in the friction that only he could provide, prompting her to erupt with such pleasure he'd leave her seeing stars.

"We may not be able to achieve six, but maybe just one?" Amelia couldn't believe she was asking, but she was.

"We should be downstairs," he said, almost to himself. His fingers outlining the planes of her neck.

"We should. But if tonight is our last night—"

"Nothing is going to happen to you." Gabriel's voice was raw and commanding.

She reached up and placed her finger on his lips, silencing the fear that lingered beneath his words. "Even so, we can't predict the future. If things don't go our way, I don't want to leave this world without having you inside me one last time. It will never be enough. A thousand lifetimes with you will never be enough, but this moment may be all we have, and I don't want to waste it."

"Then don't."

Gabriel's lips crashed down on hers, stealing whatever words she had left to say. Amelia's arms wrapped around his neck, forcing his mouth harder against her. She pulled at the root of his hair, scratching his back as she dug her claws into his shoulders. Hunger and desire tore at one another, leaving her desperate for his skin, his touch.

Fabric tearing sounded like background noise. She wasn't sure if it was her clothes or his, but it didn't matter. Suddenly his bare chest was flushed with her. Her breasts pebbled against the brisk air, hardening into lofty peaks.

Gabriel pulled back for just a moment to admire her before a growl escaped him. His lips pulled back into a possessive snarl that left her soaked and throbbing for his touch. For something hard and firm to bury itself so deep inside her, she didn't know where she began, and he ended. He forced her back onto the bed and pulled her leggings off with one swift motion. This wouldn't be love-making. Slow or intimate. This would be hard, fast, and so desperately needed by the both of them.

"Don't go easy," Amelia told him, causing his pupils to dilate even wider.

The human was barely hanging on as the wolf surged forward, prowling over her with deadly desire. She recognized his need. His hardened length was pulsing and dripping with anticipation, ready to be used and use it she would.

Without warning, Gabriel plunged inside of her quickly and with accurate precision. Amelia hissed at the sudden intrusion, but the smarting pain quickly melted into a burning desire that licked at her skin, made her brain turn to mush, and left her panting. She clung to him, her legs bound around his waist, and before she could put her hands on his neck, his fingers laced with hers and secured them above her head. Amelia flung her head to the side as he rocked her body with his, pounding into her hard and fast. She was already near release.

The battle was getting closer by the second, and their bodies seemed to comprehend that. His panting and silent curses in her ear caused her moans to grow wilder. Their bodies rubbed together, causing rough friction against her sensitive mounds, making the pleasure that much more. She could tell he was near his own release by the way he picked up speed. Meaning he was no longer focused on restraining her hands, leaving her unable to touch. She wrestled them free and wound them around his neck, forcing his mouth to hers. She wanted to taste him. Feel the pleasant sting of his teeth on her lips, the silky warmth of his tongue pressing against hers. Imprint the taste of apples and cinnamon spice until it was so deeply ingrained, she'd die with it on her breath.

The pleasure began to build to an almost uncomfortable level, threatening to spill and explode in an inferno that was sure to devour them both. She dug her nails into the tender muscle of his shoulder when stars began to shoot across the ceiling. Gabriel moaned loudly but was swiftly snatched by her kiss and stayed buried inside her, unwilling to part.

They both knew they had to separate sooner rather than later, but if this was their last moment like this, they would end it on their own terms.

Gabriel sat up, balancing on his forearms. He spread his fingers through her hair, most of which had escaped its braid. "I love you, Snow. Tonight, is not the night we die. We will have more. More endless nights of lovemaking. More screaming fights that will inevitably end with me on my knees in some form or another and countless days to enjoy ourselves because this isn't the end. This is only the beginning."

Gabriel and Amelia raced down the stairs. Her hands were cramped, replating her hair when she caught sight of her family.

Damon and Cordelia, were embraced in each other's arms. She could just barely make out her brother's voice, murmuring something in his wife's ear.

Amelia turned from them, allowing them privacy only to find Emery waiting but a few feet away, helping the last few stragglers down the stairs into the bunkers.

"Em!" Amelia called to her.

Warriors were flitting back and forth through the house, gathering weapons, securing the doors and windows. A few of the Omega's that had stayed behind were seen carrying large stacks of books and loose paper coming out of Gabriel's office and down into the basement.

Prepare for the worst, hope for the best.

"Mom! Dad! There you are!" Emery yelled over the bustling commotion. "What took you two so long?"

Amelia wrapped her braid in a bun and secured it on her head, trying to smooth down any flyways. Gabriel's hair was a rumpled mess as he drew a foot up onto the couch to tie his laces.

Emery took in their appearances and rolled her eyes.

"My parents are rabbits," she mumbled.

"Better get used to it, Em. You'll likely have a brother or sister before you know it," Damon chuckled as he and Cordelia approached.

"I've always wanted a sibling." Emery considered the possibilities.

Amelia's heart practically exploded from her chest.

Damon was right. If they weren't careful, getting pregnant was a very real possibility. Although, she wasn't certain if, after her rape and torture, if she'd still be able to have children. She had never been formally examined. Too terrified to find out what and if there was irreversible damage. But aside from all of that, they were nowhere near ready to bear another child. They had only just found each other. She wanted time with him—time with her family.

Gabriel's hand trailed down her back, rubbing soothing circles in her skin. His consciousness reached for her, rubbing against her frazzled mind. "It's okay. There's no rush. We can tab this conversation for another day."

"There *will* be another day," Cordelia told them all, ensuring each of them knew she expected them all to survive. "I should be getting down below. Be safe. All of you." She swiftly gave her mate a kiss and Amelia a squeeze on her arm before disappearing through the basement door and closing it firmly behind her.

Damon stared after his wife for a moment longer. His jade blue eyes were vacant as he stared through the sealed reinforced steel door.

Amelia studied her twin as dread began digging its claws deep in her, rooting its way into her mind. She reached out for her brother, placing her hand on his shoulder, snapping him out of his daze.

"She's going to be okay," Amelia assured him.

Damon examined her eyes, identical in color, and she felt a single drop of fear snake its way down her spine. Amelia seized his shoulders and gathered him in, winding her arms around him tightly. She squeezed him hard but not nearly as tight as his hold. She concealed her face in his neck, tears dampening his skin.

"Don't you dare think like that," Amelia growled against his flesh, causing his chest to rumble with a suppressed chuckle.

"I'd never dream of leaving you," Damon promised. He finally let her go as he gave her a strained smile and Gabriel a curt nod before turning to Emery. "Stay by your mom, kid. Don't leave her side."

Emery nodded. Her brows furrowed slightly. "I promise."

Amelia stared at his back as he left out the back doors, blending in with the shadow of the forest. She could barely make out his silver-blonde hair in the trees until he disappeared altogether.

Turning back to her mate and daughter, she detected Emery waiting, her weapons in hand. Amelia sighed gratefully as she took her knives and began sheathing them, securing them around her thighs, waist and stowing them in the pockets of her skin-tight leggings.

"You loaded up?"

Emery nodded, patting the silver daggers hidden discretely along her waistband.

"I don't like the idea of you fighting. You're too young for the front lines." Gabriel massaged his forehead, gripping at the roots of his hair.

Amelia knew what he felt without even having to tap into their bond. She had experienced the feeling more often than she'd have liked. It didn't matter how many times Emery had fought beside her. How much training she had drilled into her. The fear and anxiety never lessened. She stroked her fingers into his shoulder, giving him a slight squeeze.

"Emery has trained hard. She's been fighting rogues and evading them her entire life, but she will stay with us." Amelia gave her daughter a hard, enforcing stare. "No running off on your own. No showing off. No fancy tricks or overextending yourself. If we tell you to run or hide, you do as you're told, are we understood?"

Emery took a step back, visibly flinching at her mother's words. She inclined her head and exposed her neck, trembling beneath the effort.

Amelia gasped, jerking around, nearly stumbling on her own feet when Gabriel gripped her waist, steadying her.

"Snow, your eyes," he whispered. The words were practically forced from his mouth, brushing against the sensitive skin of her ear.

Amelia looked around wildly until she caught sight of her silvered hair in a mirror hanging from the wall behind Emery, but what was staring back at her wasn't anything she recognized. Her eyes were golden honey that practically seemed to glow, illuminating her skin with a radiant shimmer. A pounding grew in her ears, racing wildly, forcing her skin to flush a shade of crimson. Her chest began to rise and fall drastically as her heart roared all around her, drowning out the impending mayhem and chaos.

She could feel hands gripping her. Rough calluses were scratching along her skin. Gabriel and Emery's mouths were moving, but she couldn't hear anything over the blood rushing through her body as her heart rate skyrocketed and panic flooded her system. She could feel her throat begin to close. Her lungs constricted, deprived of oxygen as the air became scarce in the room. Her nails clawed at her throat, desperate for a reprieve.

Was this the end? Was this how she'd die? She was sure it was until the world stopped.

Hands forcefully seized her just as warm and tender flesh pressed down on her dry, cracking lips. Hands had her squeezed in a vice with her face pinned between them, garnering her attention. He didn't move to deepen the kiss or even hold her more gently. Something she had grown used to rather quickly in the last twenty-four hours, but instead, he held her frozen, unwilling to allow her the freedom of movement. She should be furious at him for clutching her so tightly. For pushing himself on her during her panic, and yet, her mind went blank. Her heart settled in her chest, and the pounding in her ears turned to silence.

Her panic all but vanished. Retreating into the remote recesses of her mind, taunting her that it would come at a later time. His grip on her lessened as her pulse slowed to a steady rhythm.

Amelia pulled back. His hands still rested along her cheeks and neck, but they were softer, no longer restraining her to him. He rested his forehead against hers, taking in steady breaths she forced herself to replicate.

"You're okay," he assured her.

She nodded against him. Tears pricking her eyes, she looked at Emery. "I'm so sorry, Em. I don't know what happened."

"It's okay, Mom. It's fine. Really." Emery smiled even though she could detect her hands slightly shaking at her sides.

"What happened?" Gabriel looked back over his shoulder.

Emery shrugged her shoulders. "I don't know. Mom's always been able to command me, but only to a certain degree. If I tried hard enough, I could resist some of her lesser orders. But this. This was different. It took everything in me not to get down on my knees and kiss the ground. It was like every cell in my body was forcing me to obey."

"It's never happened like that before." Amelia swayed her head in disbelief. She glanced at her reflection in the mirror and encountered her typical green-blue eyes staring back at her.

A silent sigh of relief escaped her as she took comfort in the familiar color.

"This is new territory for all of us. We don't know the full extent of your power and that goes for the both of you. We don't know if the Alpha bond has magnified that or what the repercussions are." Gabriel stroked her cheek with the back of his knuckles.

Amelia turned, taking a step back. She rolled her shoulders, shaking them out. "I'm fine. We don't have time for this." She inhaled, taking in the scents staining the air. She pushed out the mouth-watering apple cinnamon of her mate and vanilla roses from her daughter. Past the pine scent of the pack and under all the bitter fear and overwhelming determination, a rotten stench lingered, drifting closer and closer. "They'll be on our territory in fifteen minutes."

Gabriel nodded his head. His eyes were distant as though an impenetrable fog was clouded over his silver iris. He was linking the pack. Cautioning them.

"Everyone's in position."

"Good. Let's go." Amelia headed for the back door.

The house was now vacant and void of life. No more running pups, loud teenagers, or adults bustling around.

Gabriel and Emery were close behind her, just like she knew every point and curve of her knives.

Outside, the sun slept beyond the horizon, leaving a blanket of stars twinkling against the void of night. Amelia could sense her pack all around her and in some strange, baffling way, her brother's pack as well. Although she couldn't link them like she could the Twilight Moon, she could still pick out each member of the Wandering Moon as though they belonged to her as well.

All three-hundred and fifty warriors present were stationed around the perimeter and inside the territory, awaiting the rogues that were getting closer by the second.

Leaving the weathered planks of the back deck, they pushed off into the tree line, immersing themselves in total darkness. Amelia adjusted her eyes to the limited light. Luckily enough, the moon overhead was full and illuminated the space in front of them in a silver hue, but shadows still lingered and tormented them with every breath of wind.

Gabriel assumed position on her left while Emery stood on her right. She took in her mate. His skin was already rippling with the desire to shift. His hands flexing at his sides as his feet dug into the Earth, grounding himself.

Emery, on her right, was the picture of calm and collected. Her knives were balanced in the palms of her hands as she flipped them in the air effortlessly, only to catch them again by the hilt.

Goddess, did she remind her of herself at that age.

I love you. Amelia linked her mate, twin, and daughter.

Amelia reached into her pockets and pulled out two knives. The blades were the length of her forearms, glinting in the moonlight. The handles were made of textured leather to allow for a sure and steady grip. She gripped them tightly, positioning her feet shoulder-width apart.

The stench in the air was getting heavier, burning her nose hairs. Pungent enough for each wolf present to take in deep breaths, anticipating the incoming horde.

Amelia reached for the pack bond. The tie that permanently tethered her to every member of the pack. She opened the floodgates and reached into each of her warrior's minds.

Work together. Look out for one another. We are one pack, one unit. Do not let them separate you. This is our territory. Our family. Fight for what's yours.

The air grew loud as paws beating against the Earth pounded through the air. It reminded her of a heartbeat that grew faster and louder with each beat. She shifted her feet, supporting her weight and positioning her hips. She squinted into the dark as the snarls drifted closer.

"They're almost here." Emery's position matched her own perfectly.

"Then let's greet them." Amelia took off at a run into the tree line, becoming one with the darkness.

CHAPTER 41

RED DEATH

The stench of rot became overwhelming. Bile rose to the back of her throat. Amelia forced it back down as she pounded her feet into the Earth even harder. Onyx fur raced alongside her. His jaws snapped at the air in front of them as his growl vibrated through the ground. Her heart stuttered in her chest at the sound, setting her blood blazing in response. Her mate at her side fueled her with purpose and strength.

She narrowed her eyes just as the rogues broke through the brush, lunging forward.

Amelia engaged the first Rogue with her knife as it soared past her and sliced through the carotid artery as though it was nothing more than butter. Her hand whipped out, catching the next one immediately behind it. Her knife severed through flesh until it met bone. She barely granted it a second glance as they kept coming in a flurry of teeth and fur. Her breathing was timed fluently with her movements. With each breath she gathered, both her knives cleaved through meat like carving a filet.

Earlier, she had been unsure of herself. Doubting her own capabilities. But standing there, the bodies already piling around her, she knew she was born for this.

Stay human as long as you can. Smaller targets make for a more difficult kill. Choose your moment wisely. Don't let them get too close! Amelia instructed through the link.

She wasn't sure if it had been minutes or hours since the fighting began, but already she could feel the deaths of her packmates. Hundreds of lights had been illuminated around her, teaming with life, but as each was killed, a light was snuffed out, causing their collective to grow that much dimmer. The casualties were a minor distraction. The only comparison she could think of was bamboo splinters being forced beneath the bed of her nails—agonizing. But mourning for them would have to come later. She pushed their deaths aside and focused on the never-ending tide of Rogues.

Amelia struck her foot out, catching a wolf in the jaw. She bent down swiftly as she drove her blade into its chest, plunging it between his ribs and into the heart. Just as she bent down, hair caressed along the back of her neck as a faint breeze pushed past her. She spun on her heels to catch the wolf that was attempting to attack from behind when she caught sight of Gabriel's onyx fur leap in front of her and latched onto the Rogue's throat, flinging him about like a rag doll.

Standing back up, she hurdled over the stacked bodies in front of her and charged for the Rogues running in her direction. Countless wolves split through the tree line, breaking through brush and branches to attain their target. Her.

Amelia spun her body over a wolf. Even in the dark, she could see the gray, matted fur embedded with mold and feces. She was close enough to taste the stench of rot. Landing on her feet, she threw her wolfsbane knives as two more Rogues emerged from the shadows. She swiftly plucked her next set of blades out as she became overrun by three more. She dodged their claws as they attempted to swipe at her legs. Evaded their fangs when they tried to latch on her arms, clothing, anything they could sink their teeth into. She struck out, striking one in the jaw with her fist. Pain exploded in her hand, shooting up her arm and down her spine. She bit her tongue to restrain a cry and pushed through the pain.

Amelia could detect Gabriel not far behind her, catching the wolves that were trying to slip past them. Their whines were cut off abruptly as he quickly ended their lives. The sound of flesh being split from fangs, claws, and knives was an audible wet sound. One she was sure would haunt her dreams for the rest of her life.

Distressing cries rang out all around her from the pack and enemies alike. The sound of necks cracking, like the popping of a log that's been left over a fire, reverberated through the inky night. The scent of iron and putrid, rotting flesh permeated the air, choking out anything familiar and comforting.

Amelia could hear the steady breathing of Emery just beside her. Still, in her human form, her daughter was dispatching wolf after wolf without so much as a hiccup, but she knew from experience they couldn't maintain this momentum forever. Reaching out through the bond, Amelia felt for her twin. He wasn't far off, but a hundred yards to her left, but she could detect him moving farther away, chasing after rogues that were attempting to break through their lines on the West end.

Her legs and arms were lashing out. Her knives were slick with blood as the warm liquid slithered down her hands and forearms, coating her in red death. She readjusted her grip on the hilts as her skin became tacky.

Fear, her unwanted and tortuous friend, began to creep its way forward, but she stamped it out, knocking it back. She didn't have time to examine the stench of death that was surely embedded in her flesh and hair. Process the mangled corpses, their limbs torn from their bodies or throats ripped out. What her mind wanted her to recognize as organs strewn along the forest floor and blood soaking through her clothes would do no one any good.

Now wasn't the time to worry for her daughter's soul and the stain all this death might create. Or the wetness soaking through her mate's fur, dripping from his maw. Not even the bits of flesh wedged between his incredibly sharp canines. Her stomach rolled once before she snuffed it out when she experienced yet another death from her pack.

The night had merely begun, and already their losses were more than she wanted. The fear of being injured and unable to stand and defend herself, losing her mate or child, or any one of those she loved spread throughout the territory threatened to overcome her. She couldn't afford any of that, and neither could those that depended on her most. The defenseless that waited beneath the Packhouse. Their survival was dependent on their success.

Amelia jumped on the back of a wolf, threatening to overrun her daughter, and plunged her blade into the beast's back. Jerking it free, she leaped off and rolled on the ground before shoving the knife into the chest of another wolf. Emery surged forward after being relieved from the overwhelming numbers and knocked a wolf off another pack member. She snapped the Rogue's neck before looking down at the warrior. He couldn't have been much older than her but judging from the distant gaze to his eyes and the fact that she could see through to his esophagus, he was gone.

Amelia watched as her daughter closed the boy's eyes before turning her rage on another Rogue. Her daughter screamed out her anger and agony as she lashed out with her knives, carving through anything and everything within reach. Blood sprayed through the air, staining the trees and ground. She felt a wet warmth hit her cheek, arousing her from her stillness. She pushed off the Earth, her hands stuck in the dirt that had turned into thick mud, sucking her in farther before she yanked them back out, causing a sickening slurp sound. Just as her knees began to straighten out, she felt sharp talons tear into her scalp, causing her hair to ripple around her as it was released from its braided bun. Her hands automatically flew to the back of her head, where she felt jagged edges and warmth seeping from her skin just beneath her hair. Before she could turn and confront whoever had maimed her, the breath was knocked from her lungs as a large mass pinned her to the ground.

Instantly, Amelia's arms flew up protectively around her face, holding back the russet furred beast now straddling her body. The wolf snapped its jaws, missing her nose by mere inches. His breath ravaged her skin as saliva projected from his mouth as he continuously attempted to remove her head from her body. She struggled to prevent him from meeting his mark and pushed harder with her arms until they screamed under pressure. She bucked her body, kicking out with her feet and knees, trying to gain any distance she could from the savage animal. Her heart raced frantically in her chest. If only she could reach into one of her pockets and release one of her knives, but she couldn't risk her hold. If she moved even a fraction, the Rogue could claim her life before her next breath.

Her arms were no longer made of flesh and bone but now consisted of lead, threatening to collapse. Amelia gritted her teeth. A strangled scream escaped her lips as she yelled out her frustration. Her arms gave way just an inch, bending in at the elbow. She twisted her head to the side. The sound of teeth smashing into teeth rang in her ear louder than anything she'd ever heard. Her shoulders fell back into the dirt, causing the wolf to fall further against her.

This was the end. At least if he ripped out her throat, her death might be swift. His balmy breath fanned her face when she suddenly felt lighter. She elevated her head to discover Gabriel pinning the Rogue on the ground. His claws dug into the Rogue's underside, exposing intestines, and rotting stomach contents to the night air. The Rogue whined in pain beneath him, but that didn't stop the Alpha. Gabriel growled viciously in his face. The power behind it rippled around them, causing the trees to shrink away from its force just before he bit down on its throat, jerking viciously. The snap of the neck gathered the hairs on her arms as she stared at the head that was now nearly twisted, facing its spine.

Amelia didn't have the time to thank Gabriel or check his wounds that were bleeding freely down his side. She could tell his back leg was hurting as he limped on it, but that didn't prevent her mate from meeting another two rogues before they could reach them. Amelia pulled herself up off the floor, fatigue seeping into her bones. She could feel her pack struggling to deal with the number of rogues—more than they could have imagined.

"Use the trees! Your daggers! Whatever you can! Stay out of their reach!" Amelia simultaneously yelled and linked her pack.

Amelia took a step forward, prepared for another swarm of rogues when a sharp cry captured her attention. Emery stood a few feet from her with her calf in the jaws of a wolf. The beast jerked its head back and forth, tearing through muscles and tendons. Her daughter was encountering two rogues in front of her, trying to fight them off as the animal kept a firm hold on her leg.

She moved to help her, to save her when she became caged in by four mutts. They obstructed her path to her pup, effectively separating her from not just Emery but her mate as well. The pain of claws ripping into her side seared through the mind link as she watched a wolf tear into her mate's flank. She struggled to keep the rogues at bay, slashing at them with the last knife she had managed to free from its hiding place. Her eyes flitted between the rogues in front of her and her daughter struggling in the dirt. Tears streamed down Emery's face, creating visible trails through dirt and blood. Her leg was no more than minced meat in the rogue's mouth as it continued to tear through, hitting bone.

Amelia made the only choice she could. It was as easy as drawing breath in her lungs as she released the knife. She witnessed it as it silently cut through the air, lodging itself into the side of the wolf. The hilt protruded from its eye.

The Rogue's jaw released her leg before it fell to the ground with a dull thump.

CHAPTER 42

SACRIFICE

Amelia stood before the four rogues that surrounded her with nothing but her wits and her fists. In synchrony, they ambushed her all at once.

Amelia dodged the one immediately in front of her, forcing her fist up into the underside of his jaw, effectively cutting off his air supply. The rogue to her right missed her entirely as she sidestepped, but she wasn't fast enough. The rogue on her left slammed into her side, causing pain to sear her insides as her vision was suddenly blinded by white lights. A cracking sound told her she had broken at least two ribs. But that was the least of her worries as the rogue behind her nearly grabbed hold of her arm. Razor-sharp teeth skimmed her skin just as she jerked out of his reach. She looked down to find that the teeth had left scrape marks down her arms, nearly ribboning her flesh.

Amelia twisted around and snapped the canine's neck. Pissed that she had allowed him to so much as mark her body. She struck one of the other rogues in the head, momentarily stunning him. Staggering back, she pushed the hair from her face that was blowing freely in the wind. Sweat beaded on her forehead. She could feel the thick layer of perspiration, dirt, and blood that now caked her skin.

An audible gasp left her body.

Amelia fell down on one knee, bent over, nearly screaming in agony. Pushing herself up on her leg, she caught sight of Gabriel. He was being overwhelmed as well. A rogue had him by the scruff of his neck, teeth clamping down on fur and flesh. Gabriel jerked his head about, trying to shake the mongrel off.

Her neck felt like it was on fire. Flames licked her skin as she experienced his injury. While she could feel his pain through their bond, that wasn't what bothered her most. With his scruff in the mouth of the enemy, all he was concerned with was reaching her. His panic was overriding his sense of self-preservation as he tried to claw his way to her, witnessing her boxed in by three rogues.

Focus! She yelled at him, gritting her teeth. Desperate for him to save himself.

A blood-curdling scream clawed its way through her throat as she felt a searing hot pain lance down her back. Amelia turned her head over her shoulder to find her shirt in ribbons. Iron filled her nose as a wet warmth bloomed down her spine. The trees and the earth seemed to be spinning around her and she instantly became woozy. Falling forwards on her hands, desperately trying to ground herself, she narrowly avoided another swipe of claws aimed for her back. The rogues surrounding her were moving around her in a broad circle. Snapping their jaws and regarding her like a piece of carrion, reminding her of vultures.

Tears pricked her eyes as she tilted her head. Her hair was matted to her skin with blood, sweat, and dirt. She could hear a faint dripping as her essence mixed with the soil beneath her hands. Her body felt heavier than stone. Just the mere thought of moving left her feeling useless and meager. She questioned if she had the strength to endure as her arms hung limply in front of her. The growls of the rogues felt remote, unreachable. Their breath was hot on her skin, but that wasn't what she was focused on.

Amelia could barely make out Emery amongst the shadows if not for her silvered hair. Her daughter was keeping herself upright on her left leg alone, her right one dragging behind her as it struggled to heal. Two rogues were pressing in on her from the front, narrowly avoiding their claws and teeth. Somehow, she had managed to hold on to her knives and kept them at bay with blades alone. But what Emery was too busy to notice was the beast sneaking behind her, hiding in the brush.

Panic overrode her senses, fueling her veins as she made to push off the earth, but before she could launch herself between her daughter and the attacker, a russet brown she-wolf darted between them, absorbing the blow that would have claimed Emery's life. The she-wolf somehow managed to latch onto the rogue's throat, her teeth piercing skin and muscle. Lifeblood poured from the wolf's neck and into her mouth, all the while his sharp claws racking down her underside.

Amelia moved to help when the rogues surrounding her pressed in, pinning her to where she was. She reached out to the wolf, trying to notify her of the situation she was in, when she gasped. She knew that mind. Recognized the wolf that had spared her daughter's life.

Kelsey! You have to let go! Amelia shouted at her through the pack link.

Kelsey defied the order, locking on to the savage beast's throat. It didn't matter that her stomach was being shredded, ripped open, and flayed or that her life was slipping from her with each passing moment. With a final shake of her head, the rogue went limp beneath her as her fangs serrated its artery, terminating the struggle.

Emery turned to the she-wolf after having just dispatched her offenders.

Kelsey struggled to stand on her paws. The world swayed around her as she glanced over her shoulder, her hazel eyes meeting Amelia's as a knowing expression passed over her face just before they rolled to the back of her head. Her body emitted a sickening sound as it collapsed to the ground, her chest still with finality.

Emery barely had time to fasten the wolf's eyes before being attacked yet again.

Amelia watched from a distance as her old friend sacrificed herself to save her child. The woman she had imagined maiming a thousand, dreadful ways now lay dead among the carnage.

A mournful howl could be heard nearby with her passing. She would know that voice anywhere as it cried out the sorrow that swelled in her heart. She wasn't sure if it was hers or Gabriel's grief she felt. Maybe both, but it was deep and electric, frying what little nerves she had left. The woman who had received her into the pack nearly seventeen years ago, her first friend and confidant, was gone. Her mate's ex-wife, who stood loyally by his side even when his heart ached for another, was dead.

How had she even gotten out of the bunker?

Amelia's body felt numb and cold. Whether it was blood loss or the reek of death that surrounded her, she didn't know.

She struggled to stand. Her body screamed at her as her wounds stretched and pulled in agonizing directions, causing a fresh stream of blood to release down her back. Managing to stand upright, she swayed on her feet. A brisk breeze tugged on her loose hair. The knotted strands were coarse over her flesh as it dragged debris and dirt along her wounds.

Emery was fighting somewhere to her right. Gabriel was confronting his own demons, both figurative and literal. She could feel both of their wounds, bleeding and aching as though they were her own. None of them would survive much longer if they kept at this pace. She squared her shoulders even as her back screamed in agony, pulling on the existing scars and fresh marks across her flesh. Amelia raised her chin, flexing her hand as they curled into fists. The skin split over her knuckles, reopening wounds from earlier, but she bit past the stinging pain. She supported her stance and was prepared to launch herself at the three rogues that circled her when she detected a familiar scent on the wind. One that made her skin crawl so badly she wanted to peel each layer off. Her stomach rolled at the smell of petrol and cigarettes causing her back to itch fiercely. Her ears tuned into the crunching of leaves as all sound seemed to die around her. No longer could she hear snarls and skin shredding beneath powerful claws. It was as though the world itself had frozen time. The Goddess held her breath as the wind died, not daring to move.

The first thing she noted about him was the puckered pink scar down the length of his face. New mixing with old. His mousy hair was thinner than she remembered, but the smug smirk, the upward pull of his lip, was enough for a snarl to slip past her lips.

The rogues that had her pinned down began to slink back into the shadows, keeping her separated from those around her. Amelia looked to her left and discovered Gabriel pacing, caged in by multiple rogues, withholding him. His chest was rising and falling sharply as he struggled for breath. She marveled at how he managed to stay on his paws. The pain emanating from him was enough to make her hurl, but she shoved the notion down deep. He was severely injured, that was without a doubt. His ribs were fractured, one pierced his lung, threatening to collapse at any moment. Deep puncture marks could be seen along his neck, back, and side, bleeding freely.

Amelia wanted to reach out to him desperately. Heal him but given the distance and her enemy standing just before her, it wasn't an option.

The man stepped clear of the tree line and into a slight break of the branches above. The moonlight highlighted the deep scars on his face, the one's her mother left behind beneath the one she added seventeen years ago. His shit brown eyes raked along her body, regarding her like a piece of meat. She wanted to gauge his eyes from their sockets and force them down his throat for looking at her in such a way. She wanted to flay open his back like he had done to her. Shackle him in silver, inject wolfsbane into his veins and watch as he burned from the inside out.

Rage threatened to erupt from within her as she recalled every second of her torture. Every moment she spent running, hiding, and protecting her daughter from the monster before her. Instead, she bottled it, storing it for the opportune moment. She had waited almost two decades for her revenge. What were a few more minutes compared to that?

Amelia took a rattled step forward, afraid her knees would buckle beneath her, but held her ground, standing upright only out of sheer will. The rays from the moon glinted off her skin, making her pale flesh glint in its pearly light. She pulled her lips back into a tantalizing smile, baring her pearly teeth as his name burned in the back of her throat.

"Michael."

CHAPTER 43

FURY AND BLOOD

"Amelia, my sweet," Michael cooed.

Maggots crawled beneath her skin, eating away at the scars and marks of her whippings. Her fingers itched to scrub at her skin until blood was drawn to erase the slimy feeling he left covering every inch of her flesh. He paced in front of her, trying to look at as much of her as he could from the vantage point he had. She forced herself to stand still and not cover her body with her hands, even though that was precisely what she wanted to do. Imagining her feet were roots buried so deep not even the strongest hurricane-force winds could wrench her from her spot, she refused to move. Or be goaded by the monster in front of her and provide him with any sort of satisfaction that the very sight of him made her want to curl into a ball and lose whatever shred of sanity she had left.

He scented the air deeply, waving his nose in the air, categorizing each individual scent until his pupils zeroed in on her. His frown deepened, causing deep grooves to set in along his forehead.

"You've mated once again with Twilight Moon's Alpha," he grimaced. His tone suggested he was displeased with this revelation. "Unfortunate, but not the end of the world. We can work around it. Fortunately for us, your stunning daughter is unmated."

"Us?" Amelia heard herself ask. Her lips moving before her brain could process the words. Her skin bristled as she understood his meaning. Nails extended into claws as her body half transitioned into that of her other half. Rey was howling to come forward, begging to obliterate the man in front of them until he was nothing more than pink mist on the wind. "You will not touch her."

"Like we touched you?" Michael smirked. An eerie half-hearted laugh rumbled his chest. "It's too bad they destroyed your body the way they did. Such a beautiful canvas maimed and tarnished. If you had cooperated, been more willing, you could have spared yourself a lot of trouble."

"You expected me to lay there and be raped without fighting back? That would never happen." Her memories instantly surged forward. Flashes of coarse, calloused hands gripping her firmly until her skin bruised with his fingerprints. The stench of his release leaking between her legs once he'd finished exploiting her. She tried to bury them, to lock them away in the forgotten parts of her mind where they could never resurface again, but it was impossible. "I will never let my daughter be used as a breeding bitch. I'll die before that happens."

Michael cocked his head. "It would be a waste to lose such potential. The joining of our lines would make our heirs more powerful than any before. I want the both of you, but I will settle for one." His eyes wandered to the side where Emery was boxed in by multiple rogues.

A small chuckle escaped her before she forced a hand over her mouth, stifling herself. Amelia's eyes danced with amusement. Nothing about this was funny, and yet he truly knew nothing. She knew he was delusional, but this took the cake.

"You honestly believe either one of us would be allowed to bear your seed?" She chuckled again. "We are descendants of Rhea, destined with fated mates. We are incapable of bearing any pups other than our mates. It's genetically impossible."

Michael waved her off, scoffing at the notion. "Lies. You are no different from any other woman with her legs spread open. The only thing that makes you special is the blood you carry."

"I'm sorry to disappoint you, Michael, but your plan was flawed from the start. You think you're bigger than fate? Then destiny? Then the Goddess? You're dumber than you look." He narrowed his eyes on her. She could see the doubt lingering behind his pupils that were nearly black in the darkness.

"Whether you're right or not doesn't really matter. I'll enjoy trying either way," he said as his body turned toward her daughter, a sadistic smile playing on his thin lips.

A snarl twisted her upper lip. The air before her quaked in its wake. The shift was rapid. From one breath to the next, she was standing on all fours. She rose up on her paws. The moonlight illuminated the space around her as it reflected off her silver fur. Rey growled at the man in front of her. Their captor. The boogeyman that stalked them as if they were no better than prey. Now, there was no more running. No more hiding. She would defend her own until her last breath.

Rey charged forward. Michael barely had a chance to shift before she barreled into him. Somehow, he managed to keep his feet beneath him, swiping at her neck. Rey dodged the feeble attempt. Rearing on her hind legs, she came down with both paws, raking her claws down his side. Michael roared in a fury, in pain and frustration. He lashed out, causing her to growl as his teeth grazed her shoulder. She kicked out with her back leg, striking him across the jaw hard enough to snap his head back. The entirety of his neck was left exposed. All it would take was one bite. Severe the artery and watch as the life drained from his body, but before she could make the killing blow, a whimper nearly knocked the wind from her chest and her feet from beneath her.

Rey's head snapped to the side, following the familiar sound to its owner. The scent of panic and fear tasted acidic in her mouth. Her green-blue eyes widened in horror as her heart raced erratically against her fractured ribs, causing a searing pain with each beat, but none of that mattered. Unimportant and barely a blip on her radar. Not when Emery lay on the churned earth.

Her body was a collection of bruises, scratches, and bite marks. Her knives were long gone, nowhere in sight, but they wouldn't have been much help. Not when a rogue's large paw had Emery pinned to the ground, pressing firmly in her throat. Its sharp claws pierced the delicate, thin flesh. The only barrier she had between life and death. The beast's body was flush with her daughters, boxing her in beneath him, unable to free herself.

Out of instinct, Amelia glanced in the opposite direction where she knew her mate to be and what she discovered there did nothing to ease her anxiety, only heightened it. A deep gash ran along his underbelly, bleeding too quickly. She didn't know how long ago it occurred, but if it continued to bleed as it was, she knew he didn't have long before he took his last breath. Not only was she divided between her mate and child, but the pack members that were still dying all around her caused her restlessness to build. Lights were being snuffed out all around her. Their cries were echoing off the walls of her mind, reflecting their pain and their bravery. Begging for help. For some kind of relief.

The bond that connected her to each of her pack members grew, engulfing not just the Twilight Moon Pack but the Wandering Moon wolves as well. A light bloomed within her mind as a warmth spread across her chest, infusing her, completing her.

Amelia was an Alpha by birth and chosen by her pack. She was descended from Rhea and the first mated pair and blessed by the Goddess. She had her mate and her daughter. She was a mother, not just to her own blood but to all those under her care, charged to protect and preserve all life. The desire to defend flooded her senses. She wasn't weak, and she never had been. It wasn't just the knowledge of fighting and weapons that made her strong. It was love. Love for Gabriel, Emery, her twin and best friend, the pack she was raised in, and the one that accepted her with open arms. They gave her purpose. Shared in her joy and happiness, sorrow and pain, and there was nothing she wouldn't risk for each and every one of them.

A faint light stretched out, illuminating the space around her, and flooded the surrounding forest. Amelia glanced down, her eyes widening as she caught sight of her silver fur, glowing from within, releasing a purple mist that seemed to stretch and grow as though it had a mind of its own. It licked across her flesh, removing the blood from her fur, dissipating before her eyes as her body healed itself, sealing all wounds and purging any toxins that might be lingering. It expanded beyond her, penetrating the darkness, and seeking those who needed aid.

As the mist crept along the ground, curious and exploring, her glow seemed to grow brighter. If the Goddess was the moon, then she was the sun, pure and blinding, unleashing its fury amongst those that threatened harm.

The rogues shrunk back. The mongrel who had pinned her daughter was already shrinking away, whining as though the light caused him pain and tried to put as much distance between them as he could.

Emery sat up. Her eyes were fastened on her leg as she watched the flesh knit itself back together. No longer did her bones feel too heavy to lift. Instead, she felt rejuvenated and strong.

Gabriel barely noticed that his blood no longer soaked the dirt beneath him or that he no longer heard death beckoning him towards the stars. Nothing mattered more than his mate, his love, his Alpha that burned bright with fury, swathed in silver light and purple mist.

Michael shifted back into his human form, his jaw hanging by a hinge. His brown eyes were star-struck as he took her in.

"You are more stunning than I imagined. Such power," he whispered.

Amelia extended her power, pushing out further than she ever imagined. The air around her felt charged and electric. The faintest spark could set it all ablaze, but it couldn't touch her. Couldn't harm her. She commanded the power, and never again would she run from it.

She could hear exclamations from the pack in her head—one after another.

How is this possible?

I'm no longer bleeding!

The rogues are leaving!

They're fleeing through the trees!

But Amelia didn't stop. She pushed out her aura further. Continuing to test her power. Every wolf it touched, every pack member it grazed, restored them almost instantly. She was nearly a hundred yards out in every direction, and yet she could still feel more that needed her.

Without opening her eyes, the bond hummed in her bones, sending a shiver of sparks down the length of her spine. Gabriel had taken up her left flank and Emery her right. Rey finally revealed her eyes, molten gold swirling in the iris, showing her enemy her true strength.

For once, Michael had the sense to cringe, crawling backward slowly on his hands and knees.

"This isn't possible. He said you were broken and ready to be claimed," he rambled.

Rey puffed her chest, standing proud and tall. *I have never been broken, merely bruised. I've been claimed since the moment of my birth. I just didn't know it yet.*

Michaels eyes nearly bulged from their sockets as he gasped, her voice rang clear in his head.

"This isn't possible," he repeated to himself. "He won't stop. He'll keep coming."

Amelia snarled. The wind plucked the hair from his eyes. Her breath was scorching on his face with power and fury. The ground became soiled beneath him. The tang of ammonia burned her nose. Her aura continued to grow around her, but that wasn't what he was gazing at.

Around her, the air became mixed as Gabriel's blue mist expanded, and Emery's pale lavender aura blended into one.

Alone, they were strong, but together, they were unstoppable.

No one will touch me or mine ever again, Amelia promised.

Rey lunged for him. He didn't have time to blink or think or contemplate the end before her wolf shredded his body with teeth and claws. The sound of paws pounding into the earth, trying to escape her wrath, forced her head up. His blood dripped from her mouth. Flesh caught in her teeth.

Hunt them down. Kill them all.

CHAPTER 44

DARKNESS

A melia stepped back from what was left of Michael's body. She felt sticky and unclean. His blood contaminated her body as it leaked from her mouth and soaked into the ground. All that was left of the man that haunted her nightmares and chased her around the world was nothing more than scraps of flesh, deflated organs, and blood, lots of it. But that wasn't what gave her pause. The blood wasn't scarlet like that of her race, or any other living creature known to the world. This was black, reeking of death and decay long before his corrupted heart took its final beat. She spat as much of it out as she could, shifting in the process to hurl whatever managed to enter her body. It was slick and clotted, coating the back of her throat, reminding her of crude oil.

Gabriel, already back in his human form, kneeled beside her. One of his fingers dipped into the blood and rubbed it between the pads. He sniffed it briefly before stuffing his own gag reflex down.

"What is this?" he snarled.

"I don't know." Amelia sat back on her heels, sucking in as much clean air as she could. "And I don't think I want to. Whatever Michael was mixed up in is done with now."

"He made it sound like he wasn't working alone. What if there are more out there?" Emery asked the one question that hovered before them.

"Then we'll deal with it." Amelia gripped Gabriel's hand to stand when the world spun violently around her.

A painful and final howl could be heard in the distance when something vital snapped from within that destroyed her senses with a final blow, hurling her into a never-ending abyss.

Darkness engulfed her. She didn't know which way was up or which way was down.

Was she alive, or had she finally died?

All of her senses were beyond her reach. She couldn't feel, smell, or see anything. It was as though her body was being torn in two separate directions.

One, where there was peace and light. Where pain was no more, and love chased all the darkness away. Those that came before her called to her, beckoning her to join them, but something else grasped at her. Tethering her to something that felt so unreachable, so far away it was almost a fool's dream. One of her strings was left flapping in the wind. Irrevocably broken and beyond repair. But the other one. The other one enticed her closer.

Someone was calling her name. Or what she believed was her name. The voice was lovely and familiar, like a warm blanket, comforting and safe, but she didn't know its name or owner. It was mournful, nearing desperation. The crack in his voice made her angry. Whoever hurt the lovely voice brought forth a rage she didn't understand. She wanted to destroy the one who injured it. Who made it cry.

She struggled with the darkness that enveloped her in its embrace. Trying to devour her in its loneliness and despair. She clawed at it, tried to fight her way out and reach the voice that beckoned her. A slight break in the black nothingness before her opened to the point where she could barely comprehend the words.

"Don't leave me, Snow. Not now. Not after everything we've been through. Come back to me, my love. Please."

The voice cried to her. Pleading with her. But why? She wasn't going anywhere. She didn't know where she was or who she was, but this angelic voice was terrified. She wanted to brush the tears away. Lick them dry. She tried to shout to the world that she was there. Trying to fight her way through. The gap narrowed, towing her down into its depths until she knew nothing more.

CHAPTER 45

GOLDEN FLAME

E mery watched as the fire danced high above her head. Flames of gold, blood, and amber brightened the night sky, diminishing the stars twinkling against the blanket of darkness. The embers glowed hot as wood popped under pressure, sparking on the ground.

Everyone else had already gone inside. The funeral formalities were over as they released the souls back to the Goddess and burnt the bodies. Every wolf that passed from both the Twilight and Wandering Moon packs had been laid to rest. The stinking, rotting Rogues had been piled into a single mound a ways from the territory and left to burn in solitary. The smoke could still be seen rising in the distance over the tree line.

Emery watched as the body in front of her disintegrated within the flames. The heat and flame striping away everything that made the person a living being until nothing was left but bones. She wiped the tears from her face, her heart breaking. Her mother was upstairs in her room fighting for her life. She'd never forgive herself for missing this, for not being there to witness their release, to say goodbye or be there for her packs, for Aunt Cordelia.

"Were you close with one of them?"

A stranger's voice startled her, causing Emery to nearly jump out of her skin. Her hand flew to her chest, just to be sure it was still there and flopping around on the ground.

"Where the fuck did you come from?!" Emery squealed, her voice high pitched and strangled.

The man raised his hands in surrender. A small, teasing smirk pulled at the corner of his pale, full lips. "I'm sorry. Didn't mean to startle you."

Emery coughed, buying herself time to settle her heart rate and steady her breathing. "No, it's fine. I just thought I was the only one left out here."

"I was going but then I saw you standing out here all alone and wanted to make sure you were okay."

Emery looked up in his face. The glow from the flames reflected off his creamy, unblemished skin. He was tall, towering over her by well over a foot. His eyes were a brilliant gold, swirling and iridescent, almost like tiny diamond facets embedded in the iris. Hair darker than the night sky was combed back effortlessly, not a strand out of place, a stark contrast set against his milky complexion. He was perfectly tailored in a fitted suit, accentuating a thin and fit frame and his voice was thick with an accent she couldn't place.

"I'm sorry, but who are you? I don't think I've seen you before." Emery scrunched her brow, curious as to who the identity of the man before her was.

"My name is Lorenzo. I came to pay my respects. I heard it was a battle not to be forgotten." The stranger watched as the flames continued to burn.

The fire reflected off his eyes, bringing out the orange and yellow tones.

Emery watched him as he observed the pyres withering away beneath the heat. He was utterly still, calm, and indifferent. She wasn't sure what to make of him, but what she did know was he wasn't one of them.

"No, it wasn't." Emery kept her answer short, unsure of the man's intentions.

Hailey peeked behind the curtain at the stranger beside them. He was odd and she was curious. If he wasn't a wolf, then what was he?

"It was nice to meet you, Emery."

Emery frowned, turning back to face him but he was gone. If it weren't for the imprint of shoes in the dirt beside her, she was sure she hallucinated him. All that was left behind was a faint scent the wind was quickly tossing away.

Jasmine and sparkling snow.

CHAPTER 46

ALWAYS

Something beat painfully in her chest, bleeding sorrow and grief she couldn't understand.

Everything hurts.

The air that entered her lungs burned. The rise and fall of her chest made her body throb. The back of her throat felt raw as though she'd spent countless hours screaming and her mouth felt drier than the Sahara Desert. She tried to force her eyelids open, but they were glued shut.

How long had she been out?

By sheer force of will, she opened her eyes and blinked rapidly, demanding them to focus, and found herself in a dimly lit room. Their room.

A mound of pillows supported her head and back as she lay in the center of the bed. Tubes and needles connected her to an IV bag and heart monitor. Her eyes explored the room, looking for the one thing she needed. A slight breath of relief was released when they landed on his onyx hair. He was resting in an armchair by the bed, his form slumped over on itself.

"That can't be comfortable," Amelia croaked.

The rasp of her voice startled him awake, his eyes shooting open. The silver iris was swathed in a sea of red, rimmed with deep, dark shadows. When was the last time he slept? The once clean, cut-shaven face was now ragged and overgrown. His hair looked like the only grooming it received was his fingers, and she could smell him from where she lay and not in a sexy way.

Relief lightened his face before dread settled in his shoulders, causing them to droop.

"How many did we lose?" she heard herself ask, barely above a whisper.

Gabriel got up from his chair, only to sit beside her on the bed. He grasped her hand, feeling for her pulse. It wasn't until he counted a steady rhythm did he breathe a silent relief.

"I thought I almost lost you," his voice cracked.

The sound reminded her of something dark. Something that had wanted to consume her, devour her until she no longer recognized who she was, but it was his voice that kept it at bay. Kept it from truly silencing her.

Amelia forced her arm to bear its weight as she extended her hand to caress his face. The pad of her thumb brushed along the coarse facial hair, sweeping away the moisture that leaked from his star-kissed eyes.

"We could never be lost to each other. We always find our way back. Always," she promised him.

Gabriel bobbed his head before taking in a deep, steadying breath.

Amelia could feel it. Feel the tension strung tight in the air. The unspoken words that lingered yet needed to be spoken and unleashed. She promised herself no more running.

"How long was I out?"

"Ten days."

Ten days. Her mind whirled at that number.

"Why?"

An overwhelming part of her didn't want to know the answer. Dreaded to know. Something fundamental was missing. She could feel it. As though she no longer had two functioning lungs. Only one supporting her body.

A crucial, vital part was missing.

"We lost fifty-two wolves to the attack, including Kelsey. Wandering Moon lost nineteen," Gabriel informed her.

Amelia gazed at him harshly. There was more. Something he wasn't mentioning. Something that prevented his eyes from reaching hers, inspecting the intricate lines on her hands. She wanted to tell him to spit it out. Just tell her instead of dancing around it. Rip the Band-Aid off. Her mouth opened to shout at him, but movement in the corner made her freeze.

The waning moon cast muted light into the room. Deep shadows lingered, hiding from the soft lamp at her bedside, but this one moved with purpose. It rose from the ground, molding its shape into a large wolf. She watched as the beast took form. Fur sprouted from its flesh in a faint gray color that seemed to catch the moonlight. The body was faded through, non-corporal, just visible enough to see the shape and color of its eyes that lit up like glow worms. Its body seemed to stutter in the shadows as though holding its form was difficult.

Amelia clutched her chest.

A deep, shocking cold enveloped her soul, sucking her dry. This wasn't a Band-Aid. This was a bandage trying to staunch the bleeding of a major vessel, barely containing what threatened to unleash from within. A dry sob clogged her throat as she took in the wolf before her. His sides were still, breath no longer needed. His fur seemed to move in a breeze that wasn't felt in this realm and those blue-green eyes gripped hers, overcome with sadness.

"Damon," she sobbed.

Damon sat up off his haunches and approached her bedside. His paws were silent across the floor. Not even an imprint was left on the carpet. She could feel Gabriel's eyes on her. His curiosity was heavy, but he had the common sense to keep quiet. She reached out to the apparition. Her hand outstretched between them.

Damon nuzzled his face in the palm of her hand. She couldn't feel the silky fur she knew should be there or the intricate lines of bone that filled his face. It was no more than a sigh of air against her skin, but she could scent him. The scent of home, late nights sneaking out, and countless squabbles filled her senses. The boy who grew into a man at her side. The twin that never abandoned her. The brother that she loved since before she drew her first breath.

Amelia now understood the gaping void that seemed to reside within. The other half of her essence had been ripped out without care for the shattered pieces that were left behind. She wanted to scream at him. Demand from him what had happened. How could he have been so stupid as to get himself killed? Why hadn't she healed him? Why didn't he call for help? Thousands of questions raced across her mind in a blinding torrent of pain and fury. She wanted someone to blame. Wanted to scream at the world and burn it all down until the world felt an emptiness she knew would haunt her till the end of her days. Throttle the Goddess for allowing her brother to die. But none of that would change a thing.

Tears spilled down her face as waves of grief crashed against her. It was piercing and agonizing, and it devoured her. She mumbled his name in disbelief. This couldn't be it.

I'll always be with you. Always. Damon's voice echoed in her mind as his form faded into nothing.

Amelia's eyes widened as he disappeared before her. As though he was never there, never even existed. But he was. He had been. He had been a part of her since the moment of her conception, but now that bond was gone. Severed forever. Her body curled in on itself as she unleashed her heartbreak.

Gabriel climbed onto the bed, gathering her body into his, clutching her tightly. He enveloped her as though to absorb her sorrow, shield her from its depths and sharp edges, but he couldn't.

No one could.

Gabriel embraced her tightly as her mourning assaulted her relentlessly. She tore at his shirt. Her nails shifted from human to claws and back again, over, and over. Shredding his clothes, his skin, but none of that mattered. He held her tighter than ever as she screamed for her brother. Begged for the Goddess to bring him back. Pleaded to take her life instead, but all of it went unanswered. Her grief pulsated down through the pack bond, alerting every one of them to her agony.

The bedroom door burst open. Emery's heart was nearly thumping out of her chest. Her head pulsed with its own heartbeat, pounding against the boundaries of her skull. She wanted to vomit all over the floor and scream until her voice was lost forever with the rage of emotions that seemed to be spilling through the bond, and all of it seemed to be coming from one person—her mother.

She found her parents clutching one another on the center of the bed. Her father was a bloody mess. Blood covered his chest and embedded itself under her mother's nails. Amelia was calling for her brother. Whimpering into what remained of his shirt. Her body was shaking uncontrollably, fighting off the desperate urge to shift and decimate anything within reach. Her mother was on the cusp of losing herself and her humanity. Without thinking, she climbed on the bed and bound her arms around her from the other side until her hands touched the ribboned remains of cotton fabric. She stroked her silvered hair and hummed their tune. The same one Amelia had used on her countless nights when nightmares plagued her sleep. The same one Emery had used to remind her that she was no longer confined in that cell.

Emery hummed until she could hear her mother's cries turn into hiccups. Until the song of mourning rang from every inch of the Packhouse, territory, and beyond as each pack member tilted towards the skies and cried out in song, howling to the moon, honoring the Alpha that lived in the stars.

Amelia didn't know how or when she had fallen asleep, but she must have.

The water of the lake lapped against her toes. It was surprisingly brisk with winter on its way, but the frigid cold already resided in her chest. Numbing her to everything.

Leaves rubbing together could be heard over the faint billowing breeze that caused ripples over the surface of the water. She barely flinched when she heard a gentle sigh beside her. Didn't bother to acknowledge the ancient woman that looked younger than her. To hell with decorum. She didn't care about any of it.

"I'm sorry, Amelia."

Amelia snorted. Loudly. "You're sorry? For what? For allowing my brother to die? For standing by and doing nothing?"

"I'm sorry for your grief and your loss."

"You're sorry for my loss? Have you ever had someone punch a hole through your chest and show you what your heart looks like? To have a gaping void left where that person used to be?" Amelia screamed, her voice rebounding off the water.

"Yes."

The soft confirmation from the woman beside her caused her to turn. She wouldn't have believed her if not for the heart-wrenching truth that was plain on her face, from the sorrow-filled eyes to the grim set line of her mouth.

"I didn't know a Goddess could love like that," Amelia said.

"Just because I am eternal does not mean I do not come with a past—a beginning. Do not mistake me for being heartless," the Goddess advised her. "I understand you're hurting and wish to lash out, but do not mistake my presence as an omission of guilt. I have no control over who lives or dies, just as you have no control over the weather. It is simply beyond me."

The Goddesses' words did nothing to ebb the anger that was boiling in her veins. Her powers of healing and being a bright lightbulb felt useless in comparison to death. She wanted to explode. Slice a tree in half with her rage. Unleash the storm that was brewing inside of her so that all could feel her ire. Understand her loss.

"Control your rage, or you will become nothing more than the monster you defeated. Do not let them win by allowing them to turn you into something you are not," the Goddess warned her.

Amelia breathed heavily. Trying to stifle the barrage of terror she deeply wanted to release. "I don't know if I can. I feel like I can't breathe. How am I supposed to go on? How am I supposed to quiet this rage inside of me?"

"One day at a time."

Amelia whirled at the familiar voice.

The sight of him nearly knocked her off her feet. The familiar cock to his head and smirk on his lips were enough to send her heart racing. Tears overwhelmed her eyes as she barreled into him, embracing him in a bone-crushing hug. His arms wrapped just as tightly around her, stroking the ends of her hair in a calming manner.

"I can't do this without you," Amelia sobbed into his chest.

"You will. You can. I believe in you, Mia. I always have."

She shook her head. "I feel like a part of me has died. I can't do it."

Damon backed away just enough to look down. He cupped her face in his hands, forcing her to look up.

"Whether I breathe or not is irrelevant. You have the power of the Goddess within you. You can see me anytime you wish. I told you. I'll always be with you. Not even death could keep us apart."

"It's not the same. What about your pack? Cordelia and the boys? Oh Gods, the boys." Her heart bled even more as she remembered her nephews. She may have lost a brother, but they had lost their father. The youngest was only four. Too young to retain lasting memories of his father.

"Cordelia understood the risks we faced. She understood this was a possibility," Damon spoke solemnly.

"No one understands death until it happens and even then, it seems pointless. There's a difference between discussing the possibility and accepting the reality of death."

"I think on some level, I knew this was my fate. I already said my goodbyes to Cordie. The boys are in good hands. They have their mother, their pack, and you. What more could I ask for?"

"It's not fair," she cried silently. "Adrian's only fifteen. He's too young to bear the burden of being Alpha."

"That's why he won't be Alpha."

Amelia blanched. Not grasping what he meant. "He's your oldest. Your heir. Of course, he's the next Alpha."

"The title was never his. Or mine for that matter."

"I don't understand."

"You were always meant to be Alpha, Mia. But due to some archaic, misogynistic views, I was named Alpha instead. I'm correcting that mistake."

Amelia stepped out of his arms, jerking her head in disbelief. She glanced at the Goddess, who observed from the side. This was a joke. It had to be. But the Goddess merely nodded her head in agreement.

"No. I am *not* the Alpha. It was always your position. It belongs to your sons," she said with an iron will.

"You'll accept being Alpha with your mate but not over your rightful pack? Your birthright?" he questioned.

"Says who?! You?" Amelia pointed at him until she turned her venom to the woman standing beside her. "You? Because I say fuck that."

"What are you afraid of? The responsibility or accepting your fate?" the Goddess asked, her face as smooth as stone.

"Neither," Amelia spit. "I have accepted my fate and all that comes with it, but this is not fate. This is him screwing with the succession."

"You are the firstborn heir. Damon took what was not his. This is a correction," the Goddess spoke candidly.

"By seven minutes! I was born first by seven minutes! How does that even count?! I never wanted to be Alpha. Not once was that a desire of mine. I just wanted to live my life."

"So, selfish then?" the Goddess called her out. "You are refusing your birthright over an idea of freedom that was never attainable. Long gone are the dreams of traipsing around the world with not a care for anyone but yourself. Those were the whims of a child. But you, you are a woman who has seen things that would make most tremble. You have given birth under the cover of darkness and stared death in the face and laughed. You have survived unforgivable torture at the hands of your enemies and turned your scars into a weapon. You bore through the pain of separation from your mate all so your child could live. So you could give her a future that was denied her twin."

Amelia looked elsewhere. Tears burned the back of her eyes. A flurry of emotions whipped violently around inside her chest. But no matter how angry or annoyed with the Goddess she was at using her past against her, she was right. She had survived all of those things.

"But that doesn't make me an Alpha," Amelia said faintly. "How can I claim the title when all I did was run instead of confronting the threat that loomed over us all? How can I call myself the Alpha of the Wandering Moon, the first werewolf pack, and deserve that title when I know I'm not worthy?"

"You cannot fight something if you are dead, and that is what would have happened had you stayed. I saw it. It was as good as written in the stars." A warm hand pushed the hair back from her face, gently brushing against her skin. Amelia nearly startled at how close the Goddess was to her, let alone touching her, but she forced herself to remain still. "Do not fight this. This has always been your destiny."

CHAPTER 47

GUILT AND SHAME

The room was lit. The lamp on the nightstand illuminated the space, chasing away the darkness. Night blanketed the sky, abandoning the Earth in total darkness beyond the window. Her body felt stiff and heavy. A sturdy, sheltering arm wound around her back, holding her along his side. Forcing her head to tilt, she found herself looking up into the face of a sleeping angel. His eyes were fastened. Obsidian strands of hair draped across his face. His nose twitched in his sleep, along with a soft whistling snore that caused his chest to rumble. She wanted to wipe away the bruises beneath his eyes. Kiss each of them until he no longer felt tired and weary. How long had she been in his arms, screaming and crying?

A symphony of noise rose from her stomach as cramps began to set in. Her mouth was parched, and her eyes felt like someone had poured sand in them. Amelia forced her body to obey as she sat up from the mounds of pillows propped beneath them. Her limbs screamed in protest, the tendons and muscles stretched and pulled until she was certain they were tearing. She scooted her butt along the mattress until she could grasp the edge of the bed. Looking back, she checked to see that Gabriel hadn't moved. His persistent snoring told her he wouldn't be stirring anytime soon. She grabbed the throw from the end of the bed and enclosed it around herself. Somehow, she was in nothing but a shirt and panties.

Hugging the plush blanket against her chest, Amelia silently opened the bedroom door. The outside of the room was shockingly cold. Even the wood floor beneath her feet sent a frigid chill up her back. She left the door cracked open before walking through the hall and down the flights of stairs. The kitchen beckoned, drawing her closer with its still lingering smells from dinner, roasted chicken, and baked potatoes, when a familiar scent stole her attention.

Even in the dark, Amelia could make out the golden hair and drooping shoulders. The faint sound of sniffling could be detected as well as the salty taste of tears. Amelia ignored her grumbling stomach and approached with caution. The last thing she wanted was to startle her. Her bare feet were soundless against the hardwood floors, but she made sure to sigh deeply before she got any closer, signaling her presence.

Cordelia straightened as she looked behind her briefly. Her shoulders pulled back at the sight of her. Almost as though she intended to stand.

"Mia! You shouldn't be out of bed."

"There wasn't any food upstairs," Amelia shrugged her shoulders.

"I can make you something to eat." Cordelia went to get up until Amelia place her hand on her shoulder, forcing her back down on the couch

"It can wait. I haven't seen you since before the battle." Amelia sat down on the loveseat, sinking back into the conforming foam cushions before taking in her friend. Even in mourning and well past midnight, Cordelia was dressed to impress in a simple white tank-top that was tucked inside black slacks. Her golden hair was clipped away from her face. The only interruption in her manicured look was the tear tracks cutting through her foundation.

Amelia noticed the untouched drink held between her hands. By the smell of it, someone had discovered the stashed bottle of tequila.

"I didn't want to intrude." Cordelia directed her eyes on the door behind them. Her hazel eyes made a point not to look at her.

Amelia reached out and clasped her friend's hand. Spreading her calloused fingers over her unblemished skin and taking comfort in her warmth when she felt nothing but frozen inside.

"Look at me, Cordie." Amelia waited until her friend finally looked her way, silver lining her eyes. "I am so sorry."

"What do you have to be sorry about?" Cordelia scrunched her brow. Her voice soft and baffled.

"I didn't know he was hurt. I could have healed him. Saved him. But I didn't know." Grief rolled inside of her, rising closer and closer to the surface.

Cordelia set her drink down before reaching out with her other hand, placing it on top. She squeezed tightly, holding her gaze. "This was not your fault. No one could have predicted this. Damon knew the risk going into this battle. We all did."

"But you lost your husband, your mate," Amelia cried. Her voice cracked over the last word. She didn't know how Cordelia was holding it together. So composed and regal, even with tears falling from her eyes. If it was her and she had lost Gabriel, they would have had to sedate her and abandon her to a padded cell.

"And you lost your twin, your brother. I had his heart, but Mia, you had his soul. I'm just thankful that you and Emery are okay." Cordelia shuddered, silently praying to the Goddess in thanks for their survival.

"Me too. I don't ever want to see Emery that close to death again." Amelia tried blocking out the memory of her daughter in the mouth of the enemy, bleeding out on the forest floor.

Cordelia nibbled her lip as nerves wracked her stomach.

Amelia sensed her anxiety, her rising apprehension and knew something was really up when her knee began to jig—Cordelia's telling sign.

"What is it? What's wrong?"

"Damon and I talked before the battle. About what would happen if something was to happen to him," Cordelia began and went to continue until Amelia held up her hand, forcing her to stop.

"He wants me to be Alpha," Amelia finished for her.

"How did you know?" Cordelia asked, taken aback.

Amelia spotted the tequila resting on the coffee table in front of them, snatched it up and took a swig straight from the bottle. The instant burn down the back of her throat had her eyes immediately watering as she forced down the rising cough. The alcohol settled in her stomach, swallowing her gnawing hunger, and brought forth a pleasant, fuzzy feeling taking its place. She set the bottle in her lap between her legs. No sense in putting it back when she figured she'd require it for their conversation.

"I saw him. He came to me in my dreams and just after I woke up. I could see him. He was there, but he wasn't," Amelia tried to explain.

Cordelia swayed her head, clearly confused. "I don't understand. You hallucinated?"

"No. No," Amelia exhaled heavily. "Sometimes, I see these shadow-wolves. Usually, only when danger is near, they come to me in warning. But, somehow, Damon can visit me. I don't know if it's because of our bond, a power from the Goddess. I don't know. All I know is I saw him in my dream, and he told me he made me Alpha. That you two spoke about it before the battle."

Cordelia's eyes were wide with amazement. "We did. We realized after all that's happened, after digging up your lineage and your powers, you are the rightful Alpha of the Wandering Moon. He wanted to make sure to rectify that, whether he lived or not."

"Well, it's bullshit. Adrian is your eldest. It's his birthright."

"Adrian will understand. There is honor and respect in being a Beta. He will serve you well when he comes of age."

"How can you just be okay with this? You're their Luna. Your sons are the heirs. Damon was made Alpha by law and through the rites. The Goddess approved his position the moment the link snapped in place. This isn't right." Amelia couldn't comprehend how she had zero issues with this. That this was even a semblance of a good idea.

"Maybe Damon needed to be Alpha until you were ready. Maybe you had to endure everything you did to serve our packs, to become the leader we need," Cordelia insisted.

"And what about Dominik? He's just okay with stepping down. His future heirs having no chance at succeeding him?" Amelia tried to get her to see reason.

"Dominik found his mate last year. A man. I don't think he'll have any heirs to worry about, and even if he did, this has been in the talks a lot these past years. We all knew you had to come home at some point. It was just a matter of when."

"Dominik's gay?" Amelia asked louder than she'd have liked, her jaw hanging open. She only ever knew her cousin to be a bit of a sleaze. Constantly flitting from she-wolf to she-wolf.

"Apparently so, given the gender of his mate." Cordelia shrugged her shoulders.

"Well, good for him." Amelia smiled. "If he's happy, I'm happy for him."

Cordelia reached out and placed her hand over the one still gripping the neck of the bottle. "I know you're nervous, and this is a lot all at once. Less than two weeks ago, you were still on the run with no pack and no support, but you're not alone, and you never will be. We will all help you with this."

"What if I'm not any good?" she asked, her voice soft and shaking. "I don't want to fail anyone."

"You only fail if you give up, and I've never known you to be a quitter."

Amelia stared into her best friend's bright green and brown eyes. An exquisite combination of the two as they glowed in the surrounding darkness. All she found there was unwavering love and support.

"You're an amazing Luna."

Cordelia smirked, seizing the bottle from her hands, and throwing back a shot. "I've had some practice."

Amelia tried to smile, tried to find the lightness in the mood, but all she could identify was the overwhelming sadness settling in her chest.

"I miss him."

Cordelia looked back at the sound of her voice cracking. "Come here."

Cordelia set the bottle down on the table and opened her arms wide before Amelia climbed in beside her, placing her head on her friend's shoulder.

Amelia wrapped the blanket around them as they took comfort from one another. Wetness fell in her hair as her own clung to the fabric beneath her cheek. Together they mourned their friend, brother, and mate. For even though he left a vast crater in their lives and hearts, maybe one day it wouldn't be so extensive.

CHAPTER 48

TAKE OUR TIME

Amelia and Cordelia had devoted the remaining hours of the night crying and reminiscing over their youth. Retelling countless stories that usually involved sneaking off and a race to see who could break the most rules.

Amelia had never cried or laughed so hard in her life, and even though her brother's loss was a gaping void in her chest, she felt just an inch lighter.

By the time she had crawled back in bed, Gabriel was just getting up at the break of dawn. She barely remembered his lips brushing along her forehead before she drifted into a dreamless sleep. Now the clock appeared to tell her she had slept till noon. Her stomach was twisted in knots. Acidic bile took personal residence at the back of her throat. Drinking tequila until the sun came up on an empty stomach was probably the worst idea she'd had in a long while. Her head was bouncing off her skull, and from the way she was feeling, nausea would be her best friend all day.

The conversation with Cordelia played over and over in her mind. It seemed like everyone was dead set on her becoming the next Alpha of the Wandering Moon. But what about what she wanted? She had only just become Alpha of her mate's pack, but being the Alpha of two packs … how was that even possible? What if she couldn't balance it all? She still had Emery to raise, a mate to ravish, a brother to mourn, and now two packs to look after. She felt beyond overwhelmed.

Any input from the peanut gallery? Amelia asked her other half. She'd barely heard from Rey since she woke up, and it was starting to make her nervous.

Everyone else believes in you. Why can't you accept that? Rey's voice was frail and faint. As though the effort to produce words required more strength than she had.

What's going on, Rey?

I'm tired. Rey sighed. *So, so tired. The battle took a lot from me, and now, no longer having Zeke, it's a lot.*

Amelia wished for nothing more than her wolf to have a physical form outside of their body so that she could wrap her arms around her neck and stroke her fur. Not only had she lost her twin, but so had Rey.

I know. Take your time and rest. I'll be here when you're ready. She'd do anything for her wolf. Even if that meant going at things solo for a while.

You can do this, Amelia. This is what we were born to do. To lead. And you're not alone. You never have been. You have me, Emery, our mate, and two packs backing you. Lean on them. Listen to them. We can do this. No matter what comes our way, we never give up.

Rey's voice began to fade as she receded further into her mind.

Amelia absorbed each of her words. Taking them at full value and safeguarded them in her heart. She was right. She wasn't alone and never would be again. She could do this. But first, she had to run it by her mate.

Getting out of bed, she made quick work of changing into decent clothes and brushing her teeth. She twisted her hair up into a bun and left it at that. She sniffed her pits quickly. At least she didn't stink. Following the bond that tethered her heart to his, she allowed it to direct her all the way to his office door. Exactly where she thought he'd be.

Amelia didn't bother knocking. After inhaling sharply, she took in each scent until she knew without a doubt, he was alone. The only ones wafting from underneath the wood door was one's she associated with home and love. By the rise in pheromones tickling the back of her throat, she knew he could scent her too. She twisted the knob and pushed her way inside.

The office was much the same since the last time she stood in it. Except, for now, there were stacks of paper and files covering every surface in the room.

"Is there a paper shortage in New York, or are we just allergic to electronic files?" Amelia arched her brow.

Gabriel chuckled as he sorted through a smaller stack in front of him. "This is everything that was brought down to the safe rooms during the attack. Now I get to put it all back. Usually, Kelsey kept track of our records, but..." He drifted off, visibly flinching at the use of her name.

Amelia drifted closer towards him. Her feet moved without thought or hesitation. She sat on the corner of his desk and laid her hand on his shoulder, rubbing the spot between muscle and tendon.

"It's okay to miss her."

"Are you sure? I know there was no love between the two of you, and you had every reason to—"

"Gabe. She was your wife. Whether I like it or not, you spent the better part of a decade with her as husband and wife. Whatever you two were to each other, there had to be something there, and it wouldn't do either of us any good to ignore that or pretend it never happened. I did love her. She was a good friend to me. We may not have been besties in the end, but she sacrificed her life to save our daughter, and for that, I will always be grateful and have the utmost respect."

Gabriel exhaled. Whether in relief or resignation, she wasn't sure. "It's just so weird not having her here. We may not have always gotten along, but I knew I could count on her, no matter what."

"I know." Amelia moved to stand behind him and continued to apply pressure to his shoulders, rubbing out the tension that left him stiff and rigid. He twisted his head back. A small groan slipped past his lip causing her to smile softly. He had been through so much the last few days. Between her being unconscious and not knowing whether she'd wake up. The countless funerals and pyre burnings. Juggling both packs under one roof. She could feel the stress beneath his skin melt away as she kneaded his flesh with her hands.

"How are you feeling?"

Gabriel's voice disrupted her contemplation. She looked down at him to discover his eyes searching hers. Trying to uncover any facet of pain or discomfort.

"I'm okay. Drinking till the sun came up didn't help much, but I still feel sore. Using all that power ... I've never felt so drained." She felt weary to the bone. Every inch of her still ached. Just lifting her arms to put her shirt on was an effort. Each of her limbs felt heavy, as though she was physically dragging herself around by will alone. She was sure if given the opportunity, she could sleep another week at least. "I still don't understand why I was out for so long, though. I had no problem shifting back after the battle. I felt fine."

"You lost consciousness the minute your brother passed. I don't think your little battle with death had anything to do with flexing your power. I think it had everything to do with losing your brother. When Damon passed, something fundamental to your tether to this plane snapped. It became more of a battle of wills. I think if you wanted, you could have passed with him," Gabriel speculated.

His words were gentle like a cool kiss against her skin. As soothing as a babbling stream flowing over unblemished river rocks. Her hands had stilled against the base of his neck. The memory of darkness beckoning surged forward. A part of her had wanted to join, to get lost in that never-ending abyss of light and love. The place that knew no grief, loss, or hate. Where her ancestors called her name, summoning her to enter their ranks.

"I remember it," she spoke aloud. "I remember being pulled in two. One towards the light and the other to pain and darkness. I would have gone." The admittance of that fact surprised her. Up until that moment, she hadn't been sure, but now that she had uttered it out loud, it was true. She would have gone with Damon. "I didn't recognize my name, who I was, or what I stood to lose. I would have chosen the light if it weren't for you."

"Me?" Gabriel's brow scrunched. He looked like the wind was being sucked from the room. The air getting harder to breathe as she revealed her own little epiphany.

"I heard you, Gabe. I heard you telling me to hold on and not to leave you. I didn't know who you were or why you were saying these things, but just the sound of your voice breaking, I knew I never wanted to hear it again, and I would destroy anyone who made you feel that way. I wanted to avenge you and protect you. I chose you. I chose life because of you. Even when I didn't remember my own name or even Emery, just the sound of your voice was enough to make me want to live."

Gabriel stood up from his chair. The pad of his thumb was rough against her cheek as he brushed a tear from her skin. She hadn't realized she'd been crying until the current of electricity from his touch rippled across her flesh. She leaned into his hand, savoring the warmth of his body. The life force echoed between them, connecting his heart to hers forever. She swallowed with difficulty as she recalled the purpose of this visit.

"There's something we need to talk about," she started.

"Well, that's never a good way to start a conversation." Gabriel chuckled nervously.

"It's not like that," Amelia hastily corrected herself. "It's been brought to my attention that Damon's final wish was to make me Alpha of the Wandering Moon." She was never fond of slow reveals. Better to rip the band-aid off quickly.

"His final wish," Gabriel dragged out. "Alpha of the Wandering Moon. You. And we know this how?"

"Damon told me. The Goddess told me. Even Cordie. Apparently, he's wanted this for years. He was just waiting for me to come home." Amelia shrugged her shoulders as though it was nothing more than deciding chicken or steak for dinner.

"Damon told you," Gabriel repeated the words slowly, trying to figure out how that made any sort of sense.

"He came to me in my dream. Him and the Goddess. They both told me this is my destiny. As if this wasn't some sort of cosmic joke." Amelia rolled her eyes.

"What did Cordie have to say?"

"Basically, the same thing. This is what he wanted and what's best for the pack. It should have been my position all along. Blah, blah, blah."

"Amelia." Gabriel produced a pointed look that told her to take it more seriously.

"What?! What am I supposed to do?"

"What do you want to do?"

Amelia froze. No one had asked her that. Not one. Not her brother, her best friend, or even the mother of them all. No one bothered to ask if she even wanted the position.

"I want what's best for our packs. For us. I don't want to do anything that jeopardizes that."

"Jeopardizes what? Us?" By the expression he recognized on her face, he knew he hit his mark. "Snow. Nothing could ever come between us. If you want to be Alpha of the Wandering Moon, we will figure out the logistics. If you want to be lead warrior, then the position is yours. If you want to be a kitchen wench, we have plenty of aprons."

"A kitchen wench, huh?" Amelia arched a brow, smirking at the soft chuckle he expressed.

"You get what I mean. It doesn't matter what position you take or if you have none at all. It doesn't change the fact that you are my mate, the mother of my children, the keeper of my heart. You're still Alpha in this pack, and if you were to be Alpha of the Wandering Moon, then great. You can handle it. *We* can handle it."

His arms threaded around her waist, gathering her in against him. She placed her hands on his chest, leaning back in his strong embrace. Only one word stuck out like a sore thumb.

"Children?" she asked.

"I want it all with you, Snow. I wasn't there for Emery, but we're together now. I want more pups with you. I want to watch them grow inside of you and raise them together. Emery is almost of age. She can learn the ropes of the Twilight pack, even Wandering Moon. We can take the time to just be us. Mates. Take back some of the time we lost." He brushed the few wisps of hair that fell from her bun back behind her ear.

Amelia was thrilled to hear how much of a future he saw for them, but dread was present as well. Her stomach knotted tightly in her abdomen and not from the hangover that was still lingering.

"I don't know if I can have any more pups. My pregnancy with Emery was anything but smooth. It practically killed me. And after my abduction, what they did to me. I just don't..." her words drifted off, afraid to finish the sentence. A shiver ran down the length of her and not because her mate was stroking his hand down her arms.

"There's no rush. We'll take this one day at a time. I don't want you doing something you're not comfortable with. Pups or no pups, I'll always love you, and Emery will always be enough," he promised her.

Despite her apprehension, she found herself smiling.

"I want to marry you." His words wrapped around her heart in a loving caress. "I want you to be my wife and I your husband. I want to be bound to you in every way imaginable."

His words snatched the breath from her lungs. Her knees felt weak. She was certain the only thing keeping her upright was his arms locked behind her back. She wanted all of it too, and so much more. It was all she ever wanted, but something held her back.

"Slow down, cowboy. There's still so much we have to do."

"Right, of course. I'm getting ahead of myself. Forgive me, love."

She reached up, extending her fingers through his hair, relishing in the silky feel of each strand. "Let's not rush this. I want us to take our time."

CHAPTER 49

SECOND GUESS

The funerals had concluded while she slept. Since no one had any idea how long she'd be out or if she'd ever wake again, they built the pyres. Bodies can only last so long before they start to rot, and given the number of dead, time was not on their side.

Amelia had missed her own brother's funeral. Missed the lighting of his pyre and getting to see his soul depart this world and enter the beyond. She didn't get to say goodbye before their packs or honor him with his remembrance. She had been too busy fighting her own battle.

Choosing death with her twin or life with her mate and daughter.

Although she had missed the ceremony, his pyre remained. They had the ceremony by the lake, and instead of tearing it down like they typically wood after the fire died, they left it, in case she came back.

Standing before the remnants of his pyre, just mere feet from the lake, Amelia couldn't help but chuckle at the irony of the entire situation. Between the bone fragments being the only thing that now remained of her brother's earthly form or the eeriness of the lake, how calm the water looked when so much raged within, she didn't know.

The pyre that was left was breaking down by the minute. The wood was little more than ash being held together by some unknown force. One swift breeze would make it all tumble to the Earth, scattering her brother to the four winds, with not a trace left of his existence. Standing before it, she wasn't sure what to say. That was until the hairs rose on the back of her neck.

A figure apparated beside her.

The breeze didn't affect the fabric of his clothes or lift the ends of his hair. His chest was still. Oxygen was no longer necessary.

Amelia glanced towards him. Anger, grief, and resentment swarmed her, coating the back of her mouth in what tasted like battery acid.

"Shouldn't you be off doing ghostly things? Like comforting your widow or spooking Gabriel when he takes a piss?"

Damon snorted in a distinctly human way. "You sound bitter, Sis."

Amelia wanted to stamp her foot, scream at the top of her lungs, and plunge her fist into the trunk of a tree. She wanted to shout to the world how unfair it was. Why him?

"Of course, I'm bitter! You're dead, Damon. Like dead, dead. Never coming back, dead. How can you be okay with this?"

"I'm not okay with it, Mia. How can I be okay with never being with my mate again? To never hold her in my arms and tell her how much I love her. Never to play ball with my boys and be there as they grow and turn into men. I hate this. I hate that I won't be there for you at your Alpha ceremony and shift with you for your pack run. But this is better than nothing. Even if I can't wipe your tears or hold your hand, I'm still here for you. You may not always be able to see me, but I am always here. With you."

Amelia swiped at the saltwater on her face angrily, annoyed with herself and him until his words fully registered. "What do you mean I can't always see you?"

"It takes a lot of energy to be visible to you. Most of them are incapable of doing it." Damon nodded towards the tree line.

Amelia tried to follow his line of sight but detected nothing more than dancing shadows as the trees moved with the wind. A chill crept along her skin at the thought of countless wolves observing them.

"Then how can you?"

Damon merely shrugged his shoulders. "Maybe it's our bond. Being twins and our bloodline makes it possible. I really don't know." He glanced down at her, tilting his head. "Does it really matter?"

"No," she said quickly. "No, it doesn't."

Silence stretched between them. One that didn't require empty words and endless chit-chat to fill. It was comforting and familiar. Her eyes were fastened on the charred pile of wood. The white bone was the only contrast among the crumbling pyre, covered in a thin coat of black dust. His bones would be returned to Wandering Moon territory, where they would be laid to rest beside their mother and father.

"I wish I could have been there for your funeral. Watch as your spirit joined the stars." She tilted her head back to gaze at the tangled lights that shone from billions of miles away.

"It was a dull affair." His smirk caused her to chuckle, even if it did sound slightly hysterical.

"What should I do?" Amelia released her breath loudly, running her hand through the roots of her hair. "How am I supposed to become an Alpha?"

Damon turned towards her for the first time.

Being able to see through him was eerie and nearly caused her to flinch. It sent a trickle of anxiety dripping down her spine, enough to make her want to separate herself from her skin and hide. He was there, and yet he wasn't. She could see him, hear him, but the world around them no longer affected his corporeal form. As though he straddled the line of life and death.

"You already are an Alpha. Whether you hold the formal title or not. It's in your blood. It's who you are. It's why your first instinct is to protect. To fight for your pack, whether on the battlefield or in endless council meetings. You've never been one to back down against prejudice or be intimidated when things get hard. You've always faced those things head-on. Do you think most she-wolves would have survived seventeen years of rogues, fleeing your home, and moving all the time? To stay one step ahead of your enemy. You raised Emery in that chaos and still managed to produce a well-adjusted teenager that could give any seasoned warrior a run for his money. If anything, I'm afraid of what you might do sitting behind a desk. Not a lot of action. You'll get bored easily."

Amelia laughed. The sound surprised her when the situation was anything but funny. "I've had enough action to last me multiple lifetimes. I don't think I want to fight another battle again. We've lost too much and endured so much more. I just want to enjoy my time with Emery and Gabriel. Show her the territory, her lineage, and give her a chance at a normal life. No more running. No more fighting. She's never had stability, but now, I can finally give her that."

"With two packs, nonetheless."

Amelia grunted in response. She still wasn't sure how she felt taking over as Alpha of the Wandering Moon. In some ways, it felt like something crucial had slipped into place. Foundation was finally firm beneath her, and she could stand on both feet on her own. She was standing on the cusp of something she never knew she didn't have, and now that she did, she felt foolish for not realizing sooner. Being Alpha of the pack she was raised in felt right, and the fact that it did, made her want to throttle the Goddess. So much heartache and pain could have been avoided if she had known sooner.

"Don't do that."

Amelia looked up at her brother, not realizing she had been staring off into the reflection of the stars on the surface of the lake. The water rippled under the kiss of the wind. "What?"

"Don't second guess this. Don't think of the what if's and what could have been'. We can't change the past, and nor should we want to. Everything happens for a reason."

Amelia rolled her eyes, her gag reflex spiking. "So now that you're dead, I get to endure philosophical metaphors and beyond the grave advice? I think I'd rather be tortured. Again."

"Seriously, Mia. Why are you fighting this?"

"Which part? You being dead or me being Alpha of two packs?"

"Me being dead, well, that we can't change. But you being Alpha. Is it really so bad?"

"Yes. No. Maybe. I don't know," she said, exacerbated. "I'm terrified I can't handle it all. I'm afraid it'll be too much, and something will slip through the cracks, and then it'll be my fault. People's lives will be in my hands. I don't want to fail anyone."

"Even with all the power in the world, you can't control everything. You're going to slip up and make mistakes, but that's how we learn. Don't let your fear get in the way of what's right."

Amelia exhaled. A cloud of frost billowed in front of her. Winter was rapidly approaching. Soon, snow would be glittering in the evening sun, and they'd be surrounded by a world of white.

The universe waited for no one. Life goes on.

"I promised myself when I came back, I wouldn't let my fear stop me from doing what's right. I wouldn't be its victim and let it control me," Amelia reminded herself.

"So, what are you going to do?" Damon asked, but by the tone of his voice, he already knew. He knew long before she did.

Amelia turned to him and flashed him the biggest smirk she could. "I'm gonna make Alpha my bitch."

Damon bellowed. He'd be gasping for air if he actually required it. "That's my girl."

CHAPTER 50

PROMISE

Amelia kicked off her sneakers, abandoning them at the foot of the bed. She was exhausted. The entire way up the five flights of stairs, she was convinced she'd knock out right there on the steps. She devoted the last remaining hours of the day sketching out a rough plan with Cordelia, Emery, Gabriel, and other pack officials on both sides.

Tomorrow, she would leave with the remaining Wandering Moon pack and help them adjust to the loss of their Alpha, be there for her nephews, and coordinate the next steps to her succession.

She was doing it. She was going to be an Alpha of not just one, but two packs.

Amelia wasn't sure how long she'd have to be gone to establish herself, but Gabriel promised he'd visit her frequently. The first step was getting herself reacquainted with her birth pack. Then, they could figure out the long-distance thing. Emery would be dividing her time between both packs, and Cordelia would be a fundamental figure to lean on.

Amelia crawled in bed, not even making it under the covers before she sprawled out. Her clothes were left forgotten on the floor. The brisk air floated in through the cracked window, soothing against her skin. She pulled herself in until her body was flush against him.

Gabriel's arm was already propped beneath his head as he snuggled down into the mattress to better accommodate her. She breathed in deeply. Savoring his apple and clove scent.

"Penny, for your thoughts." Gabriel disrupted her drifting mind.

She rested her head on his chest. Winding her fingers through the salt and pepper hair on his chest. The sound of his heart was steady and comforting, repeatedly reminding them both that they were alive and together.

"I just can't believe I'm here. With you," she told him. "I never thought we'd have this again. To be in your arms, with our pack. Don't tell the Goddess, but I am grateful to her for giving you to me. You're probably the only man on the planet that could deal with my stubborn, thick head."

"Oh, but what a lovely head it is." Gabriel chuckled, lightly kissing her forehead. "I love you, Snow. Always."

Amelia sank further into him, burying her nose in his chest until the hair tickled her nostrils. She propped herself up on her elbow, gazing into his silver twin moons. "Promise me something."

"Anything."

Not even a moment's hesitation.

"Promise me nothing will ever separate us ever again. Not distance, the packs or whatever demons lurk beyond our borders."

"I promise."

Amelia nodded. Satisfied with the undeniable, truth that poured from him. She was home. She was safe and she was loved. She leaned over him, and for the first time in over a decade, she flicked off the lights.

CHAPTER 51

UNINVITED GUEST

The light flicked off overhead. The window glass was swallowed in darkness.

From the tree line, he could hear the cover's rustling and lovemaking ensued. His lip curled up in disgust.

Humans.

Disgusting all of them.

Especially when they reeked of wet dog.

It was bad enough he had to endure decades of the mangy, flea-bitten rogues, but pack wolves were so much more insufferable. At least rogues were lost to their instincts. Pack wolves were merely dogs with better tricks.

Michael was slain. The foolish idiot stupidly tried to confront her head-on with the weight of two packs supporting her. He was supposed to deliver her to him. Now, he had to wait. Bide his time just a bit longer. He waited centuries. What were a few more years? At least until she was vulnerable again.

He disappeared into the shadows. Blending in until he became one with the darkness. Blood was still fresh on his breath. Not a stitch out of place on his tailored look. He smirked at the thought of attaining his prize.

What a match they would be.

The story continues in the third and final installment . . .

HEATHER SMITH

DAWN

OF

LIGHT

FATED DARKNESS | BOOK 3

Read on for a preview of Dawn of Light:
Book 3 of Fated Darkness

Coming January 2022

It's been two years since the war with Michael. Two years since her brother's death and she became Alpha of the Wandering Moon Pack. Amelia is still struggling to balance being an Alpha, wife, and mother, but that's nothing compared to what lurks in the shadows.

An old enemy, an ancient evil is finally ready to make their move. After centuries of waiting, they finally seize their opening, but it's not as easy as they believe.

In the final installment of the Fated Darkness Series, Amelia must overcome daring odds, dire circumstances, and yet another life-altering choice, but she's not the only one. Emery finally comes face to face with her mate but it's no one she ever expected in her wildest dreams. Can she change his nature, or will he bring about the end of her world?

AUTHOR'S NOTES

In a lot of way's Amelia's journey is my own. *Shadow of Twilight*, we saw a young girl, feisty and head-strong thrown onto a path she never saw herself walking. While she may have been naïve, she handled each situation to the best of her ability with the information she was given. When I started writing *Shadow of Twilight* and *Dusk to Dawn* (I was writing both at the same time), it was during a period of my life where I felt out of control with no clear direction. I felt lost and hopeless. But through Amelia's story, I was able to discover the woman I wanted to be. Through her trials and bravery, I found a strength within myself that I never knew I had.

Amelia had ideas for what she wanted her life to look like and yet fate had other plans, but that's not always a bad thing. She found a passion she never knew she needed, a love she never knew she wanted, and a life she never saw herself having but fought so desperately for. That was all I wanted. When I finished drafting *Shadow of Twilight* and halfway through the first draft of *Dusk to Dawn*, I finally grew the courage I needed and went in search of true happiness.

I went back to Florida with my four young children and moved in with my parents just as I began the editing process for *Shadow of Twilight* and continued writing *Dusk to Dawn*. During this time, I battled with significant weight loss due to stress, hair loss, anxiety, and insomnia. But day after day, Amelia came through for me. She taught me that love is earned. It is fought for with blood, sweat, and tears. It is not a fairytale, handed to you on a silver platter. And, you know what, it's okay to say enough is enough and walk away. It doesn't make you weak or a failure.

Does true love exist? I believe it does. Are soul mates real? I know it is.

Dusk to Dawn dealt with more adult themes compared to *Shadow of Twilight*. It touched on torture, rape, PTSD, and depression. Now, these scenarios are purely made up and not particular things I have dealt with from experience. But I have been a victim of sexual assault. I have been pressured to do things I didn't want to do and made to feel like garbage when I said no. I have dealt with postpartum depression and general self-loathing over my weaknesses and stubbornness. I have lived with someone who experienced PTSD in varying forms and watched how that can change someone.

I wanted to take all of that trauma and turn them into strengths. While many victims may hate being told that their situations made them stronger, seeing as how they would rather have not gone through them at all, these things happen every day and there is no sense in denying that. I wanted Amelia to come out the other side, still bruised and battered and lacking self-worth, but be able to come to terms with her past and allow another through those defenses and help her heal.

Dusk to Dawn is much more than a shifter, romance, fantasy novel. It's a journey of rediscovery, whether it be love, friendship, or self-worth, it is all so important and something we should never deny ourselves no matter what anyone says.

You are worth it.

ACKNOWLEDGMENTS

I want to start out by thanking my children. Carolynn, Aiden, Evelynn, and Cameron, you are the reason I wake up. You give me purpose, unconditional love, and the drive to be my best self. To my parents, for their unwavering support this last year, and, well, let's face it, my whole life. Without you I'm not sure where I'd be but thank you for always having my back and being the amazing Gaga and Papa.

Richard. I don't know what I did in this life to deserve you, but I am grateful to all the Gods in the Universe for having you in my life. You have been my saving grace, my quiet in a storm of chaos, my soundboard, and the other half of my soul. We found each other at the right time and place, and I couldn't be more thankful. Thank you for taking my heart and fixing what was broken, for giving me all the love, patience, kindness, and attention I ever hoped for. Thank you for being my knight in shining armor, for dealing with my ups and down, for telling me I am worth it and help me to believe in myself. Thank you, my love, and here's to the rest of our lives.

To my For the Writing's group! You all are a hoot and keep me motivated. Wolfie, you are the best, love. My motivational speaker and my biggest cheerleader. I would not be where I am today if not for you. Chloe, thank you for helping me with my edits and for loving every bit of my story. Sib, for being my smut lady and the late-night chats. Ancient, for your consistency, your selflessness, and willingness to listen and help. I have become a better writer thanks to you.

Thank you to my Grandmother for your time and willingness to read my books, Brianna for giving me your scholarly advice, and Gina for being my Beta reader and finishing *Dusk to Dawn* in less than twenty-four hours. To my Instagram Beta readers, thank you for volunteering and encouraging my writing.

But most of all, thank you readers. Thank you for your support and encouragement. For your honesty and your enthusiasm. You are the reason I write! Thank you!

Heather Smith has been crafting stories for as long as she could remember. It wasn't until she was fifteen that she wrote her first novel that she had no intentions of publishing. At nineteen she wrote her first completed manuscript that is still a work in progress, but will soon turn into a four-book series.

Currently, she is working on multiple series, all fantasy genre. When she isn't writing about fantastical worlds, she resides in Hudson, Florida with her four children and spends her time attending school events, quilting, and loving on her two Labradors and four ball pythons.

Follow Heather:

Twitter: https://twitter.com/starsascending

Instagram: https://www.instagram.com/heathersmithauthor/

Website: https://www.heathersmithauthor.com